GOOD FOLK BOOK #3

PENNY REID

WWW.PENNYREID.NINJA/NEWSLETTER/

GOOD FOLK BOOK #3

PENNY REID

WWW.PENNYREID.NINJA/NEWSLETTER/

This book is a work of fiction. Names, characters, places, rants, facts, contrivances, and incidents are either the product of the author's questionable imagination or are used factitiously. Any resemblance to actual persons, living or dead or undead, events, locales is entirely coincidental if not somewhat disturbing/concerning.

Copyright © 2024 by Cipher-Naught; All rights reserved.

No part of this book may be reproduced, scanned, photographed, instagrammed, tweeted, twittered, twatted, tumbled, or distributed in any printed or electronic form without explicit written permission from the author.

NO AI TRAINING: Without in any way limiting the author's exclusive rights under copyright, any use of this publication to "train" generative artificial intelligence (AI) technologies to generate text is expressly prohibited. The author reserves all rights to license uses of this work for generative AI training and development of machine learning language models.

Made in the United States of America

Print Edition

ISBN: 978-1-960342-38-6

Dedication

For my son. Make good choices.

Content Warnings for the Plot

Discussion of child abuse (in the characters' past) including restricted calorie/food intake (might be difficult for anyone with an eating disorder). Many chapters focus on what happens at strip clubs (exhibitionism, lap dances, stripteases, crossing boundaries, etc.). Physical violence against men and women, gun violence in a law enforcement setting, bad guys ridiculing women.

Chapter One
HANNAH

"In all honesty, I'd enjoyed the horse ride more than the man ride. At least the horse had been a stallion. Looking back, my lab TA was more like a Shetland pony—hairy and small."

— Jessica James, *Truth or Beard* by Penny Reid

Wet T-shirt contests, a tiki bar, limbo poles—the how-low-can-you-go type of limbo, not the religious-waiting-room-purgatory limbo—umbrellas in every drink, and a skimpy swimsuit on every dancer. New costumes were a major expense for dancers, but all my ladies already owned bikinis. I wanted my colleagues to make money on my party, not be forced to spend it. In case you hadn't yet guessed, the theme of my retirement event was "Spring Break in September."

I'd chosen it after the monetary success of an impromptu car wash we'd had over the summer. If tonight was my last night as an exotic dancer, I wanted to go out with plenty of buck for my bang, if you catch my drift.

"Goldie! Where are you going? You haven't opened your present yet! It's waiting for you in—"

"Be back in a minute. Just need to freshen up!" I lifted my voice without turning to check which of my co-workers had called after me. They'd all been teasing me for the last week about this present of theirs, dropping cryptic hints, giving each other knowing side-eyes. Basically, teasing me and making me batty.

But now was not the time. Jogging in my stilettos, I came to a stop just inside the hallway off the main floor. I needed to catch my breath and deposit the cash weighing down my string bikini. While a Jimmy Buffett dance remix pumped over the speakers, reverberating through the walls and in my bones, I plucked the ones and fives from my body and bundled them together, not bothering to count.

I never counted until the end of my shift and saw no reason to break tradition now. My life motto was: best to not have any expectations of tips, cats, or people. But I did dash down to the dressing room to store most of the cash, leaving just a few bills tucked into the front of my costume as inspiration for other customers to do the same.

The event, which was now in its sixth hour, had been rowdy for sure, but also, thankfully, uneventful. No one had broken any rules, no one had picked a fight, no one had been thrown out. Most of my regulars had shown their faces this last week, and handing them off to other dancers had struck me as oddly bittersweet.

But . . . so it goes.

Cash dropped off, bottle of water chugged, my breath finally even, I pushed myself into the right headspace, a task that had been surprisingly difficult tonight. I blamed the contingent of firefighters who'd arrived a few hours ago. Apparently, some of the fellas from the neighboring fire stations—"nice" guys I'd gone to elementary, middle, and high school with, but whom I'd never spotted at the Pony before—had all talked and, since I was retiring, they'd figured it was their last chance to see me nearly naked.

They were right. Tonight was their last chance.

I wouldn't go out with George Padmar if the only other alternative was a rabid raccoon. A rabid raccoon would be a better conversationalist and likely have more self-control. That said, I'd let George and all his buddies look at my body to their hearts' content tonight as long as they were stuffing bills in my bikini and keeping their mouths shut.

Two more hours.

Just two more hours and then I'd be finished, done for good. I liked my boss and I liked my co-workers, but after ten years of doing this job week after week, I was more than ready for a change.

Taking one last bracing breath, I lifted my chin and plastered a smile on my face, getting into character. This was my superpower, making folks believe

I was not only unperturbed by any given situation, but actually enjoying myself and sincerely hoping they were enjoying themselves too. If there were a faking sincerity Olympics, I'd be the gold medalist every four years. That's where my stage name came from. "Goldie" was for my acting skills, not at all related to the color of my hair, contrary to popular belief.

I'd just stepped out onto the floor when Kilby—aka Fantasia—intercepted me, gripping my wrist to hold me still. "Hey, your present is waiting, gorgeous. Louis is looking for you. Another lap dance in the champagne room, all bought and paid for."

She winked, then altered course before I could respond, sashaying to one of my regulars—that is, one of my former regulars—and placing her hand on the back of his chair. Staring after her, I was careful not to frown.

My present is giving someone a lap dance in the champagne room? No. That couldn't be right.

Dismissing the thought, I didn't waste time watching what happened next between Kilby and my former regular. If someone had already paid for a dance from me and was waiting, I wanted to get it over with before another queue formed. Earlier in the evening, the line for a private dance with me had been ten-folks long. Doing three private dances back-to-back was tiring, but ten took the steam out of a girl real quick. My legs would hurt tomorrow like I'd been planting a field of turnips, make no mistake about that.

Careful not to engage in any lingering eye contact, I hopped up to the bar and waved Louis over. Louis was a fine bartender, especially considering his young age, but he'd never worked in a strip club until Hank had hired him three months ago. As such, he needed guidance and mentorship, both of which I'd be able to give him after tonight when my official role switched from dancer to club manager.

Smiling wide when he spotted me, his dark eyes warming, Louis wiped his hands on a towel and abandoned the drink he'd been making. He then jogged over to where I waited at the end of the bar. "Hey, Hannah."

I tried not to grimace. "It's Goldie. My name is Goldie on the floor."

"Oh. That's right. Sorry I keep doing that, boss." He looked contrite. "It's only you I keep messing up. Well, you and April."

"You mean, me and Shimmer."

"Yes. Sorry." He huffed, giving his eyes a half roll. "I will stop doing that to you and *Shimmer*."

Nodding, I leaned forward so he could hear me better. "Fantasia said I had a private dance paid for?"

"Yeah, about that." Louis's eyebrows pulled together and he braced his hands on the bar top. "It's the blond guy near the front—don't look yet, he's, uh, kind of scary."

I kept my eyes trained on Louis. "Okay."

"He asked and I told him I'd have to check with you, but he purchased five private dances, all in a row. He said Tina—Adore—set it up ahead of time. Is five dances in a row allowed? I didn't think it was allowed."

"Uh, no." Alarm had me automatically searching for this man who'd asked for five consecutive private dances.

Hank, the club owner and former manager, would lose his damn mind if we did that. Private dances lasted no less than three minutes but no more than five. Consecutive dances were not allowed, a bouncer was always stationed outside the door to the champagne room, and no customer could be alone with a dancer inside the room for longer. "That is definitely not—"

I stiffened.

Oh. My. God.

The words I'd been about to say died on my tongue and my train of thought derailed into a field of wildflowers and fantasy. The man hovering at the front of the club was absolute perfection. Six foot something, long beautiful body, piercing blue eyes, cliffs for cheekbones, and a granite jaw. Even the way his chin came to a rounded point felt perfect.

And I knew him.

And he was looking right at me.

Isaac.

A shock of thick, blond-white hair topped off his flawless-to-me façade, the locks now much longer than I'd ever seen them before.

Was this a joke? Or . . . *is this my present?*

In my haze of shock and thoughtlessly shameless admiration, I tried to remember the last time I'd laid eyes on the real Isaac Sylvester and not the Isaac Sylvester in my dreams.

He'd disappeared years ago, just after the motorcycle club he'd been pledging to crumbled. The Iron Wraiths were still around, but without their money man—on the run from the law—their president—currently on death row—and their second-in-command—rumored dead—they were a mere shadow of the powerful club that had reigned over Green Valley for decades.

My heart jumped to the spot in my throat where the words had died. Realizing that I'd been blatantly staring, I tore my gaze from the arresting intensity of Isaac's inscrutable gaze and redirected it to the third button on Louis's shirt, swallowing convulsively but managing to hold on to my polite smile.

"Goldie?" Louis asked.

What could Isaac be doing here, I wondered. Surreptitiously, I glanced around the floor, inspecting each of my co-workers in turn. Had they—did Tina call him? Louis had mentioned Tina. Is this—is he—some sort of going-away gift? Or a practical joke?

It was no secret among my co-workers that I had a mountain of a thing for Isaac Sylvester. In the past, whenever he'd arrived, they would tease me with quiet whispers and meaningful eyebrow raises. But as a customer, he'd never asked for me. Not once. He'd never spared me a glance either. Which, in retrospect, I'd considered a blessing. Other professional dancers plus conventional wisdom told me that developing a crush on a patron was a recipe for bitterness and a broken heart.

"Is that the man?" I croaked, then cleared my throat. "I mean, is that the—uh—the one in the leather jacket, blond hair? He's the one who wants the dances? From me?"

"Yes. Like I said, the scary-looking one." Louis sounded concerned. "But he mentioned Tina set it up, so I thought I should check with you."

Every time he came in, Isaac used to buy private dances from Tina, multiple times a night, once an hour at least. And now what? Had Tina set this up as a present for me? Was Isaac the gift everyone had been teasing me about all week? My cheeks warmed at the thought. I didn't know whether to be pleased or embarrassed or irritated.

"And he wanted the dances from *me*?" I licked my lips and tasted the cherry gloss I'd painted on earlier. "Are you sure?"

"He said he wanted you."

I caught myself just before a frown pulled my eyebrows together. This was not like me, almost losing my composure like this. I forced a small smile. It felt shaky. "You're absolutely sure? Are you sure he didn't say he set up the dances for Tina? He didn't ask for Tina? I mean, he didn't ask for Adore?" Tina was out of town. If Tina was who he actually wanted, he'd be disappointed.

"Nope. Not Adore. He asked for you specifically. He even used your full real name, first and last."

I stared at Louis without seeing him, my mind staging a riot, my heart beating at warp speed while I held my expression steady.

Each dancer I'd ever compared notes with readily admitted to having a mental stand-in, a fantasy person who took the place of the individuals who paid for a dance or stuffed a tip in their G-string. We relied on the pretend image to get through any given moment, imagining until reality blurred with fantasy. Customers who looked at us with desire or leered at us with lust were *that* fantasy person, and it helped. It helped a whole helluva lot to imagine that whatever person was in front of me was someone I actually wanted.

Tina/Adore's stand-in was Duane Winston. Piper/Diamond's was Benedict Cumberbatch. Everly/Nixie's was her husband.

My stand-in was, and always had been, Isaac Sylvester.

I rubbed my forehead, not knowing what to do. The answer should've been obvious. Logically, reasonably, I knew Hank wouldn't be happy if I did something so foolish on my last night dancing. I doubted he'd question whether I could take over as the club's manager, but this would definitely make my judgment seem suspect.

And yet . . .

My gaze flickered to the beautiful man loitering by the front of the club, his eyes on the floor as he waited patiently for a verdict. Heat exploded like a firework in my chest, smoldering embers settling low in my stomach.

I'd never broken the rules. I'd never wanted to. I'd never been tempted. Lord help me, but right now? I was more than tempted. With each of those boys from my high school earlier, I'd pretended they were Isaac.

"Did you tell him we don't allow consecutive dances?" I asked Louis, stalling. "Did you tell him there's a five-minute maximum?"

"I did. He told me that I should talk to you and mention Tina setting it up. He said you'd know why so much time was required."

My stomach dropped even as my head swam. If anyone would send me a man as a retirement present, it was Tina Patterson. She was a hot mess, but I loved her.

Louis leaned farther over the bar. "Should I tell him—"

"Tell him it's fine," I said, forcing the words out—albeit gently—before I lost my nerve. "Tell him . . . tell him I'll meet him inside the room." I smiled sweetly in an outward presentation of calm.

Louis's disquieted frown became a fretful one. "That's over fifteen minutes alone with one customer, up to twenty-five."

"I know." I tucked my hair behind my ears—a nervous habit I'd developed as a kid—but then realized what I was doing and shook my head to release the strands, scrunching the wild style back into place. "It's totally fine. I actually know him. We grew up together, old friends."

I didn't know Isaac Sylvester. In fact, I'd never spoken to him, not once, but I'd looked at him plenty when we were in choir together growing up. He'd been a reader, always bringing giant books to choir practice at the church. If he wasn't dutifully singing, his eyes were on the pages of his book. And that had given teenage me plenty of time to indulge myself in admiring him without the fear of being discovered.

"Goldie, are you sure?"

Giving Louis a sunny smile, I stepped back from the bar. "It's fine. Like I said, we're old friends. And remember, a bouncer will be outside the room the whole time. In fact, I'll ask Dave."

Louis looked like he wanted to argue, but a customer shouted impatiently for a drink. His attention divided, I darted to the side and around the back of the bar, hammering on the sunny expression more firmly to hide the knots twisting in my stomach. A regular waved me over and I winked at him. I did not stop.

I didn't want to stop or chat. Determined to talk Dave into allowing me five back-to-back private dances in the champagne room with Isaac Sylvester, I sought out the big bouncer and formulated a plausible excuse for fifteen minutes alone with Isaac, pasting on my most convincing unconcerned smile as I approached him.

Dave returned my smile with brotherly politeness, giving me his full attention and bending his tall frame toward me so I could reach his ear. "What's up?" he asked.

"I need a favor." I spoke loudly so he could hear me over the music, unconcerned that anyone nearby would be able to overhear. As far as I was aware, Dave didn't know Isaac Sylvester. Isaac had disappeared in the wind years before Dave had started working nights at the Pony. "A, uh, an old friend just walked in and I need a few minutes to speak with him."

Dave nodded, maintaining his stance bent at the waist. "Okay."

"I'm going to head in and I'd like you to be the one to stand outside the room, ensure we get fifteen or twenty minutes of privacy."

The tall bouncer leaned back, his forehead wrinkling. "Fifteen minutes?"

"Or twenty." I shrugged like it was no biggie, winning another gold medal for fake sincerity.

Inspecting me for a moment, his forehead cleared. "Okay. I can do that. No problem."

"Thanks, Dave." I gave his forearm a grateful squeeze and, with one more nod, walked around him to the champagne room, my stomach all fluttery.

I didn't want to think or give myself time to second-guess this haphazard, reckless decision. I was always the good, levelheaded one, the responsible one. I always made good decisions.

I deserve this, some errant voice in my head told me, and my steps faltered for a split second at the thought even as my heart ticked up. Resolve straightened my spine when I stepped into the private room, because I did deserve this. Tina was a good friend but, as I mentioned, she was also a hot mess. If she'd sent Isaac to me tonight, there was no telling what she'd said to get him here. But she wouldn't have held back. She wasn't circumspect at all.

She must've told him that I wanted him. That was fine with me. If he was here, then he obviously didn't have a problem with being wanted.

HANNAH

"Bravery was still bravery, no matter how clumsy the execution."

— Beau Winston, *Beard in Mind* by Penny Reid

"It's colder than usual tonight," he said—or something like it—as soon as he stepped into the room.

Nerves wound tight, I asked, "How do you want me?" like my heart wasn't in my throat, fully aware I was playing with a fire I'd been building for years.

"Pardon?" his voice asked my back.

Stapling on a façade of calm, I glanced at him over my shoulder. "Do you want my front, or back, or both?"

Good Lord, that just happened. I just asked Isaac Sylvester that question. I was moments away from giving this man a lap dance.

Isaac held perfectly still, staring at me, his thoughts an ice-coated mystery candy covered in a quicksilver wrapper of inscrutability. Several seconds passed while I surveyed this specimen of a man I'd always thought of as ideal. It wasn't necessarily his features or skin color, his hair color or height. I'd been attracted to all sorts of men. It was *Isaac.*

Something about how absorbed he became whenever he read books, how he walked, moved, carried himself, how he unflinchingly stared at people like he was engaging in an eternal game of truth or dare, the sound of his voice.

Taken all together, he did something to me. Made me feel weak in the knees and hazy.

Finally—and yet too soon—he said, "Uh, both?" and nothing about his disinterested calm appeared to be merely a façade. I swear, this man was as cold as a blizzard. So, why did that get me hot?

"All right." I nodded, biting the inside of my lip when my voice sounded a little shaky to my own ears.

I should've dated more. But it's difficult to date when you're an exotic dancer. Men were either freaked out when they found out, thinking of you like a Jezebel and condemning you as a sinner, or they claimed to be into it and expected you to immediately capitulate to their kinkiest fantasies, while also getting jealous and suspicious every time you went to work.

I'd had a few boyfriends, several of each flavor, and therefore no desire to date anyone ever again.

Perhaps if I'd had more experience with men that wasn't pretend and paid, I would be handling this moment better. But I'd sworn off relationships and hook-ups, both having been ultimately unfulfilling and a waste of my time and energy. I'd never had much time or energy to spare, especially not with naïve, unrealistic notions like romantic love. Sex was fine, but have y'all tried morning muffins?

I faced him fully. "And touching?" This question was asked to buy me some time, partially to draw the moment out and partially to get my thoughts in order. Also, a small part of me doubted this was real. Yes, I was certain Tina had sent him—Isaac had told Louis himself that he was here because Tina had asked him to come specifically for me—and yes, Tina would only send him for one reason.

But still. Nothing ever came easy. At least, not for me. Life never seemed to go the way I wanted. Could I trust this?

His head cocked a millimeter to the side and his eyes began sliding lower, making it to my chest before abruptly jumping back to mine. The tiniest frown appeared between his eyebrows, like he was concentrating. "Touching?" His tone held a bit more gravel than before.

Good Lord. How had he made that single word sound so filthy and fine all at once? "Yes," I said, impressed when I didn't sound breathless. "Touching."

"Could you be more specific?" he asked.

I quirked an eyebrow at his question. He'd had private dances before, but always with Tina. At first, I'd been jealous of Isaac's preference for Tina, back when he'd first returned to town, in his early days of pledging to the motorcycle club. I'd liked him for so long before he joined the army that when he returned and asked for Tina time and time again, it had irked.

But then, after a while, I learned to feel grateful that he never seemed to see me.

What if he'd asked for a private dance with me and it had been unpleasant? What if he'd been crude and grabby? Or smelled bad? Or said something mean? Or was violent? Or farting got his rocks off? Or if he'd displayed any number of disturbing, flawed human traits, which then made it impossible for me to use the idea of him as my stand-in? Then where would I be? I'd needed someone to put on a pedestal.

No. Me being invisible to him had been a good thing. I'd never been attracted to anyone else half as much as Isaac. Pretending while using his face and body had seen me through some experiences with customers that would've been downright repulsive otherwise.

But tonight . . .

I would never have to pretend again after tonight. I'd never have to use this man's face and hands and body in place of another's. If he proved himself to be repugnant tonight, I had nothing to lose except a few minutes.

"What did Adore do?" I asked, using Tina's stage name. "Did she touch you?" That old twist of jealousy tried to claw at the inside of my lungs but I shoved it away. I had no reason to be jealous of Tina. None of this was real. Nothing I did, or said, while I wore these clothes and called myself Goldie was real. He knew the drill. To him, I was likely as fake as my press-on nails.

Isaac's jaw ticked but he didn't answer, he just kept staring at me with those enigmatic eyes. Hannah loved his eyes. Goldie, however, loved nothing except making enough money to pay the mortgage and put food on the table.

Channeling Goldie's bravado, I lifted my hands and spelled it out, "Where am I allowed to touch you with my hands? I'll be on your lap, but when I need to balance, can I touch your shoulders? Your legs? Where?"

His steady gaze continued to arrest mine for a long moment. Then, it narrowed for a split second before glancing up at where the walls met the ceiling. He scanned the inside of the room.

Eventually, his jaw flexed and he said, "You can do whatever you want, Hannah, as long as we're close enough to hear each other."

Hannah.

He'd said my real name.

And how he'd said it, all soft, like he knew me and liked me, and we were talking about something benign and friendly. My heart flipped then raced, and

I smoothed a frown from my features before it could betray the sudden apprehension I felt.

Again, I asked myself if I could trust this. The man of my sex-dreams was suddenly here, presenting himself as a gift on my very last day as an exotic dancer. The urge to clarify the situation hit me hard.

I needed him to confirm whether Tina had put him up to this. "Did Adore tell you to come?"

Isaac seemed to hesitate, his gaze growing sharper. Eventually, he nodded once.

"And buy the five dances? All in a row?" I held my breath, afraid of his answer.

With similar reluctance, he eventually nodded again.

I breathed out. "We'll get those refunded, don't worry."

"I'm not worried," he said, all low and deep and delicious, his gaze squarely on mine. I fought a shiver.

Biting the inside of my lip, I studied him. He seemed to be simply waiting and watching, expecting me to take the lead, and I guessed that made sense. It was obvious why he was here, I'd just confirmed it. But still, something held me back.

Actually, not *something*. I knew what it was, so I asked, "Do you want to be here, Isaac?"

He didn't take even a moment to think about this question before giving me another of his silent head nods.

A rush of pleasure made my cheeks feel hot and I allowed myself a small smile. Yet one last question remained: What was he getting in return? Try as I might, I couldn't force my mouth to form the last question. I didn't want to know if she'd paid him or how she'd convinced him. Knowing would definitely deflate the fantasy.

Maybe I should just . . . *enjoy myself for once?*

A whisper of a laugh passed between my lips at the thought, but it wasn't ridiculous. How many people had purchased me over the years for someone else? How many times had I been given to a reluctant customer, paid for—part and parcel—by a friend, and asked to take good care of the fella? To treat him real nice for three minutes and make sure he felt like a king. At least five hundred. Too many times to count.

Isaac was here and, based on how Tina talked about the man, he certainly wasn't the type to do something he didn't wish to do. He was in this room because he wanted to be, whatever the reason. If he was a gift from Tina and some of the girls, because they knew he was my stand-in and they'd arranged it, then maybe I should simply enjoy my present. Not doing so would make me a hypocrite and I'd never been one to judge. I didn't have that luxury.

Decided, I gestured to the bench along the wall.

"Please sit down," I said. (Just so we're clear, *I* being Hannah, not Goldie. He might've paid for Goldie at the bar, but he'd called me Hannah just now, and so it was Hannah he'd be getting.)

Not waiting to watch him comply, I walked to the speaker controls and quickly scrolled through the playlist options, choosing a synth dance song I often used for cardio workouts. When played four times in a row, it would total just over twenty-four minutes.

I heard a scraping sound and looked over my shoulder, watching Isaac's powerful body pull a simple wooden chair from where it rested against the wall to the center of the room. *Interesting.*

The luxurious cushioned bench along one wall was typically where the customer sat, leaving the rest of the room for me to put on a little show before climbing on their lap. The bench was nice because it was easy on the knees when I straddled a customer and allowed me to brace my hands on the wall behind their back so I didn't have to touch them with my hands.

His stoic eyes on my backside and legs, he took off his jacket, tossed it to the bench, and then sat. His legs were spread wide and his arms moved restlessly, like he didn't know where to settle them.

Huh.

I walked to the door and poked my head out. "Okay, Dave. We're starting. I'll keep time too—twenty-five minutes."

The big guy nodded once, a hint of uncertainty behind his gaze as it strayed to the room behind me. "Everything okay, Goldie?"

"Just fine." I arranged my face into an unconcerned smile, grateful that Dave and Louis were relatively new to the club and its rules. "I've known Isaac my whole life. His sister is Jennifer Winston. He's okay."

"His sister is Jenn?" Dave's forehead cleared. "Well, okay then. Twenty-five minutes."

I gave him one last smile and shut the door, forcing my mind to clear itself of doubts. The time for doubts had officially passed. I only had twenty-five minutes, and I wanted to make the most of them.

Crossing to him in time to the music, I lowered to the floor and closed my eyes. I found I couldn't look at him in the moment and maintain composure. Kneeling between his legs, my hands fell lightly to his knees. I felt his body stiffen upon contact and I smirked at his jumpiness, my eyes still closed. Sliding my hands higher on his muscular thighs, I tested their size. In a moment, I'd be sitting on these massive things and it would be my legs spread wide. Good thing I was so flexible.

Halfway up, I redirected my hands to the outside of his legs, to his hips, grabbing hold and lifting my body. Moving my front upward between his open legs in a smooth motion, I let my chest slide along his groin, stomach, and chest, then I cracked my eyes open just as my forehead drew even with his nose. I lifted my chin; an inch separated our lips. His eyes immediately hooked into mine, appearing gray instead of blue in the dim light, and I momentarily lost my concentration. I stared at him. This man was so beautiful. And here. Not in my imagination, but *right here.*

My head fell back, exposing my throat, and Isaac leaned toward me, his attention dropping to my mouth. His lips parted like he'd planned on saying something but either forgot what or decided against it, his eyes undeniably hazy and hungry and . . . *my goodness.* Was the AC working? *It is very hot.*

It was so strange, having him actually here instead of existing in my mind. Already discombobulated, the way he looked at me sent all my plans straight out of my head.

He whispered something I couldn't hear over the thrumming of my heart, and I felt the air of it against my lips. His hand lifted, and I thought for a moment he was going to touch me. But then he balled it into a fist and returned his arm to the wooden armrest of the chair. He leaned away, settling back in his seat, jaw ticking and eyes devouring my neck and chest and lower.

Move! Move, Hannah. You're supposed to be dancing, not holding still.

Giving myself a mental slap, I forcefully squeezed my eyes shut again and swallowed, making my hands return to his thighs. I would give him my back first, then I wouldn't have to look at his distracting face. Turning in a practiced movement, I used my hands on his legs to leverage myself up and slide my bottom back and forth against his groin.

A puff of hot breath stirred my hair, then another. Over time, I felt the unmistakable length of him grow, harden, and strain against his jeans, swelling with each pass of my bottom and the backs of my thighs. Unbidden excitement and the thrill of power coursed through me. I bit my lip to keep from smiling, wanting to laugh. This certainly wasn't the first time a customer had displayed such obvious evidence of arousal. An erection just meant I was doing a good job. So, good job, me.

Likewise, I'd been turned on by a customer before. Usually, they had to smell good, their voice had to be deep and friendly and respectful, and they had to have kind eyes. Those seemed to be the only requirements, but folks would be surprised how rarely all three coupled together in one man.

It didn't happen often, but it did happen. I'm human after all.

And yet—tonight, Isaac, the charge in the air, the obvious strain on his control, the tension of his delectable body beneath mine—it certainly was the most electrifying experience that I could recall.

Unable to help myself, I glanced over my shoulder and opened my eyes again. He'd closed his. His eyebrows were knit together fiercely and his teeth were clamped shut, like he was in pain. Or experiencing too much pleasure to process.

The heady sight made me feel bolder and helped shove the remainder of my doubts—along with my good sense—to one side. I'd always imagined him beneath me while I did this, and to have him here, willing, eager even, I felt like I was inside my own fantasy. It was completely intoxicating and the term *drunk with desire* took on a four-dimensional meaning.

Setting my weight on his upper lap, I reached above and behind me, wanting to feel his skin. I dug my nails into the short hairs at the back of his neck, sliding my fingers down to the muscles of his upper back and letting my head loll on his bulky shoulder as I writhed slowly, methodically, and let the heat between my legs stoke the hardness between his. The friction felt sinful and wonderful and therefore forbidden.

Getting off on a customer wasn't just forbidden, it was the first of Hank's cardinal rules. *Never let yourself lose control because that's when the customer takes it from you.*

But here I was, getting hotter and hotter and wanting it, wanting the loss of control.

If I don't stop soon, I'll come. I'll come apart.

I didn't want to stop. The fever of my spiraling need and the intensity of his reaction held me hostage.

Just a little bit longer.

Ignoring the echo of restraint, I buried the last few strands of remaining wisdom, telling myself that this was my night. My party. I deserved this. I'd spent the last ten years doing everything for everyone else. I'd wanted this man for so long. I wanted just this one thing for myself. I was always pleasing other people. I deserved pleasure, too, didn't I?

Just a little bit more.

Before I realized what I was doing, I'd caressed a slow hand from his elbow to his wrist, delighting in the texture of his solid arm and threading our fingers together. I guided his large hand to the triangle covering my breast and skimmed his fingers over the center until my nipple peaked and hardened tightly. A low moan slipped past my lips at the tender, prickling sensation, the delicious heat of his palm, and the friction of his callouses. I might have been losing my mind, but I did not care. He felt so good.

Just this one time.

"Fuck," he said, the word part air, part growl as his hips jerked upward, seeking, searching. I gasped and his chest rose and fell behind me with ragged breaths. "God, Hannah. I'm here to talk—wait. Wait. Is this allowed?" He sounded just as lost as I felt.

It wasn't allowed. It definitely was not allowed and I'd never done it before, but it felt absolutely amazing.

Just a little bit longer. Just a little bit more. Just this one time.

"Hannah?"

In lieu of answering, I shifted his hand and guided it inside the fabric of the string bikini, encouraging him to palm my bare breast. His body shook with another powerful jolt and he sucked in a hissing breath. I felt a millisecond of reluctance before he surrendered to the feel of me filling his palm. His other hand lifted to mimic the first, and he squeezed, greedily massaging both of my breasts, his thumbs strumming back and forth over the tight peaks at the center.

I whimpered and his mouth found my ear. He nipped at the lobe, tonguing it, sending fire and aching need between my legs. My fingers slid behind me, down the front of his body, over the unyielding muscles of his stomach, and beneath his thin shirt, to cup him over his pants.

Another harsh sound left his lips and he abandoned my ear, his forehead falling to the back of my neck with another uttered curse as I stroked him, my hand between us.

Again, I'd never done this before at the Pony, nothing even close to it, not once. I'd never been tempted, never wanted to, but this man was the fulfillment of my fantasy and I wanted—needed—to make him feel so fucking good he'd never forget this night. Maybe he was being paid to be here, maybe he was here as a favor to Tina. But I wanted to haunt his dreams from now on because visions of him had haunted all my shifts for the last ten years. I wanted—

"Stop," he said, like the single word was ripped from him. It felt like a vicious bucket of ice and water, savagely dousing the raging carnal fire that had taken my brain and body hostage.

I held my breath.

His hands left my breasts, one removing the hand I'd placed between us and the other holding my hips still. But he didn't need to hold me still. My whole body had gone rigid.

"Jesus, Hannah. I *know* that's not allowed," Isaac growled, sounding nothing but angry. "What the hell are you doing?"

ISAAC

"I don't like to judge people. I love it. Writing people off completely was liberating."

— Cletus Winston, *Beard Science* by Penny Reid

I wasn't interested in her answer, I couldn't afford to be. This woman had me on a knife's edge. I needed to take control of the situation, not give her a chance to explain it.

Allowing no time for a response, I demanded, "Miss Townsen, immediately remove yourself from my person."

Several racing beats of my heart passed before she unseated herself and walked to the far side of the room. The music was loud, but all I could hear was the rushing of blood between my ears, and all I could feel was the painful protest of my body at her growing distance. A moment was required.

I closed my eyes in the ensuing silence. They wanted to look at her, at the curves and lines of her body, the glow of her skin, her stunning face and lips. What the hell was going on here?

As soon as I walked in the room, I'd spoken the phrase Tina Patterson promised she'd pass on to Hannah Townsen: *It's colder than usual tonight.* Per my conversation with Tina, whenever Hannah felt it was safe to talk freely, she would respond with: *Is it colder than usual? I didn't wear a jacket.*

I'd kept waiting for her to say the words.

Eyes still firmly closed, I ground out, "What exactly did Tina Patterson say to you about our meeting today?" loud enough that she'd hear me over the music.

I knew I sounded official and sharp. Given the situation, I considered harshness more than justified. I needed to get my head—both of them—back on straight.

The goal had been to engage in a friendly conversation with this woman, convince her with reason and facts to help my investigation. In any undercover operation, the agent takes cues from the contact and the confidential informant. Thus, Hannah Townsen's initial questions about front or back and touching—as though she'd been planning to give me a real lap dance—didn't necessarily surprise me once I'd confirmed the existence of the cameras in the corners of the room.

They hadn't been there the last time I was undercover in Green Valley. Perhaps the situation with Levit Traveston was more dangerous for her than I had anticipated. In the moment, when she hadn't responded to my prompt and instead initiated the lap dance, I'd followed Hannah Townsen's lead, planning to begin our conversation as soon as she was close enough to hear me without the cameras picking up our words.

The rest? Well. I wish I could say it all happened too fast for me to object, but that would be a lie. The truth was, she'd felt amazing and she'd made me feel amazing and those were both understatements. I hadn't been prepared for . . . her.

Lungs full of fire, I cracked my eyelids and peered at the woman. Hannah Townsen's exceptionally well-formed backside was still visible to me and I bit down on a frustrated groan. I needed another minute. Using the time, I closed my eyes again and recalled unsexy images from the case file on Levit Traveston, my ultimate target and Hannah Townsen's longtime regular customer.

Human trafficking. Women and children. Cargo containers. That worked. I focused on the case file I'd read last month, on what it told me. I focused on my reasons for being here, who I would be helping, what was at stake.

Calmer after a time, but also increasingly irritated, I cleared my throat, stood, and dragged the chair back to its former resting place. We couldn't stay in this room. I didn't know if those cameras were recording us. Also, I doubted I'd be able to concentrate if we remained here. We would go to my car and talk there.

Picking up my jacket, I crossed to her, draped it over her shoulders, and grabbed Hannah Townsen's wrist. Her head whipped toward mine. Not meeting her eyes—looking directly at her face struck me as potentially dangerous—I opened the door and pulled her into the main club.

The big guy I'd walked past on my way in, a bouncer who took the time to introduce himself as Dave, turned at our sudden appearance. I'd forgotten about him, which was extremely sloppy and unlike me. The man didn't block our path precisely, but he did frown and step forward, inspecting Hannah.

"Uh, Goldie? Everything okay?"

I watched as his gaze trailed to where I held her wrist and I opened my mouth, a lie formed and ready, but Hannah stepped forward in front of me.

"Oh, yes. Everything is just fine, honey," she yelled over the music, sounding perfectly at ease. Chipper even. In the next moment, her arm twisted, forcing me to release her wrist if I didn't want to cause a scene. Suspicion surged. I thought for sure she'd use this as an excuse to give me the slip. But then she surprised me by sliding her hand into mine and tangling our fingers together. "Isaac and I are just going to step out for a second." She leaned closer, resting her head on my shoulder and looking up at the big guy.

"You're leaving?" His eyes flickered to mine, conducting a quick inspection. I tried to look innocent but probably failed. I was good at looking mean, disgusted, sinister, and bored, but I'd never been good at looking innocent. In my line of work, it's important to know your limitations.

"He got me a retirement gift," she lied easily, in a way that would've convinced me if I didn't know the truth. "It's in his car. I'll hurry back, I promise." Maybe she sensed hesitation in him because she added quickly, while pulling me toward the front of the club, "Don't forget, I still have another fifteen minutes before the timer runs out on our private session, so no one should miss me. It's totally fine."

I let her lead us until we were outside, the door swinging shut behind us, congratulating myself the whole way on my foresight of covering her with my jacket. First, because it was cold outside. Second, because my brain told me this woman was so beautiful, her face alone was a massive distraction.

The Hannah Townsen in my memory had been twentysomething-ish, five eight, white skin, blue eyes, blond hair, size small to medium, and that's it. But my suspicion that she was goddamn gorgeous solidified now as she turned to face me with wide, searching eyes, her breath creating little white clouds of condensation in front of her generous mouth.

So, no. I didn't need her body out here on display, standing too close while wearing nothing but a string bikini. Why I was now noticing the oval shape of her face and the little beauty mark low on her right cheek, I had no idea. Point was, the jacket had been a brilliant maneuver in retrospect.

"Where are we going?" she asked, her tongue darting out to wet her lips.

At the quick movement, my attention dropped to her mouth and became absorbed. I realized it was covered in some sort of high sheen that revealed the true color of her lips rather than painting over it. I usually didn't notice such things. Or more precisely, I never let myself. Until tonight, I hadn't taken any notice of whether Hannah Townsen was beautiful.

I didn't understand. Why had I noticed her? Why was I still noticing?

Her lips pressed together and she swallowed. "Isaac? What's—uh—what's going on here?"

Shaking myself, I turned from the woman and pulled her after me toward my car, clipping out, "Do those cameras work?"

"What cameras?"

"The ones in the room where y'all give your *lap dances*." I slathered the last two words with disdain. Perhaps Levit Traveston's preference for Hannah Townsen had nothing to do with her beauty and everything to do with her lax attitude toward the law. The thought sobered me further and I finally started coming to my senses.

What we'd done—what she'd clearly initiated—wasn't allowed according to Tennessee state law. Each state had statutes and regulations regarding strip clubs and their operation. Her actions were a crime in Tennessee. She'd be (at best) barred from all strip clubs moving forward or (at worst) arrested and prosecuted for prostitution should her actions be made public. Or, more correctly, should I decide to make her actions public.

"Uh, yes. Those cameras work."

I nodded once. *Good to know.* Swelling anger told me I could seize the recordings immediately without a warrant since I'd been the one she'd violated and I'd been on the premises in an official capacity, didn't matter if I was plainclothes or not.

Surveying the parking lot and seeing we were alone, I opened my car's passenger side door and gestured to the interior. "Get in."

She hesitated. "Are we going somewhere else?"

"I don't know yet." I continued scanning the lot. Unnecessary in general but essential in the moment. My earlier shock had now dispelled.

Who the hell did she think she was, doing that to me? Doing that with any customer? Did she have no respect for the law? What about the safety of the other dancers? Once a club opened its doors to Johns, violence and drugs always followed.

Still visibly hesitating, the woman asked, "What are we going to do in the car?"

"Talk," I gritted out, now working hard to curtail my fury before it ballooned out of control. What we'd just done was the furthest I'd ever gone with a woman. I wasn't simply mad, I was furious. Yes, at her, but mostly at myself. How could I have let things go that far? What had I been thinking?

Abruptly fed up, I gripped her shoulder, physically maneuvered her inside the black Dodge Charger, and placed my other hand at the crown of her head to ensure she didn't accidentally hit it on the doorframe. Once she settled inside, I shut the door and walked around the trunk, taking a few extra seconds to breathe in the cool autumn air.

Being angry was just as inconvenient as being turned on when trying to get an informant on your side, conceivably more so. She needed to see me as an ally, not an aggressor. I needed her cooperation and Tina Patterson had led me to believe Hannah Townsen would be more than willing to cooperate with me.

Assuming the woman cooperated, this whole assignment would take a month, two months tops. It would be my shortest undercover assignment since my very first, but it would also hopefully be my last. Similar to my first assignment in Green Valley, I'd requested this one. And here I was, jeopardizing the case before it started due to a pretty face and great tits.

Granted, she had a real pretty face and amaz—

Doesn't matter. Never matters. She's not why you're here. Nothing about this woman matters unless she agrees to help. And then, only her safety and help matters.

Shutting the door as soon as I took my seat, I felt more in control. Hannah Townsen sat in profile, blond hair tucked behind her ears, attention zeroed in on where she twisted her fingers on her lap. Now she appeared to be the one in shock.

I endeavored to keep my tone gentle. "Miss Townsen, what exactly did Tina Patterson tell you about my visit tonight?"

She croaked out, "Nothing," then cleared her throat, adding, "Maybe you could tell me what it is you want to see me about." Her voice sounded small.

Tina had told her nothing? I found that hard to believe. Not because Tina Patterson was a paragon of reliability in general, but because she'd always been prompt in passing messages in the past.

I took a deep breath and decided to get straight to the point. "Do you know a man named Levit Traveston?"

She said nothing for a moment while I studied her features. Then, she lied. "No."

I ground my teeth. "You do know him. He's a regular of yours and has been for over twenty months."

She said nothing, just kept staring at her fingers.

"Listen, I'm an undercover agent and I need your help. And I need you to stop lying."

She flinched when I said I was an undercover agent and her gaze cut to mine, widening with what I read as confusion and disbelief.

Digging my badge out of my back pocket, I handed it to her. Hannah Townsen accepted it, albeit reluctantly, as though it might burst into flames once she did. I gave the woman a moment to look, to read and confirm, before I continued.

"Levit Traveston deals in human trafficking and illicit drugs. He's a very bad guy and we need your help to bring him in."

"I don't know anyone named with that name," she said, it sounded absent-minded, her attention still on the badge.

"I know that's not true, Miss Townsen. Things will be so much easier for both of us if you would tell the truth." I did a bad job of hiding the fact that my patience was wearing thin.

She glanced at me again, passing over the badge, her gaze now wary. "How can you know whether or not that's true, *officer*?"

Oh. I get it. She's one of those.

I stared at her. The way she'd said "officer" as an insult essentially tossed lighter fluid on the smoldering coals of my temper. Who the hell did she think kept things safe and tidy in this country? Fucking fairies?

A complete change in approach was now required.

Angling my body toward her, I invited my anger to rise completely to the surface, making no attempt to disguise it. No need to with people of her kind, who had no respect for law enforcement. "I know it for a fact, *miss,* because Tina Patterson told me so and we have photographs of you with the man."

She flinched again. "I honestly have no idea . . ." Hannah trailed off and her attention seemed to turn inward. "Wait. Wait a minute." She focused on me again. "Can I see these photographs?"

I shrugged, still glaring openly, and pulled out my phone. Navigating to the shots of them together that Tina had sent me last month when I'd first made inquiries, I showed Hannah Townsen the screen of my cell.

She blinked, a small breath puffing out of her. "If Levit Townslip is his name—"

"Levit Traveston," I corrected.

She kept on talking. "—I had no idea. I know him as Tavvy Little, or Little Gun, as the men with him say."

"You've been giving this man *lap dances* for over a year and you don't know his name?" I made sure those two words were once more coated in contempt, frustrated when my blood pressure spiked at the mere thought of Hannah giving Levit Traveston the kind of lap dances she'd attempted to give me.

Her look turned dirty and I had to assume she understood what my words implied. "I don't—I've never—" She shook her head, her eyes lifting to the ceiling of my car. After breathing out slowly, she said more calmly, "I don't give Tavvy lap dances at all. He doesn't like to be touched."

"Then what do y'all do in there?"

"He likes stripteases." Her attention lowered to her lap again.

"Stripteases," I mimicked flatly. What was that code for? Blow jobs?

"Yes. Stripteases." Sounding bored, she redirected her attention to the dark night beyond the windshield.

I wasn't going to push this woman on her criminal solicitation activities. Fact was, I still needed her cooperation and backing her into a corner wasn't going to help me get what I wanted. At least, not yet. So, I asked, "Does he also happen to borrow your phone and make calls on it during these stripteases?"

"Yes."

Good. That was the important part. "And what are the nature of these phone calls?"

"I don't know."

She was obviously lying to me again and I'd officially had it with her. "Miss Townsen, let me tell you how it's going to be."

The woman crossed her arms and I saw the muscle at her temple jump, her focus still out the windshield.

No matter. I didn't require her gaze, just her attention. "You're going to assist me with this investigation. You're going to allow the FBI to tap your phone for the next month, at least, and you're going to continue putting on your *stripteases* for Mr. Traveston. And when he asks to borrow your phone, you're going to let him."

"I'm retired. I don't do that anymore after tonight." She sniffled but her voice was steady.

"Well then, come out of retirement for Mr. Traveston. Your country needs you."

Her chest rose and fell, her chin lifting at an angle that screamed defiance. "What if I say no?"

I wasn't surprised by this question. In every way imaginable, Hannah Townsen had lived down to my expectations thus far and this reaction from her was what nearly every person has when asked for help by law enforcement. They don't care about their community. They don't care that there are bad guys and drug dealers and human traffickers. They only care about themselves and being inconvenienced. As it turned out, Hannah resembled everybody else in this regard.

Nevertheless, my lips tugged to one side. I found her question amusing, given all that had occurred tonight.

I'd wanted our conversation to be friendly. Before I'd arrived, it hadn't occurred to me that it wouldn't be. Tina had described Hannah Townsen as a sweetheart. But this woman was no sweetheart. Her actions, attitude, and lies had made a friendly conversation impossible. Now she would reap what she had sown.

"You can help willingly," I said evenly. "Or I can arrest you—right now—for prostitution."

Chapter Four
ISAAC

"Clowns, in my experience, are like cats. They can sense when a person isn't into them and then go out of their way to interact with that person."

— Simone Payton, *Dr. Strange Beard* by Penny Reid

She did look at me then. Even though the night was moonless, the outdoor lights did a fair job of keeping the parking lot illuminated. The car less so, but I did witness the color draining from her lovely features.

"Are you . . . are you serious right now?" She sounded shocked, indignant, wounded, her voice cracking. She must've thought of herself as a victim, and of me as the villain, and I'd broken her heart. And she sounded completely sincere, aided by the gathering moisture in her eyes, turning her beautiful blues glassy and liquid.

Wow. What an incredible actress. I had half a mind to applaud and I couldn't recall ever being more infuriated in my life, or as impressed. Not only did she have no ethics, or morals, or sense of responsibility and justice, the woman was a master manipulator.

"You're blackmailing me," she whispered. It was an accusation.

"I'm not blackmailing you." I couldn't keep the smirk off my face and I didn't wish to. It's not that this was funny to me—I mean, it was a little funny

—it was more that I loved when criminals were shocked by the consequences of their choices.

I'd seen and heard it all: I stole something and now I have to go to jail? I hit my children and now you're arresting me? I threatened my spouse and now there's a restraining order against me? I'm so shocked. I'm completely blindsided. I'm a victim!

I loved it. It was why I would never quit law enforcement completely, why I would never stop paying attention and forcing criminals to take responsibility. Maybe if someone had been paying attention to my family, to what my father had done to us, he would've been held accountable and my childhood wouldn't have been hell on earth every single day. So, yeah, holding criminals accountable was my favorite part of the job.

"This is not blackmail," I said, keeping my tone light. "This is an opportunity."

"You are. This is blackmail. I can't believe you're blackmailing me into helping you." Water pooled heavily in her eyes.

I breathed out a laugh at her performance and I suddenly realized why I was so angry right now. She was a pretender, and that reminded me of my father. He'd been a master manipulator, exceptionally skilled at pretending to be respectable in public, showing one face to the world and another to his family. It was the duplicitousness I hated.

Duplicitousness is part of my job, so that makes me a hypocrite, right? The difference is: My father feigned goodness to trap good people. Whereas I feigned wickedness to trap wicked people. And I could definitely live with that.

Thus, Hannah Townsen's attempts at sending me on an all-expenses-paid guilt trip were ineffective. Unmoved, I drawled, "No, Miss Townsen. I'm offering you a chance to make reparations for your criminal activities. Either do the right thing, help your government put a human trafficker and illicit drug distributor behind bars, or face the consequences of your choices. I'm giving you a second chance. As I said, it's an opportunity."

She shook her head, tears spilling down her cheeks, and my mind told me she was beautiful even when she cried.

Beware of beautiful women, my father's voice unexpectedly echoed between my ears with words he often quoted in my youth, *they're harmful to your health and your soul.* Yeah. My father had been a real piece of work. Luckily, he was now dead.

Heaving a shaky sigh, she ripped her gaze from mine and faced the passenger door, perhaps finally understanding the severity of the situation. If she didn't help me with this investigation, I had no reason to hide what had occurred tonight in the club's private room. She'd confirmed there existed recordings to prove it. She didn't need to know that I doubted the charges would stick, but maybe a stint in jail would help turn her life around. I'd seen it before, specifically with drug addicts. Without access, they got clean behind bars, they had no choice.

Studying the back of her head as the car filled with the sound of her breathing growing more labored, a twinge of empathy had me wondering if maybe, during this investigation, assuming she agreed to help, and assuming she wasn't too far gone, I could help her also. In my experience working undercover, folks rarely got involved in drugs or prostitution because it appealed to them. Usually, desperation was the culprit.

Once Tina Patterson had confirmed Hannah Townsen was Levit's preferred stripper, the field office had investigated her. I'd skimmed her file. Dissimilar to my own father, who'd grown up with a silver spoon and loving parents, this woman hadn't lived an easy life. Her father had left her momma with a mountain of debt and no way to pay it, running out with another woman. Her mother had then turned to the bottle and crashed their car while intoxicated, leaving Mrs. Townsen with probation, a permanently revoked driver's license, and limited mobility in her legs.

Hannah, at seventeen, gave up a scholarship to college in order to stay home and make money, taking care of her mother by working as a hostess at the Front Porch, Green Valley's nicest restaurant, which wasn't saying a lot, but it said something. She started stripping at the Pink Pony shortly after her eighteenth birthday as a quick way to make more money.

According to my information on Miss Townsen here, she'd put herself through college once she'd paid off the debt, and her momma had hooked up with a man to help at the farm. Recently, Hannah had graduated near the top of her class in marketing and business. Hank Weller, owner of the Pink Pony, had then offered her the position of club manager, which she'd accepted.

It was no wonder folks in town—Tina Patterson included—considered her a sweetheart. With a history of that sort, she came across on paper as a stripper with a heart of gold, trapped by the cruelty of fate and forced to pay for her parents' mistakes.

However, one point about her past hadn't made sense to me when I read her file: Why would someone who'd graduated near the top of their class from a solid four-year university accept the job of manager at a strip club? Didn't she want to get out of this place? Wasn't she ready to leave this life behind? Apparently not. I guess now I knew why.

Sex work in this part of the world paid a lot more than the salary of a recent college graduate, and that was a fact. Giving up that kind of money wouldn't be easy for someone who was used to it.

Presently, Hannah's breathing, which had crescendoed acutely when she'd turned to face the door, began to even.

The moments recalling her pitiful past deflated my ire. Along with my suspicion, I now felt a measure of pity for this woman. I didn't need to feign calm this time as I sat back in my seat, saying, "I would appreciate your cooperation, Miss Townsen. Your country needs your help in order to catch a crim —a very dangerous person." Technically, she was also a criminal, thus I avoided the word.

"I don't—" she started. Audibly clearing her throat, she faced forward again, swiping at her cheeks. "I don't know if I can help. I told Tavvy I retired. I tried to pass him off to Fantasia, but he got upset and said he wouldn't be back."

"When was this?"

"Last Saturday. He knew tonight was my going-away party and he didn't come." Her shoulders rose and fell with a shrug. "He seemed serious. I have no way of knowing whether he'll return to the Pony or not, and I have no way to contact him."

"Hmm . . ." I thought about this information, inspecting her and the veracity of her claims. Maybe she was telling the truth and he was gone for good. However, and more plausible given our interactions this evening, maybe she was lying and protecting a good source of income, and therefore her own interests. In which case, I could no longer simply tap her phone and wait for Levit Traveston to make his calls.

I would need to go undercover at the Pink Pony and keep an eye on the place, on her, and wait for a month—maybe two—to see if he showed up. If he did, I'd make sure Hannah did her part.

"You can't know for certain he'll never return." I reached forward and opened the glove box near her knees, ignoring how she recoiled from my hand and any incidental touch. "He could change his mind."

"He could," she allowed, her voice back to being small. "And, if he does, then I'll help." The way she said it made me think she did not believe Levit Traveston would return. Her promise sounded empty.

"How about this." Closing the glove box, I placed a container of tissues on her lap. "Let's make a deal. You agree to let us tap your phone, just in case Traveston returns. If he does, you put on your show and let him use your phone as normal. Do this no less than four times, no more than eight, and I won't bring you in for what you did. But I will be taking those tapes. Tonight."

"Fine." She set the tissues on the dashboard without taking one and then reached for the door handle. "It's a deal. My phone is inside, I'll go get it. And I'll grab the recordings."

"I'm not finished."

Her fingers froze on the handle. "What else do you want?"

"I need to be on-site. We need to come up with a reason for me to be here often, at the Pony."

"You want to be a dancer?" Her voice was devoid of humor though the words were obviously a joke.

"I'll pose as your boyfriend. It'll give me a reason to—"

"No!" She shook her head, her eyes squeezing shut tightly. "No. Absolutely not. That is absolutely not an option."

I released a silent sigh, willing to work with her here if she met me at least halfway. "Then give me a better idea."

"You could—you can be a—uh—uh—a bouncer!" Hannah's eyes flew open as soon as the words left her mouth. "Yes. We're, um, hiring. We need a bouncer and no one would question me hiring you in a hurry since we're short-staffed. Yes, a bouncer is much better."

I frowned my confusion. "You want me to be a bouncer? At the club?"

She nodded.

"That means I'll be on-site all the time," I filled in. How could she—how would she—be able to meet with her Johns if a federal officer was present at the club?

"Yes. I know." She grabbed for the tissue container, pulled one from the plastic flap, and dabbed at her eyes. Her voice had changed, she was someone new. Someone reasonable, calm, and professional. "As I mentioned, the club needs a new bouncer. This solves a problem for me. You can work at the club until the investigation is over and I'll time that with finding a permanent replacement. It's a solid plan."

Wait a minute. Did she think I'd work at her club and provide a cover for her criminal activities? I scowled. "Let me be clear. If I'm present at the Pink Pony and I witness you soliciting, I will arrest—"

"Mr. Sylvester!" she shouted over me, again sounding indignant. "I'm not —I wasn't—" Hannah Townsen huffed harshly, gritted her teeth, released another short laugh, and then faced me. Her eyes were caged fire, her features set and determined. "You don't need to worry about that, officer. You have my promise, other than what is necessary for helping with your investigation, I will never do *anything* like what happened tonight *ever again*. And I do mean ever again, in any capacity, paid or otherwise, with you or anyone else, as long as I shall live. I am officially done—with stripping, with dancing, with getting my hopes up, with all of it. And from today forward, I will never touch a man for any reason other than as a friend, colleague, or acquaintance. And only then with a handshake or a hug, so help me God."

My scowl became a small frown. Once more, she looked entirely sincere even though her words were completely ridiculous. Why would she swear off touching men? What an absurd overreaction. Her litany of nonsense, spoken with so much genuine fervor, was just another reason not to trust her. *More lies.*

But she'd given me what I wanted. She'd said what I wanted, promised not to solicit at the Pony. So, I ignored her nonsense and I offered her my hand for a shake. "Fine. It's settled. When do I start work?"

"Work starts tomorrow afternoon at two. I'll let the team know you're expected. Dave will let you in. Now, allow me to go grab my phone and that tape so you can leave." She didn't take my offered hand, she didn't even look at it. Instead, hers reached for the door handle again. "And if you don't mind, I'll make us both another promise, Mr. Sylvester." Popping open the door, her features and tone seeming entirely at ease, she smiled brightly and said, "I promise to never touch *you* ever again. For any reason. Not even for a handshake."

* * *

I promise to never touch you ever again. For any reason. Not even for a handshake.

Hannah Townsen's vow from last night kept echoing between my ears. It floated in and out of my awareness as I drove to my temporary housing, as I prepared for bed, as I tossed and turned and gave up on sleep, and as I attempted to read.

I did manage to pass out around 4:00 AM, but the cacophony of birdsong in the Smoky Mountains woke me up not two hours later. And there she was again as soon as I'd rubbed the sleep from my eyes.

I promise to never touch you ever again.

After a shower, instant coffee, and no luck concentrating on my book, I decided to take a drive. That's how I found myself parked in the Donner Bakery lot, staring at the tastefully decorated storefront and the long line that had already formed outside of it by 7:00 AM, when my field office contact called.

"Where are you?" Agent Beth Danforth asked by way of greeting. "Your tracker says you're at a hotel?"

"Yeah," I confirmed, not wanting to get into the details.

The Donner Bakery was an outbuilding of the Donner Lodge, which had been built and managed by my mother's side of the family for three generations, until just recently. The lodge was an all-inclusive and somewhat exclusive resort. A popular destination for wealthy families from all over the world with its farm-to-table restaurant, antique-filled cabins and guest rooms, and—of course—the award-winning Donner Bakery, which my younger sister now managed as the head baker. Or pastry chef. Or whatever her official title was.

Whatever. It didn't matter what they called her. All the awards were hers. She'd earned them all on her own.

Jenn and I hadn't talked in years. I didn't know the details of her life, but I'd always made a point to keep myself informed of the big picture stuff. She'd gotten married to a local. He was an auto mechanic. His family was nice and respectable, but he was sketchy as fuck.

No matter. According to my person inside the bakery, he treated her like a queen. If my sister, Jenn, was happy, I'd stay out of it until she wasn't.

"Why are you at a hotel? What about the safe house? Why aren't you there? Is there something wrong with it? Could you find it?" Danforth's questions were rapid-fire, as was her habit, but also a little sluggish. She sounded tired.

"I found it just fine. What's up with you? You sound ready to pass out."

I heard the shuffle of papers from her side of the call. "Budget cuts. We're down two agents, they're upgrading our goddamn database next week, I'm on my fourth week of forty hours overtime, and everyone is pissing me off. Just ignore me. Are you sure you found the safe house okay? Barner said it was in the middle of nowhere and the road up to it had spotty reception."

"I had no trouble. Let me give you a quick report on last night." I didn't remind her that I'd grown up in Green Valley and finding the government-owned parcels around Bandit Lake was not a big deal for a local. My eyes still fastened to the front of the bakery, I provided Danforth with all the details from last night, leaving none of the pertinent facts out, but trying to be succinct. She really did sound exhausted.

When I finished explaining the events, I heard her whistle. "So, you let her go for now? Don't tell me you'll push the office to press solicitation charges later. Leveling with you, we really don't have the resources for these kinds of small operations, nor do we have time for them. If you push this, I'll send it to local law enforcement. That's all I can do."

"Depends." I knew this call was official, but that wouldn't keep me from being truthful. If my logic or ethics were called into question later, I'd deal with the fallout then. As long as I understood my own reasoning in the moment, that was good enough for me. "The evidence isn't rock solid. She never verbally offered, but I believe the context and the recording should be enough to make the charges stick. If she helps with the investigation and stops soliciting Johns, I'll recommend that her efforts be taken into consideration. But if the issue is widespread at the Pink Pony, if she's just one of many who are soliciting customers, I'll recommend an additional investigation into the club and its activities. Regardless, it should wait until after we secure evidence against Traveston. He's the priority."

"I concur. You have Miss Townsen's phone?" Danforth had started typing.

"Yep. It's at the safe house. I already installed the software and will give it back to Miss Townsen today when I see her at the club." Shifting in my seat, my gaze narrowed on the two new people who'd just joined the Donner Bakery line. I recognized them as Beau Winston—one of my sister's many brothers-in-law—and his girlfriend, Shelly Sullivan. Both mechanics at the Winston Brothers Auto Shop, they wore blue coveralls and had possibly stopped by the bakery on their way to work to grab breakfast. Or maybe just to say hi to my sister.

They could stop by the bakery whenever they wanted and talk to Jenn, spend time in her company, shoot the shit. How nice for them.

"It was a good idea she had, you come on as a bouncer. Quick thinking."

I could tell by Danforth's tone that, having what she needed from our call, she was ready to end it.

"Wait, what about the protection package? When should Hannah expect your call?" Tearing my eyes from Beau Winston and Shelly Sullivan, I stared unseeingly at the steering wheel, collecting my thoughts.

"What do you mean?" she asked on a tired sounding sigh.

"It's Traveston, right? He's notorious for taking revenge. What kind of package is Hannah being offered?" Maybe, if Hannah went into witness protection, it would force her to walk the straight and narrow. At the very least, it would remove her from the environment that had led to her current circumstances.

"Let me grab the file again. I printed everything out since I might lose access for a bit. One sec." Once more, I heard papers shuffling, then she was back. "Nothing. There's nothing in the file regarding protections for Miss Townsen."

"Why the hell not? She's a witness, isn't she? Where's the protection package?"

"The specialists don't consider her a witness. We don't need her to testify, we just need to tap her phone. They haven't taken her safety into consideration. Why? Do you think they should?" Danforth sounded bored. I got the sense my questions irritated her.

I cursed under my breath and could've kicked myself for not asking about this earlier. I'd assumed, since Hannah was always in the room while Traveston made his phone calls, she'd be considered a witness and would be offered a protection package. Those conversations didn't usually include me. They were done by the field office after I obtained the witness's consent to assist.

"Fine. If there's no protection, then how probable is it he'll be able to trace the information we gather to Miss Townsen?" A sense of righteousness had me asking the question despite Danforth's shitty attitude. "What kind of precautions have we taken on her behalf, to keep her as the source anonymous? There's got to be something in there."

"Uh, let me see . . ." Danforth remained silent for a few moments, then sounded as though she was reading when she said, "'The court will be petitioned at the time of warrant to maintain a blind on the source of the recordings.' That's it. That's all it says."

I cursed again. "So, you're telling me that's it? That's all they're doing? They're going to ask the court to keep the source anonymous? What good does that do? The defense will still have access to the evidence. They'll put two-and-two together. Traveston will know right away it was her. It's not enough. You need to push them for more."

Now Danforth sighed dramatically, loudly. "Sylvester, I've got a huge caseload here, a system upgrade next week that's going to be an absolute nightmare, and you want me to . . . what? Request a protection package for a small-town stripper who's also soliciting on the side and who we don't really need as a witness? Is that the best use of tax dollars?"

"I'm not—"

"You asked for this assignment for some reason. Fine. You got it. But don't tell me how to do my job or how I should allocate resources. I'm down two agents. My hands aren't just full, they're tied. If Miss Townsen feels unsafe, then maybe she should look for a different line of work when this is over. I don't—we don't—have the time or resources to save everyone, and putting

Traveston behind bars is the priority. He's moving a lot of cargo—*kids*, Sylvester. Little kids."

My attention focused on the line of customers outside the bakery just in time to see my sister emerge from the building. She held a tray covered in muffins and wore a ponytail and an apron. Her smile resembled a sunbeam as she chatted up the customers. Folks laughed, returned her grins, and fawned over her. She was a celebrity. At the very least, I could see she was beloved.

When she reached Beau Winston, she gave him a big hug, then hugged Shelly Sullivan. I blinked at the wholesome scene and willed a blanket of apathy to descend, suffocating any useless longing that might rise within me.

"Danforth," I tried again, my voice devoid of emotion. "I'm not asking for a protection package. I'm asking you to reach out to the analysts and legal to request something better with the handling of the evidence. They can suggest that handing over the evidence—the actual recordings—to the defense would put Han—Miss Townsen's life in danger. See if they can blind not only the source, but the evidence itself. That seems reasonable given the fact that we're discussing a human life."

"Fine. Fine, I'll do that. Is there anything else? Otherwise, I have to go."

"No, nothing I can't handle my—"

She hung up.

Chapter Five
ISAAC

"Laws varied depending on the place and time, required documentation, due process, and interpretation. You couldn't count on the law to serve justice."

— Scarlet St. Claire, *Beard Necessities* by Penny Reid

After my call with Danforth, I left the bakery and drove around the valley, taking only mountain roads while Hannah's vow kept repeating in my head. *I promise to never touch you ever again. For any reason. Not even for a handshake.*

Why was I thinking about it? And her? And why had I suddenly taken note of Hannah Townsen when, in all my years undercover, I'd never allowed myself to notice any woman while on assignment.

Years back, when I was deep undercover in Green Valley and Tina Patterson used to be the conduit through which I received information and orders from the local FBI field office, Hannah Townsen had been merely one of many dancers at the Pink Pony, all of whom I also didn't notice beyond cataloging their physical features: height, size, approximate age, skin color, eye color, and hair color.

But not lip color. Not face shape. And not beauty marks.

After several hours on the winding mountain road, I accepted that I hadn't really looked at Hannah—not ever—until she'd surprised me in that private room last night.

Kneeling between my legs and sliding the front of her body against mine in a movement so smooth and lithe and sexy, she'd startled me. Her face had been an inch from mine at the beginning of her performance. I'd detected the sweet smell of candy, or cherries. It had been disarming, and my mouth had watered, also startling me.

But most disarming? The way she'd looked at me in that room. I played the moments over and over in my mind as I left behind the aimless mountain roads in order to make it to the Pink Pony by 1:50 PM. Hannah Townsen had looked at me last night as though she wanted me. Badly. As though she knew me, saw me, and had never wanted anyone or anything more. It had been more intoxicating than any alcohol, more mesmerizing than any hypnotist's show.

Parking in the Pink Pony's lot, I told myself to be on my guard with her today, not to fall for her tricks or appearance of goodness. One would think I'd be good at this after so many years working undercover, but I was nowhere near as hardened against it as most of my colleagues. Something for me to improve, I reckoned.

Grabbing my book from the passenger seat, I flipped it open to where the bookmark lay and read, no longer troubled by Hannah's vow. My timekeeping behaviors changed based on whatever person—whatever cover identity—I was pretending to be for any given assignment. If my cover was a lazy slob, I'd be late and not give a shit. If my cover was uptight and tense, I'd arrive early. Interestingly enough, I'd discovered over the years that folks hated people being early more than they frown on people being late.

Today was a rare occasion where I was Isaac Sylvester, and Isaac couldn't abide tardiness. And since I knew being early flustered and annoyed folks, Isaac always appeared right on time.

Arriving at the Pink Pony ten minutes before 2:00 PM, I read my book for nine minutes, and then approached the front door at 1:59 PM. Since the door was unlocked, I opened it and strolled inside. With the dimness of the interior a harsh contrast to the bright early-autumn day, my eyes required an adjustment period. I blinked, discerning a mostly empty main room save for a big shape sitting at the bar and a smaller shape behind it.

When my vision cleared, I recognized the big shape as the same guy who'd been standing outside the private dance room last night. The bartender turned out to be the smaller shape and he pulled some sort of face upon spotting me, ceasing whatever murmured conversation they were in the middle of, and lifted his chin. In contrast, the big guy glanced over his shoulder and stood, sending me a wide smile and extending his hand.

I remembered his name from the previous night when he'd introduced himself. "Dave," I said, accepting his handshake. Firm, but not bullish. A quick up-down, then release.

"Isaac." He tossed his thumb over his shoulder. "This here is Louis. He's our only bartender. We're looking for a second if you know anyone. Louis has only been here a few months, but he can also answer questions."

"Thanks." I leaned to the side to give Louis the bartender a nod in acknowledgement. The younger man stared at me with what could only be described as wary curiosity.

"Our third team member isn't here right now. Joshua is off on medical leave. Man, we really do appreciate you starting so soon."

I openly inspected Dave. He wasn't from around here, but his Yankee accent didn't put me off any. Rather, his friendly words and straightforward demeanor, paired with the memory of his protective concern for Hannah last night, won me over immediately.

Don't get the wrong idea. It had nothing to do with Hannah. He clearly cared about the dancers in general. It was his job to protect them and I respected how seriously he took the responsibility.

I allowed myself a small smile. "Oh? Y'all hurting for help?"

Hannah hadn't been lying last night about needing a bouncer. At least that much was true.

"Yes." Dave chuckled. "But not just any help. Good help is what we need."

"Hard to find good help?" I slid my hands in my jeans pockets, not letting on I was fully aware of Louis's continued stare. He could stare all he wanted.

"Almost impossible." Dave hit the center of my chest with the back of his hand, the familiar gesture a surprise. "I'll be honest, we were a little worried when Hannah told us she'd found a new bouncer and he'd be starting today." He leaned closer and glanced at Louis, possibly to draw him into the conversation. "When Hank was in charge, all bouncers and bartenders would be part of the interview process. But you being Jenn Winston's brother buys a lot of credibility, ya see? So, what I'm saying is, tell your sister I say hi, and welcome to the team."

Ignoring his comments about Jenn, I asked, "You think it's a bad thing or a good thing? I mean, Hannah taking over from Hank Weller?" I wanted to gauge how much these two might know about Hannah soliciting customers.

I didn't expect them to admit much—in truth, I expected them to dodge the question or give me some nonanswer—so I'd crafted it to be pointed enough for unconscious body cues to reveal their true thoughts.

"Are you kidding?" Grinning, Dave hit me again with the back of his hand.

"Best thing ever! Am I right, Louis, or am I right?" The big guy strolled back to the stool and sat.

"Best thing ever," Louis confirmed, a small smile taking over the younger man's features, his expression becoming hazy as he looked past me and at nothing but his own thoughts. "Hannah is . . . amazing," he said with a sigh. "We all love her."

I didn't frown at that, but I wanted to. Either she had these men fooled and they had no idea what she'd been up to in that private room, or they had absolutely no problem with it. How could they not know she was soliciting for sex? Dave didn't appear to be the ignorant or naïve sort. Louis, on the other hand, struck me as someone easy to manipulate. Maybe he was her partner.

Then again, recalling last night and her convincing performance of distress —and everything else—Hannah Townsen's ability to fool both men remained a real possibility.

I made a noncommittal sound and nodded. But before I could take a seat, Louis extended his hand, the suddenness of the movement demanding my attention.

"I'm Louis," he said, even though Dave had already named him.

"Yeah. I heard." I accepted the shake. His grip was aggressively tight and he didn't immediately release me.

"We didn't realize who you were last night." His statement sounded as though it had a double meaning.

I glanced at Dave. His eyes were on his shoes but he wore a small, rueful-looking smile.

"Who am I?" I asked the bartender, wondering if we were engaging in two different conversations. This guy was younger than me, maybe twenty-two or twenty-three. Just a kid.

Louis crossed his arms, his eyes moving down my front—perhaps he was looking for a name tag or something—and then back to mine. His smile didn't look mean, it looked sad. "Listen man, like Dave here said, we need the good kind of help. I don't care who your sister is as long as you do your job well and don't lead Hannah on or anything."

"Louis." Dave's tone resembled a warning.

I echoed Louis's statement as I tried to process its meaning. "Lead Hannah on?"

"You know." He lifted his eyebrows meaningfully, sounding entirely reasonable, beseeching even.

I shook my head, wondering what lies Hannah had told them about me. "You'll have to spell it out."

"Just shut the fuck up, Louis," Dave said with a good-natured laugh, rolling his eyes, his Yankee accent thicker. "Stop it with the dramatics. You're all adults. You're not her white knight and you're not her little brother. You don't need to defend her hon—"

"Damn right I'm not her brother." Louis stood straighter, dark eyes hardening as he added a lament under his breath, "If I was her brother, I think I'd drown myself."

What the—?

I had so many questions, but the sound of footsteps pulled our collective attention to my left. The unexpected sight of Hannah Townsen exiting the back hallway made me stand straighter. I mean, Hannah was expected, but this version of her wasn't.

She didn't look a thing like she had last night, covered in body glitter, wearing a ridiculous excuse for a bathing suit, and sky-high stilettos. In contrast, today she wore a relaxed-fit black skirt that reached her mid-calf, a button-down gray shirt that was all buttoned up, a black cardigan, sensible black clogs, and glasses. Her hair sat in a tight bun on the crown of her head, everything in opposition to the wild style from the night before.

This woman reminded me of a librarian. *A very sexy librarian.*

Actually, no. She reminded me of my seventh-grade English teacher. And that was an especially inconvenient thought since I'd been infatuated with my seventh-grade English teacher.

Grinding my teeth, I batted the pointless thought to the side as best I could. It persisted, an irritating truth, as she ventured closer, her friendly smile just as disorienting as her new appearance. Last night, my brain had immediately bought into the fantasy, had been disarmed and charmed stupid by it, and my body had reacted in kind. Even when we'd stumbled out into the parking lot and she'd turned to me with those wide, searching eyes, I'd still been under her spell. That's how believable she'd been.

Clearly, I was susceptible to Hannah Townsen's brand of showmanship.

"I see you've met Dave and Louis? That's great." She gave me an approving nod, her features bright and open, resembling nothing of the distressed, indignant woman from the night before. She looked happy to see me.

Happy. To see me. I'd always wanted to live in a book, and now I was inside V.E. Schwab's *A Darker Shade of Magic*.

No, no, no. This wasn't an alternate dimension. This woman was a chameleon. She was maybe the best actress I'd ever met. Similar to my father,

her antics would probably have me questioning my own sanity from time to time. Her new appearance and this moment was a good reminder.

"Miss Townsen." I gave her a differential nod, successfully shaking off my earlier surprise. She was smart, I knew this.

She made an adorable face, wrinkling her nose. "Don't call me that. Call me Hannah, please. Are you ready to fill out your paperwork? Or do you need a bit more time with Louis and Dave to get acquainted?" While she spoke she moved to a nearby table and removed one of the chairs from the top that had been placed upside down on it.

I felt my lip curl in response to her act but I shouldn't have been surprised by this new character of hers. What had I expected? Hannah to come out here as the club manager in pasties and a G-string? Did I expect her to give me the cold shoulder in front of her employees when she'd just hired me? No. Of course not. The woman had to keep up appearances.

"We can do that, Hannah." Dave stood from his stool, crossed to her, and removed another chair from the table. "You and Isaac should go get his paperwork done. Louis and I got this."

Louis came out from behind the bar. "Yeah, we got this. But you could always bring the paperwork out here if you want our company." I didn't miss his flirtatious tone or the wink he sent her.

I wanted to frown, but—again—I didn't.

"Well, okay then. Come on." She waved me forward and turned, walking back to the hallway she'd just exited, apparently assuming I would follow. Which I did.

My long steps caught up with her shorter ones, but her clogs were much louder than my silent footfalls. I cleared my throat, wanting to alert the woman as to my proximity without startling her if she turned suddenly and found me closer than expected.

Her back stiffened and she picked up her pace, saying lightly, "I forgot to ask you to bring your ID, social security card, and a utility bill for verification of address. Sorry about that."

She kept up the act even while we were alone? *Interesting.*

"I don't have a utility bill or my social security card on me."

"That's fine. You can bring them in on Thursday for your first shift."

"My first shift is Thursday?"

"Um, yes." We'd reached an office and she walked inside, gesturing to one of two chairs in the small space.

Actually, the office wasn't small, but it was packed with furniture, leaving only a small amount of floor space in comparison to its size. A desk with various papers, two computer screens, a keyboard, and a mouse sat along the wall next to the door. There were no pictures, no trinkets, no personal touches. Heck, there wasn't even a stapler. Presumably, this was Hannah's desk, where she did most of her office work.

The other two uninterrupted walls also had a good-sized desk each, the tops of which were completely empty. The one directly across from Hannah's had a chair, the only chair in the office other than the one in front of Hannah's desk. In the far corner sat a tall shelf full of binders, random manuals, and books.

She didn't close the door, instead opting to leave it wide open. "Dave is the shift manager for the front house team. When I told him you'd be starting, he added you to the schedule according to his assessment of staffing needs. I believe you'll be working Thursday through Sunday on any given week."

"I see." I thought about that and it seemed fine to me. Traveston had made a habit of coming only on Saturdays. As long as I was scheduled to work on Saturdays, I didn't care about the rest. Actually, the more I thought it over, this arrangement suited me fine. My cover would have more credibility if Dave was the one deciding when I worked and if I worked more than just Saturdays.

"Here we go." Hannah, not sitting, gestured to a tablet and stylus on top of, what I assumed was, her desk. "Please pick up the tablet and stylus, Mr. Sylvester."

I glanced between her and the devices, eventually picking them up.

She backed up two steps toward the hallway before speaking again. "It's not password protected, you can just power it on. As you can see, the first two pages of the document package are the offer letter with salary and benefits. The second page has the position description. If that all looks agreeable to you, I'll leave you to fill out the paperwork on pages three through ten. Take all the time you need. Please don't hesitate to ask any questions and, when you get a chance, I'll need that ID so I can copy it for our files."

While pulling out my ID, I nodded and inspected her openly, impressed with the consistency of her latest character performance, the script she'd written for herself, how professional she sounded and looked. Her mannerisms were also steady and calm, as though I was any run-of-the-mill new hire. She would've made a great undercover agent. Too bad her ethics were so flexible.

I held my ID out to her.

She gave me a tight smile and gestured once more to her desk. "Please put the ID on the desk."

This earned her a slow blink. *Oh. I get it.* She was treating this no-touching business as seriously as a religious vow. Not having the time or energy for her antics, I ground my teeth and placed my ID on the desk. She waited for me to sit down before stepping quickly forward and snatching it.

Settling in my seat, I said, "I do have a question, Miss Townsen."

"Please, call me Hannah. Everyone else does and it would be odd if you didn't." Fiddling with my ID, she wrinkled her nose and the action made her look adorable all over again.

Her adorableness grated on my nerves, but I swallowed my annoyance before asking, "Is Tina Patterson working today?"

"Uh, I don't believe so, no."

"When does she work next?" I had a bone to pick with my longtime acquaintance and she wasn't answering my calls. She'd promised to prep Hannah for our meeting last night, tell Hannah I was an undercover agent and needed her help. I suspected that Tina hadn't prepped Hannah at all and I wanted to know why.

"I believe she's out of town until Thursday and back to work on Friday, but we can double-check. All employee schedules are posted in the breakroom on the big cork board." She gestured to someplace behind her with a thumb tossed over her shoulder. "In a few weeks, I'll also have them up online, making it a bit easier for folks to swap shifts. I can show you now, or when you're finished with your paperwork. Your choice."

"After is fine," I said, watching her openly.

"Okay. Sounds good." She smoothed a hand—which I noticed was shaking slightly—down her skirt and took another step backward. "I'm going to go make a copy of this and—uh—check on some things in the dressing room. If you need me—that is, if you need help, not that you need *me*, just holler. It's just around the corner, but off-limits to anyone except dancers. So, just . . . holler." As she spoke, her cheeks turned bright pink. And every time her eyes met mine, they darted away.

"Fine." I didn't point out that she was technically no longer a dancer.

"Okay. Good. That's good." Her unnecessary response sounded a little breathless.

I waited and stared unabashedly. Meanwhile, she loitered in the doorway, sneaking peeks at me for another few seconds, then stepped to the side and darted out of view.

Obviously, the façade, which she'd held up admirably, had begun to crack. I made her nervous and that was good. If Hannah Townsen worried I'd spill her secrets, have her arrested, make good on my threats, maybe she'd cooperate without any problems.

Taking a moment to study my surroundings, I frowned at the stack of books piled on her desk, reading the titles out loud to myself, "*Handy Home-ownership*; *Plumbing Basics for New Contractors*; *Electrical Essentials and Safety*; *Install, Remodel, and Repair: Doors and Related Hardware*."

Only confused by the selection of titles for a minute or two, I reminded myself that Hannah had taken over just recently. These books had probably been left in the office by her predecessor, Hank Weller.

Dutifully, I turned my attention to the tablet, skimming the offer letter and position description. The compensation package and benefits were impressive, more than I'd assumed. I filled out the new hire paperwork to the best of my ability. This was the first time I'd filled out new hire forms other than for my enlistment into the army, if those counted as new hire forms.

Reading the Pink Pony's paperwork was a novel experience. My commanding officer had helped me fill out my college applications and I'd been recruited straight out of college for the DEA. The agency had handled the completion of my paperwork, including my security clearance.

The sound of a knock on the doorframe had me looking up. Hannah hovered outside the office, a small, patient smile on her pretty face. "How's it going?" she asked softly. Her arms were full of clothes, shiny ones, lots of netted fabric.

I frowned. "What are those?" I glanced at the clothes she held to her chest.

She followed my gaze to the sparkly mass in her arms, and then stepped into the office. "Oh, uh, these are costumes that need mending."

I watched her maneuver in the small space, placing the costumes on a shelf in the corner. She also seemed excessively careful not to make any contact with me, pressing herself against her desk in order to remain several feet from where I sat. Forget a religious vow, this was holy orders.

"How's the paperwork? Do you need more time?" Hannah Townsen placed my ID on the desk rather than handing it back to me, all outward display of kind attentiveness. She then hurried to remove herself from the office, returning to the open doorway with quick steps.

"I'm finished," I clipped out, this act she put on once more reminding me so much of my father. In public, he came across as kind and reasonable and generous, timid even. Feigning kindness—using it as a weapon to gain folks' trust, make them lower their guard—pissed me off more than anything else I'd encountered during my years working undercover.

Razor Dennings, the scary-as-hell former president of the Iron Wraiths and my main target during my last undercover assignment in Green Valley, never pretended to be something he wasn't. He was evil. He didn't sugarcoat it. I'd been anxious to put him away, but I'd been able to bide my time, ensuring it was done right, by the book.

But with folks akin to my father and Hannah Townsen, the "pretenders" as I called them, they made me irrationally angry. I had no patience for pretenders, and I decided to limit our interaction moving forward, a necessary step if I didn't want to bite her head off every time she spoke.

Standing, I picked up the stylus and tablet and held them out to her.

"Please leave them on the desk." She pointed to the desk where they'd been earlier and where my ID now resided, because of course she did.

"Don't you need the tablet? To process my paperwork?"

"No." She lifted her fingers, perhaps to tuck hair behind her ears, but she ended up patting her bun instead. "It's all synced up. If you filled out the forms on the tablet, they're already in my database."

"Your database?"

"The employee database I built." She backed into the hallway, giving me a wide berth to exit, but pointed at her desk again. "Right there, next to where you put the tablet, that stack of papers. See it? That's your onboarding and new employee packet. I'll also email it to you. It contains all the basic stuff—like setting up insurance, who we suggest for retirement planning, that sort of thing—but also Dave's and my contact info, should you have an emergency and need to call in."

At the mention of her contact info, I remembered her phone. Withdrawing it from my back pocket, I held it out to her. "That reminds me, I believe you left this in my car last night." If she wanted to play pretend even though we had no audience, then so would I.

"Thank you. Please"—she cleared her throat, lifting a hand in a vague gesture, not making eye contact with me—"leave my phone next to the tablet. Thanks."

"Sure thing," I drawled, fighting the urge to roll my eyes. After placing her phone on the desk, I picked up my ID. "Anything else I should know? Anything else on the desk I need to pick up?" I asked, returning my ID to my wallet.

"Just, on Thursday, don't forget your utility bill and social security card. Also, our quarterly employee meeting is next Sunday—a week from today—and you'll be introduced as our newest staff member."

I huffed a short laugh, tucking my wallet away. "Is that really necessary?"

"I think so."

"Oh, yeah? Why's that?" I leveled her with a look, communicating with my glare and tone how I felt about her wasting my time with all this pretending.

Her chin lifted, and she drew herself up taller, a little frown marring her forehead, an expression ten times more adorable than her nose wrinkles earlier. "Because, Mr. Sylvester, no matter how long you're on staff, I have seventeen talented dancers and they need to know that you'll have their backs if things get out of hand on the floor or in the champagne room. This job, for us, can be scary sometimes. Anything we can do to make it easier on the talent, we do. The relationship between dancer and bouncer needs to be fostered, it requires trust. How can they trust you if they don't know you?"

Well. She had me there.

"Fine. I'll be at the meeting next Sunday." Giving her a single nod, I acknowledged her point, reminding myself that even my vile father made a good point once in a blue moon. "Anything else?"

"That will be all," she said, crossing her arms and glaring at me, giving me the sense my attitude disappointed her, I was a very naughty boy, and she'd deal with me later.

I turned and left, giving her one more severe frown on my way out because part of me enjoyed her stern act. A lot. And the sudden, involuntary hope—that I'd see a similar expression on her beautiful face in the future—really pissed me off.

Chapter Six

ISAAC

"In my experience, the only undertaking more difficult than forming new habits is breaking old ones."

— Billy Winston, *Beard Necessities* by Penny Reid

"Hey, Isaac. You made it," Dave the bouncer greeted me once I stepped foot inside the club. It was noon. He'd asked me to come earlier than the regular shift time so we could get some training in before the club opened.

"Dave," I said, pulling off my jacket. It wasn't hot inside but I was hot.

"You okay?" he asked, venturing closer. "Something happen?"

I shook my head, but didn't try to wipe the scowl from my features. "I might've overdone it on the Cooper Road Trail this morning. But I'm fine."

I'd encountered Drew Runous on the Cooper Road Trail on Monday morning, and then every morning so far this week. He didn't stop or acknowledge me other than with a surprised double take on Monday and a short head nod when we passed each other on the trail each day since. Drew was the federal game warden assigned to this part of the Great Smoky Mountains National Park and Ashley (Winston) Runous's husband, and therefore Ashley was the sister to my sister's husband, Cletus Winston.

Confusing, right?

You see, akin to any small town in the USA, everyone knew everyone, and half the folks were related to the other half. I'm not sure how it is in any other part of the world since I've never traveled beyond the east coast of the United States, if you don't count my time in the army, which I didn't.

Anyway, "seven degrees of Green Valley" was how I thought about it. There were only three degrees of separation between me and Drew Runous in here: Jenn, Cletus, Ashley.

However, and ironically, there were only two degrees of separation between me and Drew Runous in the federal government. His primary training officer had been my primary training officer's roommate at the Naval Academy some thirty-odd years ago. I hadn't been aware of this connection until just recently when I'd met with my former training officer and asked him for advice on my future career options once I left undercover work. He'd suggested I become a training officer and had told me of an opening in Nashville.

Which was why I'd spent every hour of every day this week studying for the upcoming trainers' exam. That is, every hour when I wasn't sleeping, exercising, reading my latest book, or—for some godforsaken, unknown reason—sitting outside the Donner Bakery on the off chance I'd spot my sister, Jenn.

"Well, let me see." Dave took my discarded jacket and placed it on the bar top. "Let's get these chairs off the tables first and I'll talk you through a typical night, what to expect."

I followed the big guy over to the tables and we began unloading them while he rattled off, from his perspective, how a normal night might proceed. I was only half listening. My mind was still back in the Donner Bakery parking lot.

At first, I'd stopped by my sister's workplace just to confirm she was doing well, the first time being last Sunday, when she'd walked with muffins up and down the line of customers. Then, I'd stopped by Monday after my run and I saw her again, walking from the bakery to the lodge. Tuesday, Wednesday, and today it had been more of the same—she'd popped out to hug someone in line, or she'd come out the front to hand someone a bakery box, or she'd walked out to her car, retrieved something, then walked back in—and I couldn't believe how lucky I'd been. I'd seen her every day since Sunday, five times total.

She looked good. She looked happy. I was glad. I really was.

So, why my chest felt tight and my nerves were raw now, I didn't understand. Or maybe I did.

After this present assignment, after the weeks or months of paid time off I planned to take, and assuming I passed the trainers' examinations, I would assume a different name when I applied for my new position with the government. This identity was waiting for me and I would have to cut off contact with everyone known to Isaac Sylvester in order to assume it.

Which meant my time in Green Valley now was my last chance to make things right between us and say goodbye.

Long ago I'd accepted the two of us would never—could never—know each other. She lived and worked in this community. Her home was here and I would never be able to return. Even though the Iron Wraiths were mostly disbanded, a few former members remained, and they weren't the pleasant sort. They wouldn't take issue with me being a bouncer at the Pink Pony, that tracked for my former cover story, but any attempt on my part to mend fences with Jenn would only invite her a world of trouble. I couldn't exit her life for good right after making it difficult.

If only she would move to a different city, we might—

"Isaac! Good. You're here." Hannah's voice yanked my attention out of inattentive self-reflections and toward the back hallway. She and Louis had just turned the corner and were walking together toward the bar. Today she wore torn, baggy jeans, tennis shoes, her hair braided in two long pigtails, and a plain white long-sleeve T-shirt covered in paint stains. No glasses. The sight pulled a deeper frown out of me.

Her steps seemed to falter at my expression and she pivoted gracefully, taking two steps closer to me while Louis continued his straight line to the bar.

"Did you bring that utility bill and your social security card so we can complete your paperwork?" she asked, her tone polite and professional.

"No," I said, probably glaring at her.

"Oh. I see." She rocked back on her heels and looked me over. "Uh, when do you think you'll have a chance to bring it in?"

"Tomorrow." I set down another chair. It hit the floor, making a loud sound I hadn't necessarily intended.

Hannah flinched at the sudden noise. "O—okay, that'll be fine."

Standing still, I waited for her to say something else or leave, acutely aware of Louis's and Dave's silent attention on us.

When she didn't, just kept on eyeballing me as though she was trying to decide whether to speak or not, I ground out, "You want something else?"

"No. No, nothing." She held up her hands and took a side step toward the front door of the club. "Just remember, you said you'd be at the staff meeting on Sunday. It's at noon."

"I know," I said, and I acknowledged inwardly that my threadbare patience with this woman wasn't really her fault. Well, it wasn't her fault *today*.

Giving me one last tight smile, Hannah turned and fast-walked across the main floor to the short passageway leading to the front door. I heard the door open, then close. I breathed out, frustrated with myself.

Lord help me, but just the sight of her set my teeth on edge.

"You know . . ." Louis called from the bar and waited until I faced him to continue, "you're not going to make any friends here if you keep treating Hannah with disrespect."

My eyebrow quirked at that. "Pardon?"

"Just now, when we walked out here." Louis lifted his chin toward the back hall. "You were rude."

"Okay, okay. Calm down, Big L. Maybe Isaac is just a quiet guy." Dave stepped forward, his hands up, and I assumed the nickname Big L was applied ironically. "Hannah hired him, right? So, she knows him. Let's just trust her, let her handle the management issues, and stay out of it, huh?"

Louis grumbled something unintelligible which I didn't ask him to repeat. He also sent me a few anthrax envelopes with his eyes while Dave grabbed me by my shoulder and took me on a tour of the floor. I did my best not to zone out as he continued his overview of what to expect on any typical Thursday night.

I ignored Louis. Obviously. But I felt sorry for him. He liked Hannah, had a thing for her, that much was obvious. Handing one's heart over to a pretender always ended in disaster. Poor kid. He'd learn. Eventually.

True to his word, Dave finished his spiel detailing a typical night, then moved on to atypical nights, special event set up, and what to do if we reached capacity before closing. He spent the next several minutes showing me where we could set up rope lines if people needed to wait outside.

I spotted Hannah again as soon as we set foot outside the club. Now I was the one doing a double take. She was standing on a ladder—mind you, no one was holding it for her, which was foolish and dangerous—and as far as I could tell she was painting the exterior cinder block. Dave, meanwhile, didn't seem to find anything amiss with her actions and went on for a bit about line procedures outside, including between the two of us, who would be assigned to the line and who would be assigned inside.

According to Dave, in the past the club had never reached capacity. But since Hannah took over, it had occurred three times in the last two months.

"She's been juggling both roles, you know, as a dancer and managing the place. Just this last week, for her retirement party, we had so many people at one point, we had to set up the ropes for two hours. Luckily, I had a friend who was free and could help out during that time, otherwise we would've been screwed."

"Why didn't your friend take the job here? As a bouncer?" I asked, my attention snagging on Hannah again. I held my breath as she climbed down the ladder and it wobbled unsteadily, then yelled over to her without thinking, "Would you please get someone to hold that ladder for you? It's not safe to be climbing up and down with it set on gravel!"

She turned at my hollering. Clearly, I'd startled her, and she yelled back, "No need. I'm all done with the ladder." Paying me no mind, she turned her back, bent over to pick up a brush and a paint can, and returned to her work. After using the brush for a little, she took a few steps away from the area she'd been painting and seemed to be analyzing it.

I glared at her and the nearby ladder. She better not be lying again. Ladder safety was no joke and no one seemed to take it seriously.

Dave's chuckle brought my attention back to the big guy. He was looking at his shoes, something I noticed he did quite a lot while smiling.

"Uh, anyway. About my friend who helped last week, he works for a private security firm—same place I used to work—and isn't in town permanently. We can't rely on him to help often. I don't know if it's a sign of things to come, but Hannah is banging with that social media stuff."

I nodded, my eyes seeking out Hannah and the ladder. She'd placed the paint can on one of the steps and was dipping the brush in it.

Dave hit me in the chest, drawing my attention back to him. "Hey, let's go back inside. I'll show you the champagne room, where to stand, what to look for, that kind of thing."

Agreeing with a nod, I followed him inside while my brain rewound and caught up with everything he'd told me outside, which led me to ask, "What do you mean social media stuff?"

"Yeah, you know, like spreading the word online about the Pony, getting it out there, making this place seem like a landmark. She added that mural to the front of the building. Did you notice?"

My feet stopped walking. "Wait. Hannah painted that?"

I had noticed it today when I drove up but had been too preoccupied to pay it much mind other than to think, *Huh. That's nice.* It was a painting of a Pegasus-type horse. The horse was of moderate size relative to the huge wings on either side of it. They were beautiful, reminding me of angel wings.

He nodded, looking proud. "That's right. She did a good job, right? It's not finished yet but people are already coming by just to take photos in front of it, tagging this place on social media and shit."

I could imagine people wanting to stop and take photos in front of it. What

I couldn't comprehend was Hannah Townsen being the one to paint it, even though I'd just seen her out there with my own eyes.

"Yep. She's going to set up some lights so people can take photos at night before they come inside." He paused here to chuckle. "I was like, who's going to want to take photos in front of a strip club, right? But, wrong. I was wrong, she was right." He glanced at me sideways. "I know what you're thinking."

I seriously doubted he knew what I was thinking.

"I sound judgmental," he went on. "I guess maybe I do. I'm not into any of that online crap, but if I was out there taking photos in front of strip clubs and posting them publicly, my mother would have my balls."

"You work here. Does your mother know that?"

"Sure she does." He opened the door to the champagne room—the room where Hannah had given me her very memorable version of a lap dance—and we walked inside. "My ma has been here, a few times actually. Comes with one of my former clients whenever she's in town."

"Former clients?"

"Like I said, I used to work for private security." He took us over to one of the walls and removed a cushioned panel that had been invisible to me until he touched it.

"But you stopped to work here?" I asked, watching him open another panel, this one was metal and appeared to be electrical plate facing.

"Yeah. Well, no. Well, kind of. It's a long story. I still do security for some old friends when they ask, but this is where I work most of the time. The pay is good. Not as good as private work, but I got tired of the travel."

"Your mom has been here, knows you work here, but would have your balls if you took photos here?"

"Yeah. Makes sense to me. She doesn't want me posting photos with strippers. I'm her son. That doesn't make her look like she raised a good son. I get it." He shrugged again. "What can I say? My mindset is old-fashioned."

I didn't respond to that. I didn't think his mindset about posting photos with strippers was old-fashioned. What I didn't understand was how his mother could visit the place and be okay with him working here.

Turns out, he didn't need me to ask.

"It's like this." He faced me, placing his hands on his hips. "She's met Hank and she's met the dancers. She knows them and sees they're the good sort. If I post a photo of me with my work colleagues and friends, that's what she sees, that's what I see. But that's not what the world sees, ya see? The world sees strippers, not work colleagues. Not friends. Not dancers. Just strippers. Hell, the more you work here, the more you'll understand how they're not even really humans to most people, you know?" His laugh this time sounded sad.

Dave's words reminded me of Agent Danforth's rant last Sunday morning. *And you want me to, what? Request a protection package for a small-town stripper who's also soliciting on the side and who we don't really need as a witness? Is that the best use of tax dollars?*

"But I'm glad to see all the Pink Pony posts on social media and that Hannah's mural—among many of her efforts—is making this place more popular. Looks like times are changing," he said, handing me the metal plate. "This here is the control box for the cameras in this room, but the monitor is set up in the office next to Hannah's."

I nodded absentmindedly, again only half listening while he went over how to do a systems check with the cameras. When we finished, he replaced the metal plate, the cushion panel, then showed me how to find and remove it. I made a mental note that this room would not work for a quick phone call to check in with Danforth. The cameras made that impossible. I'd have to ask Dave at some point where I should make a personal call if needed. Should I step out to my car? Or what?

But, mostly, my mind was still on our conversation from earlier, the mural, his mom, and how—in his words—society didn't treat the dancers like people.

I stopped him before we left the champagne room, not wanting Little Louis to overhear. "Wait a minute, let me ask you something."

"Go for it."

"That mural, Hannah painted the whole thing?"

"So far, yes."

"Because she wanted people to take photos in front of it? For social media?"

"That's what she said." He nodded.

"How'd she know it would work? What made her so sure? Seems to be a lot of work she's doing for this place, especially when—as you said—people don't usually post photos publicly with strippers or at strip clubs." I couldn't help but ask, this woman made no sense to me.

If he was surprised or irritated by my questions, he didn't show it. "I mean, these online influencers who are taking photos out front don't really cater to the teacup-and-pearl-clutching crowd, ya know?" Dave snorted at his own statement. "Anyway, it's been good. It brings in a different kind of clientele, those that are curious and want to have fun. We're now having twice monthly ladies' nights instead of every other month. The girls wear more clothes and do more dancing. Everybody has a good time. It's like a party, or a dance club. Nice change."

Doubt and suspicion had me asking, "And you credit Hannah with all this?" Something didn't add up.

"Yeah. Of course. She's the one who pushed through the changes. Don't get me wrong. Hank was a good boss and everything, good mentor for the dancers, but he never thought outside the box with the business, almost like he didn't care if it made money or not as long as the dancers were protected and *they* made money."

I nodded, understanding what he said. But still, something was off. What Dave said about Hannah, what Louis believed about Hannah, what Tina had told me about Hannah all contradicted what I knew to be true about her.

Dave interrupted my thoughts, adding, "Truthfully, if it didn't serve to piss off the locals, Hank was, at best, kind of disinterested in the Pink Pony. But not Hannah. Seems like Hannah's going to take this on more from a business perspective in the modern sense. According to her, a business needs a social media presence. It needs a brand. She said she's going to open an online store, start selling merchandise, and give a cut to everyone. That's a smart lady right there."

"Yeah. She is smart," I agreed easily. I already know this. But being smart didn't make her good.

"She just graduated from college, did you know that? Near the top of her class." Dave turned back to the door and opened it.

I followed him out of the room, shutting the door behind me, remaining silent. Dave clearly didn't need me to speak or prompt him unless I had a specific question. He enjoyed talking and volunteering information, which suited me fine.

"She knows the latest research and what works and what doesn't. We're all proud of her, lucky she's here. Did you know, we wanted to throw her a graduation party but she didn't want it. Instead, she insisted on a retirement party, said it would make everyone more money. That's what I'm talking about, she's always looking out for us."

"Don't tell me you got a thing for Hannah Townsen and you're gonna warn me away?" I bumped his arm with my elbow.

"Ha! No. Hannah's not—how do I put this? She's not my type." Dave strolled unhurriedly to the bar, surveying our surroundings as we went.

"What's your type?"

"Truthfully, I like my ladies to be exciting." He sat on his normal barstool.

I stood by the stool two down from his. "And Hannah isn't exciting?"

Dave glanced at the ceiling. Apparently, this matter required contemplation. "Hannah is the what-you-see-is-what-you-get type. She's mellow. Sensitive. Kinda brainy. *Lots* of baggage that isn't her fault. I think of her like a little sister, someone who needs taking care of, watching over."

I couldn't help but think she really had him fooled. "You're saying she's boring?"

"No, no." He paused, thought a moment, then contradicted, "Maybe a little." He laughed. "I mean, she's not boring. She's a nice lady. But to date? Nah. I need more excitement, more verve. Chaos. Like take that Tina Patterson. Now *that's* my type."

That made me laugh. Dave laughed too. I liked this guy, despite his alarming taste in women.

"Just so you know—"

I jumped back from the bar because this statement came from Louis, who was suddenly there, having just popped up from behind the bar like a barely-legal jack-in-the-box.

"Jesus!" Dave covered his heart with his giant hand. "You scared the crap outta me, Louis!"

Louis went on, ignoring Dave, "—I got a thing for Hannah and I got no compunction about warning you away."

Irritated, mostly because he'd startled me with his abrupt appearance, I slid my eyes to his. "Were we in the middle of a conversation, Louis?" I knew I sounded belligerent, but whatever. This kid was annoying. "I didn't know we were in the middle of a conversation."

"Pardon me. I'm just saying, for the record, I got a thing for Hannah. But she doesn't date anybody, so she's not going to be dating you either." He crossed his arms, tone hard.

"All right, Louis, that's enough," Dave said on a tired-sounding sigh. "Let's put the dicks away until the hen party next week."

"What's the problem? I'm just saying she doesn't date." Louis's voice raised and therefore cracked. "So, if that's the reason why you started working here, you should know from the start, that's not going to work on her, no matter who you are—or were—in her past. She's not interested in you *that way*."

I had no idea what he was talking about. Hannah and I had no past. And what I should've said in response was, *I have no interest in Miss Townsen.*

But, for reasons unknown, what came out of my mouth was, "Not interested in me? You really think so?"

Louis's eyes seemed to flash with something akin to frustration and I could see he didn't believe his claims were true. He doubted them, he doubted Hannah wouldn't hook up with me first chance she got. Furthermore, he considered me a real threat to Hannah, assuming I was here to take advantage of her. Use her.

My mood soured. Just what the hell kind of lies had she told this kid about me?

Dave cleared his throat, standing, grabbing my shirtfront, and pulling me after him. "All right, all right. Enough of this. A few things to know about the bar. You can keep your jacket, hat, gloves, and even wallet if you want in the basket under the counter—just here." He reached over the side of the bar top and pulled out a wicker basket with a knit hat and scarf inside, gave it a shake, then put it back. "If someone needs a medical mask, like they're coughing all over the place or their immune system doesn't work right and they ask for one, we keep those behind the bar. Let me show you around the rest of the front area. You know how to use a defibrillator? 'Cause you'll need to. We have cardiac arrests in here all the time. Come with me."

Chapter Seven
ISAAC

"Love sometimes means calling another person on their bullshit, even if doing so requires an awkward, uncomfortable conversation, like this one we're having right now."

— Jethro Winston, *Beard Necessities* by Penny Reid

My first night as a bouncer at the Pink Pony was eventful. Or, at least, I considered it eventful. Dave said it was, and I quote, "No biggie."

First, several couples—all of whom looked totally normal, could be any couple dressed up for a date night—arrived early in the evening and stayed the whole night, making out hot and heavy during most of the stage performances. In all my time coming to the Pony, back in the day when I was undercover with the Wraiths, I'd maybe spotted only two or three couples *ever* at the club. Definitely not multiple in one night.

Second, later in the evening, a few businessy-looking guys dressed in suits and several local firemen arrived. Not together, but within about fifteen minutes of each other. One woman who'd entered earlier as part of a couple talked the firefighters into taking off their shirts. When I questioned this, Dave had shrugged and said it was allowed. The club was exempt from local nudity and decency ordinances and had to comply with laws specific to its operating license. That meant, as long as the club owner was on board, customers could take off just as many clothes as the dancers.

The woman sat on each man's lap in turn, rubbing herself all over them, sliding their hands up her skirt, but not too far. After a while of that, she had the business guys pay the dancers to give her lap dances while they watched.

As far as I could recall, nothing similar had occurred when I'd been undercover, stopping in to liaise with Tina. Then again, I usually only stayed long enough to make my visit seem believable, and I hadn't been paying much attention to the customers beyond their physical descriptions.

Tonight, now that I was paying attention, I couldn't believe my eyes. Dave had laughed it off, saying, "That lady is always like that. She talks guys into paying for her lap dances. It's her thing."

See now, I've worked undercover for over a decade, seen some crazy violent shit and some crazy sex shit, but all that shit had been at private motorcycle clubs or cartel compounds, where, in context, with a bunch of depraved, criminal exhibitionists, the behaviors didn't seem strange to me at the time.

Even undercover, even playing a part, I'd never been able to bring myself to act the part of an exhibitionist. At the Wraiths' compound, the most I'd done with Tina in the public space was kiss and grab her for show, and let her kiss and grab me also for show. Then, I'd take her to my bedroom, we'd talk and play card games for an hour, she'd mess up her makeup and rumple her clothes, and we'd go back to the bar area.

These people tonight and their showoff behavior seemed shocking as hell. I hadn't expected preppy, normal-looking couples, businessmen, and local firefighters to let loose at a place of business where nearly anyone was free to walk in and see them. These people weren't criminals. They were just . . . people. By all outward appearances, law-abiding, tax-paying, productive members of society, getting freaky with each other.

The firefighters didn't seem to mind the woman using their laps, nor did the businessy-looking guys mind paying for her dances. Neither did her boyfriend mind—or whatever he was—maybe because he had a constant stream of attention from most of the club's dancers. Apparently, he was a big tipper.

Third, about two hours before closing, one of the firefighters walked up to me and said, "Hey Isaac. You working here now?"

I nodded, trying to place him. He looked vaguely familiar.

Everyone seemed to know me. My father had been the local high school principal, my momma had been a big local employer, and my sister was a beauty pageant contestant turned local celebrity. Rarely did I know or recognize people, however. I knew I was antisocial, even more so as a kid, preferring books to the company of people, so I wasn't surprised he knew my name and I couldn't place him.

After an attempt at engaging me in conversation, which I stonewalled, he asked me if a dancer named Goldie was working. If so, to send her out. He wanted a private lap dance.

Dave overheard and good-naturedly chimed in, "Goldie retired, bub. She's no longer working at the Pony."

Later, to me, after the guy walked back to his friends, Dave explained that Goldie was Hannah's stage name.

My attention remained on the firefighter for the rest of the night while involuntary images of Hannah—dressed in her string bikini and stilettos—doing to him what she'd done to me on Saturday flashed through my mind. Had she looked at him just the same? As though she wanted him so badly, she might die if he didn't touch her?

She probably did. I admitted inwardly that this sourness on my tongue might've been resentment. Then again, I was self-aware enough to wonder why it also tasted akin to jealousy. Apparently, it's hard to tell the difference sometimes.

When the night was almost over, and per Dave's advice, I borrowed his keys to unlock a cramped storage closet and call Danforth. Keeping the door cracked—according to Dave, it auto locked and there was no way to open it from the inside—I left a quick voicemail update on the events of the evening. Despite how much I'd witnessed, the check-in was quick because there wasn't anything to report relevant to the case.

As I was leaving the closet, I spotted a large box of condoms—a wholesale amount of condoms—in various sizes, sitting on one of the shelves.

"Unbelievable," I muttered, pushing through the door and rolling my eyes. That woman was shameless, but at least she was safe about it. *Whatever.*

Dave, Louis, and I walked each of the dancers to their cars as soon as they were ready to go. I didn't see Hannah, and I didn't ask about her either, figuring she must've already left.

* * *

I arrived for my second shift at the Pony earlier than necessary Friday afternoon and took a moment to really look at Hannah's mural. As far as my limited exposure to art and artsy things went, I thought the painting was good. To my untrained eye, it looked professional. But what did I know?

I'd never been into art. Growing up, it wasn't something my father thought boys should do or needed to know about. My major in college—GI Bill paid—had been criminal justice. I'd taken exactly one humanities class in art history and felt uncomfortable most of the time, especially when all those naked Renaissance paintings were flashed up on the big screen in the lecture hall.

Hannah's mural didn't make me feel uncomfortable. It made me smile. I especially appreciated how she'd painted the wings. Folks wanting to stop and take photos in front of it made sense to me, regardless of where it was painted. And wasn't that the great thing about beauty? If something was beautiful, if it moved you, the location didn't matter, nor did the source.

Similar to that one Marcus Aurelius quote: "Dwell on the beauty of life. Watch the stars, and see yourself running with them." When we appreciate the beauty of the stars, we're not thinking about what they're made of or how far away they are. We're simply admiring them as something beautiful.

I decided to do that with Hannah's mural. I admired it, independent of the source or the artist.

Driving around the building, I drove in the gated employee lot and backed into a spot that gave me a good view of the back door. Really, other than an old —and I mean vintage, from the 1970s—red Ford pickup truck, I had the pick of the lot since it was so early. I wanted to catch Tina on her way in. And since I was so early, I read in my car for a time, looking up at intervals when other cars pulled into the lot.

Tina's was not one of those cars. I noted that Hannah hadn't arrived either. It wasn't until half an hour before my shift that I spotted Tina Patterson's Lexus drive through the gate. I knew it was her car because, when we'd last spoken on the phone, she'd told me one of her regulars had bought her a black Lexus with gold trim.

I said, "Tina," as soon as I drew even with her shoulder.

Not breaking stride, she glanced at me and smiled. "Twilight."

I grimaced. Twilight had been my pledge name during my assignment with the Iron Wraiths. I'd remained a pledge during the entire assignment, never patching in to the club. Tina had made fun of the name often. Apparently, she was still making fun of it.

"Piper told me you started working here as a bouncer." She winked at me. "Everyone is in a tizzy. Welcome to the club."

"Thank you," I said flatly, opening the building's back door for her. I followed her in. The breakroom was empty, assuming Louis wasn't hiding inside one of the kitchen cabinets, ready to pop out and sass his elders. "We need to talk."

"Go for it, babe." Her short legs carried her quickly to the back hallway and I followed. We'd already passed the closed door to Hannah's office, and another closed door that I knew held the video-monitoring equipment inside. Just before we made it to the dressing room, I tugged on her elbow to make her hold still.

"Tina, what did you tell Hannah about my visit last Saturday? Did you give her the code?" I made sure to lower my voice. I could hear the dancers in the dressing room, but no one seemed to be nearby. Even so, I didn't want to take any chances of being overheard. What we needed was an office, a room with a door I could close.

"Code? What—" She stared at me in plain confusion for a few seconds, then her hands flew to her mouth and her eyes widened comically. "Oh! Shoot! I forgot."

"You forgot." I wasn't surprised. She'd confirmed what I knew already.

"Yeah. Sorry." She singsonged the word *sorry* and paired it with a flap of her eyelashes.

I stepped closer, lowering my voice to a whisper when noises coming from the dressing room increased in volume. "How could you forget? You never forgot when you helped with the Iron Wraiths' case."

"I dunno." She shrugged, not lowering her voice. "Y'all were paying me that time."

"Are you saying you forgot to tell Hannah about my visit because I didn't pay you?"

"I don't know, Isaac. I just forgot, okay? Sheesh." With a roll of her eyes, she turned and sauntered further down the hallway.

I had more questions for Tina. We weren't finished yet.

Catching up to her in three strides, I bit out, "Fine. You forgot. Okay. But I have something else to ask you."

"I'm all ears."

"Not here. Come with me." Taking her by the arm, I led her past the dressing room and into a vacant office I'd been told used to belong to the club's former accountant.

Releasing her arm, I closed the door behind us and faced her. "You gotta be honest with me, Tina."

"About what?" Sipping from the iced coffee in her hand, she set her purse on a desk along the far wall, turned, and leaned against it.

"Is there prostitution going on here?"

She flinched then shot up, placing the iced coffee on the desk behind her. "What? What are you talking about?"

Of the strip clubs in this part of the world, the Pink Pony had the best reputation. Over the last week, I had to wonder if Hannah wasn't the only one soliciting folks. Had things changed so much since I'd last been in town? Was the Pony now just as notorious as the G-Spot? That would be a real shame.

I paced a few steps closer. "It's an open secret that the G-Spot—"

"Wait." She waved her hands in the air to stop me. "Are you asking me if any of the dancers here are selling themselves for sex?"

"Correct, that's what I'm asking."

She seemed to struggle for a moment before loud-whispering, "No! Absolutely not! What the hell is wrong with you?"

"Tina."

"Don't *Tina* me." She rushed forward, her words quiet but furious. "Why would you even ask that? First of all, most ladies here have families, are married with little kids. Some of the others are trying to put themselves through college or grad school. It's understood, no one is expected to do that here, there's never pressure to do that here, because it's simply not allowed. If a dancer here wants or needs that kind of income—short-term or long-term—they go elsewhere and pay a stage fee. Some go to Vegas for a few weeks or down to south Florida. No judgment, but not here."

I tried to absorb this information, parsing through her statements for the facts. "Are you saying the dancers here do solicit, but just not in this club? They go to Vegas or south Florida?"

"Isaac, stop being such a Boy Scout." She leveled me with an impatient look. "The point is, it never happens here at this club. Never. Hank had a zero-tolerance policy for solicitation on the premises. If he found out, you were barred from dancing here ever again. And as far as I know, only one person broke the rule. They were kicked out that night and not allowed to return. He never wanted someone to feel pressured and if one dancer does it, the rest will feel the pressure. So, just trust me, it would never happen here."

"But Hank isn't around anymore."

Her head rocked back on her neck. "Are you saying you don't believe me?"

"I believe you believe what you're saying."

"But you think it's happening at the Pony?" Tina's gaze searched mine, narrowed. "Well, you're wrong."

"Personal experience tells me differently."

"Personal experience?" Tina gave me a once-over, then crossed her arms. "Care to share?"

"Fine. Hannah Townsen."

Her suspicion cleared, leaving only confusion. "What about Hannah?"

"She solicited me last Saturday."

"Solicited you?" Tina appeared to be genuinely perplexed.

"Yes."

She made a face, like my answer was spoiled milk. "Fine, Twilight. Why don't you tell me what happened. And don't leave anything out."

So, I did. I told Tina all about it, leaving out none of Hannah's statements, questions, movements, or hand placements, or the fact that I'd—as per Tina's advice—paid for five lap dances in advance. I also told her about Hannah pretending to be indignant in the car, how she'd lied and pretended, acting shocked when faced with the repercussions of her actions.

Tina, fully absorbed in my story, stared at me with wide eyes. But then, when I finished, she threw her head back and laughed her ass off. A switch had been flipped. And boy, did she laugh. She laughed and laughed. And every time I thought she would stop laughing, she'd look at my scowl and laugh some more.

I patiently waited for her to calm down. I could be patient with Tina because I liked Tina. Tina was fundamentally honest about what she wanted and who she was. Okay, yeah, she sometimes lied. But both things can be true at the same time. My point is: She never pretended to be someone she wasn't. She wasn't perfect, she wasn't bad, she wasn't good, she was just a person. And she'd helped me out, saved my skin a few times back in the day. So, yeah, I liked Tina.

That is, letting her laugh at me wasn't necessarily bothersome until it went on too long. Her drawn out knee slapping and swiping at her tears of hilarity, pointing at me and shaking her head, it all eventually got on my nerves.

"Okay, okay. Pull it together." I leaned my shoulder blades against the door and sighed. "What the hell is so funny?"

"You're such an idiot," she said, still giggling. "You're so sexy and so stupid, it would be charming except stupid guys are a huge turnoff. I can't believe how stupid you are, though. Don't you read all those books? Didn't you graduate from college? And you're this stupid, how?" She chuckled, shook her head, and sighed.

Insults were Tina's love language, thus I wasn't bothered, but I did want to be let in on the joke. "Fine, Tina. How am I stupid? What am I missing?"

"Hannah Townsen wasn't soliciting you for sex, dummy." Her pretty brown eyes twinkled at me. "She was offering it to you for free."

"What?"

"She's into you, turkey brains. You're her—you know—stand-in. You always have been." Then to herself, she chuckled, "I really can't believe she did that. Good for her."

I straightened from the door, Tina's words making no sense. "I'm her what?"

"Stand-in." Tina paired this with an irritated sound, then went right back to talking to herself. "Seriously, good for her. I didn't think she had it in her. I'm actually proud. Get it, girl."

"Stand-in? What's a stand-in?"

"You know, a *stand-in*." This time she said it louder.

Through gritted teeth I seethed, "Repeating the word over and over ain't going to help me know what it means, Tina. I'm ignorant, not hard of hearing."

She made another sound of irritation. "Fine, ignoramus. It's a person you think about—like, a fella you're really attracted to—that you imagine all other people are, don't matter if the customer is a woman or man. We do this when we're on the floor or giving a private dance or whatever. All of us do it. I've never met a dancer who didn't do it. You're Hannah's stand-in. She puts your face and body on everyone, imagines you when she's touching people or dancing for them. Get it now?"

I stared at Tina, again trying to absorb this information. My brain experienced a lot of difficulty this time, so I blurted, "Are you implying Hannah imagines me when she—when she's with other men?"

Tina shrugged. "I don't know if she thinks about you when she's having sex with her boyfriend, if that's what you—"

"Wait. Hannah has a boyfriend?" A surge of heat climbed up my chest and clawed at my throat while a sense of cold heaviness made my stomach plummet.

"No, no. That's not what I'm saying." She waved an impatient hand through the air. "Listen, I meant, when she *had* a boyfriend. She's had boyfriends, they've come and gone. She doesn't have one now, but when she did, I don't know if she pictured you when she was with them. That's all I'm saying."

"But with customers?" I prompted, still trying to wrap my mind around this.

"Correct. With all customers. Men and women. I know for a fact she's picturing you instead of them when she dances, and has been for over ten years." Tina strolled back to the desk where she'd placed her bag and picked up her iced coffee, shaking the plastic cup and rattling the remaining ice. "I think—no, I know—she's had a crush on you since y'all were teenagers. Maybe even before that. Girl has it bad."

I tried to recall everything that had happened between Hannah and me last Saturday, every word spoken, every glance, every touch, every sound. What I recalled made my breath catch and my chest ache. Was this—could this be true? Had I been wrong about Hannah this whole time? Making faulty assumptions and treating her in kind? Had I presumed duplicitousness when she'd been nothing but genuine?

"Don't faint. I won't catch you." Tina sounded beyond amused. "You must've thought she was faking those tears in your car. I bet you were a bastard to her all week, weren't you? Don't deny it. You hate liars more than anything. How mean were you? Be honest." She sounded as though she might burst out laughing again.

My eyes sliced to hers. "Are you messing with me right now? Hannah has a thing for me? She wasn't lying or pretending?" I couldn't name this feeling inside myself. It felt both bad and good, and therefore intensely aggravating.

"I absolutely am not messing with you." Her lips twitched but her eyes told me she was serious. "Hannah has always had a big, and I mean massive, thing for you." Tina snorted. "I bet she thought—oh my God." Tina started laughing again, but then she abruptly frowned and made a tsking sound. "Poor Hannah."

"What? What did she think?" My nerves raw, something unknown had taken up residence in my chest, tight and heavy and restless.

"It might be my fault," Tina said around the straw in her mouth, grimacing.

"What is your fault?"

Her grimace intensified. "See, it's possible—given what you said about your conversation that night, her questions about whether I sent you, if you wanted to be there, all that—it's possible she thought you were her retirement present."

Chapter Eight
ISAAC

"I'd come to realize that if I feared what I couldn't control, then I would fear everything."

— Scarlet St. Claire, *Beard Necessities* by Penny Reid

"A—a present?" I parroted, feeling every bit as stupid as Tina had accused me of being. I could barely keep up with this conversation. Hell, I wasn't keeping up, I was falling behind. "Hannah thought you sent her a man as a present? Who would do that?"

"Who wouldn't?" she asked. Apparently, this question was entirely reasonable to Tina. "I've done it before. Hank used to send dancers to Beau Winston all the time as a way to say thank you for being a good friend."

I'd always considered Hank Weller a complete weirdo, and this confirmed it. Who sends people as presents? That was dehumanizing and . . . *fucking gross.*

"See, I told her—we all told her we'd arranged a surprise for her. I bet she thought you were it." Tina sighed and then spoke again, mostly to herself. "I bet she was real disappointed when she opened that desk set we all pitched in for. Fantasia—that is, Kilby—even had her name engraved. It was expensive as hell because the place charged by the letter."

Tina went on, lamenting the cost of engraving, but I wasn't listening. I was too preoccupied feeling sorry for Hannah and the rest of the folks here, that they existed in a world where people were apparently *gifted*, and I struggled coming to grips with the truth.

Except, if what Tina said was true—

"Hey, if no one is soliciting out of here, then what's the deal with all those condoms in the storage closet?"

"Horny couples," Tina said.

Requiring more of a justification, I stared at her and waited.

"Oh, honey. How can you still be so sheltered?" She gave me a look, making me think I was equal parts precious and stupid. "The condoms are for horny couples," she repeated, louder.

I sent her another glare. "Again, Tina, I'm ignorant. Not hard of hearing."

"Fine, fine. Gracious, I'd forgotten how inexperienced you are." Gathering a deep breath, she said slowly, "Ever since Hannah started targeting—and I mean the advertising kind of targeting, not the gun and bullet kind of targeting—toward couples, we've been getting more and more coming in. It's been great for business. The presence of women customers always makes male customers spend more, they want to show off or something. Anyways, the guys up front, Louis in particular, were getting asked all the time whether we had condoms as the couples were leaving. So, Dave asked Hannah to start stocking them in the bathrooms. And that's why we have condoms in the storage closet and in the bathrooms."

That . . . made sense.

"Do you get it now, precious? Or do you have more questions for me? In case you didn't know, condoms go on a man's penis to protect—"

"I get it, I get it," I growled.

She smirked. "Well, you were still a virgin when you left town last time. I don't want to take for granted you know what condoms are for. By the way, are you? Still a virgin?"

Sending her a dirty look, I turned away. In the next moment, as reality caught back up to me, I speared my fingers through my hair, spinning slowly in a chaotic circle, staring without seeing. "Fuuuuck."

The way Hannah had looked at me, that had been real.

The way she'd touched me, she'd wanted that. She'd wanted me.

And her reaction in the car, when she'd cried, that had been real, too.

If this were the case, if her words and reactions had been real, then I needed to rethink every conversation, every interaction with Hannah Townsen. Not just the events of last Saturday. And for damn sure, I needed to apologize.

"This is madness," I said to no one. I knew in the past I'd messed up worse while working undercover, but I honestly couldn't remember when it had felt this serious.

Part of me tried to rationalize it: So what? So what if I hurt her feelings? Folks get their feelings hurt every day and folks die every day. Life is tough. I'd been approached, hit on, and propositioned by people before, why should I care about rejecting this particular person?

Not only did this attempt at rationalization not help, it made me nauseated. These were things my father might say when he hurt me, my sister, or my momma. According to my father, any perceived mistreatment was him teaching us essential life lessons: *Better get used to it, buttercup. Stop being so sensitive. I'm doing you a favor. Toughen up.*

I wasn't perfect. At times, I questioned whether I was even a good person. But no matter what, I'd never be my father. In the past, when I was myself and not working undercover, I'd rejected advances many times, but I'd done so as gently and graciously as possible no matter who was hitting on me. I would never knowingly hurt someone, and then call it good. *Because, hey, that's just life.*

Tina jabbed a finger at my chest, bringing my attention back to her. "It's not madness, Isaac. This is what happens when people don't simply say what they want. She's wanted you, like, forever. And then you were there all of a sudden, paying for five lap dances on the last night of her dancing career. Hell, I don't still hold a torch for Duane Winston, do I? I played my cards and lost, but at least I don't have regrets."

"Then who is your stand-in?" I asked, suddenly curious.

"Still Duane Winston, always and forever." She gave her head a single nod and chewed on the straw sticking out of her iced coffee.

"Wait, what?"

"Yep. He's still my stand-in, but I'm not longing for him. I'm not pining for the man. I'd never date him again, and I wouldn't lose control if he showed up."

"So, if Duane Winston showed up and paid for five lap dances, what would you do?"

"I'd be all over him." She grinned and wagged her eyebrows. "But I'd clarify things first, I'd spell it out: just sex, nothing else."

My lip curled. "Tina, Duane Winston is married to your *cousin*. They have a baby."

"So?" She wrinkled her nose. "If she was keeping him happy, he wouldn't show up and ask for five lap dances with me, would he? That's not a me problem, that's a them problem. Like I said, I'd never date him or lose control or beg him to take me back. But I'm supposed to turn down an orgasm buffet because he's married? Nope."

I rolled my eyes and exhaled. I'd forgotten what Tina was like. I mean, I knew what she was like, but I'd forgotten how different we were on a fundamental level.

Shaking her cup, she rattled the ice again. "Why are you rolling your eyes at me?"

"Where you see every individual as an island of personal responsibility, I don't. No one is an island, Tina."

She harrumphed. "Why am I responsible for other people's choices? Live and let live is what I say."

"Because we live in a society, Tina. We're all responsible for making sure this country, and society, reflect the best we're capable of, or at least collectively working toward it. And sometimes that means helping out misguided folks, or people who are having a weak moment." I didn't want to soapbox, but she'd asked.

"Then tell me, what do you think I should do if my married former boyfriend wanted a fling? Send him back to his wife?"

"Exactly."

She snorted and crossed her arms. "Fine, fine. That's easy for you to say. But what would you do if a woman you desired, and had desired for most of your adult life—a married woman—came to you for one night, no strings attached?"

I didn't even need to think about it. It's what I'd wished my father's mistresses had done. "I'd have compassion for her and her husband, for their kids. I'd encourage them to get a divorce or work it out, not cheat and lie. Complying with someone's destructive impulses isn't ever the right answer."

"You're making her weakness your responsibility." She flicked her hand at the wrist as though she was tossing away invisible garbage. "I am not responsible for other people's bad decisions."

"Her weakness is her responsibility, true. I'm not disputing that. But a bartender doesn't serve someone they know is an alcoholic, do they? If you know your compliance—passive or active—hurts people, you should always choose the path that doesn't hurt people."

"This is a dumb conversation. And how would you know what you'd do in that situation? You've never even had sex with anyone! I still say it's not my responsibility." She pulled her bag back on her shoulder. "And my iced coffee is gone. And I'm finished talking to you. And—and"—she held up a finger and pointed at my face—"don't give me that look, Twilight. If Hannah had just confessed when y'all were teenagers, you would've turned her down and she would've been happier. Saturday never would've happened if she knew where you stood, that's for sure. She can still use you as a stand-in, ain't no rule against it. No one needs your consent to fantasize about you. She gets to do that no matter what you want or think about it, and I get to keep using Duane even though he's married with a kid. Or do you think that makes me a bad person, too?"

"I never said you were a bad person, Tina," I said softly.

Tina wasn't bad, but she had more than enough people telling her she was. In the past, I'd witnessed it firsthand too many times to count. I wouldn't add my voice to the chorus even if I did think so—which I didn't—because then she'd drown me out.

If she drowned me out, we'd never be able to talk and challenge each other's perspectives. I appreciated her willingness to share her perspective, especially when it contradicted mine. She'd helped me rethink many issues I'd taken as fact. She was, and I hoped always would be, a good friend.

But Razor Dennings? My father? Levit Traveston? Those were bad people. Evil people.

"You don't need to call me a bad person, I can see it in your stupid face," she grumped, pushing me to the side and making for the door. But then, at the last moment, she spun and gripped my arm. "Oh. Crap. Isaac! Don't tell Hannah I said anything."

"Pardon?"

She gave my arm an insistent shake. "She let you believe she was a prostitute, right? She didn't try to tell you different? Explain herself?"

I hesitated, ensuring I understood the questions, then nodded.

"Well, since she'd prefer you assume she's a prostitute than admit she's got a crush on you or explain how you're her stand-in, clearly she doesn't want you to know. Lock it up tight and pretend you have no idea."

Tina couldn't be serious.

Before I could ask whether she was serious, Tina said, "I'm serious. Don't let her know you know."

"Then why did you tell me?!" I seethed, keeping my voice low so I wouldn't shout and twisting out of her grip. "I can't pretend I don't know she's not a prostitute, Tina." At the very least, I needed to apologize. I *needed* to.

"Excuse me, you were gonna find out anyway. You can't work here and not hear it from somebody. Aren't you an investigator? You're, like, a detective, right? Something like that. You'd find out sooner or later. Don't get mad at me for answering your questions. You asked, I answered."

Louis's statements from yesterday surfaced in my mind, something about who I was to Hannah. Even before that, when I'd first met the young bartender and he'd been salty as a Triscuit.

"Louis knows," I said and realized at the same time. The kid had it bad for Hannah. No wonder he was always giving me looks that oscillated between dirty and sad.

"Of course Louis knows. Everyone who works here knows. It's not a secret."

"Everyone knows?" I choked on the question.

"Sure. We all know who each other's stand-ins are. It's not like we're ashamed of it. Everyone does it to get through the day." She frowned, studying me, then shoved my shoulder. "This is the other reason I told you about being Hannah's stand-in. You're a self-righteous asshole, Isaac. Like I said, there's nothing wrong with having a mental stand-in. How the hell else am I supposed to give George Padmar a lap dance without gagging? I work for tips, don't I?"

"Sorry, Tina. I have to tell her I'm aware of the misunderstanding. I need to apologize," I said, knowing I sounded stubborn. "I'm not going to pretend I don't know."

Her bottom lip pushed out. "Isaac, can't you just stop being a bastard to her? Or just be a little bit of a bastard, so she doesn't know you know the truth. Walk the line, find a good balance."

"Tina."

"I've helped you out so much in the past. We're friends, right? How can you betray me like this?" she whined.

"You're friends with Hannah and you spilled her secrets."

"Because they're not secrets! Like I said, everyone knows." She clasped her hands beneath her chin and peered up at me pleadingly. "Fine. Apologize. But wait two weeks. Can you do that? For me?"

Lifting my eyes to the ceiling, a growling sound reverberated from my chest. "Fine. Fine, I'll wait."

"When you do apologize, make sure you don't let on I was the one to tell you about it. I'd be so embarrassed. Please."

"You? You'd be embarrassed?" I lifted an eyebrow at this dubious claim.

"Well. Not embarrassed exactly." She smirked. "But it would be super inconvenient."

* * *

Tina needn't have worried. Even though I spotted Hannah later, it was obvious the woman was avoiding me.

She came out to the main floor before we opened and speedwalked by me without making eye contact, wearing baggy overalls, her braided pigtails, and carrying a small toolbox. She approached the bar, spoke to Louis, then returned to the back hall without sparing me a glance.

Hannah didn't come out again, not as far as I knew. That night, about a half hour before my shift ended, and again borrowing the key from Dave and standing in the cramped storage closet, I left my voicemail for Danforth, doing my best to explain that I'd been mistaken about Hannah. I left it as, "I grossly misread the situation and her intentions. Miss Townsen is not currently soliciting customers, nor do I have reason to believe she ever has or plans to. I misunderstood, it's my error, my misread of an innocent situation. Please remove those statements from the record."

The next time I spoke to Danforth in person, I'd ensure she removed my mistaken claims from the case record. If I was going to pester Danforth about anything else, it would be to follow up on the plan for ensuring Hannah's safety once we secured the recordings of Levit Traveston using her tapped phone.

When Dave, Louis, and I escorted the dancers to their cars Friday night, I noticed Hannah's office door was shut and locked, the light off, just as it had been on Thursday. I figured she must've left early since there was only that vintage red Ford truck left in the lot when I closed and chained the back gate. On my drive home, I decided I would ask Dave during our Saturday shift which car belonged to her.

Chapter Nine

ISAAC

"Duct tape is man's answer to electrons and protons. It's how we keep matter together."

— Cletus Winston, *Truth or Beard* by Penny Reid

Even though I was exhausted I didn't sleep well. I'd promised Tina I would wait two weeks to apologize. I would wait two weeks. But come the Friday after next, I'd find a moment alone with Hannah to tell her how sorry I was, and I'd use the time between now and then to plan my words.

Early the next morning, as was becoming my habit, I drove over to the Donner Bakery and parked on the far side of the lot, spreading out the materials for the trainers' exam. The textbook open on the passenger seat, I'd intended to be good and study. Instead, I spent the time glancing at the front door of the bakery for a sign of Jennifer while thoughts of Hannah kept interrupting my good intentions.

Movement caught my attention in my rearview mirror and I heaved a sigh. My sister's husband approached my door, holding two cups of what I assumed was coffee. Turning my head toward him as he knocked on the window, I frowned at his unkept beard, hair, and sharp eyes.

"Come out here," he said, stepping back from the car. "I have coffee for you."

I wasn't exactly pleased to see him since—in no universe—did I, or would I ever, like this guy. You see, Cletus Winston was a pretender. He pretended to be full of nonsense, but his nonsense was a shield and a mask. I hated that he and Jenn were married. She deserved so much better.

But it was a rare opportunity to check in on Jenn, assuming he'd give me a straight answer if I asked. Figuring my chances were fifty-fifty, I opened the door, stepped out, and shut it behind me, crossing my arms against the cold.

He looked rumpled. His jacket had white marks on it, making me suspect he'd been working with paint or clay. His pants were also covered in the stuff, and his boots were two-inches caked in still-wet mud. But then, Cletus Winston usually looked various shades of messy. What my sister found attractive about this haphazard-looking schemer, I had no idea.

"You pick which one you want," he said, holding both cups at chest level. "Then, if one is poisoned, the victim will be random."

"Is one poisoned, Cletus?" I asked flatly, already tired of him and this conversation. He wouldn't poison me with coffee offered in broad daylight outside a busy bakery. If Cletus wanted me gone, he'd be a fucking schemer about it and no one would ever find my body.

"Depends on your definition of poison," he said reasonably. "Some folks would consider coffee poison all on its own."

Since I was tired of the instant garbage at the safe house, I chose one of the offered cups at random. "Thank you," I said, bringing it to my lips for a sip.

He muttered something similar to, "Don't thank me yet."

I lifted an eyebrow, planning to question him about the statement, but then the taste of the coffee hit my tongue and I turned my head to spit it out. In the next second, as the full flavor coated the interior of my mouth and throat, I gagged, wishing I hadn't turned my head and instead had spewed it all over him.

"What the hell—?!"

Cletus faced the bakery, bringing his own cup to his lips and taking a sip. "Don't you like it? It's my own recipe."

"Is that vinegar? Did you put vinegar in my coffee?" I hoped I had a bottle of water somewhere in my car. Or bleach. Or anything to get this taste out of my mouth.

"Apple cider vinegar. But the hint of sweetness is blackstrap molasses."

"I didn't taste any sweetness," I snapped, opening the lid to pour out the disgusting concoction on the gravel. In my car, I hunted for a water bottle, found one, straightened, and slammed the door shut.

Rinsing my mouth, I glared at my sister's husband while he sipped his coffee, unperturbed and seemingly unsurprised by my reaction.

"How'd you know I'd take the left one?" I asked.

"I didn't. They're identical."

I grimaced and decided to cut to the chase. "What do you want, Cletus?"

"I have two questions for you, Isaac," he said, his tone lofty and philosophical.

Instead of responding, I leaned against the car and crossed my arms, waiting for him to go on.

He took a sip from his cup, licked his lips, then said, "Several years ago, near Halloween, your sister's BMW was stolen. You stole that car, didn't you?"

This was not the question I'd expected him to ask and my disorientation kept me quiet.

"It was 'cause of the banana cake in the front seat, right?" He lifted his cup toward me, watching me from the corners of his eyes. "That's why you stole it. You wanted that banana cake."

Rubbing my forehead, I sighed. "Yes, I did want that banana cake. But that wasn't the reason, it was just a bonus."

"Did you steal her car to piss off your daddy? It was brand-new, right?"

"No. It wasn't to piss off my father."

"Then enlighten me." He faced the bakery again.

I debated how to answer, or whether to answer at all. But I suspected if I didn't assuage his curiosity about this matter, he'd be silent when I asked after my sister.

"The King brothers—you remember those assholes?"

He nodded. "I do remember those assholes. Proceed."

"They'd disabled her car alarm. They had, uh, plans for her. I stole the car, which meant she had to drive my momma's instead. My momma's was an older model, but it had all the bells and whistles, unlike Jenn's. Improved antitheft features, including a panic button."

"I see." He lifted an eyebrow at this. "Well, now I don't feel guilty at all."

"You don't feel guilty for what?" Eyeballing Cletus, I took a big gulp of water, wishing I had gum to chew.

"How I dealt with those King boys last year."

"Boys? Aren't they older than you?"

"Age is just a number, Isaac. Don't let age hold you back." He lifted his cup toward me again. "Get that tattoo. Wear those miniskirts. Buy that comic book."

"Whatever you say, man." Turning my eyes and body toward the bakery so he wasn't in my direct line of sight, I kicked at the dirt instead of kicking him. Jenn wouldn't appreciate her husband coming home with bruises, and I didn't want to show up at the Pony for my shift with bruises either. This man was a dirty fighter, always had been, and followed no one's rules but his own. "Is that all you wanted to ask me, Cletus?"

"That was the main thing. Thanks for answering. I've always wanted to know." He slipped the hand not busy with his coffee into his jacket pocket.

I frowned at the cup he held as a gust of wintry wind hit me right in the face and everywhere else my skin was exposed. I'd been too hasty, discarding the hot coffee. It was cold out here and the heat from the cup would've warmed my hands.

"What's the other thing?" I asked, trying to keep my teeth from chattering.

"The other thing is about your plans for the future."

"My plans," I echoed robotically, shifting my weight from foot to foot. It was too cold for the clothes I wore. I needed a better jacket. My last assignment had been in Florida and it had been hot as the devil's ballsack all day, every damn day. And every night. There'd been no escape. Just the memory of the oppressive heat made me stop shivering now.

I didn't know how people lived like that, being hot twenty-four hours a day. What had Louis said about Hannah being his sister? Something about drowning himself if they were related? That's how I felt about living in the heat forever. I'd rather drown myself than live like that.

"Yes. Your plans." Cletus twisted at the waist to face me, interrupting my musings. "Are you planning to stay in town? Or are you just passing through? And, if passing through, when are you leaving?"

Seeing no reason to avoid the questions, I said, "I'll be here for another two months at the most."

"Then you're leaving?"

"Then I'm leaving." I left out that my leaving this time would be for good. He didn't need to know about all my plans. "Any other questions?"

"Nope. All done." He shook his head and took a sip from his cup.

"Fine." I crossed my arms. "Then I'm going to ask you a question, and since I answered yours, you have to answer mine."

Keeping his eyes forward, he said, "Seems fair."

I gathered a deep breath and asked, "How's Jenn?"

I didn't keep tabs on my sister via the internet. I'd tried years ago, but those first photos she'd posted on social media as the "Banana Cake Queen" made me feel sick. That persona wasn't her. It erased her. I suspected they were my mother's efforts to capitalize on Jennifer's blue ribbons for baking at the state fair.

We had been each other's only friends growing up. She'd been my confidant and I'd been hers. Jennifer was just as shy as me, and seeing her put on display like that—for the entire world to discuss and tear down—pissed me off. I didn't care about the Banana Cake Queen. I cared about my sister. Thus, I hadn't searched for details about her life on the internet for over seven years.

Which meant, frustratingly, I could only rely on Cletus Winston for information regarding how my sister was actually doing.

"Good," he said, then nodded somberly.

I waited for more. He gave me nothing. "Cletus."

"Yes?"

"*How* is my sister?" I ground out. "And I need more than just *good.*"

"Fine. She's very good."

I huffed a laugh. I should've known. He was a sneaky shithead. "You're a sonofa—you're a real asshole."

His eyebrow cocked and he glanced at me. "I appreciate you not calling my mother an untidy name. And to show my appreciation, I'll tell you a story—"

"Great. Can't wait."

"—about Jenn."

I glanced at him and rolled my lips between my teeth, stopping myself from speaking. If I said anything else, he might change his mind.

"So, once upon a time, I took Jenn on a hike. I think you know it. You walk down the trail until you get to a stream with rocks on the bank, all different colors. And you're deep under the tree canopy. It's about twenty minutes north of the auto shop."

"I think I know it," I confirmed.

"Well, she told me about her brother, who she said used to be her best friend before he disappeared one day and joined the army, leaving her all alone with her control freak of a momma and dark triad father."

A pang of guilt hit me hard, right in the chest. I ground my teeth against the ache, but I said nothing.

I'd never explained to my sister or my mother why I'd left, because I was of two minds on the subject. Until I reconciled them, there wasn't anything to say.

Was I sorry I'd left her? Yes.

Did I regret it? No.

Would I do it again knowing what I know now? Definitely, yes.

Did I wish I was a stronger person, a smarter person, who would've found a different, better way to keep my sister and mother safe? Also yes.

As it was, I didn't deserve her as a sister any more than Cletus deserved her as a wife.

"Talking about you that day made her melancholy," he went on, his eyes seeming to lose focus. "She cried. Made me want to release a roll of armadillos into your underwear drawer at the time."

"What's a 'roll' of armadillos?"

"Roll is the collective noun for armadillos, just like the collective noun for a group of people with leprosy is leper colony, Isaac. Keep up." He huffed impatiently and gave his head an exasperated shake. "Anyway, talking about you now makes her just as sad as it did way back then. Thus, I never bring you up. And you know what else?" His eyes sliced to mine.

I met his glare. "What else?"

"*No one* brings you up. She doesn't bring you up, not any more. It's like you never existed."

His statements resounded between us, essentially a door being slammed shut. Maybe it was for the best. Why make myself a nuisance now right before I was leaving forever?

I nodded, swallowing around a thickness, then croaked, "Makes sense."

Before I knew what was happening, Cletus Winston withdrew his hand from his pocket and flicked me—hard—in the forehead.

Flinching, I stepped away, covered my forehead, and adopted a defensive posture. "Ow, Cletus! What the hell—"

"What in tarnation is wrong with you, turkey brains? It doesn't *make sense* for a woman's brother never to be mentioned, for him never to see her, never to visit, call, write, acknowledge her glorious presence. Not unless that man has subscribed to the manosphere, or insists on storing rice in silos for longer than two years. In which case, good riddance."

I stared at him, nonplussed, part of my mind stuck on the fact that he and Tina Patterson had used the same insult—turkey brains—to describe me in less than twenty-four hours. What were the chances?

But also . . . *what?*

"Well, what the hell do you want me to do, Cletus?" I raged in return. "Are you here inviting me to dinner right now? Is that what this is? Are y'all putting me on your Christmas card list?"

"Do you want to be on our Christmas card list? Where should we send it?" He was either taunting me or was genuinely curious. Impossible to tell.

Rubbing at the sore spot in my chest, I grumbled, "Forget it." I turned and opened my car door as another gust of wind bit at my nose, lips, neck, and chin.

"You're leaving already?" he asked, facing me.

Not answering, I sat in the car, shut the door, and ignited the engine.

He bent at my window and knocked. In my peripheral vision, I saw his hand wave. "So, I guess I'll see you tomorrow, right? Same time? You want coffee or something else? Tea? I have a good recipe for tea."

Ignoring his nonsense, I left the spot. But when I made it to the stop sign, I glanced in the rearview mirror. Cletus Winston stood in the middle of the parking lot, facing my departing car. Just before he lifted his cup for another sip, I saw he wore an intensely-satisfied-looking smile.

Man. I really hated that guy.

Chapter Ten
HANNAH

"Sometimes, things are sad and unfortunate. But finding the funny in a situation can make the sad and unfortunate more bearable."

— Duane Winston, *Beard in Mind* by Penny Reid

"Anyone heard from Tina?" Pacing between the makeup stalls, I checked the clock on my phone for the umpteenth time. She was late.

"Not me." April glanced at me in the mirror and offered a sympathetic smile.

"Me neither." This came from Laney.

"That's 'cause y'all weren't working yesterday, but I was." Nora swiveled in her chair to face me. "Didn't you see her yesterday? She was here."

I hadn't seen Tina at all yesterday even though I'd been looking for her everywhere. Which made me wonder whether she'd been avoiding me on her first day back from vacation. Tina was a notorious ghoster if she felt guilty about something. She was also the only dancer I hadn't yet spoken to, to explain about Isaac being the club's new bouncer.

"Did she say why her phone's off?" I asked, checking the time again.

My fellow dancers had teased me when I'd told them the news last Sunday morning before he arrived to fill out new hire paperwork. They'd immediately stopped their teasing when I clarified the situation. Namely, that he was here temporarily, doing the club a favor since we were so short-staffed at the front of the house, and also that Isaac had no idea about my silly, longtime unrequited crush.

I'd explained how we really needed his help and I didn't want him being teased about being my stand-in. He might get frustrated and leave before we filled the bouncer position with someone permanent. This information seemed to sober the dancers' silliness. I had their promises not to mention it—even as a joke, even to me, even in passing—until a new permanent employee had been hired.

"When I talked to Tina yesterday, she said she accidentally left her phone behind during her vacation and had forgotten to charge it when she got home." Nora turned back to the mirror and picked up her eyeliner. "Maybe she has it on her today?"

I nodded while thinking through things. I didn't reckon I should trouble Serafina—our chef—or her staff, nor Dave, Joshua, or Louis. They weren't as rambunctious as the dancers, who were always looking for ways to keep the mood fun and light. Dave wasn't the sort to gossip, neither was Joshua. And Louis . . . well, he had a crush on me and he was obvious about it. I doubted he'd tell Isaac about him being my stand-in.

"I've already tried calling a few times," I said. "She's not picking up." My gaze absentmindedly scanned the room. Piper's confused expression reflecting back at me in the mirror caught my attention. "What's up, Piper? Do you know something about Tina?"

She shook her head quickly, her features clearing. "No, boss. Just, uh, thinking about what to make for dinner this week. That's all."

"Did you try that recipe I sent you?" April crossed to stand behind Piper's chair.

Their conversation transitioned into a sharing of simple dinner ideas and I mostly zoned them out, checking my phone again.

"Hey, sorry to interrupt," I interjected into their discussion as I backed up toward the door. "If Tina does come in, can one of you let me know?" She was cutting it close.

"Sure thing, boss." April gave me a short salute.

Antsy, I power walked to the door and yanked it open, coming face-to-face with Tina.

"Oh my God! You scared me." Her hand flew to her chest and she closed her eyes, then she added on a light laugh. "I swear, I almost pissed my pants."

I placed my hands on my hips. "I need to talk to you."

"Can't right now, boss. I'm running late." Her eyes opened but didn't meet mine.

"Make time. It's important." Blocking her attempt to enter the dressing room, I reached for her wrist.

She leaned to one side, avoiding me and protesting, "But—"

Not waiting for an excuse, I grabbed for her again and dragged her down the hallway and to my office. Closing the door behind us, I stood between her and the exit. She didn't look at me. She looked around the office like she'd never seen it before. Weird.

"Tina, listen, I have a favor to ask."

"Sure. What is it?"

Instinct told me to keep blocking the door. "I'm not sure if you know or noticed yesterday, but Isaac Sylvester works here now as our new bouncer."

"Oh, yeah. Piper told me." Her tone was conversational and I was surprised by her lack of surprise.

I frowned. "Piper told you? When did Piper tell you?"

"Uhhh, yesterday, when I got back."

"Really?" Strange. Piper hadn't said anything just moments ago when I'd asked if anyone had talked to Tina.

"Can we hurry this up? Like I said, I'm already running late and I'm not finished with my makeup." She turned and sat heavily in the second office chair, sighing in her special brand of beleaguered.

My frown deepened. I'd expected Tina to tease me about Isaac once she heard the news. "Is anything wrong, Tina? Are you okay?"

"I'm fine. Are we finished?"

Inspecting her, I saw something was wrong. She seemed on edge. But I had to trust she'd come to me when or if I could help. Pushing Tina Patterson never ended well.

"It's about Isaac," I went on. "I've already spoken to everyone else and I need to ask that you don't let on that he's my, you know, stand-in. While he's here, please don't tease me or him about it. You see, we need—"

She stood, cutting me off, "Okay. Sounds good. I won't."

I reared back, inspecting her again, stunned by her easy agreement. "You—you won't?"

Tina gave me a small smile that looked sympathetic. "I won't. I promise."

"What do you promise?" I narrowed my eyes.

Holding up three fingers, she said, "I cross my heart and promise, from this moment forward, I will not tell Isaac anything about your massive lady-hard-on for him. Nor will I tell him that you've been using his face and body as your stand-in since you started working here. Satisfied?"

Surprised again, I nodded. "Yes. I am. But don't you want to know why I don't want y'all to tell or tease him?"

She shook her head, walking around me for the door and opening it. "No need. I get it."

"You do?"

Facing me again, Tina dropped her fingers from the doorknob, stepped closer, and lowered her voice. "I know Isaac is here undercover. He doesn't technically need to work here for the assignment, but it's a win-win since you need the help. Right?"

I lifted my chin, absorbing this information I'd almost forgotten. Tina had been the one to send him to me on the night of my retirement party. Of course she knew he was here undercover.

She went on, "And I know him better than anyone here. He doesn't like to be teased. If folks kept bringing it up, he'd quit and just run his investigation off-site. Before his parents decided to homeschool him, he was teased and picked on in elementary school. Plus, his daddy picked at him constantly, called it good-natured teasing. He can't abide teasing of any sort now. We need the help at the front, and we can't afford to be down another body since Joshua's still recovering and won't be back for another two weeks. Makes sense."

I marveled at not only her abundance of good sense and quick summary of the situation, but also how I'd felt no pang of jealousy at the reminder of Tina's friendly, familiar relationship with Isaac. Well, maybe a little pang, but nowhere near as bad as in the past.

I understood why. Isaac had been treating me like crap, being rude and whatnot, since last Saturday. The way he looked at me, like my mere presence offended him, meant I'd been avoiding the man. Whereas prior to Saturday, I might've sought him out just to sneak a peek at his face.

But before I could thank Tina for being so reasonable, she snapped her fingers and said, "Before I forget, have you fixed the handle to the storage closet yet?"

Not this again.

"No, Tina. No, I did not *fix* the storage closet handle. It's already fixed." I'd had it up to my eyeballs with folks using that closet for reasons other than storage. Before I'd been forced to install the lock, I'd tried a number of tactics to discourage people from using the storage closet for personal reasons.

Paper towels had been on sale at the wholesale mart about a month ago and

I'd filled the closet to the brim with them, hoping the lack of space would discourage people from using it, hoping they'd feel claustrophobic. Not only had it not worked, but one of the short-order cooks had placed the paper towels on the tiny bit of empty floor space remaining, put a blanket on top of the pile, and had taken a nap. The week before I added the new lock, one of the dancers had used it for a quick smoke break.

No matter what I did, they just wouldn't listen.

"And I'm not gonna change it," I said, repeating myself for the hundredth time. "Y'all shouldn't be using that space to hide, nap, make private calls, or whatever. I made it self-lock for a reason. If you need to make a call, use one of the stalls off the dressing room, or step outside to the gated lot, or use the spare office. If you need a nap, use your car."

"Hannah," she whined. "The storage closet is the most private area in the—"

"I'm not changing the lock and that's final." Only Tina continued to push this issue. Everyone else had at least pretended to accept my verdict. I knew Dave still used it for private calls, but he was smart enough to leave the door ajar, and as long as it was just him, fine.

Drawing herself up to her full height—which was four inches shorter than mine—she lifted her chin. "It's a safety hazard, Hannah. Serafina got locked in two weeks ago."

"It's not a safety hazard, Tina. If Serafina had kept the door open, like she knows to do, she wouldn't have gotten locked in. But she closed the door to take a nap." Other than me, Dave, Hank, and Serafina, no one else had a key to the storage closet, and now I was questioning whether or not to limit access further. "I've told y'all over and over, don't use that storage closet for anything but storage."

Giving me a rebellious side-eye, she grumped, "Well, maybe I'll ask Dave to fix it so it doesn't auto lock."

"I could change it if I wanted, Tina. I just don't want to. Do not ask Dave to mess with it or I won't schedule you for any shifts this month."

"You know how to fix it? So it doesn't auto lock?" She sounded like she didn't believe me. Tina always seemed to doubt me and all other women when we claimed to know how to do handy things, like adding a new light fixture in a room, replacing a doorknob, hanging a door, switching out weather stripping, etc.

Not rolling my eyes even though I wanted to, I said, "Tina, you seem to think screwdrivers know and respond to the level of testosterone in a person's body. A screwdriver doesn't care if I'm a woman or a man, it works just the same."

"Are we talking about the tool or the drink?" This question came from the doorway and we both turned to find Hank Weller, our old boss and technically still the current owner, standing in the hall.

Before I could react, Tina faced him and reached for his arm, pulling him into the office. "Hank! Tell Hannah to put the storage closet back—"

Removing himself from her grip, Hank held up his hands. "You're meowing up the wrong tree, gorgeous. I don't work here anymore. Talk to the lady. She writes your paychecks."

Making a short growling sound, Tina pushed past Hank without a word and marched out. A few seconds later, we heard a door slam, presumably to the dressing room as she entered.

Hank smiled. "She took that well."

I snorted. "I think you mean, she took that well considering she's Tina."

"Yes. That's what I meant." His smile grew, and soon we were both grinning at each other in commiseration.

We'd done this often over the last decade. Some people have "work husbands" or "work wives," but I'd always thought of Hank as my "work brother." I didn't have a real brother. I had no siblings at all, no family to speak of other than my mother. Sure, I had one maternal cousin, but she'd gone off to college a few years before I didn't, and we hadn't spoken since. Last I heard, she'd gone west for medical school.

"How are things, Hannah?" he asked quietly, giving me a bracing smile.

"All right. Come on in." I waved him forward as I sat in my chair. "I'm guessing you're here because of my message?"

I'd sent him a text message earlier in the week asking him to stop by. In typical Hank fashion, I saw he'd read it but he didn't respond. Hank had this extremely irritating habit of only responding to messages in emojis and he knew I wasn't a fan. Therefore, whenever I texted, he would leave it on read and respond with a phone call when he could. Or, like today, simply show up.

"Yes, ma'am." Hank took the other seat in the space, not bothering to shut the door.

Rotating in my chair to face him, I folded my fingers on my lap and prepared to switch gears, getting my thoughts in order.

But before I could figure out how best to broach the topic, he asked, "Have you been living here? How long? And why?" He didn't sound unhappy or judgy about it, merely curious.

Oh well. So much for organizing my thoughts.

I nodded. "That's what I wanted to discuss with you. It relates to Jethro Winston."

"What does Jethro have to do with you living here?"

"I know he's been a silent partner for a long time, and he does all the upgrades and new construction on the property. Right?"

"That's correct, more or less. But we hire out for electrical and plumbing."

"Do you think he would be open to building out the east side of the building and adding an apartment?"

"An apartment?"

"Yes." I rolled my seat closer to his, taking no mind that our knees bumped. "It could be for the club's manager."

"You mean, it could be for you." He lifted an eyebrow and his lips tugged to the side, but his voice was still free of judgment.

"That's right."

Hank studied me for a long moment, his eyebrows drawing together. I stared back at him plainly. I had nothing to hide, no ulterior motive.

Eventually, he asked, "What's going on? Why'd you move out of the farmhouse? Are you and Jedd at odds?"

"No." I waved away his question. "I like my mother's man just fine, but he and my momma need their own space. She's happy, and I'm happy for her. It's just, well, I turned twenty-eight this year. It was well past time that I moved out." My mother had found her happiness with a really lovely man who happened to love farmwork. Good for him.

I, however, did not enjoy it. Nor did I enjoy the smell of manure every time I stepped outside. I'd meant what I said, it was well past time that I moved out.

"But didn't you pay both mortgages on that place for, like, a decade or more? What happens to the farm? How are you protecting that investment?" Hank pushed. "Did you get anything in writing about who owns it?"

Finally understanding the nature of Hank's concerns, I relaxed back in my chair and crossed my legs to the side. "Oh. I see. No, Hank. My mother owns it."

"No, Hannah. No. How can you just leave?" He leaned forward, clearly agitated. "That's a lot of money to walk away from. I won't let you—"

"I didn't walk away from it."

He made a frustrated growling sound. "Hannah. I don't care if she's your mother, you have to get money stuff in writing—"

"They took out a loan, a new mortgage, and paid me back."

Hank sat up. "What?"

"They took out a new mortgage and gave me all the money. My momma paid me back all the money I put into that place, paying off the debt and the mortgage."

"Oh. Well." He frowned, finally leaning back. "There will be tax implications."

I tried not to smile. As long as I'd known him, Hank was a businessman first and foremost. But unlike what other folks thought about Hank Weller, he was the most rigidly ethical businessman I'd ever met. He didn't let anyone take advantage of him, everything was about checks and balances and keeping score and who owed who and settling debts.

Which was why his new relationship with Charlotte Mitchell made no sense to me. She was a single mother of four cute kiddos and everyone always assumed Hank hated kids. You could've knocked me over with a feather when I realized the nature of their relationship. Not only had he fallen ass over ankles in love with the children, he'd ruined himself (in a good way, in the best way) for the mother. Which was the main reason why I was now in charge of the Pink Pony and he was now a silent partner, who I'd soon be buying out if everything went according to plan.

I never thought I'd see the day Hank Weller cared about other people's opinions, but I'd seen it. He needed to be respectable for his new family, not because Charlotte had asked him to—she didn't care—but because he wanted it.

"There won't be tax implications." I shook my head at his statement. "It was done as a gift—last tax year, this tax year, and the last payment will be after the first of the year. I don't have to pay taxes on it. This might be sudden to you, but it's been in the works for a while, even before I decided to move out."

"So they haven't paid you back all the money," he said, like he suspected as much all along.

Hank may have changed for Charlotte and her kids, but obviously with everyone else, he was still the same shrewd, suspicious, miserly yet ethical businessman as before.

"Anyway." I huffed a laugh, needing to get this conversation back on track. "Do you think Jethro would help with building an apartment at the club? I feel like I could do the electrical, tile, and plumbing if he could do the foundation, framing, and drywall."

Ignoring my question, he asked, "What did you do with it?"

I knew he meant the money, and I knew he wouldn't drop the subject until he was satisfied I hadn't been taken advantage of or hadn't been reckless. So, I answered, "I invested it in an index fund for now."

"Hmm." He leaned all the way back in his chair, studying me. "Real estate would've been better."

"I don't have time for that right now. And I don't want to do upkeep on a property—on land—even if it's just a small lot. I've had enough farming and mowing and yard work to last a lifetime. Also, the kind of place I want, I can't afford yet in this area."

"You want to live in the club? Until you can afford a place you want?"

"Yes. Then I can save on living expenses, put that money toward a down payment on a house, bide my time and wait for a good deal."

Finally, he nodded. "That makes sense."

"I don't mind sleeping in the dressing room if needed. It's just—once I do move out—that apartment could be revenue generating. It could also be used for one or more of the dancers, if they need a safe space to stay, or a place to stay until they get back on their feet."

This was a fine line I was walking with Hank. He'd made it clear to every person who worked at the Pony over and over that he wasn't running a charity. You worked for what you had, within the rules he set, and in return he provided a safe environment, a solid paycheck, mentorship if requested, and a found family who looked out for its own.

Hank Weller didn't need money, he already had buckets of it in the form of a sizable inheritance from his parents. But he was also odd. He'd never touched the inheritance other than to buy ridiculous trinkets for people, and he had paid his own way through an Ivy League college by stripping. Then, one semester before he graduated, he dropped out of school, took all the money he'd earned as an exotic dancer in New England, and opened the Pink Pony as a way to mortify his parents, their friends, and the whole of Green Valley's high society.

Since then, he'd invested his returns into real estate. The Pink Pony was now a very small part of his portfolio. He didn't need the money, he'd defined the payment plan for me to buy him out, and yet he still treated every aspect of the Pink Pony as a business.

"Fine." He stood, still nodding. "Okay. I'll talk to Jethro. He's got his hands full right now, but if you have schematics, maybe y'all can meet next month to go over the plan. How does that sound? You okay in that dressing room for a few more months?"

"Yes!" I jumped up and stuck out my hand. Hank wasn't a hugger, but he liked shaking hands to seal a deal. "I can wait a year if needed, just as long as there's an apartment at the end of it." Just the thought of my own apartment made me feel giddy. Walls I could paint however I like, a space I could decorate and call my own.

He accepted my handshake but didn't move our hands, instead holding mine and openly studying me. "Dave told me the numbers are up and y'all had a line a few times last month."

"That's true. Do you want to see the numbers?"

Hank stepped closer, squeezing my fingers, his eyebrows pulling together again. "Hannah, are you sure this is what you want? Managing the Pony and living here, too? I saw that mural you painted as I drove in. It's beautiful. Are you sure your talents aren't being wasted? Why don't you try looking for a job again?"

I gave him a small smile. "You know I tried to get a job everywhere. No one will hire me if I'm honest about my work history. And the one place that did . . ." I lifted my shoulders in a resigned shrug. "Well, you know the story."

His features darkened. "That sonofabitch manager. I wish you'd tell me his name."

"Why?" I chuckled without mirth. "What would you do? Beat him up for making stripper and sex jokes after he found out I worked here?"

"Yes, and beat him up for making untoward advances, too."

"Come on now, Hank. You know as well as I do, if I don't want to be harassed in the workplace and if I want to be taken seriously, then maybe I shouldn't have been born a woman, let alone danced at the Pony in order to put food on the table. Really, I had it coming." I tried to make a joke out of it, minimize it, play the sarcasm card like it didn't bother me. What else could I do? I was an unlucky person. But, from now on, I was determined to stay in my lane, keep my head down, and keep quiet.

Hank looked pained. "Hannah, you—if you would—I think you should try again. Leave the Pony off your resume and maybe try looking in Nashville. Or even further."

"Seriously. Let it go. I have." I dropped his hand. "Working here, managing things, this is the best opportunity I'll ever get, and I'm grateful for it."

"But is it what you *want*?"

"It doesn't matter what I want, Hank. It only matters what I can get. Don't be pushing me to dream big, we both know my life doesn't work that way. Either I can be miserable wishing for what's unattainable, or I can make the best of what's possible." And that was the truth of my existence in a nutshell.

My former boss stuffed his hands in his pockets and he opened his mouth like he was about to argue the point, but a throat being cleared pulled our attention to the doorway.

Isaac.

His gaze loitered on me for a beat and I gave myself an internal round of applause for not flinching under the weight of it. Isaac's attention then shifted away and, even though his features didn't perceptibly move or alter, something about his stare seemed to communicate an intensity of dislike as it came to rest on Hank.

"Isaac Sylvester," Hank said, standing straighter and frowning. "Why the hell are you here?"

Apparently, the dislike was mutual.

I stepped forward even though my instinct was to hide behind the bookshelf in the corner until Isaac left. "Mr. Sylvester is our new bouncer."

Hank's frown swung toward me. "What the—"

"Joshua is on medical leave, as you know, and with the increase in customers we are very, very short-staffed in the front. If you recall, I'm still hunting for another bartender since you left and Louis is by himself."

Lifting his chin, Hank inspected me with unhappy features then finally gave a short nod. "Whatever. Not my business who you hire, Miss Townsen. Nor are the messes you create with bad staffing decisions. Just as long as you identify and train the two new dancers for the male revue and hen nights coming up, I've got nothing to say."

I did not roll my eyes, nor did I smile at his surly statements. It was just typical Hank Weller sass. After so many years, I was used to him.

Sucking in a deep, bracing breath for courage, I faced Isaac and stapled on a polite expression. "Can I help you with something?"

His glare of dislike shifted again, returning to me, and I worked to hide my surprise when the hostility behind his gaze appeared to completely dissipate in an instant, again without his features altering in any perceptible way.

"Dave wants your approval to rope off the west side of the floor for a party," he said, blue eyes solely focused on me, his voice softer than I'd ever heard it. The combination of his focused attention without hostility plus his gentle tone hit me right in the chest, making it ache with a familiar—albeit recently dormant—longing.

But I didn't get a chance to respond or react because Hank stepped in front of me and said, "Don't bother her with that. She's a busy woman. I'll do it on my way out."

The next thing I knew, Hank had pushed Isaac out and shut the door behind him, leaving me alone with my suddenly disordered thoughts.

Had Isaac just been . . . nice to me? Did that just happen? He'd been polite, right? Or did I imagine it?

Giving my head a quick shake, I sat and decided to push all thoughts of Isaac Sylvester from my mind. It didn't matter if he was nice to me today, he'd be a jerk tomorrow. *You imagined it. He thinks you're a liar and a prostitute.*

Yes, I must've imagined it. I decided there was one silver lining to his misconception of my intentions: Isaac's rude behavior had already filed down the sharp edges of my crush. Perhaps, by the end of his time here, my feelings would finally scatter into the ether of my teenage years, where they belonged.

Chapter Eleven
HANNAH

"Compassion without love felt suspiciously like pity."

— Beau Winston, *Beard in Mind* by Penny Reid

I spent the remainder of the evening on tenterhooks, but not because of Isaac. Tavvy—Levit Traveston—had only ever frequented the Pony on Saturdays. If he showed up at all, it would be today. So, when my momma's number popped up on my caller ID, I took the call, happy for the distraction in the moment.

"Hello, Momma. How are you?" We hadn't talked in a while. I was anxious to hear how things were going with the farm and Jedd and the new horses he'd brought to the stable.

"Hey, baby. I'm grand. How are you? Is now an okay time to call? You're not dancing, are you?"

My stomach sunk and I forced my voice to remain even as I replied, "No, Momma. You know I don't do that anymore." But then I bit my lip because the words had technically been a lie.

I would be dancing if Tavvy showed up.

Mother had been over the moon when I'd informed her I would be retiring from exotic dancing. But then she'd come crashing back down to earth when I explained I'd still be working at the Pony. She never really said it outright, just a few frustrated comments here and there, but I knew she hated me working here. She'd always hated it, swallowing the reality of our situation like a bitter pill.

"Good. Just checking," she said, sounding more relaxed.

Biting my bottom lip to keep from saying something I might regret, I glanced at the time on my computer screen. I'd answered her call less than a minute ago but now I felt anxious for it to be over.

"How's Jedd? Did he get those horses?" Infusing my tone with lightness, I pasted a smile on my face. Folks can always hear a smile over the phone.

"Oh, he did! And, baby, they are so beautiful. A momma and her foal." My mother spoke for a while about the horses and her man, something sweet he did, something funny he said.

I caught myself genuinely smiling a time or two because she sounded happy. But when we hung up after sharing *I love yous*, I felt mostly hollow.

I loved her but I didn't know how to fix this fractured relationship. She wasn't currently doing anything wrong. She was sweet and kind, funny and caring. Yes, she'd made mistakes in the past. She'd also been punished for them. I didn't wish to see her punished any more, I didn't want her to struggle any more. I wanted her to be happy.

But no matter what I did or tried to tell myself, talking to my momma and being around her made me feel awful. Angry at her and my father for their choices. And then I felt angry at myself for getting angry.

It was like, I felt wrong. I was *wrong*. Guilty of the crime of bad luck and desperation and subsequently sentenced to a life of paying for it.

* * *

I wasn't sure whether to be relieved or disappointed when closing time came around but Tavvy had not.

The sooner I let Tavvy borrow my phone while I put on my show, the sooner Isaac would leave me in peace. On the other hand, I had no desire—no matter how much Tavvy paid for the privilege—of stripping for the man. As a general rule, I usually preferred stripteases to lap dances, but something about Tavvy had always been off. He paid me plenty, tipped me like a high roller, but he always brought the clothes I'd be stripping out of along with him. They weren't dirty or anything. In truth, they usually still had the tags on. But they were . . . bizarre.

One time, he brought me an Easter bunny costume to strip out of, complete with a stuffed carrot, giant head, and big mitts for the hands. A few times, it was a pantsuit like my grandmother used to wear, always pastel green with a floral blouse. He asked me to keep on the thick-lensed glasses with a chain at the ear parts. The shoes were brown orthopedic loafers, and the stockings were various colors of calf-height compression hose, a real son of a gun to remove. Other times, it was cargo pants, a tank top, a running jacket, sport socks, tennis shoes, and a full hiking backpack.

His requests—and he always had a request—were also odd, like: keep the bunny head on, strip without taking off the backpack, take off the compression hose just with your toes, that kind of stuff. And often he laughed at me—pointed and laughed—as I tried to fulfill his weird demands.

Whatever. It only ever lasted three minutes, he never touched me, and he paid a bundle. But still, strange.

Point is, because I'd been preoccupied and expecting Tavvy, mentally preparing for his strange requests, I lost track of time and forgot to close my office door all the way. So, when a knock sounded on the doorframe, interrupting my deep focus and startling me, my hand flew to my chest as I gasped, "Cheesus!"

"Pardon me," came a deep, rumbly voice.

My eyes lifted to the door even though my brain already told me who I would find. *Isaac.*

Inhaling for calm—I realized this had now become a habit whenever Isaac appeared—I craned my neck to check the hall behind him for any eavesdroppers. I rolled my chair back from the desk, putting a little extra distance between where he hovered and where I sat.

"Uh, hello, Mr. Sylvester. May I help you?"

He leaned a shoulder against the doorframe. "We didn't talk today. Or yesterday."

Alarm made me stiffen. "Oh! Am I supposed to check in with you daily? About the—" I cut myself off and checked the hall behind him again. Even though I saw no one, I decided to whisper the last word. "The *case*."

He lifted a hand, his expression and tone free of hostility. "No. It's only—"

"Tavvy hasn't shown up, as far as I know, but you would know better than me since you're at the front." Why was he being polite? *He probably wants something.*

"Correct. He didn't show up tonight," he said, now looking and sounding downright friendly.

My eyes narrowed. I wouldn't read into it. Maybe he'd had a good day. Maybe he got lots of tips. Maybe his favorite sports team won.

With a tight smile, I nodded slowly and waited to see what he would do or say next, endeavoring to remain still under his inspection.

We spent several long moments with him staring and me wishing he'd take this new, perplexing attitude and simply leave, before he asked, "Don't you need to be walked out?"

"No, thank you. I have things to do here." It wasn't a lie. I did have things to do here. I'd been in the middle of setting up the new online scheduling system. I wanted it finished before the staff meeting in the morning.

"I'll wait for you."

I glanced at him—found his eyes still fastened to my face—then away. "I don't need to be walked out."

"I'd feel better if I walked you out."

Rolling myself back to the desk, I set my suddenly sweaty hand on the mouse and my gaze on the computer screen. "There's no need. I don't need to be walked out."

"I'm not leaving until I walk you out."

Blaaaah. *No use hiding it.*

Releasing the mouse, I wiped my hands on my jeans and swiveled toward the door, leaned back in my chair, crossed my arms, and met his gaze. "There's no need to walk me out because I live here." Maybe I sounded a little belligerent about it, maybe I didn't. I couldn't tell. The man was making me more nervous than usual.

"Pardon?" He straightened and I could see I'd confused him.

"I live at the club. So, you see, you don't need to walk me out. I'm not leaving."

"You live here?" He took a step further inside my office.

"I do." I stiffened but didn't roll my chair back.

"Why?"

Huffing, I glared at him even though he wasn't—for once—glaring at me. "Is that a question asked in an official capacity?"

He seemed to ponder this, his features still free of aggression, then said, "Yes."

"Fine. I live here so I don't have to pay anyone rent." My stomach rumbled and I pressed my forearms against it, realizing I'd forgotten to eat dinner. *Great. Now I'm nervous and hangry.*

"Why don't you live with your momma?" Uninvited, he walked fully into my office and sat down in the seat situated at the desk across from mine.

In order to face him, I had to turn in my chair and ended up rolling to the side again. It was the only way to ensure our knees didn't touch. "I don't wish to live at my momma's house and I don't believe this line of inquiry is at all relevant to your investigation. So, I guess, I'm not answering any other questions about this subject." I nodded at the assertion, then added for good measure, "Without my lawyer present."

Isaac's eyes seem to brighten and, if I wasn't mistaken, his lips compressed, twisting just a smidge to the side. "I see," he said evenly and I got the sense he was trying his darndest not to laugh at me.

Whatever. I was hangry. If he arrested me now, then they'd probably feed me in jail, right?

Shifting in his seat like he was settling in for a nice long chat, his gaze swept over me. "I overheard some of your conversation with Hank Weller."

This statement brought me up short and I couldn't stop myself from asking, "What part of the conversation?"

"About looking for a job, about being hired somewhere only to quit because of your manager, and about settling for what you can get rather than what you actually want," he said, all *la-dee-dah* and *as you please*, like confessing to eavesdropping was no big deal. Who did that? Especially when the topics Hank and I had discussed were incredibly personal in nature.

I felt my face grow hot while we exchanged stares—his openly assessing, mine stunned and embarrassed—until I couldn't hold his gaze any longer. Nor could I stand his company any longer.

No wonder he'd been polite when he'd interrupted my conversation with Hank this afternoon. Isaac felt sorry for me. He pitied me. My chest was suddenly full of ice, burning and painful. What had occurred when I attempted to apply for jobs elsewhere wasn't a secret at the Pony, but what he'd heard wasn't for his ears.

At a loss, I stood, walked to the bookshelf, and contemplated what to do next. The more I thought about it, the angrier I got. I would prefer his hostility over his pity. If I'd wanted his pity, I would've tried to explain my point of view last Saturday instead of letting him think I was a prostitute. But here he was, pitying me anyhow.

Well, screw it. And him. And his pity.

He may've been an undercover agent, and he may've been my mental stand-in and unrequited crush, but that didn't give him the right to know anything about me. He was an outsider, he was untrustworthy, and I wanted nothing to do with him ever. Period. The end.

I heard Isaac make a rustling sound just before he spoke. "Hannah, I want to—"

"Mr. Sylvester." I faced him, interrupting whatever he'd planned on saying, too angry to bring him into focus clearly, and knowing I was maybe three minutes from bursting into tears. "I wasn't lying, I do have things to do.

Unless there's something to discuss related to the investigation, or you have questions about your job here, you should head home. It's very late. Good night."

My office descended into silence. Again, I could feel his regard move over me, but I didn't meet his stare. I wasn't in the mood for his scowls and sharp words, or his pretend friendliness, or his casual bringing up of topics he had no right to bring up. It was the end of the week, I still had the staff meeting tomorrow to finish prepping for, and I was wrung out.

I wish he'd just leave!

Eventually, he also stood, and I felt relief when he ambled toward the hall. I remained standing, planning to lock myself inside and have a good cry as soon as he left, whenever that happened. The man was currently moving at a snail's pace.

But then, instead of leaving, he shut the door. My eyes flew to his.

If I wasn't mistaken, his eyes were full of what looked like remorse as he reached in his front pocket. "I want to, uh, give this back to you." He pulled a thumb drive from his pocket—*the* thumb drive I'd given him last Saturday with the video of my misguided lap dance on it—and held it out to me.

Gripping the desk behind me, I dropped my gaze to the carpet and made no move to accept the thumb drive. In fact, I made no move at all.

After several seconds of me doing nothing, Isaac placed the drive on my desk. "You don't need to keep cooperating with the investigation if you'd prefer not to. I won't force you."

I didn't understand what was happening and this abrupt offering felt like a trap. Or maybe it was simply more pity. Whatever it was, I wanted no part of it.

So, I said, "I promised I would help."

He shuffled a step closer. "I know I coerced you. I want to give you a chance to decide for yourself if—"

Without looking up, I lifted my hands to stop his advance. "I will keep my promise. I consider this matter closed. We will proceed as you've dictated. No need to rehash it. Please don't bring it up again."

Another long moment of quiet passed until I heard Isaac clear his throat before asking, "Is there nothing else I can do for you?"

The softness of his tone set the fine hairs on the back of my neck standing even as my stomach dropped. I hated this. I wish he'd shove his pity where the sun didn't shine. But mostly, I wish he'd never overheard my conversation with Hank.

"Not a thing," I said dully. "Have a safe drive home, Mr. Sylvester."

Isaac opened the door, loitered for a few seconds while I stared at the carpet. Eventually, he said, "Good night, Hannah." And pulled my office door closed.

I stood there unmoving for I don't know how long. Then I sat down and cried. Then I dried my eyes, microwaved some leftovers for a late dinner, and got back to work.

* * *

My phone rang at UnGodly-O'Clock on Sunday morning and I answered it immediately. "Hello?"

When you have a family member with a chronic health condition, like my momma has had since her accident, your body becomes conditioned in a variety of ways. One of those ways was going from fast asleep to awake and ready to respond to whatever emergency in the span of five seconds.

"Hi, Hannah? This is Hazel Huebner down at the Donner Bakery. How are you?" Hazel's sugar-sweet and laser-beams-of-sunshine voice sounded from the other side of my cell phone, jarring and antagonistic given my sleepy frame of mind.

But still, thank God it wasn't Jedd calling about my momma.

"What's up?" Placing my hand over my heart, I leaned back in bed and closed my eyes. I'd put a bed in my former changing room. In addition to the big dressing room, each of us dancers had been given a small, seven-by-seven-foot space, an upgrade made to the Pink Pony by Hank some six or seven years ago. The mattress sat on a platform I'd built about four feet off the ground, which gave me space to store my clothes and whatnot under the platform. Unfortunately, this meant I only had three feet of clearance between me and the ceiling.

"Well, I wanted to reach out because we had a cancellation on a very special cake this morning and Jenn immediately thought of y'all down at the Pink Pony. It's baked and decorated and ready if y'all are interested."

My eyes flew open again and I bit my bottom lip, wracking the inside of my brains for the right words. "Uh, well, to be honest, Hazel, I don't think we have the budget for one of Jenn's cakes."

Jenn was Jennifer Winston, formerly Jennifer Sylvester, before her marriage to Cletus Winston, and she was famous for her cake. Specifically, banana cake. Since she'd been entering her banana cake at the state fair, no one else had taken home the blue ribbon, not even close. Now her cakes were famous everywhere and her social media following was off the chain. She had millions of followers. Folks all around the world bought her cakes and they certainly weren't cheap.

More than once I'd wanted to pick her brain on how she'd built the Donner Bakery into a recognizable global brand using the power of social media. She was magic, or her cakes were magic, or something over there was magic.

"No, silly!" Hazel giggled. "She don't want you to pay for it. It's free."

"Oh!" Thoughtlessly, this news had me sitting up and I hit my head on the ceiling. "Ow!"

"Ow?"

"Uh. No. Sorry. I said oh, not ow. Sometimes my *oh*s come out sounding like *ow*s. Anyway." *What are you doing, Hannah? Stop trying to explain yourself. Why are you making up an excuse?*

I hated that I did this, but it was a difficult habit to break. I'd spent the whole of my twenties thus far trying not to feel inferior to everyone else near my age and around town. My overexplaining, or lie-explaining, to cover up minor things came so naturally now, I couldn't catch myself before I did it. Worse, even with my instinctual lie-explaining, I was still a terrible liar.

"Anyway," I said again, rubbing my forehead and plastering on a smile so I'd sound friendly and not in pain. "If it's free, then we'll definitely take it. The timing is amazing since we're celebrating this quarter's birthdays today. I can be there in a half hour."

"No need to drive over, honey. I can walk the cake out to Isaac."

I stopped rubbing my forehead, certain I'd misheard her. "You'll—you'll walk it out to whom?"

"Isaac. Jenn's older brother? He's in the parking lot again this morning. He's here every morning, actually. Word is, he's been working at the Pony. Is that true?"

"Uhhh." I rolled to my side, quickly debating whether I should admit Isaac worked for the Pony or if doing so would make him mad at me all over again. I stalled by asking, "Where did you hear that?"

"Everyone knows, Hannah. This town is smaller than a pond. Then I'll take it out to the big guy and he can drive it over. How does that sound?"

"Uh, I—I guess—"

"Good. Good. Talk later, gorgeous. Bye!" She hung up.

Chapter Twelve
HANNAH

"'You are so adorable. I just want to take you home and put you in my pocket.'
I'd prefer her pants, but I guess I'd settle for her pocket."

— Sienna Diaz and Jethro Winston, *Grin and Beard It* by Penny Reid

Sleep felt impossible after the strange call from the bakery. I got up, showered, and dressed, but I couldn't help the direction of my thoughts. If Jenn Winston wanted to give her brother a cake for the Pink Pony, why didn't she just give it to him? Why have her bakery minion call me first? And why was Isaac in the parking lot of the Donner Bakery if not to see his sister? In which case, why call me before giving Isaac the cake? Round and round went my thoughts until I felt dizzy.

Fortunately or unfortunately, I didn't have to wait long for answers. I'd just finished pouring myself a cup of coffee when I spotted Isaac open the back door of the breakroom off the employee lot. Propping the door open, he paused, turned, and spent some time trying to pick up a big fancy bakery box, so big that I couldn't see the whole thing from my vantage point. Then he couldn't quite keep the door open while also maneuvering the box inside.

He didn't spot me at first and I considered making a run for it. After our awkward interaction last night, I didn't wish to talk with him at all if I could help it. However, sympathy for his struggles had me setting down my coffee and walking over.

I planned to reach for the bakery box so he could prop open the door. "Let me help with—holy moly!"

Isaac turned his head toward my exclamation. As his squinty, frustrated eyes connected with my shocked round ones, the furious-looking lines between his eyebrows relaxed.

"Hannah," he said, standing straighter. The action almost caused him to drop his burden.

Spreading my arms, I gripped the end closest to me to stabilize it. It was at that point I realized how flimsy the cardboard was.

"When she called and offered to give us a cake for free, I wasn't expecting it to be the size of a whole dang zip code!" I took turns gaping at Isaac and at the monstrous-sized box. "This is the biggest cake I've ever seen!"

"*She* offered?" Isaac asked, sounding incredulous as he slid his hands on the underside of the box toward the other end. "She called you and offered? You didn't order this? Wait—be careful. You have to support the center or else it might bend."

"What? Are you out of your mind? I can't afford a Donner Bakery cake!" I hollered, working to maintain my balance while supporting my side of the box with one hand and sliding the other toward the center. "And, by 'she,' if you mean Happy Hazel from the bakery calling on behalf of your sister, yes. Hazel called me—wait, can we just—can we take a moment and get this beast inside first before we talk? How heavy is this? Good Lord!"

This was a very heavy cake in a very flimsy box. The short side of the bakery box barely fit through the doorway without being tilted, and the long side had to be seven feet, at least.

Isaac kept his foot at the bottom of the door to keep it open while also not blocking the opening with his body, but that meant, as I pivoted and backed into the kitchen, he had to contort himself in order to support his side and the center. Meanwhile, as I walked backward, I hit a cluster of chairs and stumbled.

"Ah! Don't push." Nearly falling as I tripped on the chair legs, I almost dropped my side. "Wait a minute!"

"Are you okay?" His side dipped as he asked the question.

"I'm fine. Keep your side up!" The last thing we needed was the cake sliding out on his end and depositing itself on the gravel just outside the back door.

I glanced behind me. The chairs surrounded a table, which was covered in paper plates, napkins, and utensils.

"Give me a second to set the edge of the box down on the table and I'll move this stuff off. Then you can just push it inside while I hold the door."

"Do we have to set it on the table?" Isaac called from outside, his body still contorted to keep the door ajar.

Pressing my lips together as I caught sight of him again, sudden laughter threatened. He looked truly ridiculous, his head just visible above the box, one leg outstretched at the door, the other barely balancing. It looked like he was playing a ridiculous game of Twister: one hand on the side of the box, one hand toward the center, one foot on the floor, one foot propping the door open.

Quickly composing myself, I stepped to the side in order to place the edge of the box on the table. "If you want to get this over with as quickly as possible, then let me—"

"Wait!" A hint of panic entered his voice. "If you do that, if you lower it, I can't hold both the cake and the door. I won't be able to reach the door with my foot."

Shoot. If he didn't hold the heavy door, it would swing shut and crush the flimsy box. I lifted the cake back up, a renewed urge to laugh forcing me to close my eyes. It was no use. My shoulders began to shake.

"Hannah?"

"I'm thinking!" I endeavored to mask my laughter. Hopefully he wouldn't hear me—

"Are you . . . laughing?"

I guess I failed.

"I'm sorry!" Eyes still squeezed shut, I gave myself over to the hilarity of the situation and laughed openly. "It's just that, I didn't even order this stupid cake and now it's trapped us and we can't move. We're going to die here, holding a seven-foot cake."

To my surprise, Isaac's rumbly laughter joined mine, and that felt like permission to laugh harder.

I sniffled, shaking my head. "It's like, how did you even get it here?"

Around his own laughter, he said, "Very slowly. I had to—to put it on top of my car, and strap it—"

"Don't say anything else!" Picturing Isaac Sylvester strapping this giant, delicate box to the top of his car and driving five miles an hour up winding mountain roads, I was in great danger of losing it.

"What is going on in here?" Serafina's question had me opening my eyes and turning toward her voice.

"Oh thank God!" I sniffled again. "Serafina, hold open the door! Quick."

Serafina sent me a side-eye as she drifted over to the door much slower than the urgency in my voice dictated. But, whatever. We now had a door holder.

"Isaac, now that Serafina is holding the door, you can let go. Good. Serafina, can you hold the door and support the center of the cake? Yes, just like that. Let's lower it and I'll place my side on the table and just—yes. There we go." Sighing my relief as soon as the edge of the box met the table, I hurried to collect the items covering the tabletop and relocate them.

Once finished, I called to Isaac, "I'm ready. You can slide it in now."

"That's what she said," Serafina deadpanned.

Though I tried to ignore her, the comment made me flustered. Likely since it was said about Isaac. And me. And him sliding—whatever!

Moving another table to accommodate the box, I helped guide the length of it to the new table, ensuring the weight was equally distributed between the two surfaces and the center was supported, willing the heat warming my cheeks to dispel.

"Whew. There now." Grinning at the sense of accomplishment, I placed my hands on my hips and looked up just as the back door closed. "That wasn't too bad."

Isaac, looking right back at me, lifted an eyebrow at my statement. It took my brain a few seconds to register that he was also smiling. At me. It wasn't big, there were no teeth involved, but it was definitely a smile.

"Thanks for your help," he said, all low and soft.

"My pleasure," I said. Or, I think I said.

He drifted closer, still wearing his little smile, his eyes still on mine, his voice still deliciously low and soft as he said, "You showed up just in time."

"Are you saying I rescued you?" The words arrived without me thinking. If I'd considered them first, I definitely wouldn't have said that.

Luckily, his smile grew, just a smidge. "You did rescue me. How can I show my appreciation?" He was very close now. If I reached out, I would touch him.

A new warmth, a nice kind, flooded my neck and cheeks. I felt my grin morph into something dreamy and slight as we looked at each other and, try as I might, I couldn't think. Nor could I tear my eyes from his. Like yesterday, they lacked hostility, and they were so darn pretty and interesting when he didn't act irritated by my existence. Like those pictures of the glowing northern lights, spectral blue and green, I could've stared at them—at him—for hours.

He leaned forward, his smile waning from his mouth but still warming his eyes, and he whispered something that sounded like my name.

But then Serafina said, "So, you're Isaac," and broke the spell.

I blinked away first and reality rushed in. Where was I? And how did I get here? And . . . had I just been staring like a fool at Isaac Sylvester? *Flirting* with him?! The man who thought I was a manipulative liar and pitied me to such an enormous extent that he gave me back the evidence of my supposed crime?

Yeah. Him. Fork it all!

My good sense wrestled with the urge to be embarrassed. But why should I? It wasn't like I'd stared at him for hours. It couldn't have been more than a few seconds. Ten at most. No biggie. I was okay, it was okay. And, by the way, if he didn't want to be stared at, maybe he shouldn't be so handsome. He was likely used to stares. He probably didn't even notice my stare. WHATEVER!

"Yes. You're Serafina," I heard his voice say, no longer soft and low.

I walked back to my discarded coffee and watched the two shake hands while I debated whether or not to make a quick exit or put cream and sugar in my cup.

Just as I turned to leave without sweetening my coffee, Serafina asked, "When did you start dating Hannah?"

I froze, a lump jumping to my throat, then faced them, almost splashing my coffee in my haste to say, "Oh no. We are not—"

Just as Isaac responded calmly with, "A few weeks ago."

I snapped my mouth shut and stared pointedly at him. He still looked at Serafina with an unconcerned expression, while I sensed Serafina's glance shift to me.

"Well, isn't that nice," she said, her mouth curving. If I read her expression correctly, it communicated something like, *GET IT, GIRL!*

I opened my mouth to contradict and Isaac spoke again. "But she wants to keep it a secret from everyone. You understand. The club needs the help up front and she asked me to step in for a few weeks, until she could find a permanent bouncer."

"Oh. I see." Serafina nodded. "So, if people know you're dating, then they'll think she's giving you preferential treatment. But really, you're helping her out."

He nodded, his eyes sliding to mine, holding. I stared back, disbelieving. He smirked. I scowled. His eyes narrowed but his smirk became an amused-looking smile.

Well. Goodness. So happy I could amuse him.

"Don't worry, Hannah." Serafina walked over to the coffee machine and pulled out the carafe. "I won't tell anyone. But they'll suspect something is up, since it's—you know—*him*."

I felt my eyes bulge, a flare of panic joining the hard lump in my throat. Rushing forward, I grabbed Isaac's arm and tugged him toward the hall. "That reminds me, I need to speak with you about, uh, that issue. Come with me, please."

He allowed himself to be led and that was good, but it was also bad. I didn't know where we were going. My office seemed too close to the break-room and I didn't want us to be overheard. I couldn't take him to the front, in case Louis or Dave had already arrived, nor the dressing room, since those were off-limits to men except on hen nights.

My feet kept walking and before I understood their intent, I'd shoved him inside the storage closet—yes, that storage closet, the one I told folks to stop using for anything but storage!—and followed him, careful to prop the door open so we wouldn't be trapped.

With some effort, he turned in the tiny sliver of space and faced me. His features wholly relaxed, he looked at me, like he was waiting for me to explain myself.

Me!

Huffing out fire, I crossed my arms, paying no mind to how one elbow bumped into a big box of condoms on my left and the other elbow nudged a package of bar napkins on my right. "What the heck was that? We're dating now?"

"You look very stern right now, Hannah," he said, still smiling, his eyes dancing over me.

"Well, of course I look stern, *Isaac*," I seethed through gritted teeth. "I'm very frustrated. And confused."

"Us dating was the original backstory for this assignment," he said evenly, like this explained everything.

"The *original* backstory. We agreed to change it. You're a bouncer here and that should be enough."

Isaac's gaze swept down then up my body in a way that made me feel suddenly self-conscious. But before I could fully react to his odd perusal, he said, "It's important to be flexible in undercover situations and you suddenly hiring me last week makes more sense if we add the dating element."

Not sure what I would say, but knowing I needed to contradict this assertion, I opened my mouth to protest.

He spoke before I could. "People are already questioning why you hired me so quickly and this could undermine the investigation and my cover, especially since Levit didn't show up yesterday."

"Who? Who is questioning it?" I demanded.

"Louis brings it up every day, and he's loud about it. I can sense everyone else giving me long looks of suspicion. Now, why would they do that unless they're doubtful of my cover story?"

"Because you're my st—" I snapped my mouth shut just in time, my brain catching up before I revealed too much.

His eyes narrowed again and the side of his mouth curved. "What? I'm your what?" he asked, looking entirely too interested in my answer.

Chapter Thirteen
HANNAH

"If anyone knows how to stop worrying about stupid shit, please give me a call."

— Scarlet St. Claire, *Beard Necessities* by Penny Reid

Pressing my lips together, I gave my head a tight shake, pretending to be a frozen brick wall. I would not give this man another reason to pity me. I'd rather he forever believe Hannah Townsen to be a marauding mastermind than know about my ridiculous *feelings*.

Isaac waited, and waited. And waited. Dipping his chin and trying to catch my eyes, a frown began to form between his eyebrows.

When my silence persisted, he sighed. It sounded tired. "Fine. Don't tell me. But listen, it's not just folks here and their doubts. I might need to be here longer than previously anticipated. You promised to help—a fact you reiterated last night though I offered to you an out—and helping means doing everything necessary to make my cover appear as believable as possible. Right?"

"Yes, but—"

"And why would I work here at the Pony? Why would I return to Green Valley at all? I need a good reason to be here. *You* are a very compelling reason."

He had a point about needing a reason for returning. Except, wasn't his sister here? "Okay. Fine. Then what about Jennifer?"

The change in him was immediate. All that odd warmth he'd been tossing my way was abruptly blanketed with a layer of ice. "What about her?" he asked, and even his voice sounded cold.

"Couldn't she be your reason for returning to Green Valley? According to Hazel, you're at the Donner Bakery and Lodge daily. Why can't you use your sister as your excuse for coming back?"

Isaac's chest expanded with a deep, silent breath as we watched each other, me waiting for his answer and him a frozen brick wall. Ha. Our roles had reversed.

Finally, he cleared his throat and glanced away. "She's not an option."

"Why?"

"I can't use her as part of my cover story." His voice had turned husky and he wasn't meeting my eyes.

"Why?"

He seemed to struggle, then murmured, "She doesn't want to see me."

I stiffened in surprise, really taking a moment to look at him. His efforts to mask his inner turmoil were admirable, but I could see everything. Perhaps if I'd been anyone else, someone who hadn't spent two hours every week of their adolescence memorizing his face, the micro-expressions, the shifts in mood illustrated by kaleidoscoping shades of eye color, I wouldn't have spotted his anguish.

My first instinct was to comfort him, to reach out and give him a hug. My second was to fiddle, to interfere and try to fix this fractured relationship between the two siblings. Perhaps they simply needed a mediator? Someone to bridge the gap. At the very least, he needed better PR, a hype-man (or woman), a person to sing his praises to Jennifer Winston and encourage the woman to crack the door to her heart.

And maybe he read some of my thoughts in my features, because in the next moment he crossed his arms even though the action wasn't fully possible given the tightness of the space.

"Also," he went on gruffly, "if I make contact with her, try to make amends and reenter her life, there's a chance my old Iron Wraiths brethren still scattered around the area—from when I was deep undercover a few years back—might consider her fair game since we're blood related. It would be the same story for anyone I married, any kids I had. Even though the club is basically disbanded, the entitlement remains."

"I see." Considering this information and him, I twisted my lips to the side. "But they wouldn't see me as fair game? If we pretend we're dating?"

He shook his head. "No. It's always considered casual without marriage."

Since I had him here, basically trapped as I stood between him and the door, I indulged in a bit of unabashed staring, then finally conceded, "Okay. Fine. We can add secretly dating to the cover story. But I—"

He interrupted, "By the way, you touched me."

I blinked at this statement, confused why me touching him had anything to do with anything. "I touched . . . ? Oh!" Taking a step back, I held up my hands. "You're right. I did. I'm sorry." Darn it all! I'd made a vow to never touch him. I'd meant that vow. Shoot.

He took a step forward and grabbed one of my hands, holding it in both of his. "Don't apologize. You should touch me. It gives more credibility to our cover story."

I didn't know what to pay attention to first: his words, his face, or where he held my hand cradled gently in his.

"I mean, us dating," he explained. "Us dating is why I returned to Green Valley and why you hired me so quickly as a bouncer. It addresses any potential doubts about why I'm here. The stronger the cover story, the safer you—uh, we'll both be. It's what's best for the investigation."

My mouth opened again but I didn't know what to say, or if I needed to clarify anything at all.

While I struggled to sort through the threads of the conversation and how I felt about it, he stepped fully into my space, thereby hijacking all my brainpower. I had no choice but to focus fully on him and what he might do next. Isaac lifted a hand and cradled my jaw, slid his long, calloused fingers into the hair behind my ear. His palm was warm, the pads of his fingers textured, and he smelled fantastic. I couldn't have stopped the small sigh that escaped my lips if I'd had ten years to prepare for this moment.

One side of his mouth tugged upward again as his eyes glittered down at me. "You should touch me," he said, using that soft, low voice of his. "And get used to me touching you."

* * *

"Hey, Hannah. You have no chair." Serafina, the last to arrive at the quarterly staff meeting, took the remaining empty seat. "Where are you going to sit?"

"She can sit on Isaac's lap," April hollered.

I would not blush, nor would I react, even though I wanted to send April a reprimanding look. Of the dancers, she had the driest humor and therefore the driest delivery.

Unfortunately, Louis piped in with, "Or mine," patting his legs and diffusing the old awkwardness with brand-new awkwardness.

"That's an HR violation," Tina said, earning her a few chuckles, distracting from April's and Louis's teasing. "We can grab a chair from the main room if needed but y'all be serious and let Hannah speak."

"It's fine. I'll stand." This was my first quarterly staff meeting since taking over as manager. Giving the room what I hoped was an unruffled smile, my gaze swept over everybody gathered in the breakroom and I found April grimacing. She mouthed, *I'm sorry. I forgot.* Seeing her contrition helped my nerves settle.

But then I made the mistake of glancing at Isaac and my heart took off all over again.

You should touch me, and get used to me touching you.

The recollection of our encounter this morning in that tiny closet had me feeling hot. How I'd been able to walk out of that small space on my own two legs, I had no idea. The memory of his touch still burned my cheek. And the way he'd looked at me? I should've been dead and buried by now. The fact I still breathed and stood and had thoughts in my brain felt like a miracle.

Currently, the man in question lounged in the second row with his legs spread. He shifted as our eyes met, scooting forward an inch in his chair. If I didn't know better, the movement seemed like an invitation to actually use his lap as a seat. Worse, his stare not only remained free of his previous disdain from earlier in the week, it looked amused. Warm. Inviting. Something like that.

Blinking uncontrollably, I redirected my attention to the paper in my hands, hands which I willed to remain steady. "I'll make this fast."

"That's what she said," one of the dancers—it sounded like Kilby—called out. More chuckles.

I exhaled a short laugh, shaking my head and knowing my cheeks were turning pink. First Serafina this morning, now Kilby. These kinds of jokes occurred often with this crowd.

"All right, I walked right into that one. Fair enough." I cleared my throat, and then I made my announcements, starting with updates on the final mural reveal event.

There wasn't much else to cover since Hank's handoff to me had been done via email, all my new plans had already been communicated by email, and everyone seemed fine with everything. I went over some of the usual topics as well as reiterated the major changes I had planned: upcoming schedule of hen parties and ladies' nights, recommendations for new male dancers to take over the empty spots, status of Pink Pony merchandise, and referral codes for commissions.

Tina volunteered to lead the search for new male dancers and everyone scribbled notes about the commissions codes. Soon enough, I'd reached the second to last item on the agenda and I found I needed a deep, bracing breath.

"Before we get to this quarter's birthdays, I want to introduce, uh, our new bouncer for anyone who hasn't met him this last week. Isaac Sylvester is local to Green Valley. His background includes, um, two tours with the US Army overseas. He's well trained to deal with any level of emergency, keep y'all safe, and I believe he's more than qualified to assist Dave and Joshua at the front of the house."

"And he's scary looking, so that helps," Piper chimed in, her words not sounding like a joke.

"Yes, thank you, Isaac, for being scary looking. We appreciate it." Nora, who was sitting next to Piper, turned in her seat, presumably to look at him. "Unlike Dave, who is everyone's best friend."

"Hey, now." Dave, grinning, shrugged. His gaze slid to Tina. "What can I say? I like people."

"Isn't your sister that fucking banana cake princess girl?" This question came from one of Serafina's line cooks, a dainty-looking but foul-mouthed woman by the name of Jessica Mays. We called her Maze in order to distinguish her from the other two Jessicas on staff. Plus, the name really suited her.

"She's married now, Maze. She's not a girl." This came from April, who'd stood to stretch.

My attention cut to Isaac and I watched him squirm for a few seconds, his expression turning remote. Eventually, he said, "We are related, yes."

"That's actually a good segue to our last order of business," I rushed to cut in, wanting to save him from a conversation he clearly wished to avoid.

Turning, I gestured to the massive rectangle box on the kitchen counter behind me. Dave, Louis, and Isaac had relocated it earlier to make room for the chairs and had removed the top of the box. "Jennifer Winston made today's birthday cake. One third is banana cake, one third is carrot, and the last third is double chocolate."

I faced the room. Almost everyone had stood at the mention of cake and they were now pressing forward, crowding me and the counter, wanting a better look, and talking over each other in their excitement.

"Oh wow."

"Now that's a cake."

"Look at that. It's too pretty to eat."

"Speak for yourself. Is smells fucking fantastic."

"Can we take some home, Hannah? I've never had her cake before."

"Me neither."

"Me neither."

"Me neither."

"Me neither! I've always wanted to try it."

"Why haven't you tried her cake?" This murmured question came from Isaac, the only person still sitting, and earned him everyone's attention, likely to see if his question had been in earnest or not. He met their gazes with open curiosity and repeated himself. "Why haven't you tried her cake? The bakery isn't far."

When it became obvious his question had been serious, a few of us traded looks. *Strange.* Did he have no idea about Jennifer Winston's fame? The price of her pastries? The demand for her desserts?

"Uh, well, firstly, her cakes are incredibly expensive," Nora said haltingly, like she wasn't sure whether his question had been sincere. "Over a hundred dollars for a small one, if you're lucky enough to get on her schedule, which is impossible. I heard she gets orders from all over the world, every continent but Antarctica."

Isaac's frown looked thoughtful and his focus seemed to turn inward as the conversation continued without him. The cake was sliced, first and second helpings were had, all while my co-workers took turns trading rumors about Isaac's sister and the infamy of her baking superiority.

"I heard she baked the queen's birthday cake," Tina said, licking a bit of frosting off her fork.

April leaned forward. "Which queen?"

Tina pointed her fork at April. "That European one."

"Doesn't every country in Europe have a queen?" Serafina, holding her second slice of cake close to her chest like she was guarding it, took a sip from her coffee cup.

"Why do they like their queens so much?" Dave asked the room. "What's the deal with having a monarchy in modern times? It's like having a mascot for a country. Why does a country need a mascot? Get yourself a badass animal mascot like a bald eagle. That's what I say."

"Tennessee's Banana Cake Queen baked a cake for *the* queen." Piper grinned happily, her shoulders coming up to her cheeks. "That's how it should be. I love that."

"Good Lord, that is fucking delicious cake!" Maze, after her third helping, tossed her plate into the garbage. "That shit is heaven on a fork, and I don't even usually like cake. We should freeze the rest of it and save it for sad days." Walking by Isaac on her way toward the kitchen, she clapped a hand on his shoulder, winked, and said, "Tell your sister she's a mighty fine baker, and you can quote me on that."

Chapter Fourteen
ISAAC

"My momma once told me, you don't need to be pushed in order to fall. I don't think you'll need to do much pushing."

— Duane Winston, *Truth or Beard* by Penny Reid

I began to doubt Tina's claim that Hannah Townsen had a "thing" for me.

Maybe *doubt* wasn't the right word. More like, since Tina told me about it, I experienced an odd sense of restlessness whenever I considered the possibility. I also caught myself listing reasons why it might not be true while also creating another list of reasons why it probably was true. Using Hannah's every movement when we shared the same space as evidence for the lists, I closely observed her interactions with others versus how she interacted with me. As a byproduct of my observations, I took note of the details that, when combined, made Hannah Townsen unique.

Employing the roundabout methods I've learned while working undercover assignments, I questioned the club's employees about her, including her likes and dislikes. I wasn't sure why I did that. Perhaps knowing the woman's preferences would either confirm or refute her supposed fondness for me? The investigation yielded results.

She preferred movies made in the twentieth century to those made in this one; she loved the Donner Bakery morning muffins and their French roast coffee, and treated herself to both on her birthday; her taste in music was eclectic. She didn't seem to have a favorite band or song, as far as anyone seemed to know. Same with books. I found this last point frustrating. How could someone not have a favorite song or a favorite book?

Some blank spaces still remained in my mental dossier of Hannah, but I felt I knew her much better now, even beyond her favorites and preferences.

For example, during these interviews and from my observations, I also discovered: Hannah had the respect of her co-workers for being straightforward, honest, hardworking, and a good listener; the woman was a locked vault when it came to secrets and was the holder of everybody's; when she felt uncertain or nervous, she'd lift her fingers to tuck her hair behind her ears even if her hair was pulled back; faced with emergencies, she was smart and quick on her feet, solutions focused instead of reactionary; she'd never traveled anywhere outside of Tennessee and North Carolina; she'd taught herself how to lay tile, basic plumbing, and fairly complex electrical work out of necessity since neither she nor her momma could afford to hire help at their farm; and the woman had no concept of ladder safety.

It was her disregard for ladder safety that plagued me on my days off. Three times since I'd begun working at the Pony I'd spotted her climb a ladder without a proper partner to hold it, usually on Thursdays, which tended to be the least busy night of the four that I worked. This made me wonder if she also used that ladder on Mondays, Tuesdays, or Wednesdays when I wasn't around.

Over a week after the staff meeting, my mind periodically drifted to picturing Hannah lying on the gravel after falling off the ladder, something broken, unable to call for help. Which was why I stepped foot in the Donner Bakery early Wednesday morning, requesting a morning muffin and a cup of French roast.

Contrary to what Cletus Winston had threatened, he'd been scarce since our last encounter. And other than Hazel telling me I needed to transport that stupid cake to the Pony, I hadn't talked to anyone from the bakery until this morning. Nor had I spotted my sister.

I bought the muffin and coffee with a lump in my throat, hoping I'd see Jenn but not surprised when I didn't. The name tag of the woman who processed my order read *Joy*. She was very chipper. Unsurprisingly, I didn't recognize her, but she recognized me and called me by my name.

With a gray cloud over my head, I drove to the Pony on my day off. As I suspected, Hannah was out front working on her mural, standing on an unsteady ladder set on gravel, no holder in sight.

This woman.

Grunting my frustration upon exiting the car, I carried the paper bakery bag and the coffee, gripping both in one hand so I could hold the ladder steady with the other as soon as I reached her. I took note of her overalls, boots, baggy sweater, and hat. Those braided pigtails she favored stuck out beneath the hat, lying like thick ropes over her shoulders.

Hannah must've heard me, presumably the sound of my boots crunching over the rocks, because she twisted as I approached and watched me walk the last fifteen feet, her pretty pink lips parted and her blue eyes rounded in what I interpreted as surprise.

"Isaac?"

"Hannah," I gritted out, setting my foot on the bottom rung of the ladder—with meaning—as soon as I could.

She twisted again, turning to peer at me beneath her, those braids hanging down. I had the sudden urge to give one a yank.

"What are you doing here? You don't work today."

"Holding your ladder. Here." I lifted the muffin and coffee up.

Hannah frowned at the offering, then at me, but set down her paint brush to accept both items. "What's this?"

"Breakfast," I said, affixing my eyes to the mural on the wall now that she'd straightened. Her ass was exactly at my line of sight if I faced her body. Being a gentleman, or trying my best to be one, it didn't seem suitable to look.

Besides, her overalls were baggy. There wasn't much to see.

I heard the bag rustle. "Is this the Donner Bakery morning muffin?" She sounded breathless.

I grunted as an affirmative.

A pause, then a quiet and reverent sounding, "Thank you, Isaac."

"You're welcome," I said, probably gruffer than the situation called for, especially since her tone had me standing straighter and feeling oddly lighter.

I felt her attention fixed to the top of my head while I stared at her mural, spotting new elements I hadn't seen before. Were they new? Or had they been there all along and I'd simply failed to notice?

"Isaac." Hannah's voice cut into my thoughts.

"Mm?"

"Are you really going to just stand there and hold the ladder for me?"

"Correct," I said, still absorbed in the details of her painting. The wings now had flecks of gold, making the spots shimmer in the morning light. When I had a chance, I wanted to back up and see the full effect.

She huffed. "All day? Don't you have anything else to do?"

I'd liked looking at the mural from inside my car, I'd liked how it made me feel. But, you know what? Looking at it up close like this, taking note of the details, it felt like something different, something new. An entirely different piece of art.

"Isaac?"

I shifted on my feet, realizing I'd been too absorbed in the painting and hadn't heard her question properly. When I couldn't recall her words, I grunted again, hoping it would suffice.

"Isaac Sylvester. A grunt isn't an answer."

The sound of her stern reprimand pulled an automatic smile out of me but I caught it before it spread too far. "Nothing is more important than ladder safety, Hannah. Get back to it. I'll just, uh, stand here quietly." Clearing my throat, I added in a murmur, "And keep you safe."

* * *

"Why does the whole kitchen staff think you and Hannah are secretly dating?" Tina slid onto the stool next to mine, bumping my arm with hers. She must've arrived recently. Only two or three customers milled around the main area and it was still early yet.

Over a week had passed since I'd first held Hannah's ladder. Buying coffee and a morning muffin for her had become part of my daily routine. I only did it because it gave me peace of mind, knowing she wasn't using that ladder without someone to hold it. The muffin and coffee gave me an excuse to check on her. If I didn't check, I would've spent my days fretting.

You might be wondering, *Well, okay. It makes sense on the days she uses the ladder. But why bring her food on the days she doesn't use the ladder?* First, how was I to know whether or not she used the ladder every day unless I checked? And second, I brought the coffee and muffin on the non-ladder days only because I didn't want it to seem weird when I brought the coffee and muffin on the days she did use the ladder. Obviously.

Whatever. Point was, being a responsible officer of the law, the woman's flippancy for ladder safety wasn't something I could ignore. Therefore, I had to bring her muffins. And coffee.

Also, buying the muffins and coffee gave me a real reason to stop by the bakery every morning, allowed me to walk inside as though I were a regular customer. Granted, I hadn't seen Jenn since her husband's interference a few weeks ago . . .

I told myself I did not buy the muffin and coffee because Hannah seemed to really like them and always acted pleased and surprised each time I passed her the bag and cup.

"Thank you, Isaac," she'd say, just as quiet and reverent as she had the first time. Similar to that first time, her words and tone always made me feel lighter, taller, stronger . . . but that wasn't the reason. Sure, it was a nice start to the day, and thinking about it now would've made me smile all over again if my eyes hadn't been currently locked with the bartender's.

And my brain reminding me recently about other undercover agents meeting their spouses during an investigation had absolutely nothing to do with Hannah either. I knew a few agents who'd fallen for their significant other while deep undercover. It wasn't against the rules, but it also wasn't encouraged. Meeting my future life partner while undercover wasn't something I ever thought would happen to me.

Not that it was happening to me now.

Because I wasn't thinking about Hannah in that context, assuming she'd be open to the idea of us dating. Not that I wanted to date her. I didn't want to date her . . .

See here, I'm just saying, *if* something did happen with me and Hannah—or someone else who wasn't Hannah—while I was undercover on an assignment, it was allowed. That's all I'm saying.

Moving on.

Presently, Louis leaned against the far end of the bar near the whiskeys and bourbons, too far away to hear Tina's question about the kitchen staff's belief that Hannah and I were dating. The younger man had been knifing me with his eyes all day after I found him aggressively flirting with Hannah this morning. They'd been unloading boxes. She'd looked aggravated and flustered, gritting her teeth, her eyes tired.

Hannah had said nothing during the five minutes I'd observed them quietly from where I stood, concealed from view. Didn't Louis realize Hannah had too much to do? She did not need this barely legal bartender stressing her out with his unwelcomed advances. According to Tina, everybody knew Hannah fancied me. Not Louis.

The youngster, incapable of taking a hint or reading the room, needed to be set straight. Thus, I stepped in and set him straight. And now he was pissed.

"Hey." Tina waved her hand in front of my face. "Earth to Isaac. Why are you and Louis staring at each other like you want to get into a face-punching contest?"

"I put him in his place this morning and he's salty about it." Tearing my eyes away, I turned my attention to Tina and answered her first question. "And I told Serafina we were."

Tina frowned. "'We were' what?"

"You asked why the kitchen staff thinks Hannah and I are secretly dating. It's because I told Serafina that Hannah and I were secretly dating."

"Oh!" She leaned back and inspected me, perhaps wanting to see me better. "Why would you do that?"

I lifted my shoulders. "For a few reasons."

When I said nothing else, Tina raised her eyebrows expectantly. "You're not going to tell me?"

Chewing on one of those little brown plastic cocktail straws, I debated whether—or how much—to tell Tina.

Adding Hannah and me dating to the cover story hadn't been a spur of the moment decision, but telling Serafina before the staff meeting had been. After bringing that cake safely inside, the way we'd been looking and talking to each other in front of the chef, there was no way Serafina would believe nothing was going on between us. Again, Hannah's alleged regard for me wasn't a secret at the club.

For my part, I'd been momentarily mesmerized by Hannah's grin. I thought Hannah was beautiful before, but when she smiled like that, I was stupefied. Embarrassing, yes. Nevertheless, the truth.

Another reason for adding dating to the cover story, Hannah's cold reception when I'd attempted to make things right and give her back that thumb drive. Liars and pretenders were predictable because they always worked with their own benefit in mind. Whereas an honest person wasn't predictable when they lacked confidence in the undercover agent assigned to keep them safe. Since Hannah wasn't a pretender, I couldn't have her withholding information because she didn't trust me.

Related, that vow Hannah had made—to never touch me—and how seriously she'd taken the promise rankled. I didn't blame her, given how I'd behaved and what I'd said that first night. But in retrospect, knowing what I did now, I didn't like the idea of Hannah expending any extra effort for my comfort, going out of her way to evade my notice, when she already had too much to do and not enough time. It didn't seem right.

Add to this the fact that her avoidance of me didn't make me comfortable. In truth, her avoidance also rankled.

Ultimately, as I eyeballed my friend, I decided to tell Tina none of this.

Instead, I checked the time on my watch and changed the subject. "How sure are you that Hannah has a 'thing' for me, as you called it."

"Very. If you don't believe me, ask anyone. Why?"

I wasn't sure why I'd asked, so I didn't respond to her follow-up question.

"Don't tell me you think I made it up? Or that you're developing a *thing* for her in return?" Tina snorted. "Come on, Isaac. Why would Hannah Townsen's decades-long hard-on for you make any difference to your psyche? You got lusty looks from women coming out of both ears, always have."

Again, I didn't respond. If I knew the answer to that question, I wouldn't be bringing Hannah muffins every morning and fretting over her approach to ladder safety. Or feeling rankled by her vow not to touch me. Or resisting the urge to tug her pigtails every time she wore them. Or yelling at young bartenders for making inappropriate suggestive remarks to her. Or thinking about her body in that bikini she wore the night of her retirement party, and how she'd looked at me, and touched me, and encouraged me to touch her.

I rubbed my eyes, not liking how much time my brain spent thinking about Hannah Townsen. I should put a stop to it. Soon. Maybe tomorrow.

"Don't tell me your white knight instincts are giving you heart eyes for Hannah?" Tina poked at my shoulder.

I sent her a glare. "I don't have white knight instincts." And even if I did, why would I try to rescue someone right before Isaac Sylvester disappeared from existence? Right before I walked away from this job, this identity, and assumed new ones?

She made a raspberry sound with her lips. "Whatever. Everyone on this planet has white knight instincts, every man, woman, and child. In some people, like you, it stays buried until they meet someone they both admire but also wish they could rescue. But let me tell you, Hannah doesn't need or want to be rescued. She's been rescuing herself for years and is really fucking good at it."

I knew all this. Hannah was . . . well, she was impressive. Akin to the staff at the Pony, I'd come to respect the woman. She had talent, and not just for painting. She was a good manager, had a good head for business, knew her stuff, worked hard. Friendly, kind, patient, empathetic. So, yeah, I respected her a great deal. And, admittedly, I admired her.

But unlike the rest of the staff, and very unlike myself, I'd been daydreaming about getting Hannah alone so I could also . . . disrespect her.

That's not true. Louis also wants to disrespect her.

The thought had me cutting Louis another glare. Busy making a drink for one of the few customers this early in the evening, Louis didn't look my way.

"What'd you set Louis straight about earlier?" Tina nudged my shoulder a second time. "I swear, if looks could kill, he'd be six—no, twelve feet underground. Beneath a lake."

"There's something I don't understand," I changed the subject again.

"What's that?" she asked, letting me.

"How, exactly, does a person buy another person as a present?"

"Oh brother." Tina rolled her eyes. "Are we back to this again?"

Tina's version of events regarding the night of the retirement party mostly made sense given what I'd observed about Hannah in the last few weeks. I didn't know whether or not Hannah had feelings for me any deeper than surface level or if she liked anything in particular about me as a person. She liked the way I looked. That much was certain.

However, this one detail didn't sit right.

"Why do you think—what I mean is, why would Hannah think I was a present? What was she thinking? That you'd paid me to be there?" And if so, recalling that night and how far she'd taken things, wouldn't that make me the prostitute?

"Whatever, Isaac." Tina rolled her eyes again. "You do realize this is my job, right? I don't see anything wrong with it, so don't be acting all high and mighty about my *job*. If you don't like what I do, you can keep that shit to yourself. If I'd thought of gifting you to Hannah before her party, I definitely would've tried to talk you into it. You would've been cheaper than that desk set for sure."

"I would've said no," I mumbled.

"But should you have said no?" She tilted her head to the side, sounding doubtful as her eyes moved over me. "If you want my thoughts on the matter, you should've gone with it. You've seen Hannah all dolled up. She's gorgeous. She would've taken good care of you since she likes you so much. And what are you waiting for anyway? Just saying, you could do worse for your first time."

Tina was right about one thing, Hannah was gorgeous. I didn't know what to do about this strange dichotomy of thought, liking Hannah so much but also thinking about doing things to her—with her, for her—that weren't at all respectable.

Abruptly, sitting there in the bar, chewing on that little brown cocktail straw, the weight of my thoughts over the past few weeks felt too heavy. I was so tired of debating the matter while not being able to do anything about it. Theoretically, that changed today.

I'd promised Tina I'd stay quiet for two weeks and that promise had expired this morning. Now I just needed to figure out—other than apologizing—what I wanted to say to Hannah.

"Don't have any response to that, do ya?" Tina sounded extremely satisfied with herself. "Then I have a new question for you: If I wanted to gift you to Hannah now, what would you say? Yes or no?"

Shaking my head, I tried to stay focused on our conversation. "I understand how y'all do it with the lap dances and such, making fellas feel special since it's your job, but it's not my job. I would never let someone buy me as a present." As much as I worked to keep my attention on the conversation, my thoughts disobeyed, telling me I wouldn't let Tina or anyone else gift me.

If I'm going to be a present for Hannah, I'll be the one doing the gifting. Not anyone else.

"Who said I would pay you? Free is cheaper than what we paid for that desk set." She huffed, throwing her hands up. "There you go, being a self-righteous asshole again. Well, I've been gifted loads of times, and it's a great ego boost. Maybe try it." She stood from the stool but then bent close to my ear to whisper, "And I don't mean for sex, obviously. I mean lap dances, stripteases, that kind of thing. Just to spell it out for you, *officer*. 'Cause, in case you're still confused, giving a lap dance don't make me a prostitute."

"It wasn't just a lap dance with Hannah. She—" I bit back the urge to explain myself, instead shaking my head and saying, "Never mind."

Draping her arm along my shoulders, Tina set a hand on her hip and peered down at me. "You're a prude, Isaac. Loosen up. This ain't ancient times. What you and Hannah did isn't the end of the world. And having sex doesn't mean you have to wear a scarlet letter."

I leaned back to inspect Tina's face. "You've read *The Scarlet Letter?*"

"What? What's that?" Her arm slid from my shoulders and she adjusted the halter top she wore, pushing her boobs higher.

"You said scarlet letter. Have you read the book? Or where did you hear that term?"

Her nose wrinkled. "It was in a movie with Emma Stone called *Easy A*, about a girl who'd let guys say they slept with her if they paid her money. Brilliant idea, right?"

I'd seen that movie. It had been listed as a remake of *The Scarlet Letter*, a book I'd enjoyed reading in college. The story had challenged many of the notions I'd been brought up with and I'd appreciated the expanded worldview.

But I disagreed with Tina. Getting paid so people can lie about you wasn't a brilliant idea. "Why is it a brilliant idea, Tina?"

"Because you get paid to do nothing. Plus, who cares if a person likes sex. Why is that so shameful?"

I swiveled in my stool to face my friend. "But they told lies about her."

"So?" She lifted her chin defiantly. "Who gives a shit what other people say if you know the truth?"

I opened my mouth to respond but then closed it. She had a point.

Tina's eyes moved beyond me and scanned the room. "Listen, I got to work, but one more thing before I forget. I need to ask you a favor."

"What is it?"

"There's some hen parties coming up—you know, bachelorette parties? And we're short two male dancers."

I didn't like the look in her eyes or the direction of this conversation. "No." I shook my head. "No way." She couldn't be serious.

"Why not? I'm sure I can find someone for next month, it's just the ones coming up that are giving me trouble. Come on." She plucked at my T-shirt. "Don't be shy. Everyone can already see your shape under these thin T-shirts. You're a sexy beast, why hide it?"

I huffed a disbelieving laugh. "No."

"It's no big deal and it pays a lot. All you have to do is stand there in your boxers. You don't even need to dance. Well, maybe a little. But I've seen you dance, I taught you, and you'll do great." She was pleading now. "We just need one more guy. A warm, chiseled body. Please?"

"I thought you said you needed two?"

"I did need two. Dave agreed to fill in one of the spots." She lifted her hand toward the entry, presumably to where Dave probably stood. "Now I just need one more guy."

"Dave agreed?"

Wait. Of course Dave agreed. I'd seen the way he looked at her. If Tina asked, he would've agreed to anything.

"Yeah. What's the big deal?" She lifted one shoulder. "He's done it loads of times before."

I almost choked on this information, but she wasn't finished.

"I'm telling you, it's standard procedure that when one—or more—of the regular male dancers can't make a hen party, the club bouncers fill in. If Joshua were well enough, he'd do it."

Already shaking my head again before she'd finished, I faced the bar and gave her my profile.

"Isaac?"

"No."

"No?"

"No. I'm not filling in." I stood, deciding to go check on Dave at the front. How could she even ask me? It wasn't because of the money, I didn't care about that part. I simply didn't want strangers looking at my body, not for any reason. Hell, I didn't want anyone looking at me like that.

Unbidden and instantaneously, a scene played out behind my mind's eye:

Hannah watching me unbutton my shirt, reaching forward to help, the shirt hitting the floor, her hands on my body, sliding down my bare stomach to my pants, slipping inside, touching—

I'd spent my whole adult life trying to avoid exactly this kind of situation, wanting a woman this way. My father used women, said they were only good for one thing, mistreated them, cast them aside when he grew tired or inconvenienced by their existence in his life. He never looked at a woman except with lust or greed.

Think of women as a resource, he'd say. *Don't get too attached. For high-value men like us, women are akin to money, only useful for spending. And once they're gone, you can always get more.*

Was it gentlemanlike to think about Hannah touching me? Us being intimate together? I didn't think so. But at the same time, was it wrong? Hannah had used me as her stand-in for years. Would she mind if I thought about her—and us—like this? I had no idea.

Worse, I didn't know whether *I* wanted it. I thought I never would, but now I wasn't so sure.

Tina hustled to block my path, filling my vision like a bucket of ice water to my imagination. "Twilight—"

"I said no," I ground out, ensuring my voice brooked no argument, restless and still frustrated by the involuntary flash of imagery.

Tina's expression flattened, her eyes narrowing to a glare. "Fine. Whatever. I'll find someone else."

"Do that," I said, walking around her and shaking my head at the mere thought.

In what universe would I ever agree to take my clothes off in front of strangers? Tina Patterson had to be out of her damn mind.

Chapter Fifteen
HANNAH

"I just feel sorry for men now. It must be frustrating to be so feeble and limited."

— Jennifer Sylvester, *Beard Science* by Penny Reid

"What are you doing?" Tina asked from behind me.

"Shhh! I'm checking the hall." I flapped my hand, using the gesture for *keep it down*.

We'd just finished meeting about her design ideas for the Pink Pony merchandise and the status of finding replacement dancers for hen nights. Her ideas for the merchandise weren't bad and she still needed one more replacement to fill the vacant spot on the male revue lineup. The meeting now over, it was time for her to go. And I needed to pick up the latest mending from the dressing room. But not yet.

Not allowing myself to be rushed, I continued to peer through the sliver I'd created by opening my office door a scant inch. Counting to five, then counting to five again, I waited. Over the last two days, this had become my habit every time I left my office.

After a beat, Tina asked, "Why?"

"Seeing who's out and about." I couldn't tell Tina I was checking for Isaac. She'd make fun of me.

"Hannah, why are you checking the hall? Are you trying to avoid someone?"

My shoulders bunched. Damnit. She'd guessed correctly.

"You are!" She tugged on my arm, forcing me to face her. "Let me guess. Isaac."

Avoiding her stare, I shrugged noncommittally and said, "You can go."

She didn't leave. "Why are you avoiding Isaac?"

I looked everywhere but at her. They were friends and Tina didn't know how to keep a secret.

Tina gave my arm a shake. "It's obvious you're avoiding him. Every time he's entered a room recently, you leave it. And you're keeping your door shut all the time now. But why? Why are you—"

"Because he's being weird!" I pulled out of her grip and threw my hands up, suddenly not caring if she'd tell Isaac I said so. "He's being weird and it's better if we interact as little as possible. Okay?"

She looked like she was fighting a smile. "Okay, baby. How is he being weird?"

"He's—he's being nice," was all I'd admit in front of Tina Patterson.

But it was the truth. Isaac was being nice, very nice, and his niceness flustered me, gave me ideas I shouldn't have. Most frustrating, I'd been well on my way to being cured of my lifelong Isaac Sylvester crush, and then he'd done a one-eighty and turned into an entirely different person: returning the thumb drive video footage, telling me he wouldn't coerce me into helping him, laughing with me about that giant cake before the staff meeting, adding us dating to his cover story.

Well . . . not an entirely different person. He was still stoic, and quiet, and stared at everyone with that eerie, unsettling intensity, like he was on the precipice of daring folks to an arm-wrestling contest if they looked at him sideways.

"Isaac being nice?" Tina nodded like this was serious. "You're right. That is weird. Okay, what did he do that was nice?"

Deciding I could tell Tina since none of it was top secret, I shut my door, rather than leaving it cracked, and crossed my arms. "Fine. Listen to this. I was adding finishing touches to the mural out front last Wednesday and he showed up on his day off, brought me coffee and a muffin from the Donner Bakery, and insisted on holding my ladder for the whole afternoon. Wouldn't take no for an answer."

"He did? What did y'all talk about?"

"*Nothing*," I said, convicting him of niceness with my proof. "See? He didn't chatter at me, didn't expect me to entertain him. He just brought me food, coffee, and held the ladder. It was very strange. And helpful. Then he showed up again on that Thursday, and again Monday, Tuesday, Wednesday, and Thursday of this week, just to give me food and hold the ladder."

"Oh! I see. Well, what else?" Tina stepped back and half sat, half leaned on the empty desk across from mine, her eyes wide and attentive.

"I was unloading boxes last Friday with Louis. And you know how Louis is always trying to flirt with me even though I've told him over and over it's inappropriate?"

"Yeah. I'll talk to him, too, if you want. But, what happened with Isaac?"

"Isaac appeared out of nowhere and, in no uncertain terms, ordered Louis to watch his mouth, show some respect, and go back to the bar."

"Louis listened to him?" Tina asked, then made a face at her own question. "What am I saying, of course he did. What happened next?"

"Before I could reprimand Isaac for being rude to Louis—"

"Was he rude, though?" Tina paired the question with a head tilt.

"Kind of, but not really," I said—because I'd been building up to it, maybe not using the same words, but giving Louis a professional reprimand of some sort—and continued my story, "Isaac then helped me unload the rest of the boxes without saying another word. Just, quietly unloaded boxes with me until we were done. It's been more of the same every day. Like, and this is a really weird one, he showed up last Sunday near closing, walked right in this office, picked up the pile of mending, and repaired the tears and stitches. All of them."

Tina's eyes grew big. "He what?"

"See what I mean? He picked up the costumes that needed repair and set to work. When I asked him what he was doing, do you know what he said?"

"No! Tell me." She leaned forward, like this was the best gossip she'd ever heard.

"He said"—I cleared my throat so I could lower it to an approximation of Isaac's baritone—"'You already have too much to do. Let me help. I can do this.'"

Tina gasped.

"I know!" I whispered loudly. "He's brought me a muffin and coffee every day, no matter if he's working or not. The last two days, he left them in the breakroom. And it's the morning muffin, Tina. The *morning muffin*!"

Tina gasped again. "The morning muffin is your favorite!"

"I know!" I said again. In the past, I'd only allowed myself to buy the morning muffin on my birthday, and now this man was giving me a morning muffin every day? I didn't like it one bit. My life was not a morning-muffin-every-day kind of life. It was more like a soggy-cereal-with-expired-milk kind of life. "No good can come of this." I infused my tone with mournfulness and leaned against the door behind me. "What can I do other than avoid him?"

What I didn't tell Tina—because it was top secret and possibly my imagination—was that I'd caught Isaac looking at me several times in the weeks since the staff meeting and his gaze hadn't felt hostile or friendly. It had felt . . . big. Heavy. Meaningful. Confusing. I'd told myself I was dreaming up stories, and yet it kept happening.

The niceness I could deal with. But those looks? They had me all twisted up and turned around. Yes. Avoidance was best.

Tina's shocked expression gave way to a mischievous smile and, despite my obvious anguish—or maybe because of it—she started to laugh. "You're right. That is all very weird for Isaac. But, Hannah, most people don't avoid their crush if he's being nice. And that makes you the weird one."

"I don't trust it, Tina." I gave my head a firm shake. "You know how it is. I don't trust kindness without a known purpose. If he wants me to do something for his investigation, if he needs a favor, I wish he'd just ask instead of buttering me up with muffins. I've tried to tell him I don't know why Tavvy hasn't shown up these last few weeks. Maybe Isaac doesn't believe me?"

"Or maybe it's not like that." She stood and crossed to where I fretted, twisting my fingers. "It sucks that a guy can't be kind without you thinking it's about something other than them just being nice. Or maybe you're right. Maybe Isaac got to know you better and has decided he likes you. Maybe he does want something from you and it's your body."

I bit my thumbnail and stared unseeingly beyond her. "No. That can't be it. He must need a favor for the investigation or something."

Tina snorted, which I ignored, and shoved me out of the way. She opened the door completely, muttering something like, "You are just as cute as he is and I think you deserve each other, that's what I think . . ."

Her voice trailed off as she disappeared down the hall, leaving me alone with an open door and my muddled thoughts. But I couldn't hide in my office forever. Isaac may've finished last week's mending in one go last Sunday but a fresh pile of it waited in the dressing room for me right now.

Resigned, I turned without checking the hall and marched in the direction of the dressing room. I'd taken maybe two steps before a stampede of wild chickens—that is, nearly naked dancers—came running from the direction of the main room, filling the hallway and laughing hysterically. Before I could press myself against the wall to get out of their way, big arms wrapped around me from behind, spun me, and twirled us back toward my office.

"Sorry, Hannah!" someone called out, followed by a chorus of apologies.

"Sorry. Didn't see you there!"

"My bad, Hannah! We're just in a rush."

"Sorry, Goldie baby. In a hurry."

It all happened so fast, it took a moment for my mind to comprehend what had occurred. I looked up and found Isaac caging me in, his face turned away and in profile as he used his big body to protect mine, not moving even after all the dancers were out of sight and squawking in the breakroom.

Finally turning his gaze on me, one arm holding my body tightly to his, he lifted his free hand to smooth my hair from my face, his eyes searching mine. "Are you okay, Hannah?"

I nodded. Too shocked to speak. Plus, the way he'd said my name made my knees feel weak.

Isaac's lips tugged a scant few millimeters to the side. "Are you sure? Did I bump you anywhere when I turned you?"

I shook my head, ignoring the ache at my crown because he smelled so good. He had bumped my head against the wall. It stung and it was beginning to throb just a little. But I wouldn't tell him that. He was so close. Too close. This was the closest we'd been since the lap dance catastrophe. He felt just as good now as he had then until—

Until he accused me of solicitation and made sure I knew how repulsive he found my touch.

Abruptly, I became aware that he'd lowered his gaze between us and I followed his sight line, realizing my hands were open-palmed and braced against his muscular chest, my right hand over his heart.

I immediately balled them into fists and tucked them close to my own chest. "Pardon me. Sorry. I—sorry."

"Don't apologize," he said, removing himself an inch but not letting me go. "You can tou—"

"No." I wiggled and pushed at him with my forearms, forcing him to back up more and let me go. "I am sorry. I should've looked where I was—well, anyway." *Ahhhh!* I could feel that my face was bright red. My chest was tight with some suffocating sensation, and I didn't know what to say while he stared at me and appeared so concerned.

"Sorry," I croaked out at last and made to move around him.

"Wait. Hannah." His hand closed around my wrist and tugged, forcing me to spin again and face him.

The inexplicable sense of being trapped by his fingers around my wrist—and his rescue moments prior, and his silent help these last few weeks, and his muffins and coffee and lack of hostility—abruptly clawed at me. Hissing in a breath between my teeth as though burned—because it did burn—I twisted out of his grip, yanking my arm back with more force than necessary. I looked up at him again. It felt safer to look at him now that several feet separated us.

He wore a frown, his jaw ticking, his glare unhappy. And he was giving me one of those *looks*. Heavy. Meaningful. Confusing.

Then he blurted, "I'm sorry."

That had my frown deepening. "You're sorry? What for? You just saved me from getting run over by those wild chickens." I lifted a hand toward the breakroom, where I could hear them squawking and laughing.

"Are you sure I didn't bump your head?" He took a step forward, his frown now appearing equal parts concerned and frustrated. "And can we talk after work? There's something I need to—"

A big round of applause sounded from the main room and instinct had me raising my hands, palms out, and taking two steps back. "I'm fine. Thank you. You, uh, better get back to it. Sounds like things are loud out there."

With that, I turned and I fled into the dressing room, ignoring the pile of mending waiting for me in favor of shutting myself in my changing room, crawling into my bed. I'd been right. I couldn't hide in my office forever. Hiding under my covers at least part of the time was much better.

* * *

I woke up with a headache Saturday morning and it persisted all day long, only clearing up near closing. Thus, I spent the whole day in my office, working on graphics for merchandise, fixing bugs in the scheduling system, running payroll, that kind of thing. No one bothered me and I didn't check the breakroom for Isaac's morning muffin and coffee.

Maybe if I ignored the problem, it would just go away. Wouldn't that be nice?

As I finished up payroll, I mused how it was a shame about the muffin and coffee. When Isaac left, I'd never be able to eat a morning muffin without my thoughts turning to him. How ironic, by bringing me my favorite things, he'd ruined them.

I huffed a sad laugh, shaking my head at myself just as a knock sounded on my door.

"Who is it?" I called, saving my work.

"Isaac."

My eyes closed and I sighed.

Not standing, I rolled my chair over to the door, opened it, then rolled back to my desk. "What's up?"

I felt his eyes on me but I didn't meet them. I didn't wish to.

"You disappeared yesterday," he said from the doorway, not entering the office.

"Uh, yeah. I had an early night. What's up?"

"I'm here to apologize," he announced, sounding determined.

That made me frown. Turning in my chair, I leaned back and looked at him. "Why? What happened?" Just like his tone, he appeared determined.

Taking a step forward, he closed the door behind him, which had my heart beating quicker.

Remaining near the door, he faced me. "I realize now I misunderstood the situation the night of your retirement party. Due to new, compelling information, I know you weren't soliciting me. I'm sincerely sorry for the assumptions I made, that you were being untruthful and such. I'm sorry."

"I see," I said, studying him, trying to think. I did not feel relieved by this news. If anything, anxiety began to swell and my mind began to race.

His words sounded rehearsed. Careful. Of course, I was curious how he'd come to this conclusion, what "new information" he'd been privy too. And yet, a sixth sense told me not to ask. Over the years, I'd learned it was best to listen to this sixth sense. Taking risks was way overrated. At the first sign of trouble, best tuck tail and run.

So, instead of asking any questions, I said, "Okay. Apology accepted. Thank you. Have a nice night."

His eyelids lowered by half and the corners of his mouth tugged downward, like my response disappointed him. At his change in expression, my heart ticked up again and I braced myself for . . . something.

"Hannah," he said, like it was the start of a conversation and he was about to spell things out despite me not asking him to. Like he *wanted* to spell things out.

I stood, panicked. "No need to explain." I paired the shrill statement with a lifted hand. "It's fine. We're good."

"I think I should explain."

"Please don't," I begged.

But he was already talking. "It's impossible to work here and not be made aware of certain information." His head dipped and his gaze grew heavy with meaning. "About you. And about me."

Apparently, after offering me nothing but silent help for weeks, the man of few words had found his voice and a topic he wished to discuss, and no amount of me attempting to dodge the subject was going to work.

Mortified and feeling like a fly caught in a web, I sent up a prayer to the heavens.

Please. Please God, please don't let Isaac know. Don't let him find out about my ridiculous crush and how I used his image in place of my customers'. I will move back to the farm and shovel horse shit every morning, even during the hellacious heat of summer, if you keep this information from his ears until the day I die. Please. And Amen.

It was too late. I could see the truth of it written across his handsome face and apologetic expression and I wanted to disappear. He knew. He knew that he'd been my stand-in while I'd been a dancer. He knew about my crush.

Breathing out a tremendous breath, one that felt both deflating and agonizing, I closed my eyes and gave him my back. Tears stung my eyes. Just like when he'd overheard my conversation with Hank weeks ago, a humiliation so deep and wide and painful stole my breath.

Until it didn't.

Because Isaac knowing the truth didn't matter. Just like his pity didn't matter. I'd been avoiding him and that's just what I would keep on doing. His discovery changed nothing.

It's not a big deal. If I have a roof over my head and food in the fridge, nothing is a big deal. Emotions can be controlled and ignored. Minimize, minimize, minimize.

"Whatever. I don't care what you know, or found out. But if you're worried about me—you know—doing something untoward, don't be." My words arrived robotic, monotone. I couldn't deal with this. "If there's nothing else"—I waved my hand in a vague gesture, sighing again and giving him my profile —"I'm really tired."

The room descended into silence. He didn't move. After a time, I glanced at Isaac over my shoulder and found him staring at me with a peculiar expression, intense and open, one I couldn't quite place. I decided to interpret it as guilt. Or more pity?

"Really, Mr. Sylvester. It's no big deal. All dancers have stand-ins." I faced him but couldn't bring myself to lift my gaze above his neck again. This conversation had worn me out. "We should just continue on as we have been until the investigation is over."

"Continue on as we have been," he repeated, then made a sound like a laugh. "I don't think that's possible. Not for me."

"Why not? This is the third Saturday since you started working here, you've been here for a full month as of tomorrow. Tavvy may never show up. You might be leaving sooner rather than later. No big deal."

"Maybe it's not a big deal to you, but it is to me. And something's got to give." His eyes seemed to heat as they moved over me. Was he annoyed? I had no idea. And I was too tired to consult my memory's codebook on Isaac's micro-expressions in order to interpret his mood.

But then he added, "I think maybe I owe you. And paying you back will settle things between us. It'll help me feel . . . settled."

"Ha!" I sat on the desk behind me, amused at the thought of Isaac Sylvester owing me something. "Really? Well, I'd say those morning muffins and coffee make us even. You can stop bringing them in, if that's why you've been doing it. Your guilt is misplaced."

"Guilt isn't why I've been bringing the muffins and the coffee, Hannah," he said, his voice low, a little hard. Maybe frustrated.

"Oh? Well, anyway." I wasn't going to ask why he'd been bringing them. Something about his last statement plus how he'd said my name unsettled me. I decided it was best to avoid the subject. "My point is, you don't owe me anything. But I am sorry if, uh, learning the truth made you feel uncomfortable. Like I said, I promise, I won't—"

"Don't make another of those vows," he said, his voice near a growl.

"What vows?"

"About never touching me."

"Oh. I wasn't." Now I laughed. "I was going to say, I won't—you know—use you like that again, as my stand-in. I am sorry if it made you uncomfortable."

"You already said that, and you using me as your stand-in doesn't make me uncomfortable."

This information was not good for my mental health. I couldn't swallow, and I began to spout nonsense. "Oh? Well. Then. Fine. Okay. I see. And. So. Anyway. Good to—uh—know."

"Hannah." He took a step toward me, then another.

"Hmm?"

"Please tell me what I can do to make us even. What would you like me to do?"

Nervous energy had taken the wheel so I blurted a joke, "You could give me a lap dance."

Oh my goodness, that was very unprofessional. Yes, my co-workers joked like this all the time, but I opened my mouth to apologize.

Before I could, he said, "I don't know how to do that." His advance had stalled and he sounded earnest. Like he was considering it.

But . . . he couldn't be taking my joke seriously, right? I smiled tightly, almost certain his earnest delivery was sarcasm, aka another joke.

I was just about to clarify when he added, "But I do know how to kiss."

Alarmed by the continued sincerity of his tone, I stood and announced, "I apologize. That was unprofessional of me and—"

"I don't work for you. You're not my boss, I'm not yours. I don't care if you're unprofessional with me."

"Well," I squeaked out, his words flustering me. "This is my workplace, and—"

"But it's also your home. You live here and you're off work. Your shift ended hours ago."

"Even so," I tried again. "That was a joke. I was joking."

"I wasn't."

We traded stares and a shiver raced down my spine while my thoughts ran around in circles. *Was him saying he wasn't joking a joke? That had to be a joke.*

Perplexed, feeling caught, and wanting desperately to diffuse the situation, my nerves decided to make another joke. "Well, then. Since I'm not your boss and we're both off work, it would have to be a few shirtless kisses and I'd get to touch you wherever I wanted for the length of five lap dances. So, twenty-five minutes." Just for good measure, I laughed.

He didn't laugh. Isaac seemed to consider my statement for a moment, and in that moment I decided we were, in fact, being silly together and he was trying to help me feel less awkward by also joking about my crush on him, because the alternative was ridiculous. *Never in a million years would Isaac Sylvester kiss me in order to make up—*

I didn't get to finish that thought.

Isaac reached behind his head, pulled his shirt at the neck, and tugged it off, leaving him shirtless and me gaping. I stared at him, afraid to say anything. There existed a very real possibility that I was dreaming and if I said anything, I would wake up.

But, shouldn't I wake up? This dream feels dangerous.

Holding my eyes, giving me that heavy, meaningful, confusing look I'd wanted to avoid, Isaac closed the remaining distance between us, plucked my hand from my side, and placed my fingers on the very center of his bare, hot, hard chest.

"I'll be very disappointed if you don't let me kiss you," he said, his voice near a rasp, his eyes dropping to my mouth. "Should I keep time? Or will you?"

Chapter Sixteen

ISAAC

"Like it or not, sometimes the only way to win is to surrender."

— Cletus Winston, *Beard Necessities* by Penny Reid

My first kiss had been with someone I hadn't necessarily wanted to kiss. It happened a week after my twenty-second birthday, before I'd decided on a life of voluntary pre-marital celibacy but after I'd started seriously considering it as an option. My reasons weren't religious. By my early twenties, I didn't think intimacy before marriage was the wrong choice for other folks, nor did I care, but I was coming to think it was the wrong choice for me. I'd never liked the touch of strangers.

I'd been on break, out with a number of my fellow soldiers, and I met a woman at a bar outside of Atlanta. I can no longer recall what she looked like, but she'd been the quiet and shy one in her group, as had I. There's a comfort between shy people, a shared sense of belonging to the outskirts and the edges.

By happenstance, I'd ended up in the seat next to hers. As the night went on and we both drank a few beers, our conversation had flowed better and our shells began to crack. Before closing, she'd pulled me over to the short, dark hall leading to the bathrooms, shoved me against the wall by an out-of-service telephone, and kissed me. I hadn't expected it and I was really bad at it. I know this because she told me so, teased me after until I felt my ears burn. But she also said I was sexy as hell, and that I should look her up after I had more "life experience."

I assumed she meant, after I had more experience kissing women.

The only other person I've kissed is Tina Patterson, and that was out of necessity, for the sake of an assignment. She wasn't somebody I wanted to kiss and I've only ever had platonic feelings toward Tina, like a cousin or a sister—

Scratch that. Not a sister. I wouldn't kiss my sister if a gun was pointed at my head. It would scar us both for life and we already had too many scars to count.

Tina was like a very distant cousin. Or a good, solid co-worker. A fellow soldier. A friend. She'd taught me how to kiss because she refused to fake it, loudly complaining about my lack of technique once we were alone in my room at the Dragon Biker Bar compound. While we played cards or checkers, she'd explain in great detail what I'd done wrong and how to fix it.

Ultimately, she'd given me kissing lessons, talking me through it. She also taught me how to dance in that room, preaching about the importance of dancing if I ever wanted to be a good husband. Equally unprompted, she shared random tidbits of information about the female anatomy.

For example, "The reason it's called a pussy is because you should pet it like a cat. Soft, long strokes unless directed otherwise."

Another, "Concentrating too much on the center of something, whether it be a boob or a vagina or an ear, is the fastest way to wear that part out. Don't spend all your time rubbing nipples and clits. You need to build up to it, tease a woman, work around the outside and gradually approach the middle. That's how you get her wet."

And, "If you really like a woman, offer to go down on her early and often. It's how she'll know you're boyfriend material and it might convince her to give you a real chance if she's on the fence. But don't cuddle after sex with someone you don't see yourself with long-term. It'll confuse her, make her think you like her a lot, and that's mean."

And another, "Touch a woman like you mean it. No one orgasms with a second-guesser."

Tina had claimed I would thank her later someday. The kissing instructions, the dance lessons, the abstract advice, it had all been technical in nature, like learning how to safely load and unload a weapon, or how to make a recipe. You had the tools, the ingredients, and the instructions.

But nothing had prepared me for this moment, right now, with Hannah, and the rush of raw, savage *want* clouding my thoughts and clearing my vision.

It was too late to second-guess my plan. Which, in retrospect, had been faulty, flawed, and foolhardy. I'd told myself that making things even with Hannah would remove the spell she'd cast on me, check a box, cross an item off a list, complete a task we'd left unfinished since I'd interrupted her mid-lap dance four weeks ago.

Confronted with the reality of this moment, her upturned face, full pink lips, eyes filled with wonder and uncertainty, hand on my chest and her body so very close, all the lies I'd been telling myself went silent, leaving only the truth: I wasn't doing this to make us even or settle a score or dispel a curse. I was doing this because I wanted to. With her. Very badly.

I wanted Hannah, simple as that.

So much so, I was willing to risk being teased for being bad at it. But something told me Hannah wouldn't tease me. She was one of those rare people who considered the other person—always—before speaking. Not because she wanted to manipulate them or exploit them, but because she cared. She didn't wish to hurt folks if she could help it. She also didn't let folks push her around.

I trust her. The thought rang like a trumpet between my ears. Maybe she only liked the look of me. Maybe my feelings for Hannah ran deeper, were more involved than hers. That was okay. She was a good person. She'd be gentle with me when she let me down.

"Isaac . . ." she whispered, my name sounding like a plea and strumming a harmonious chord low in my stomach. I liked it, how she said my name. I hoped she'd say it again, just like that.

Lowering my mouth to hers, I didn't miss how she angled her chin, stretching her neck to receive me, and I smiled at her willing anticipation just before our lips finally met.

The warmth of our connection created a sudden jolt, another harmonious chord low in my stomach and at the base of my spine, but louder. And urgent. She felt so fucking good, a desire akin to a craving, but fiercer, impulsive, flooded my body and mind, driving out restraint and replacing it with pure and distilled focus, absorbed solely with satiating the newly awakened hunger.

Earlier, when I'd mapped out how this would go, I'd decided to keep my hands to myself unless she asked me to touch her. I'd planned to give, not take.

Those plans forgotten, my hands were on her now, sliding under the hem of her shirt, eager for the feel of her skin. The memory of her breasts filling my palms, how essential, how necessary that felt, drove my fingers up her torso, the movements thoughtless, and she gasped, which allowed my tongue entrance into her sweet, hot mouth. And that, too, was so fucking good.

Instinct had me pushing her back, stepping between her open legs and forcing them wider, sucking and licking her lips and tongue, massaging her over the thin, rough lace of her bra. She tasted amazing and felt amazing, but the more I touched her and tasted her, the bigger the craving grew in strength and intensity, making new demands, forming new ideas. I needed more. I wanted to touch her in new places.

I want inside her, whether it be my tongue or fingers or—

Before these thoughts had fully formed, my hands were already lifting her skirt, palming her ass, and I heard her gasp again. The craving in me panicked, feared I'd moved too far too fast, but it was instantly soothed, stoked anew as her fingers reached for my fly and made quick work of unfastening it. One hand on my bare back to pull me closer, her other reaching inside and stroking over the thin fabric of my boxers.

"Fuck." The expletive was spoken against her mouth and I felt her lips form a tremendous smile.

I wanted to see it. I wanted to see her face as she stroked me. Did she like it? Did her hands crave my skin? Did she feel lost to it like I did? Like no path existed except surrender? Did her body push her to touch and take and feel just as forcefully as mine did?

I gripped the hair at the back of her head and pulled, forcing her chin up. Her lips were red and roughened, swollen. I liked this evidence my kiss left behind, I liked that she looked altered, and her gaze was free of its earlier uncertainty. I liked how hungry she looked, the intensity of her focus as her eyes clashed with mine, the challenge in them when she reached inside my boxers, gripped my cock, and gave me a very firm, purposeful stroke.

A breath shuddered out of me, the very core of me shaking and vibrating, that harmonious chord deafened by the sound of blood rushing between my ears and the twisting, intense ache of pleasure where she held me in her hand.

"You said I could touch you wherever I wanted," Hannah whispered. "And I'll be very disappointed if you don't let me."

Another breath pushed out of my lungs, one of surprise at how she used my earlier words against me. We stared at each other as she kept touching me *just right* with expert fingers, and everything I'd thought felt so fucking good prior to now blurred together, expanding and stretching on a canvas of linked sensations. The craving panicked again, more muted this time, but fear crept in —that ours was a one-time thing, that she would never want me after this moment—squeezing my windpipe and constricting my chest.

Hannah must've seen it because her hand slowed and sobriety entered her eyes. "Isaac? Am I—are you okay?"

"I think I need you, Hannah," I said without thought, certainly not meaning to speak the words out loud or burden her with them.

Her eyes widened, then softened, her head tilting to the side. "Okay," she said, her voice like honey. "You can need me, if you want."

She'd never looked so beautiful and she didn't understand what I was saying, what I meant. But that was fine. In fact, it was good. *Better this way.* But I knew, if I continued allowing her to look at my face, Hannah would see things there she shouldn't, things that might inconvenience her.

I kissed her again, soft and slow, luxuriating in the feel of her soft lips and mouth even as I tensed, every muscle flexing, my hips rolling in an unconscious rhythm, pushing into her hand. My body responded in ways I'd only ever experienced while alone and in private, but better. Everything felt so much better with Hannah.

Her kisses grew more insistent, firmer, harder. Her arm came to my neck and anchored me. I was going to come. I was going to come in her hand and I didn't care. I wanted her touching me when it happened, I wanted her covered, dripping, soaked. The turn of my thoughts made a helpless, short sound erupt from my throat. Spikes of pleasure-pain gathered at the base of my spine then released, rushing forward, and I couldn't breathe. Everything stopped, then started, moving too slow and too fast, and that canvas of sensation became too vibrant, too colorful, chaotic and perfect, until I was spent, exhausted, my mind blank.

I don't know how long we stayed like that. But Hannah was there the whole time, holding me, kissing me with growing gentleness until nothing remained but our shared panting breaths, her tenderness, and her soft, pleased smile.

"You are so sexy when you come," she whispered, like it was a secret just for us.

I supposed it was. No one but her knew what I looked like, what I felt like, what sounds I made. It was a secret. Ours.

Slowly, I became aware that my boxers were wet and I didn't fucking care one fucking bit. I'd wear wet boxers for the rest of my life if she was the reason, and I'd do so in a great mood with a big smile on my face.

Well. Maybe not a big smile. I'd been told my big smile, the one I'd tried putting on for pictures and such, worried people.

A sound, a *giggle*, as unexpected as it was musical, had me lifting my head and taking stock of the situation. Namely, my hand placement. Both were inside the back of her underwear, grabbing her bare ass, sandwiched between her body and the desk she sat on. At some point, though I didn't recall when,

I'd removed her shirt and pushed her skirt up around her waist, revealing a matching teal lace bra and underwear set. And her legs were spread, accommodating my hips. And her skin was flushed. And her nipples were hard as rocks, the little rose-colored pebbles pushing against the lace. My mouth watered.

I closed my eyes, grinding my teeth because, Jesus fucking Christ, my body was quickly recovering and had *ideas*. Worse, my brain upstairs began concocting new plans: dates, places I wanted to take her, books I wanted us to read together, what we'd do for our first anniversary, what we'd do for our second, how I'd ask her to marry me, how—

"Are your hands asleep?" Hannah scootched and leaned forward, obviously trying to shift her weight to allow me to remove my fingers, but this caused her breasts to brush against my chest, and the friction sent another one of those awesome, torturing jolts through my body.

"Don't—" I said, my jaw still clamped together.

"Oh! What'd I do?" Her hand in my shorts slipped out and the arm around my neck went lax, starting to fall away.

Removing my hands from her glorious skin, I opened my eyes and caught her wrists. "I'm—I'm sorry. I made a mess."

Her smile was immediate and brilliant, another musical laugh. She twisted out of my grip and I stepped back on autopilot, sensing she required space.

"Just give me a sec," she said.

I watched dumbly as she leaned to the side and opened the second drawer down on the right side, pulling out a package of baby wipes. Hannah then proceeded to clean her hand with a few wipes. She'd left the drawer open. Inside, I spotted baby diapers, a tube of ointment, and a folded cloth with little cartoon trucks all over it.

She must've followed my gaze and understood my confusion because she said, "A few of the dancers have babies. We use this desk as a changing table. It's full of baby and toddler supplies."

I gave my head a subtle nod, clearing my throat and saying, "Makes sense." It was also a good reminder that many of the *ideas* my body had would make babies. Isaac and Hannah babies.

Does Hannah want babies? I looked at her again. She'd stood from the desk and twisted at her waist, tossing two wipes into the trash like maybe she did this sort of thing every day. Then she picked up the package and held it out to me.

When I remained still, she wiggled it in the air. "Here. Take it. Unless you want to clean up in the bathroom?"

Oh. Damn. Of course.

My cheeks heated at my stupidity and I accepted the wipes, turning my back to her as I pulled myself together as best I could. The fog of desire had me in limbo, neither receding fully nor charging to the forefront, my mind flooded with fragments of overlapping thoughts.

I thought I'd be okay after whatever happened between us. Was I okay? I didn't know. I couldn't shake the sense of being exposed. My movements were clumsy. Cleaning myself up in this way, standing here in her office wiping up the mess with fucking baby wipes, a mess I'd created, it made everything that had happened between us seem absurd in retrospect. When I turned back around, would she be laughing at me? Would she find it all absurd as well? A grown man using baby wipes. How could she not laugh?

An encroaching coldness ushered in confusion, which opened the door to self-recrimination.

But before regret stepped fully forward, the feel of Hannah's hands on my waist, sliding around to my stomach, the front of her body connecting with the back of mine, her skin warming my skin as her cheek came to rest between my shoulder blades—*her* touch—halted and reversed the rising chaos. She hugged me from behind and I felt the press of her chest rise and fall, a warm puff of breath.

"The twenty-five minutes isn't over yet," she said, probably trying to sound defiant. But that forced defiance did a bad job of masking vulnerability. "We still have about seven minutes and I want to cuddle."

Warmth replaced the encroaching cold and my resultant grin was compulsory. The knots of doubt began to unravel. Inhaling deeply, because I finally could, I tossed the messy wipes in the same trash can she'd used and took my time buttoning and zipping my fly. She held on to me the whole time, her arms squeezing tighter when I tried to turn, as though she worried I might pull away.

"Hannah, let me turn around."

"Why?" The question was muffled, her lips moving against my skin and tickling me.

I grinned again, and again it was compulsory. "Hannah, honey. Let me hold you, too."

Her arms gave a short spasm, like my words surprised her, then she relaxed her hold, allowing me to turn and gather her to me. Wrapping her tightly in my embrace, I tucked her under my chin. She was soft everywhere. Warm. Like the best dream. This, also, felt good. So good. Great. Fantastic. Like nothing we'd done so far. And special. Meaningful. An answer to a question I hadn't been brave enough to ask.

But I needed to ask, not just her, but also myself, *What were we?*

Once this assignment ended, I'd planned to take some time off and wrap up any lingering personal affairs for Isaac Sylvester before I assumed my new identity. Where did that leave us? What kind of future could we have?

A short one.

One thing was for certain, I wasn't about to decide anything on my own. She had a say, if she wanted one. The first step would be to find out if she wanted one.

"Three more minutes," she said, pairing the words with a sad sounding sigh.

I smoothed a hand from the crown of her head to the tips of her hair, not knowing how to start this conversation. I'd never had one like it before. "Hannah."

"Hmm?" She snuggled closer, rubbing her cheek against my chest.

My heart did something funny and I had to clear my throat before continuing. "Let's, uh, stop keeping time."

Her body tensed, going from soft and pliant to rock-hard in an instant. "What does that mean?"

"How about you—uh—" I had to breathe out past the nerves that had gathered at the back of my throat. Why was this so hard? She'd just given me a hand job and she was currently wearing nothing but her underwear. Clearly, she liked me. Or something about me. Right? So, shouldn't this be easier?

Exhaling sharply, I tried again, "How about you and me—

"Hannah! Are you in there?" Dave's voice was followed by a sharp knock on the door.

We both turned our heads toward the sound, then looked at each other wearing identical frowns.

"Hannah?"

Removing herself a step from the circle of my arms, she called back, "What is it, Dave? I'm busy."

"Tavvy is here. And he's asking for you."

Chapter Seventeen
ISAAC

"The magnitude of disappointment was directly proportional to the magnitude of expectations."

— Scarlet St. Claire, *Beard with Me* by Penny Reid

Hannah immediately sprang into action: pushing my shirt at me, opening her office door, and shoving me out.

I'd always been told I possessed an above-average response time, a rapid-adapting mental flexibility, and an impressive cool when faced with unexpected developments, emergencies, and high-pressure situations. In the past, I'd credited my father's mind games for this proficiency, staying one step ahead of his chaotic manipulations had been necessary for survival.

But there had been one time—other than now and when Hannah had given me that lap dance—when I'd been unable to stay focused and calm. During my first assignment in Green Valley, I'd run into my younger sister at the grocery store while I'd been surrounded by my Iron Wraiths brethren. They'd started toying with Jennifer, coming on to her, trapping her against the grocery aisle and looking at her like she belonged to them. I'd panicked and I hadn't remained cool or collected, reacting without thinking, spouting bullshit our father used to say to us growing up, trying to scare her into running away. Luckily, she'd made it out just fine and my actions had finally convinced the Wraiths there existed no remaining bond or love between us.

Unluckily, the person who'd come to Jennifer's aid back then was none other than her now husband, Cletus Winston. At the time, I didn't know they were involved, or even knew each other. He'd popped up out of nowhere and has been by her side ever since, the sneaky bastard.

Then and now, the rush of adrenaline clouded my sense, making me stupid and clumsy.

I allowed myself to be pushed and shoved by Hannah. I couldn't think, trapped in the momentum of the sacred moments we'd shared while Dave and she exchanged a hurried conversation.

"What does he want? Any costume?" she asked, her voice steady, standing in her bra and underwear like her body was no big deal.

Dave handed a wrapped bundle to Hannah, saying, "It's a nun's habit this time."

Hannah nodded, accepted Dave's bundle, and closed the door.

He turned to me and gave me a pat on the back. "Come on. It's five minutes to closing, place is almost empty, but I gotta stand at the champagne door. You need to cover the front." If the big guy found a shirtless me stumbling out of Hannah's office surprising, he made no outward sign of it.

"You're—she—" I struggled. I was struggling. "She—Hannah is—how, why is she—"

Dave's forehead wrinkled as I fought to form a cohesive thought, but then his expression cleared. "Oh. Right. Hannah is technically retired, true. But she told me weeks ago that if this one VIP customer came back, she would see him no matter what. And to let her know ASAP. He's a weird little guy, but it's fine."

I stared at Dave's unconcerned expression. It was not fine. Hannah, *my* Hannah, would be in a room with Levit Traveston and his guys, basically alone, for three to five minutes. Levit Traveston, the highest identifiable perp on the food chain for the Wells Gang, aka the organized crime group responsible for most human trafficking in the southeastern USA and Caribbean, the syndicate that had stepped in as soon as the Iron Wraiths scattered.

And it was my fault. I'd asked—no, I'd *forced*—her to do it.

I felt like I was going to be sick.

* * *

"You started the timer, right?" Louis, the baby bartender, stood on my right side, arms crossed, eyes trained on the door to the champagne room.

"Yes, Louis. I started the timer. And Dave has a timer, too." Kilby, or

Fantasia if you used her dancer name, stood on my left side, arms also crossed, eyes also trained on the door to the champagne room.

During my mindless march down the hallway to the main floor, I'd run into Kilby on her way out and asked if she could stay a bit longer. According to Tina's preliminary information on the club months ago, Kilby worked my job—that is, bouncer—during the hen parties and this information had made me curious about her past. After some digging, I'd discovered she'd been a parole officer before she changed her last name and started a family. A few weeks ago, when I asked Kilby about the career switch, she told me dancing paid about three times as much, was significantly less dangerous, less stress, and the hours allowed her to spend more time with her kids.

"I started a timer too, and he's got"—Louis lifted the black, circular stopwatch, glared at it as if it owed him money—"two minutes and twenty-two seconds left."

"Two minutes and twenty-two seconds," I murmured. A lot could happen in two minutes and twenty-two seconds.

"A lot can happen in two minutes," Louis said grimly.

I looked at Louis. He looked at me. We stared at each other and I read his expression. He didn't like Levit. He never had. The guy worried him, made him nervous. This explained why Kilby had agreed so readily in the hall earlier as soon as I'd said, *VIP customer by the name of Tavvy.*

For once, it seemed the baby bartender and I were on the same page.

"Why don't you like this guy, Louis?" I asked, working to subdue a spike of alarm. Levit looked normal, much more normal than his mug shot.

Louis turned his glare back to the door of the champagne room. "He has her dress in costumes that are hard to take off."

"And she told me he laughs at her." This came from Kilby. "He looks like a normal guy, right? But when she dances for him, he puts her in stupid costumes and laughs at her when she takes them off. It's weird, sadistic. That's why I don't like him and why I'd volunteered to take him on when she retired. I can deal with being laughed at, but I didn't want anyone else here to have to deal with it. He's creepy."

This wasn't information I'd known prior to right now. Kilby was right. He was creepy and sadistic. I needed to calm down. It would be best if I remained calm. As an undercover agent, things only went to shit—as they had all those years ago when I encountered Jennifer in the Piggly Wiggly—if I didn't stay calm.

But I needed to do something. I couldn't stand here waiting for Hannah to finish, my imagination filling in the blanks of what might be happening behind that closed door.

"I'm checking video monitors," I said, my feet already moving in that direction.

Both Louis and Kilby called in unison, "Good idea."

Jogging between tables and down the hall, I told myself to calm down, and I did. Me losing my cool wouldn't help Hannah if things went south.

Making it to the security office in less than thirty seconds, I rushed inside and hit the power button on the screen monitoring the champagne room. Immediately, four views of the space appeared. Levit and two of his associates sat on the cushioned benches. Levit seemed to be talking on a phone, not even looking at Hannah.

And Hannah . . .

I swallowed a lump of something foul tasting, but forced myself to watch, keeping my eyes trained on Levit and his guys even though my attention wanted to stray to Hannah, inspect her body and movements for signs of injury or distress.

I'd been deluding myself. Kissing Hannah earlier hadn't been about getting her out of my system or settling a score between us. I liked her. I admired her. I cared about her and what she thought. A lot. I wanted to be with her. For the first time since leaving home at eighteen—and maybe even before that—I didn't want to be cautious. In fact, caution didn't feel like an option this time. I was more afraid of missing out on a chance with her than I was afraid of any possible negative consequences. I couldn't stop thinking about her. And now she was in a room with that scumbag because of me.

I tried turning up the volume but the only thing the speakers caught was the song. None of Levit's conversation was audible.

At intervals, Levit seemed to pause his conversation and point at Hannah. And laugh at her. It was mean. He and his buddies were ridiculing her. And I couldn't remember ever wanting to pound someone's face in more. Not even my father's.

It was the longest ninety seconds of my life.

By the time it was over, when I watched Dave open the door and step inside, Levit pass Hannah her phone, all smiles while he pulled out a wad of cash, I'd found my calm because I had no choice. He needed to be behind bars as soon as possible and the only way to make that happen was by focusing on my job.

I made a copy of the video footage. I uploaded it to my phone. I sent it to

Agent Danforth. Then I returned to the main floor. Hannah was nowhere in sight.

"Where's Goldie?"

Dave turned at my question but it was Louis who answered. "She left with Fantasia."

I assumed that meant Hannah and Kilby had gone to the dressing room, or maybe her office. Regardless, she was safe now.

"And—uh—that Tavvy guy?" I glanced between Louis and Dave, not caring who answered.

"He's gone." Dave tossed a thumb over his shoulder. "It's usually like this. He comes in for a few minutes, then leaves. Sometimes he pays for a few private dances, but he has to wait fifteen minutes between each of them. House rules. We're closing, so he didn't have time to stay."

"Anything odd about his visit this time?" Again, I didn't care who answered.

Louis, wiping a glass with a towel, shrugged. "Other than the fact that he hasn't been here for a long time, like weeks, nothing."

"He asked for Fantasia when he and his guys arrived," Dave said, sitting on a stool at the bar. The place was now empty of customers. "But I think it's because the last time he came in—when was that? Like a week or so before her retirement party, I think—Goldie told him she was retiring, and if he wanted a dancer he should ask for Kilby. I mean, Fantasia. Tavvy seemed surprised when Goldie showed up instead tonight. Happy, but surprised."

This all tracked, made sense, and raised no red flags. I would go check on Hannah, but first I had a phone call to make and a voicemail to leave for work. Asking Dave for the storage room key, I left the two guys at the front to clean up.

Danforth had been dodging my questions about Hannah's safety for weeks, saying she would pursue the issue once we got usable intel from Hannah's cell. Levit had finally shown his face tonight. He'd used Hannah's phone. Everything he'd said had been recorded. I'd done my part. Hannah had done her part.

Now Danforth owed me answers.

* * *

Danforth called me back Sunday morning first thing. I'd just pulled into the Donner Bakery lot when my phone rang. I immediately swiped at my screen. "Danforth."

"I guess you had one hell of a night last night, huh?" She laughed, clearly in a good mood. "Did you see the transcript yet?"

Swallowing that same foul-tasting lump as the night before, I grunted. I also switched off my wipers and cut the engine.

"I can't believe he trusts that stripper so much. Assuming this intel is legit, we have him on thirteen felony counts." She went on and on about kidnapping, commerce laws, and state lines. Danforth wanted to discuss the evidence first. I knew that and I let her.

Despite cringing every time Danforth referred to Hannah as "that stripper," I kept my responses short, mostly grunts. Restless and ready to move past the damning transcript of Levit's call and get to the issue of Hannah's safety, I knew arguing with Danforth about her tone, language, and lack of respect for our confidential contact would prolong our conversation at best. At worst, Danforth would get cagey about Hannah's safety and be less likely to give a shit.

Finally, she asked, "How likely do you think it might be that Levit is testing that stripper, making sure her phone is still a secure, viable method of communicating with his subordinates?"

"Before we get to that, I want to know what the plan is for Hannah Townsen's safety. You said we'd discuss how the evidence would be masked as soon as we received intel. So, what's the plan for Miss Townsen? How are you prioritizing her safety?"

"Oh, yeah. Yeah. I don't see that being a problem. I spoke to Griggs about it, incidentally last week, and he said they should have no issue with the judge. I promise, we can demonstrate a need for sealing the evidence—source and recordings—it's a no-brainer."

Letting the back of my head connect with the headrest, I closed my eyes. "Good. That's good." Danforth had a good track record for being reliable about this kind of thing. She rarely made promises. If she did, she kept them.

I didn't think Hannah was at the Pony right now, otherwise I would've been there already. After I'd finished leaving my daily voicemail for Danforth last night, I found out that Hannah leaving with Kilby meant that she'd gone home with Kilby.

I'd been worried about her last night, both during the time with Levit and when she left without saying goodbye. Sleep had been elusive, my thoughts returning to Hannah, wondering if she was okay, wondering how she was feeling. Had she found sleep difficult too? Was she upset about Levit? Was she upset with me? If she was upset, I hoped she'd let me comfort her. Maybe I'd buy out the bakery of the morning muffins today. Hannah deserved all the muffins every day. Not just one.

"You sure this isn't Levit testing her? If so, I'll confirm with the team. We're already treating this like real intel. We can move on this now, intercept the next cargo drop. Miss Townsen is probably finished, no need for her continued involvement."

"There's no evidence that this is Levit testing her. My contacts at the club didn't see anything odd about his behavior. According to the head bouncer, he came in asking for a different dancer, which made sense given that Han—uh, Miss Townsen had told him she'd be retiring. When Miss Townsen showed up instead, he seemed genuinely pleased and things proceeded as usual."

I recalled the moment he'd spotted Hannah last night, the big smile he'd given her, and the feeling of relief when he hadn't pulled her into a hug. I'd remained out of sight until they walked into the champagne room, since I was new on staff and I didn't want to raise any suspicions with Levit and his crew. I did note he hadn't touched her at all, just like she said he wouldn't.

Kilby had been right last night. Levit appeared normal upon first glance and second glance and third glance. His appearance was benign, but his behaviors were sadistic and made his nine-to-five, working-in-an-office dad vibe creepy. With no context, he looked like a dude out on the weekend with two other dad friends, all three fellas gray at the temples, dressed in cargo pants and button-down shirts from the Gap. In this way, he reminded me of my father.

My father had also looked benign, shorter than the average man, approachable, nonthreatening, with kind eyes and thinning hair and a dad's fashion sense. Whereas I was over six feet, born with broad shoulders, and had been told I looked scary too many times to count.

You never know about a person. Until you do.

Rubbing my forehead, I opened my eyes and stared forward. The autumn leaves left on the trees surrounding the bakery and lodge were a blob of muted orange, purple, and yellow against a gray sky, blurred by raindrops streaking down the windshield. Odd how cold and wet weather muted everything. Sounds, colors, smells . . . thoughts.

I was glad Hannah hadn't slept alone at the club last night and had a friend she could stay with, but the news of her premature departure had been frustrating. Texting her hadn't been an option. I'd bugged her phone myself. All messages and calls were recorded. I could've found Kilby's number and called her, but . . . what right did I have? We weren't together. We weren't dating. *Yet.*

A fact I would attempt to rectify as soon as possible. Hopefully starting today with a bakery full of morning muffins.

"Great," Danforth said in my ear. "I'll let you know when the raid is over. We're all rushing to get ready since the ship he mentioned is scheduled to arrive on Friday."

That had me sitting forward. "Wait. Five days?"

"Yeah. I know, right? Too good to be true. Assuming all goes well, your last day will be Friday. Unless you think you should pull out before—"

"No. No, I should stay put." I paused, telling myself to lower my voice, not sound too invested. "In case he returns this week, shares more details about the drop."

It wasn't against the rules to become involved with someone during an investigation, even if that person was my confidential contact. Actually, it wasn't all that unusual. I knew of two agents who'd met their spouses while working undercover. The biggest issue was what happened after marriage if they'd met during an undercover assignment. The civilian would have to leave their life behind, adopt a new identity, a new background, for the safety of the agent and themselves. Criminals have long memories.

I could pursue things with Hannah without restriction from the higher-ups, no problem. I'd spell things out for her and I knew it was a lot.

But the timing . . . Five days. *That* might be a problem.

Five days to demonstrate how I would be a good choice for her in the long term; five days to explain how her life would change if she wanted something permanent with me; five days to come up with a plan that didn't put her under undue pressure or rush her into a decision. Did I tell her everything at once? From the get-go? Or spread it out? I didn't know.

I wished I had someone to discuss this with, someone to help me sort it out.

"Okay. Makes sense for you to stay until the drop," Danforth said, then changed the subject to the matter of close-out paperwork, deadlines for submission, and how much paid leave I had accrued. I only half paid attention.

Five days. I only had five days left at the club. Five days to prove to Hannah I deserved a chance for a spot in her life before I had no reason or excuse to see her. Five days to figure out how to explain what needed explaining. Just five days.

I'd have to make every moment count.

Chapter Eighteen

HANNAH

"Your mistakes and missteps will reinforce people's unflattering ideas about you, and your good deeds will be explained away by nice weather."

— Jackson James, *Totally Folked* by Penny Reid

It wasn't my birthday, but I wanted to buy myself a morning muffin and coffee. I'd taken Kilby up on her offer to stay at her house due to the emotional whiplash of being intimate with Isaac and then having to strip for Tavvy. I hadn't wanted to be alone last night at the Pony. Luckily, I'd taken my truck to Kilby's last night, so I didn't need to bother her for a ride.

On my drive to the bakery, I worked myself up into a fine lather with some high-quality self-talk: I worked hard. I deserved muffins. I could buy myself a damn muffin if I wanted, whenever I wanted. And another thing! I didn't need to wait for someone else to buy me a muffin. Who are these people who sit around waiting for other folks to buy them muffins? Silver-spoon-using, not-a-care-in-the-world lazybones, that's who. Well, some of us have to work for our muffins, including me, and there was absolutely nothing wrong with that!

By the time I pulled into the parking lot, I didn't have to think about slamming the truck's door. I just did it. Marching to the front, I paid no mind to the rain or how soaked I would be when I eventually walked through the door. As usual, there was a line outside. Unlike me, everyone else seemed to have an umbrella. Whatever! I didn't care! If I wanted an umbrella, I'd buy myself an umbrella. Maybe I didn't want one. Maybe I wanted to get wet . . .

I understood what I was doing. I was getting myself good and mad before seeing Isaac later today. If I was already mad at him, I wouldn't be disappointed no matter what Isaac said or did. Getting mad feels good. Being disappointed feels bad. If I was already mad before seeing Isaac, he wouldn't be able to disappoint me. See how that worked? Don't y'all call me a genius all at once.

I didn't know what I'd been thinking, giving the man a hand job in my office? And then asking him to cuddle? What was wrong with me? *Almost two decades of being hot for just one guy, that's what's wrong with you . . .* He had me under a sex spell or something. I swear, I was not this stupid. But Isaac's bare chest had made me stupid. And his eyes, how he'd looked at me. And his kisses. It all added up to a stupidity ray gun of sexiness.

Standing in the frigid late-October downpour, I pulled the hood of my jacket further forward to cover more of my face even though I felt warm around my neck at the memory of his kisses. It wasn't a rain jacket, it didn't repel the water, but it would have to do because it was all I had. And that was fine, too. Some folks didn't even have a jacket, let alone a car and a job and the ability to buy themselves a muffin whenever they wanted. I had no right to be sad or disappointed. I should simply be grateful for the bountiful blessings I'd been given . . .

I also understood what I was doing now. Minimizing my uncomfortable emotions until they seemed like a speck in comparison to what others faced was a fantastic way to never allow myself to have feelings about anything, let alone experience sadness or disappointment. Also genius.

For more mental health tips and strategies, don't follow me or hit subscribe. My advice isn't healthy. I'm a mess. But at least I was a mess with a jacket who could afford muffins.

"And that's what's important . . ." I muttered, wrapping my arms around my torso tighter, and reminded myself for maybe the hundredth time in twelve hours that I didn't even really know Isaac Sylvester. I'd had a crush on the idea of him since I was eleven. I'd had a crush on the idea of him when he returned to town. And I had a crush on the idea of him now. Period.

I used to study everything about him, take note of the books he read and read them too, admire the sound of his singing voice, memorize his mannerisms. As a teenager, he'd always seemed hungry. If anyone brought food to one of the choir gatherings, he'd get in line last and finish whatever everyone else had left behind. Unless his daddy was there. If his father showed up, he'd eat nothing.

But what did I truly know about adult Isaac Sylvester other than how sexy he was? An undercover agent for the federal government, used to be in the army, seemed to find comfort in rules. And he apologized when he made mistakes. He liked to silently hold ladders, move heavy boxes, and repair costumes. He knew his sewing stitches. He wasn't a big talker. And he was a fantastic kisser.

"That's it. That's all I know," I muttered to myself, but then I became aware that the split-splat of rain around me sounded different and I blinked myself out of my internal musings, realizing an umbrella had been placed over my head. I looked up.

Isaac.

Standing next to me holding an umbrella, Isaac Sylvester looked pissed. Or more correctly, his features were blank except his eyes, which looked like they could melt iron.

Leaning close, his voice a gravelly whisper, he asked, "What the hell are you doing?"

I lifted my chin proudly and prepared to announce that I was buying my own damn muffin this morning when he dropped an arm around my shoulders and made his own announcement, "You're coming with me."

Holding the umbrella more over me than himself, Isaac propelled us forward together toward the main lodge. At a fork in the sidewalk, he split off to the right, never breaking stride. I allowed myself to be steered and I had no defense to offer for my complicity. I was wet, cold, shivering, and he'd appeared out of nowhere with an umbrella, his stupidity ray gun of sexiness, and apparently a plan.

Whatever. I was ready to get this over with—whatever *this* was between us—so I could put my head on straight and stop thinking about him.

We'd made out yesterday in my office. It had been very sexy. I'd liked it. I'd liked the way he looked at me. I'd liked making him come apart. I loved how he felt in my hand. I loved his hungry kisses. And I'd really liked it when he said, "I think I need you."

But, again, what did I know about this man? It would be silly to have expectations. He was an undercover federal agent. He would be leaving any day now, four weeks at the most. We had no future.

After two more forks and an unexpected walk through the woods, during which the path disappeared, we arrived at a cabin set off from the rest of the grounds. The front door plaque read, *Honeymoon Suite.*

I frowned at the sign because I was fairly certain the Donner Lodge's Honeymoon Suite wasn't this cabin. The real Honeymoon Suite was two stories tall with a massive deck, sat at the highest point of the property, and had a long driveway leading up to it.

The only reason I knew all this was because it had been photographed for *Lodge and Resort* magazine last fall and one of the dancers had brought the issue in, excited to see Green Valley represented in a print magazine as impressive as *Lodge and Resort*, which was part of the global Kradernast family of magazines.

But this cabin in front of me now sat on the edge of the mountain at approximately the same level as the others we'd passed earlier on, not high above them. Even so, I bet the view would've been spectacular if the whole valley below hadn't currently been obscured by mist.

"What is this place?" I asked.

"It's the original Donner cabin." Isaac released me, folding my hand around the umbrella's handle and stepping out from beneath it.

"What does that mean?" I watched him kneel and fish around several discarded clay pots at the exterior corner of the cabin before returning with a key.

"It's maintained but for family members' use only. Only me, my momma, and—uh—Jennifer are allowed to use it." Isaac made straight for the door, unlocking it, then turned, grabbed my hand, and tugged me inside.

"Leave the umbrella out here," he said, pivoting once all of me but my hand was inside. He uncurled my fingers from the handle, tossed the umbrella a bit away from the cabin, then closed the door, the sound of rain subsiding to a rumble against the roof instead of a rush all around us.

Stepping straight into my space, he grabbed the zipper of my jacket and tugged it down, pushed my jacket open and off. "This is soaking wet, Hannah," he said, the words accusatory.

If I was in any doubt of his feelings regarding my wet jacket, Isaac's glare confirmed his emotional state: intensely irritated.

I wrapped my arms around myself when he stepped back, my wet cotton shirt providing no warmth. He hung my jacket on a row of hooks by the door, then added his rain jacket next to it. As my eyes moved over him dressed in a black thermal, jeans, and the boots he was in the process of toeing off, I noted his shirt was completely dry except for at the wrists.

"Take off your shoes," he said, indicating to my feet with his chin. "And your socks. By the look of it, those are soaked too."

My teeth started to chatter and I did as instructed, but not because he told me to. I removed my shoes and socks because it wasn't polite to wear dirty shoes or wet socks in someone else's house.

We're not in a house. We're in a hotel cabin that only three people are allowed to use.

Shoes and socks removed, I'd just turned my head to look around the dim space when I felt my feet leave the floor and my body go horizontal. My arms flailed for only a split second before they instinctively encircled Isaac's neck. He'd picked me up, bridal style, and now carried me through a living room, down a hall, and into a bedroom, apparently too impatient to let me walk on my own two feet.

Depositing me at the side of the bed, Isaac removed himself several steps and turned around, giving me his back. "Take off those clothes, leave them on the floor, and get under the covers to warm up. This unit has a clothes dryer."

I stared at the back of his neck, confused by his words. No, that's not right. His words made plenty of sense. What didn't make sense was that he'd turned his back to me, like he was giving me privacy. He'd seen me in a string bikini last month. He'd seen me in my see-through bra and underwear just yesterday. And now he was giving me privacy?

Or maybe he doesn't want to look.

My stomach felt colder than my skin as I pulled my arm from the wet sleeve and I forced a laugh I didn't feel. "No need to give me privacy, Isaac. You've already seen everything."

He didn't turn around, but he did put his hands on his hips. "Giving others privacy is about more than not looking, Hannah. It's about space and respect."

My movements paused because his words hit me like a blow, right in the center of my chest. I found I had to stiffen my chin to keep it from wobbling and blink several times to clear the strange and sudden sting of tears from my eyes. As the rest of my clothes joined the wet shirt on the floor, I couldn't help but think the same could be said about oneself. Giving yourself privacy was about space and respect.

Had I ever given myself those things? No. But I didn't have that luxury, did I?

Numbly, I tugged back the covers and slipped inside, pulling them up to my neck and turning away from Isaac. "Okay. I'm under the covers," I said, then burrowed deeper. My brain told me the bedding smelled like Isaac—like lye soap, sandalwood, and sweetness—and I wondered if he slept here all the time, if this cabin was where he stayed when he was in town.

His relationship with his sister was a mystery. I'd heard they'd had a falling out when he was back in town and hooked up with the Iron Wraiths, but now that I knew he was working undercover the whole time as a federal agent, I assumed that was all staged for the sake of town gossip. Now he was using his family cabin, which lent credence to this assumption.

Then again, he didn't seem to know much about his sister's baking infamy or celebrity status. So . . . what was going on between the siblings?

My musings were interrupted by Isaac's movements as he retrieved my clothes and I heard him mutter something like, "Be right back." His light footfalls disappeared after a few seconds, leaving me alone in the dim room.

If it had been brighter, if a single light had been illuminated, if the rain hadn't darkened the sky outside the windows and French doors and I'd been sleeping better the last few nights, I probably wouldn't have fallen asleep.

But it was dark and I was tired. I thought maybe there was no harm in closing my eyes. Just for a little bit.

* * *

For me, waking typically occurred in stages. My little room and bed back at the club didn't have a window or other natural source of light. Thus, I'd hooked up a sunlamp to a timer. It brightened the space according to the sunrise, following the natural rhythm of the seasons. Usually, due to the light, my brain would already be stirring before my alarm went off. The sunlamp made getting out of bed easier than using just an alarm to wake up. This method helped my brain work better earlier in the day, too.

Therefore, at present, when I became aware of the brightness around me, I kept waiting for my cell phone's alarm to go off. My mind woke up completely and still no alarm. Confused, I opened my eyes, and the room that greeted me wasn't my room.

The walls were navy blue and paneled. Or maybe it was blue wallpaper that looked like panels. Hard to say. All the furniture appeared to be real wood, fine and antique, reminding me of the furniture that used to decorate my family's farmhouse when my grandparents owned the property. My momma had sold it all in order to pay the mortgage.

The overstuffed, fancy armchair in the corner was white fabric with a blue print of historical scenes and people. French or Victorian toile was what it was called, if I wasn't mistaken. But more importantly, Isaac Sylvester sat in the fancy chair reading a book.

I frowned at him and the room. The events of the morning—waking up at Kilby's after only three hours of sleep, slipping quietly out of her house and driving to the Donner Bakery to buy my own damn muffin, Isaac's umbrella and surprise hijacking—returned to me all at once.

Careful not to make a sound, I studied him, his quiet absorption, how one large hand supported the spine of the book while the fingers of his other hand fiddled absentmindedly with the top corner of the pages. He'd done the very same thing when he was a teenager. The intensity of his focus, the expression he made, the way he'd bite down hard on his lower lip and then release it softly, it was all the same. Looking at him now gave me an intense sense of déjà vu.

Except, this Isaac wasn't the same Isaac as before. That Isaac had been quiet because he was sensitive and shy, blushed easily from embarrassment, and always stood or sat in the shadows, at the back of every crowd. He only spoke to be polite, saying *please, thank you,* and *pardon me* more than any other words. He'd always been small for his age. The size of his hands, feet, shoulders, nose, and eyes never matched the rest of him.

Whereas this Isaac had grown into his larger features, was much bigger and broader, so tall he towered over me. He also didn't speak much, but when he did, his words were either sharp or blunt, not often polite.

Yesterday in my office, he'd been very sexy, pushy but also respectful. He'd kissed me and seemed to have enjoyed himself. I wondered, was I a fling? Is that what he wanted from me? And, if so, would I be okay with that?

Abruptly, his eyes cut to mine and it felt like diving headfirst—or maybe falling headfirst—into a big body of water. I'd never seen the ocean in person, but the crash of waves I'd heard in TV shows and movies reminded me of this feeling right now, being caught staring by Isaac.

Instinctively, I looked away, swallowed tightly, endeavored to find my wits, then looked back. Isaac's eyes were still on me. Outwardly unperturbed. But there seemed to be a whole universe of thoughts behind his gaze.

"What time is it?" I croaked, thankful I could use sleep as an excuse for the rough quality of my voice.

"You've been asleep for three hours." Isaac placed a bookmark between the pages of his novel and set it on a small side table. "It's not yet noon."

I nodded and shifted in the bed to sit up, bringing the comforters with me to cover my chest. "I need to get to the Pony."

"Why? It doesn't open until four." He leaned forward, placing his elbows on his knees.

We swapped stares while I tried to think of a reason and came up empty other than the truth: I didn't like being away from the Pink Pony because the Pink Pony was the only place where I felt safe and valued. I didn't like going out in public anywhere in Green Valley. Folks gossiped about me to my face, so I knew they also did it behind my back after I left. I didn't like my family's farm. I hadn't felt safe there ever, not even as a kid. My parents' dysfunctional marriage meant it had never felt like home, and definitely not when the land had become an albatross of debt for me to manage and payoff.

Coming to the bakery this morning to buy a muffin had required me to psych myself up.

The Pink Pony had a locked gate, steel doors, people who didn't judge me, people who valued me but didn't need me in order to survive. And plenty of food. I could stay there for weeks, months even, without ever needing to step outside.

When I didn't say anything, Isaac's shoulders rose and fell. He stood. "Be right back."

Pushing myself up more completely, I watched him disappear down the hall. Since I had nothing else to do, I continued documenting the room.

The two windows and the two white French doors along one wall were currently the only sources of light. Another door, likely to an ensuite bathroom, was set on the far wall. Above me was a large cobalt blue chandelier with glass lilies disguising the light bulbs. It was turned off, but I imagined it was dramatic when powered on. The room was classy and fancy yet cozy and comfortable.

A picture hung on the wall behind me but I couldn't tell what it was from my vantage point, nor did I want to get out of bed to see it better. I was warm and comfortable and didn't want to move at the moment. The mattress was divine, soft but supportive, and the two layers of feather comforters were heavy in a good way. I didn't think the sheets were silk. I checked a few times, kicking my legs slowly and using my fingers to test the texture. They had to be cotton but they felt just as soft as silk. Luxurious.

I would've asked about the brand except I knew myself. I wasn't buying nice sheets for my bed. What would be the point? I never had trouble sleeping at the end of any given day.

Movement in the hallway caught my notice. Isaac, holding a tray laden with dishes, was on his way back, his attention on a mug. Not stopping until he stood next to the bed, he bent and placed the tray on my lap.

"Careful. The tea is hot. So is the soup," he said, straightening and pointing to a bowl of chicken noodle that looked homemade.

I didn't precisely gape at him, but I'm sure I came close. It was on the tip of my tongue to ask what in tarnation was going on when he sat down facing me on the bed, his backside near my knees, and braced an arm over my legs, his hand near the middle of the mattress.

"Eat." He inclined his head to the set of silverware on the tray. "Before it gets cold."

Once again, we stared at each other. If I wasn't mistaken, those tiny curves at the corners of his mouth were his version of a smile.

I didn't smile. I was too confused.

I wasn't confused about him pulling me out of the rain. I wasn't confused about him drying my clothes and encouraging me to warm up in this bed. I wasn't confused about him letting me catch up on sleep, I knew I looked tired. Nor was I confused about him making me food. I understood all of that.

What I didn't understand, for any of it, was why. Before I accepted another act of kindness, no matter how grumpily delivered, I needed to know what he expected of me in return. Did he need a favor? Or was he buttering me up for a fling? What did he want from me?

"What are you doing?" I asked, not eating.

"Feeding you."

"Why?" He might've had me under a sex spell of some sort, but I was tired of feeling jerked around, tired of the cold then hot, then back to cold again. I wanted—needed—answers.

One of his eyebrows lifted a scant millimeter. "Have you eaten today?"

"Why are you feeding me? Why are you asking if I've eaten? Why are you pulling me out of the rain and drying my clothes? Why are you bringing me a coffee and muffin every morning? What do you want from me?"

Isaac bit his bottom lip, an echo of the familiar action I associated with him reading books. He seemed to be considering how to answer. I leaned back in the bed, crossed my arms above the comforter covering my chest, and waited. I would let his soup get cold if he didn't spell things out. If he needed a favor, it was well past time he asked. If he wanted a fling, he needed to say so.

His smile seemed to turn rueful and he withdrew his hand from the center of the bed, turning his body toward the French doors.

Isaac made a sound like a light laugh, giving his head a shake. "I think I must be really bad at this. It's my first time."

"What's that? What are you bad at? What is this?" I waved a hand over the food.

"I like you, Hannah. I like you a whole lot," he said, his smile falling away as he leaned his elbows on his knees once more, giving me his profile. Isaac rubbed at the center of one hand with the thumb of the other, his attention focused on his palm, continuing haltingly, "What I want from you, and the answer to your question is, I want you to like me in return. Ideally, a whole lot. I'd like to—uh—court you."

His confession paired with the vulnerability in his voice momentarily took my breath away. My stomach swooped, a swirling tightness fluttering up to my chest and expanding outward like a starburst.

Court me?

He wasn't finished. "I'd like to take you out on a date this Tuesday to spell things out, talk things over, if you're willing. We both have the day off and I wondered . . ."

Seeming to brace himself, he turned his head and peeked at me, apparently gauging my reaction and worried about what he'd find.

Faced with his shyness and wholesome request and sincerity, it was hard to contain my smile. It was also difficult to keep the rush of liquid emotion from my eyes. Of the two, I decided to focus my energy on banishing the odd tears, allowing the smile to fully take over my face.

Isaac straightened like he was surprised, his eyes bouncing between mine and my mouth. He turned his body toward me again, his own smile returning like the dawn. It wasn't a big grin like mine, but it was genuine and soft and sweet.

Apparently encouraged by what he saw, he continued his abandoned thought, "I wondered if we could go for a hike, then out to dinner. My treat." How could someone so stoic and stern also be so astonishingly cute?

"I'm free Tuesday. A hike and dinner sounds nice," I croaked out, feeling oddly emotional. Clearing my throat, I picked up the spoon. "I guess, then, I should definitely eat this soup." Wondering how I was going to keep the food in my mouth when I couldn't stop grinning like a fool, I stirred the soup.

He rolled his lips between his teeth. Eyes warm, he nodded.

I took a few bites, feeling my cheeks heat with each spoonful. But not from embarrassment. Embarrassment was heavy and hurt. This, whatever it was, made me feel like I might float off the bed, and the ache of it felt good.

Isaac seemed content to silently watch me eat, which didn't feel weird or odd. After so many weeks of his silent help, I guessed I'd grown used to his quiet presence. And you know what? I ate that soup. And the bread slathered in butter. I drank all the tea and the juice. I left no crumbs. I didn't want to leave him in any doubt that, what I knew about him, I liked a whole lot.

Yep. He had me under a spell. A sex spell, a cuteness spell, and a sincerity spell. *Oh well.*

Chapter Nineteen

HANNAH

"I'm a firm believer that if a person needs a hug, you give that person a hug. So many times I've been in a situation where I needed a hug, and instead had to settle for a good cry on a pillow at the end of the day."

— Jennifer Sylvester, *Beard Science* by Penny Reid

Isaac had been making eyes at me all day.

He'd made eyes at me when I ate his soup, when we left the cabin holding hands, and when we both arrived to the Pony and walked through the back door, which he held open for me. He'd made eyes at me when I strolled into the front area and checked in with Louis about the liquor order, and when I welcomed Joshua back and introduced Isaac to Joshua.

And he made eyes at me late during his shift when I literally bumped into him in the breakroom.

"Pardon me," Isaac said, catching me by the shoulders.

When I lifted my head he—you guessed it—made eyes at me.

"Sorry about that." I tried to meet his gaze, but every time I did it felt like a firecracker was going off in my chest.

His hands fell away slowly, like he was reluctant to let me go, and his attention lowered to my lips. "Don't apologize."

"But I bumped into you."

"I don't mind," he said, his tone sending a shiver down my spine.

Have I mentioned I loved his voice?

And I loved how he hadn't backed away or placed any distance between us. And I loved how his eyelids seemed to droop low and heavy as he stared at me. And I loved how I got the sense he was thinking about lovely, dirty, wonderful things. At least I hoped so, because that's where my mind had gone.

Feeling hot, I could do nothing but stand there, knowing nothing but nonsense would come out if I tried to speak again. Because I wanted to—

"Get a room, you two."

I started at the sound of Serafina's voice and the smattering of chuckles that followed her teasing statement. I hadn't realized anyone else was in the room. Several dancers stood near the fridge, watching us with identical expressions, eyebrows raised and half smiles. Likewise, Serafina and two of the line cooks were lounging at a table, drinking coffee, legs crossed, attention affixed on Isaac and me.

Refusing to be flustered—or rather, *more* flustered—I took a quick step back and tried to remember why I'd walked in here to begin with. At a loss, I looked at Isaac for help, but he wasn't making eyes at me anymore. He scowled at Serafina, perhaps not enjoying her commentary, and the flash in his glare reminded me of what Tina had said a few weeks ago: *He doesn't like to be teased.*

The chef's eyebrows shot up and she lifted her hands. "Whoa. Sorry, big guy. My bad. Sorry."

Isaac's eyes narrowed further, glinting dangerously, but he said nothing, threading our fingers together and pulling me out of the breakroom and straight to my office. What he planned to do, I would never know because Tina sat at my desk, her feet propped up on its surface.

"There you are." Tina's legs dropped and she stood, setting a hand on her hip. "I need to talk to you. Have you been hiding from . . ." Her words trailed off as she made a big show of looking from our joined hands to Isaac's face, then to mine.

Any instinct I had to withdraw my fingers was nixed by Isaac squeezing my hand tighter, and he met Tina's smirking smile with one of his plain stares.

"Are you looking for me? Or Hannah?" he asked.

"For Hannah." She leaned a hip against my desk like she was getting comfy. "But first, when did this happen?" Tina moved an acrylic-tipped finger between the two of us.

I didn't usually let others do the talking for me, not anymore. I'd been a quiet, shy kid, but life circumstances hadn't allowed me to continue following the path of my inherent nature. When Isaac had chewed Louis out last week, it was a relief but also unnecessary. I would've—calmly, politely—told Louis to maintain appropriate boundaries. I simply hadn't gotten around to reminding the young bartender. Again. For the millionth time.

But right now? I gave Isaac's hand a little shake, hoping he'd interpret the movement correctly: *You do the talking.*

Tina's relationship with Isaac remained a mystery to me. They were friendly. But she'd always been cagey about whether or not they'd ever been more than friends or whether she had feelings for him. Regardless, Tina was my friend, and I didn't wish to damage that friendship.

Isaac seemed to stand straighter after my small gesture, and he took a small step forward. "A bit ago," he drawled, his tone funny.

I glanced at him, found his lips curved in a strange-looking smile. Uncertain what *that* look meant, since I'd never seen it before, I studied Tina. Her smile was bigger but seemed similar to his as they looked at each other.

"Good for you, Isaac," she said, appearing and sounding proud, but then added, "She's the best. Take excellent care of her or I'll slash your tires."

My eyes bugged out but I otherwise stood like a statue as Tina's attention swung to me. Her expression didn't change. She still looked proud. "And good for you, Hannah. You got a good one. I know you'll treat his overly sensitive heart with care. Your tires are safe from me. But you should thank me."

"I—I should—thank you?"

She nodded once, as though bestowing a blessing. "You are most welcome. I did what I could. Now, getting to business." She rubbed her hands together, her gaze bouncing between us once more, then she said, "Oh. Now. Wait a minute. I can work with this."

"Tina." He said her name on a sigh, like she exhausted him.

Ignoring Isaac, her whole demeanor changed and she gripped my free arm. "Hannah! I have the most terrible news ever. And I'm so sorry, I know you were counting on me to help you find two replacements for the hen party this week, but there's simply no one else who can help other than Dave. Joshua is back today, but he's in no condition to dance. There's no one else. No one at all!"

My head tilted to the side subtly as I listened to her extremely dramatic performance. Why she was making a big deal out of this, I had no idea. "Tina. Calm down. The party this week has been moved to next week. I'll talk to Hank and explain the situation. He'll—"

"Yes! Exactly! Hank." She shook my arm. "I'm just so worried about you and what Hank might say. I know you're still new in your role here, managing things, and this is going to make you look really bad. I mean, really, really bad. In a word, completely incompetent."

Releasing Isaac's fingers so I could pry Tina's off my arm, I set her away. "'Completely incompetent' is two words. And, sure, Hank'll be upset, but it's not like—"

"And this puts you in such a terrible position." She brought her fingertips to her lips, her eyes tearing up. She sniffled. "Who knows if you'll keep your job after this? What will you do? Where will you go? I guess you'll just start dancing again when he fires you. Maybe at the G-Spot since you won't be welcome here no more."

I rolled my eyes. "Tina, I think you're—"

"I'll do it." Isaac grabbed my hand again and tugged.

Facing him and certain I'd heard wrong, I asked, "Sorry, what?"

"I'll do it. I'll fill in for the missing dancer."

A flash of an image, of Isaac's body on display for a room full of excited women, made my stomach drop. They would love him and I suspected I would hate it. "Isaac, I don't—"

"Oh, thank you, Isaac! You've saved Hannah so much trouble. I'm texting Hank right now." Her phone appeared from thin air and she began typing out a message with her thumbs, all while she skirted around us for the door and continued rambling. "You're such a good boyfriend, helping out this way. You'll win the boyfriend of the year award for sure, if there were such a thing. Best boyfriend ever to your girlfriend, Hannah. This lovely lady right here. I'm sure your girlfriend will show her appreciation by doing something real special for you, something involving her mouth, and getting down on her knees."

"Tina!" he growled.

"I meant praying, Isaac!" Tina bolted out the door, jogging in her stilettos and squealing like Isaac might grab for her. As soon as she was a good distance away, she tossed over her shoulder, "Oh my goodness, where is your head at? I meant *praying* for your well-being with her mouth while kneeling. Jesus Christ! Get your mind out of the gutter." Turning around, she walked backward and grinned. "I wasn't talkin' about putting your big cock in her mouth! Though she should do that, too, if you ask—"

Isaac pulled me back in the office, shutting the door and cutting off Tina's nonsense. I watched his shoulders rise and fall before he faced me. The tips of his ears were red.

"Sorry about . . . her," he ground out, not quite making eye contact. "She thinks she's funny."

Goodness, he was adorable when he let himself be embarrassed and shy instead of mad and sullen. I knew he didn't like to be teased, but the devil on my shoulder wanted more of this cuteness.

"She is right though." I tapped my lower lip with my index finger as though giving the matter deep thought.

His eyes cut to mine. Held. Isaac Sylvester seemed to be holding his breath.

I suppressed my smile, infusing my voice with solemnity. "I should thank you, show my appreciation. You are helping me out of a very tough spot." It wasn't that tough of a spot. Hank would've been irritated but fine. I could handle Hank Weller, no problem.

But this was fun. I watched Isaac's Adam's apple bob with a thick, audible swallow. He said nothing, simply stood still and stared at me, like my words held him transfixed.

Stepping into his space, I backed him up against the door, reached around his side, and locked it. Licking my lips, I lowered my gaze to his mouth. "So, should I?"

A breath puffed out of him and, if I read him right, he looked overwhelmed. His lips were parted. His eyes had grown hazy and dark.

But then he tore them away. Blinked. Breathed out. Cleared his throat three times. "Uh, Hannah, we should talk bef—"

I clapped my hands together and closed my eyes. "Dear Lord in heaven, I pray for Isaac Sylvester's well-being. Please look after him and keep him safe during next Wednesday's hen party, from the excited women but also from Hank's bad attitude. Help him and guide him. Amen."

I cracked open one eye, unable to halt my grin. "Sorry I didn't kneel," I said, and I couldn't have stopped my giggle if the end of the world were at stake.

Isaac's eyes were narrowed, but a closed-mouth smile tugged at his lips and he was shaking his head. "Oh. I see. You're funny, too."

I laughed harder, backing away, happy to see his cold blue eyes bright and dancing.

He reached for my middle, catching me, sliding his hands up to my ribs. "Soooo funny."

"Ah! Isaac! That tickles—ah!" I twisted, giving him my back. He pinned me in one of the room's corners, the pressure of his fingers making me jerk and laugh.

"Okay, okay. Truce. Truce!" Facing the corner, I lifted my hands in the universal sign for surrender.

Isaac immediately slid his arms around my waist and lowered his chin to my shoulder, turning his head to whisper in my ear, "I really like your laugh," like it was a secret.

"You do?" His words left me feeling a little shy.

He nodded, nuzzling me, tickling me in a different way that made me shiver.

"You don't mind me teasing you?" I craned my neck and tried to catch his gaze.

"No." He brushed his lips lightly just beneath my ear.

"I thought you didn't like it when people teased you."

Isaac lifted his head, making eyes at me. "I reckon you might be the only person who can tease me whenever, and however, you want. And I'll like it."

Feeling emboldened, I turned in his arms and hooked mine around his neck, pressing a quick kiss to his lips, opening mine as I retreated to tell him that he could tease and tickle me any time he wanted.

The sudden shift in his gaze as soon as I stepped back made the words die in my throat. A switch had flipped and that hungry look from yesterday returned. In the next breath he pressed me against the wall and covered my mouth with his, hot and devouring and so, so skilled. His hands slipped under my shirt and gripped me, massaging a path upward to my breasts.

As my wits scattered under his capable mouth and palms, I suspected Isaac's *making eyes at me* today had actually been his version of showing restraint, a restraint that had apparently snapped as soon as I'd pressed my lips to his. And now my back arched as I pushed myself into his hands. We kissed and groped in a frenzy.

Soon he had my jeans unzipped. Soon his shirt fell to the floor. Soon he pushed his fingers into my pants and cupped me over my underwear. I gasped at the firm pressure, tilting my hips forward and wishing for friction.

"You feel so hot here," he said, the words sounding dazed. "I want to touch you, inside. Can I?"

It was still work hours for him. Technically, my day was over but his shift hadn't ended. Today was Joshua's first day back. They might need Isaac's help at the front. There were a hundred reasons I should turn him down.

Instead, I whimpered, clawed at his arm, and nodded, wanting his touch more than being responsible and not caring whether I would regret it later.

But before I could reap the rewards of my negligence, a knock sounded at the door and Joshua's voice loud-whispered, "Goldie. Dave said to come get you. That Tavvy guy is here for a dance."

* * *

I must've been out of my damn mind this afternoon.

So what if Isaac liked me? So what if I took some time and got to know him? That didn't change the fact that we had no future. And not because of his job or history, because of mine.

"You okay, Goldie?" Dave asked the moment we were out of earshot from Tavvy and his guys. He held my arm and walked me toward the back hall. "Need anything?"

Dave had never liked Tavvy after finding out that the man ridiculed me when I stripped. I honestly didn't care, but it did seem to bother the big guy.

I'd been asked to do worse. Dressing in a weird costume—tonight's had been a beekeeper—and being laughed at hardly registered. I didn't care if he laughed as long as his money bought groceries, paid a mortgage, or contributed to my nest egg. If I could give George Padmar a lap dance on the night of my retirement party for a fifty, I could deal with being laughed at for a hundred, plus helping Isaac with his investigation. No biggie.

The reason for my low mood wasn't really about Tavvy's visit. It was about the facts Tavvy's visit had re-illuminated. Isaac's stoic acceptance as I'd left the office earlier probably meant he was jealous. He might even pout when I saw him later. His childishness was a reminder of why I'd sworn off dating. Period.

"I'm fine, Dave. Thanks." Giving his hand a pat, I twisted my arm out of his gentle grip and continued on my own.

Let's say, for the sake of argument, Isaac decided to stay in Green Valley after his assignment ended. Let's say he decided he'd been sincere earlier today and actually wanted to date me. Experience told me any relationship between us would end one of two ways: Either my stripping for Tavvy as part of the investigation would make Isaac jealous, or it would turn him on. Likewise, my history as a dancer, us running into my old clients around town and in nearby cities, would either make him jealous or turn him on.

It would be one or the other. It always was.

Morbidly, I was curious. I marched to my office holding my phone, Tavvy's tip, and wearing nothing but pasties and a thong. I'd bet this whole tip that Isaac was the jealousy guy. He'd ripped into Louis last week for the younger man's suggestive remarks. And Isaac's quiet stoicism—especially when Joshua had come to drop off the costume for Tavvy's dance—reminded me a little of the last jealousy guy I'd sorta dated.

Or rather, that guy's quiet stoicism had reminded me of Isaac's when Isaac had been younger, which was why I'd given that guy the time of day. That guy had demanded I quit the Pony during our second date. He said he couldn't handle it, the way other men could just look at me, at my body, that I touched them. He said it made him crazy and he didn't want to share.

But, you know, at least jealousy guys were honest.

Shutting my door, I set my phone on my desk and put the hundred in my drawer, peeled off the pasties and thong, then searched the office for my clothes.

The other flavor—when men were *into* it—was a huge turnoff. They spouted bullshit about female autonomy, feminism, sexual agency, lack of shame, but in reality they treated me like a sex toy and saw women as less human than dogs. It made me feel even more like an object, like I existed only to fulfill their kinks and fantasies, and since we were dating, they'd succeeded in tricking me, making me think they actually cared, getting all the perks for free. Gross.

Then again, maybe Isaac is the into-it guy. He'd asked me out this afternoon after Tavvy's first visit in weeks last night. I couldn't ignore the timing. Had witnessing my career choices up close been a turn-on?

As I kicked off my high heels, pulled on my real underwear, and hooked my bra, my brain started placing new bets regarding which reaction Isaac Sylvester would give me when we next spoke.

I hope he's not the into-it guy. I hope he's the jealousy guy. If Isaac was the into-it guy, it would taint my memory of him, what we'd done yesterday, how sweet he'd been at his family's cabin, and the sacredness of my longtime crush. That would make me really sad.

I'd just put on my shirt when a soft knock sounded on the door. Before I could ask who it was, a voice sound from the other side. "Hannah?"

Isaac.

Ugh. My stomach hurt.

"Just a sec," I called back, tugging on my jeans but ignoring my socks and shoes. He'd put his shirt back on silently and left the office without a word when Joshua had interrupted us. When I walked out to the main floor wearing the beekeeper costume Isaac had been nowhere in sight.

He'd probably been sulking. Now he's here to sulk and make demands.

Why was it that men always made their feelings my responsibility? My burden to carry?

Giving myself another moment to breathe deeply and prepare, I shook out my hands, straightened my spine, and opened the door. But I couldn't look at him. Not yet.

Stalling, I paced to the pile of mending and pretended to sort through the costumes. "What's up?"

I heard the door close, then, "Are you okay?"

"I'm fine." I turned to give him a tight smile, not allowing myself to really look at his handsome face. He'd been so cute earlier, I wanted to remember him like that. "How are you?"

He drifted closer. "Do you . . . Are you okay? Did Levit hurt you?"

"No." My shoulders bunched as I braced myself for what would undoubtedly come next.

Isaac nodded. "I was worried," he said. Then he huffed a laugh heavily seasoned with relief. "Really worried."

I blinked. Then I stared at him openly. "You were worried? Why?"

"Levit Traveston is a dangerous person. Extremely violent. I—" Isaac pressed his lips together in a frown, paused, then added, "I hope you don't mind, I watched on the video monitors. I wanted to make sure you were safe."

He didn't look mad. He looked honestly relieved. "I was fine. He's never touched me."

"I know it's part of your job—or it was—and if it had been anyone else, I wouldn't have watched."

"Oookay . . ." What was happening here? Was he . . . jealous? Or . . . *What is happening?*

Isaac gathered a deep breath and nodded, his eyes flicking down then up in another inspection. "As long as you're okay."

"I'm fine." Where were his demands?

"Then . . . I'll let you go." Isaac gave me a tight smile, turned, and grabbed the door handle.

On instinct, I stumbled two steps forward, reached out, and grabbed his shirt, stopping him before he opened the door. "Wait."

He looked down at me over his shoulder, his forehead wrinkling, again with concern. But not jealousy. And definitely not arousal.

"Are you . . . ?" I didn't finish the question because I wasn't certain what I wanted to ask.

Isaac turned completely, which meant I had to let go of his shirt. He caught my hand before it could fall and held it gently in his. "What is it? Did something happen?"

"No. It's just—" Again, I didn't continue. I had no idea what to say. So, I huffed. "Isaac."

One of his eyebrows quirked at the sound of his name and the side of his mouth curved up. "Hannah?"

I knew what I wanted to ask. *Why aren't you jealous? Or trying to get me to reenact the striptease I gave tonight?* But those weren't the right questions, not really.

So, I blurted the right one, "Do you actually like me?"

"Yes," he responded immediately, taking no time to think about my question.

I frowned, frustrated. He didn't make any sense. Pulling my hand from his, I crossed my arms, feeling like I needed the extra layer of protection. "Well, if you like me, then why are you okay with me stripping for someone else?"

He didn't frown, but two lines appeared between his eyebrows. "Uh . . . isn't it your job?"

I flinched back, feeling oddly let down, my chest hot and tight.

Now he did frown. "What are you really asking me, Hannah? Do I want you stripping for Levit Traveston? No. I don't. He's mean as fuck and dangerous. Your safety is important."

I lifted a hand and pointed in the general direction of the champagne room. "But what if it wasn't Tavvy? What if it was—what if it was Louis?"

His eyes narrowed into slits and his voice deepened to a near growl. "Are you planning to—"

"I'm not planning anything. And I'm retired anyway, except for Tavvy since I promised to help with the investigation. I'm just saying, you asked me on a date earlier. What if we run into one of my former clients? Or if we were dating and I wasn't retired, if I was still dancing for money, would you be okay with it?"

Isaac stared at me. Not a glare, a stare. And I could see he was thinking about it, considering the question, giving it real thought.

Suddenly, I wished I hadn't asked. In reality, there existed no right answer to this question for me. Since my dancing for other guys clearly didn't turn him on, I could cross that concern off my list. *Thank goodness.*

However, if he was okay with it, I'd feel sick, like I didn't matter to him. If he wasn't okay with it, I'd feel like he didn't trust me and made his feelings my problem. I didn't know how the non-single dancers did this. My co-workers had relationships but they never talked about the good, stable ones, only complained about the bad ones.

Now it was too late. I could see by his expression he had an answer ready.

If I could've done so gracefully, I would've covered my ears and sang "Old MacDonald Had a Farm" to drown him out. Instead, I could only brace myself.

Here we go. This is the day my crush on Isaac Sylvester ends, once and for all. I'M SO SAD!

"I suspect you and I are very similar," he said, looking uncomfortable. Isaac paused and cleared his throat, then went on, "And so, I would likely feel exactly the same as you would feel if dancing here—stripping for other women—was my occupation or I ran into a client outside of work while we were on a date." Isaac's tone was free of judgment, but not of emotion. How he managed to sound both reasonable and passionate at the same time, I had no idea. But he did.

I watched him silently, once more at a loss.

His chest rose and fell with an expansive breath. "I wasn't going to tell you this, burden you with it, but you asked." My longtime crush took a step forward, entering my space but not touching me. "When I said at the cabin I wanted to court you, I meant it sincerely. And when I said I liked you, that was an understatement. We have a great deal to discuss, about the future—hopefully our future—what's possible, what you want, what I can offer . . ." Isaac's eyes strayed from mine, slowly moved over my face, down to my lips, chin, cheeks, hair, like he was taking his time and documenting my features, as though it might be his last chance to do so. "You're very capable, hardworking. You're smart. Talented. Compassionate. Honest. Trustworthy. And if you felt like these talents were best put to use by being an exotic dancer, if that's what made you happy, if it gave you fulfillment and joy, then I'd be happy because you're happy. Or, to be perfectly honest, I would do my best to be happy for you. I spent a good chunk of my life trying to be something I wasn't for my parents. I wouldn't ask someone to do that for me."

Isaac's gaze finally returned to mine, the set of his mouth grim. "I'd likely wrestle with jealousy now and then. The idea of you touching other guys doesn't appeal to me. It would certainly help, though, knowing I'm your stand-in, and every time you touched someone you were thinking of and picturing me instead."

My eyes stung and my vision had grown blurry. Only capable of gaping at this man, I blinked and felt a tear roll down my cheek.

His attention dipped to follow the tear and his hand lifted to my cheek. Catching it with his thumb, he swiped it away.

"I'm sorry if I'm the reason you're crying," he said gruffly, his frown looking both repentant and severe. He moved restlessly, his feet shuffling, his gaze searching mine. Eventually, he blurted, "Damnit, Hannah. Would it be okay if—may I hug you?"

I nodded, stepping forward and pressing myself against his warm, hard wall of a chest, more tears falling, my chin wobbling like an old wooden wheelbarrow.

And as Isaac held me tightly, smoothing his hands up and down my back and arms at intervals, I had two thoughts in my brain.

First, today would not be the day my crush on Isaac Sylvester ended, once and for all.

Second, how could someone be so sweet and perfect?

Chapter Twenty

ISAAC

"Well, don't un-weird yourself on my account. I like you weird."

— Jethro Winston, *Grin and Beard It* by Penny Reid

"Did you read the transcript?" Danforth sounded tired. "And why aren't you at the safe house?"

"I read the transcript early this morning." I slipped outside the Donner family cabin as quietly as possible, not wanting to wake Hannah. "Out of concern for our contact's safety, and since I don't have approval to take them to the safe house and it's not an emergency situation, I brought them to an alternate location. They're still asleep."

Hannah had become "our/the contact," "they," and "them." I wouldn't use her name or any other identifying details moving forward with Danforth during our phone conversations, just to be safe.

Hannah had allowed me to take her to the lodge after our conversation last night. I'd used the excuses of wanting to be near her, wanting her to get a good night's sleep, and wanting to spend time with her in the morning. All true, but none were the primary reason I wanted her to spend the night somewhere other than the Pink Pony. Traveston had showed up two days in a row after being gone for weeks, a huge deviation in behavior, far outside his normal routine. Extra caution—regarding both Hannah's safety and the investigation—was justified.

"How much did you tell the contact?"

"Nothing. I didn't have anything concrete to tell them last night other than my suspicions, not until I checked the transcript." Hannah had seemed drained after our conversation in her office, I saw no benefit in worrying her with unfounded suspicions. "Now that I've read the contents, I plan to tell them everything when they wake up."

After work, I'd driven her to the lodge, walked her to my family's cabin, and left her at the door, telling her to relax, make herself at home, and call or text me if she needed anything. Her messages and calls were being monitored by the local office's monitoring team. If I didn't see them right away for any reason, someone from monitoring would see them immediately and send help.

I heard Danforth sigh. "Do you think they'll still assist with the investigation?"

"I don't know. I guess we'll see." The sun hadn't yet made its debut but the forest had already come alive. Two wood thrushes whistled their bickering birdsong back and forth, a cranky morning conversation. I wondered if they hadn't gotten much sleep either.

The first thing I did last night after leaving Hannah was call Danforth from the car and record my nightly voicemail detailing my concerns. The second thing I did was drive to the safe house, log in to the regional office's secure system, and check the transcript from Hannah's bugged cell phone.

Levit Traveston had been tipped off. Somehow, he knew we were aware of the shipment this Friday, the time, the date, and he'd used Hannah's cell to order a change in ship, port, and fraudulent manifest records. This switch had been the reason for his unexpected visit to the Pony.

The good news: I had more time in Green Valley working undercover at the Pink Pony, and Traveston hadn't identified Hannah's phone as the source of our intel. But overall, this was extremely bad news.

"Epstein must have a plant at the regional office." Levit Traveston's code name was Epstein. For obvious reasons. "Nothing has been sent up the food chain. I'd planned to send everything today. Either that or Epstein has access to our system." Danforth sighed again. "What a fucking mess."

"I don't think so, I don't think Epstein has access to the system. It's a recent upgrade, too new." Walking a few feet down the forest path, I found the tree I used to climb most often in my childhood and leaned my back against it. "And if Epstein's organization had a back door into the system rather than a person at the office, they'd have access to raw intel and would've known right away where the transcript came from. Our contact can barely hear anything. On-site surveillance picks up nothing of what Epstein says. Only the device is a plausible source." In this context, *device* referred to Hannah's cell and *on-site surveillance* referred to the cameras and microphones in the champagne room.

"Just to be safe, I've pulled down the latest evidence and wiped it from our logs this morning. Only you, me, and the head of monitoring know of its existence. I also modified the other one and changed it into a summary rather than a transcript. Just in case Epstein's contact accesses it, it'll look like a confidential contact statement rather than a transcript of a recorded conversation."

I nodded, pleased she'd started masking the evidence without requiring me to ask. However, even with the masking measures Danforth had taken and our adopting extra security measures during check-ins—like the use of code names—eventually Traveston's insider would figure out where our intel had originated, whose phone we'd tapped. That is, if we didn't find the insider first.

"What will you do?" I stepped away from the tree after a big droplet of water from the leaves above fell on my face.

"What can I do? I have to keep acting like the job is a go, prepare the reports, prep the team, pretend like nothing has changed until we set a trap, find the leak," she growled. "We'll have to go through the motions and raid a site we know is clean. You might be stuck there for months. I don't have time for this."

Again, I was pleased Danforth had decided to take this approach.

The priority now was not letting it slip that we knew Traveston's plans had changed. Doing so would not just put Hannah under suspicion instantly, it would also undermine the entire investigation. Hannah's phone remained the only source of dependable intel, more reliable, more cost-effective, and safer than placing someone undercover with Traveston's organization.

Secondarily, we needed to catch his insider and root them out before they could identify Hannah or damage the investigation further.

"Stay put for now. And you have my approval to take our contact to the safe house should, in your estimation, the situation justify it. But let me be clear, this contact is still not a witness. When this case wraps, your protection of them ends. Got it?"

I glanced up at the sparse canopy above me, whatever remained of the autumn leaves after the early frost last week. Yellow mixed with gray in the sky as the sun's first rays peeked over the mountain to our east. The bickering birdsong surrounding me grew louder.

Danforth must've picked up on something, either during our conversation today or in my nightly voicemails, a shift in my relationship with Hannah. The senior agent was overworked but remained sharp.

"Marty?" Danforth prompted. Marty was my code name for this job. Technically, it was Marty McFly. Danforth had picked it. As a fan of 1980s films, she thought it was hilarious. I knew she was using it now instead of my real name because the regional office had been compromised and she didn't want to take any chances. "Do you understand, McFly?"

Gritting my teeth, I glared at the black oak, beech, and dogwood tree trunks directly in front of me. Maybe she was using the code name to be safe, but obviously she was also using it to call me stupid.

In theory, Hannah and I now had more time, the investigation wasn't wrapping in five days. Yet, the matter of our relationship—defining it to our mutual agreement and satisfaction—felt urgent. I would have months of paid time off coming my way after this case wrapped. How I spent it was none of Danforth's business.

"I understand what you're saying," I said, the maximum I would concede.

"That doesn't sound like an agreement."

Officially, on the record, I understood and would yield to what Danforth dictated. Hannah didn't qualify as a witness and therefore wasn't eligible for protection after the investigation wrapped. Off the record, no matter what it took, I'd keep Hannah out of harm's way.

"Don't tell me—" Danforth snapped, cut herself off, then continued quietly, "Listen, you're just about to retire from this field. Your record is exemplary. I know about your plans. Don't bring baggage into your new life that opens you up to exposure."

I kicked at the mushy ground, grinding an orange-colored leaf into the mud. "If we made it official, my protections extend."

By *making it official*, I meant marriage. And by *protections extend*, I meant my lifelong protections as an undercover federal agent, my access to unlimited new identities and restarts. If my identity were ever compromised, my spouse, kids if applicable, and me would all be relocated, given new backgrounds.

At the end of this assignment, and if Hannah wished to, she could adopt a new identity and join me.

The huff Danforth heaved sounded equally cartoonish and loud, so loud I held the cell away from my ear until her voice could be heard. "You're an idiot, McFly. Falling for a s—" Again, she cut herself off.

My fingers holding the phone were cold. I shifted the device to my other hand.

After reading the transcript at the safe house in the middle of the night I'd been wired and restless. I'd grabbed an overnight bag, drove back to the lodge, slipped in the cabin, and lay on the couch in my clothes. I hadn't been able to sleep at all at first, not until I resolved to marry Hannah—if she agreed, if she wanted—should her safety become compromised. It was as though my brain needed a way out for her should the worst-case scenario occur.

Being married didn't mean we had to live together or be together. It might tie our futures together for a time, but only until the present danger passed. It would, however, necessitate that she leave Green Valley with me.

Danforth ended the call after promising to touch base later in the day after I briefed Hannah. I needed to determine what she—as our key confidential contact—wanted to do about the emerging situation, how much involvement she felt comfortable with moving forward. When I walked back inside and down the hall to check on her, Hannah still slept soundly. That was good. After today, she might not rest well for a while.

Since I knew sleep was impossible, I brushed my teeth and took the forest path to the bakery, not bothering to change out of my dirty clothes. The sound of the shower might wake her up.

Issues with Levit Traveston relating to Hannah's immediate safety had eclipsed my personal concerns. But on my short walk, now that I'd touched base with Danforth, a different kind of agitation set up camp in my chest.

During the drive to the lodge, Hannah had been mostly quiet and I didn't push. She reconfirmed our Tuesday date, saying she looked forward to seeing me this morning for her daily muffin and coffee. But she'd seemed sad, or drained. Low energy.

While I stood in line outside and eventually inside the bakery, I replayed our conversation several times from the night before, about us dating and whether I'd be jealous if she was still a dancer. She'd said very little during the discussion, but she'd asked a lot of questions. I couldn't figure out what I'd said to make her cry. She'd let me hug her and she'd hugged me back; she'd been easily talked into sleeping at the cabin; but I couldn't shake the sense I'd overlooked a critical piece of evidence that would unlock this mystery.

"Hi, Isaac! We missed you yesterday!"

Shaking off my internal musings, I found Joy the Donner Bakery worker flashing the same expectant smile she'd been giving me every day since I'd started buying Hannah her morning muffins and coffee.

"Morning muffin and French roast," I muttered, lifting my chin toward the bakery display.

Joy didn't make any move to grab either the muffin or the coffee. "Are you sure that's what you want today?"

I considered the question, thinking back to yesterday and my impulse to buy Hannah all the morning muffins instead of just one. Hard to know whether this type of gesture would be met with appreciation or awkwardness. I wanted to buy her *all* the muffins, but would she want all the muffins from *me*?

Sometimes giving people things caused them problems. Good intentions or not, I didn't want to be the source of problems for Hannah. What I wanted was to contribute to her self-directed solutions.

"That'll be it." I pulled out my wallet.

"Are you *sure?*" Joy leaned a little over the counter, her smile growing stiff. "Are you sure there's not, I don't know, maybe something you're supposed to do while you're here?"

I stared at the dark-haired woman, waiting for her to spell out whatever cryptic hints she'd tried to drop.

Her smile fell and she frowned, the expression looking strange on her face, like maybe frowning only happened once in a blue moon. Then she took a few quick steps away and she waved me over toward the register. But instead of asking Hazel to ring me up when I got there, Joy walked around the counter and toward the kitchen, waving at me again to follow.

Glancing at the people in line behind me, I found no help. They were all absorbed in studying the bakery case, fretting over which items to order. Never mind the fact that they'd had nearly a half hour to decide while we'd been standing outdoors in line.

"Well?" Joy called, sounding impatient. "Are you coming?"

Returning the wallet to my back pocket, I debated what to do. The bakery was Jennifer's domain. Did she want to see me today? Had she discovered I came to the bakery every morning and had she asked Joy to bring me to the back? I swallowed past something hard, wiping my hands on the legs of my jeans, and decided to follow the short woman to the kitchen.

If Jennifer wanted to see me, obviously I'd jump at the chance. If she wanted to talk, I'd listen. If she had questions, I'd answer them. But I'd take my lead from her.

I walked to Joy, then followed behind as we stepped into the bakery kitchen. The place was empty of people but all taped up with plastic. It covered every surface—horizontal and vertical—except the wooden countertops.

Given the state of the place, clearly prepped for construction of some kind, Jennifer was likely alone here, and that was good. It would give us time to talk. My hands had been tied when my father kicked me out, I couldn't contact her without risking her safety. When I'd been here undercover, the only way to help her was to keep my distance. Moving forward, I couldn't live in Green Valley and see her often, but maybe I could figure out a way to bend the rules.

Perhaps she could come see me wherever I settled, or we could meet elsewhere. Eventually. If she wanted.

Joy opened a door at the back of the kitchen and I braced myself, wondering how I'd explain everything if she asked. My hands were still tied in a sense, and nothing good would come to her from knowing me now, but selfishly I still wanted to see her, hear how she was doing, but only if she wished to—

"I've been expecting you." Cletus Winston spun slowly in the office chair, facing me, and stroking a gray-and-orange palm sander like it was a cat. "Hello, Isaac."

I slid a side-eye to Joy but was too slow. The woman had already scurried back to the shop.

"What do you want, Cletus?"

"It's not what I want, it's what I need, Isaac."

"What's that?"

He stood, walked the three steps to me, and placed the sander in my arms. "I need you to sand these countertops. Come on."

Cletus walked past me into the kitchen. I lifted my eyes to the ceiling. This wasn't happening. I didn't have time for this. I needed to grab that muffin and coffee and make it back before Hannah woke up.

Following him out, I shifted the sander to one hand. "I don't have time to help you, Cletus."

"Sure you do. And you're not helping *me*. You're helping yourself. Where your heart is, your time is spent."

"I have to get back—"

"To Hannah Townsen?" It didn't sound like a guess. Lifting an eyebrow at my expression, he smiled. "No, you don't. Jenn is taking good care of Hannah this morning, no need to fret."

"Jennifer—Jenn is—"

"That's right. Since you didn't introduce your sister to your paramour—and I mean paramour in the secret sense, not in the salacious one—Jenn felt called to intercede."

"Are you telling me this was my sister's idea?"

Cletus, still smiling, turned, picked up a ventilator mask and goggles from the bare counters, then pushed them at me, necessitating that I juggle the three items in my arms. "Since Jenn is your only relative not dead or on the lam, I feel confident you'll fulfill your familial obligations to her, your worthy ancestors, and this here family business your *sister* has been managing all on her own while you've been off galivanting with criminals."

"I haven't been—"

"No thanks necessary. That frosty look in your eyes belies the truth. You're utterly unable to comprehend the glorious opportunity you've been given. Please, please"—he held up his hands—"save your thank-yous and accolades. You'll need your strength. This is a big kitchen."

I grit my teeth.

Strolling around me once more, Cletus made a show of taping up the door leading to the main bakery shop, rambling as he did so. "I'll leave the back door open to the outside and turn on the fan for ventilation after I head out, but wear the mask. You can't grovel properly later if you're coughing. There's some work coveralls in your size in the office if you're particular about those clothes. When you're finished, feel free to join Jenn, Hannah, and me at the Winston homestead." Turning, he made a show of looking me over, and then sniffed indignantly. "The three of us have been invited to brunch with the Diaz-Winstons. The soiree ends at three. I suggest a shower and a shave before you arrive."

Chapter Twenty-One

ISAAC

"But time, as they say, heals all wounds that aren't affected by sepsis or gangrene."

— Simone Payton, *Grin and Beard It* by Penny Reid

Counters sanded, wiped down, and oiled twice; floor mopped and re-mopped; plastic removed from all surfaces, I'd left the bakery kitchen around 2:00 PM, rushed through a shower, and hadn't bothered shaving.

But now, dressed in a suit Cletus Winston had demanded I wear and freshly shaved under his supervision, I followed him out the kitchen door of the Winston house and on to the back porch. Most people inside the house were their own bosses, which was probably why they could gather and have a fancy brunch on a Monday, treating any day of the week like it was a holiday.

The screen door slapped shut behind us, pulling the attention of the women sitting in rockers and Adirondack chairs around a raised metal fire pit.

One of those women was Hannah. Another of the women was Jennifer. Both were looking right at me. My sister didn't seem surprised to see me and I noticed the Winston family's only daughter sat to her left, eying me with dislike and suspicion.

I sighed silently.

"My advice is as follows." Cletus, angling himself closer to my ear and keeping his voice low, gripped my upper arm. "Apologize first. Let her have her say. Apologize again. Let her keep talking and listen to her. Apologize for whatever she says you did wrong, without equivocation, and mean it. Stick to the facts, don't make excuses. Let her talk, listen, apologize. Let her talk, listen, apologize. You see the pattern? But don't, for the love of God, interrupt her."

The women were engaging in their own quiet conversation, stealing glances at us as they stood and folded the blankets they'd been using around the fire. I watched as they each took turns giving Jennifer's hand a squeeze, seeming to leave her with encouraging words.

Cletus stepped away and opened the kitchen door, presumably to hold it for the ladies as they filed past. I moved to the side so I didn't block their path, acutely aware of the dirty looks and side-eyes sent my way.

The only two exceptions to this were Simone Payton—an FBI forensic scientist who'd helped me break open the Iron Wraiths case, now married to the youngest Winston if I wasn't mistaken—and Hannah. Simone gave me a tight smile that felt like quiet sympathy. From her look I surmised none of these women sending me stink eyes knew I was an undercover agent, which meant they all still believed I'd been an actual Iron Wraiths recruit.

Hannah didn't simply pass me by. She broke off and grabbed my fingers, giving them a squeeze. "Hey," she said, smiling up at me. "You made it."

"Are you okay?"

Hannah gave me a funny look. "I'm perfectly well, thank you. And how are you?"

She seemed well and I allowed myself to take another look at her. I didn't know if her clothes were borrowed, too, but the pink dress ending mid-calf fit her like a glove and the shawl—a darker shade of pink than the dress—was the same color as her lips. The white heels made her legs look fantastic.

"Isaac?"

I returned my eyes to hers. "Sorry."

"Why are you sorry?"

"You look very pretty."

She grinned. "Don't apologize for that. You do, too. Where'd you get this suit?"

"Cletus made me wear it."

Giving my hands one more squeeze, she let me go with a wink. "I guess I should send him a thank-you note."

I probably shouldn't have, but my attention dropped to the dip of her waist, the flare of her hips, and the curve of her ass as she walked away and inside the house, my stomach slowly sinking as soon as she disappeared from view.

Just seeing her had improved my mood and settled my nerves. How strange was that? To be buoyed by another person.

Cletus stepped into my line of vision, narrowed his eyes meaningfully, then turned and marched into the house, closing the door and leaving me and Jennifer alone on the porch. Gathering courage with an inhale, I lifted just my eyes. My sister sat perched on the rail of the porch, her arms crossed, and stared at me with features free of expectations.

Well, that wasn't exactly true. She stared at me like she expected me to disappoint her.

Not sure what to do with my hands, I pushed them into the pants pockets of my borrowed suit. "How are you?" I asked ineptly, but I had to start somewhere.

"Peachy. You?" she snapped, the words sharp as a whip.

All the scripts I'd practiced in my head, all the words I'd planned to say and practiced over and over abandoned me. Only Cletus's advice remained. *Apologize first.*

This situation was desperate enough to take Cletus Winston's advice.

"I'm sorry."

"What are you sorry for?"

Too many things.

I walked toward her. "Leaving."

"And?" She angled her chin, looking unimpressed.

"Treating you poorly when I came back to town." I stopped four feet from where she sat, still rigidly glaring at me.

"I think you mean, treating me worse than a stranger when you came back to town."

The blow landed and I swallowed my wince. "Yes. I'm sorry."

"Are you? Then why'd you do it?" She sounded mad and she had every right to be, but the show of anger surprised me. We weren't allowed to be mad growing up, Jennifer most of all. If she got mad, if she gave any hint of back talk or contradicting my father, she'd be punished. "Why'd you leave *the day* after your eighteenth birthday, Isaac? Why didn't you tell me your plans? Why'd you drop off the face of the earth? Did I matter so little to you? And, if so, why are you here now? What changed? Why do I matter now?"

Per Cletus's advice, I waited until she paused, waited until I felt certain she'd finished so as not to interrupt.

I tried to remember all her questions, in order, so I could answer them according to her preference. "I am sorry," I began haltingly, in case she had more to say, not wanting to talk over her if she did. "I didn't know I'd be leaving that day, I had no plans to do so."

Jennifer's head tilted an inch to the right, her glare losing some of its sharpness in favor of confusion. "How could you not know you were leaving?"

"Our father woke me up early and told me to get in the car, he didn't say where we were going. He drove me to Nashville and dropped me off downtown with my birth certificate, social security card, the clothes on my back, and that's it. He told me not to return and to not contact you or Momma unless I wanted my bad luck to transfer to y'all, that he'd make you suffer for my disobedience."

He'd likened his leaving me in Nashville the day after my birthday to God pushing Jonah in the Old Testament out of his comfort zone and into the belly of the whale for disobedience. My father used religion and religious stories only to justify his hateful treatment of us and call it love, never as a guide for living his own life.

I stone you because the Bible tells me to. I turn my back on you because the Bible tells me to. I am intolerant of you because the Bible tells me I must take a stand. I demand honor and obedience because the Bible says you owe it to me. But loving God? Taking care of the poor and needy? The Good Samaritan and the Woes of the Pharisees? He never brought up those passages.

He quoted a book he'd never read, never studied, just pulled out the parts that justified his point of view and memorized them, pulling out passages like drawing a sword to cut and shred our confidence and dignity. The man was a master at twisting reality, picking and choosing what parts of religion suited him and what parts to ignore. He could've written a dissertation on the subject.

Jennifer slowly stood from the railing as I told her more of the story—again, sticking to Cletus's advice and relating just the facts: How I'd slept on the streets for a few weeks, how I'd eventually stumbled across an army recruitment office, how I'd used the public library to get my GED so I could enlist. How the army had saved my life. How I'd attended virtual college and earned my AA while overseas.

I also told her how, once I had access to a proper amount of food, I'd grown five inches. She listened patiently and pressed her hand over her heart and rubbed as though the spot hurt. But when I told her how the GI Bill had paid for my bachelor's degree, her small smile was immediate.

"You graduated with a bachelor's degree?"

"I did."

"That's so wonderful. Where? What was your major? Literature? Did you like it? Did you make friends? I bet you did a lot of reading."

Her questions made my heart ache. She wanted to know about me. I couldn't help but think I didn't deserve these questions. I wasn't here to rekindle our sibling bond, I was here to apologize and say goodbye.

Breathing through the tightness, I said again, "I'm sorry. I'm so sorry."

"Isaac—"

"You've always mattered to me, Jennifer. I know my actions don't appear to back up that claim, but you do matter to me. When I left—when he left me in Nashville—I was small and weak. And not just my size. I was a small and weak person. I felt powerless. And I believed him, that he would hurt you both, if I tried to reach out. I was so scared of him."

Jennifer gave me a short, jerky nod, not looking mad anymore. She just looked sad. "I know. I was scared of him, too. And he was worse to you, harder on you than he was on me."

"He was hard on you, too," I countered.

He'd been horrible to her, belittling her as being stupid, praising her if she lost weight, even though, in retrospect, now that I was an adult, I knew we'd both been underweight our whole childhood. He'd praise her for her looks in one breath then tell her in the next that girls were responsible for the lust they inspired in others. He pushed my momma to enter her into beauty pageants then berated her for being talentless and foolish.

She couldn't win with him. Maybe an insignificant skirmish, but never a battle and never the war. None of us could ever win with him. But that's how evil, manipulative people force you to keep playing their game.

Wanting to finish answering her first set of questions, I said, "The DEA recruited me out of college and I took the transfer from the DEA to the FBI's undercover division so I could have the assignment with the Iron Wraiths here, in Green Valley." Cletus already knew I was undercover, and had for a few years now. Because of this, I assumed Jennifer knew as well. "I wanted to be close by, keep an eye on you, until I could figure out how to help you get out from under his control."

"But you picked an assignment that made it impossible for us to know each other!" She charged forward a step, her features twisting with misery. "Pledging yourself to a gang like that meant you wouldn't be able to talk to me or Momma without putting us in danger. So, you cut us out. How, exactly, was that helpful?"

I didn't point out that my previous assignment wasn't the only obstacle standing in the way of our relationship. The complex nature of my chosen career path also created a barrier. I planned to retire from this field soon, and adopt a new identity. But until I did and some significant time passed, contact between us would only place us both in danger.

"Ensuring your freedom from our father seemed like it was more important than anything else at the time."

"Even more important than having a relationship with me?" Her voice wavered. "How can you say that?"

"Yes, because I knew what he was like. And I knew I needed someone powerful on my side in order to convince him to leave you be."

Even after pulling myself out of the situation in Nashville, with five more inches and muscle on my frame, tours overseas in the army, a college degree, a savings account, and a job, approaching my father on my own still scared me. By myself, I would not be enough to intimidate him. What could I do on my own? Nothing. What could he do to me? Everything.

"He still had you and Momma under his thumb when I returned and he didn't know I was undercover. He thought I was patching in for real, and that's what I wanted him to think."

"Why?"

"I knew I could use my association with the club to frighten him, to get him to leave y'all alone." As though pulled, my feet shuffled forward. I wished she'd let me hug her. She'd always liked hugs from me and my momma growing up, used to come in my room and cuddle in the middle of the night when she was a toddler. The only time I'd talked back to my father or had been willful with him had been to protect her.

"I don't understand. Why didn't you—why not just tell Momma?" Jennifer crossed her arms again, but her tone was curious, not angry. "Why go undercover and join a dangerous organization?"

"He was never going to let y'all go otherwise."

She sighed, visibly confused. "I was already in my twenties when you came back. I could've left with you—"

"You couldn't have left and you know it. You were still fully under his control, at his mercy." I let my voice raise, just a little, because she wasn't being honest about how things were, how controlling he'd been and how imprisoned she'd been.

Jennifer's lips parted and her eyes moved between mine. I saw acceptance there, a shadow of memory. "You're right," she said quietly. "He controlled me, even though I was an adult, I had no freedom, didn't think I had a way out and I was desperate, acting irrationally. But that year, things started to change. And Momma found out about his cheating and left him. Things changed."

It was my turn to sigh. "If you think he let you go of his own volition, then you are mistaken."

"What does that mean?"

Leaning against the porch post, I shoved my fingers through my hair, suddenly feeling tired. "There were two guys at the club I . . . befriended, as my alter ego. Drill and Burro. Burro was the information guy and helped me document our father's misdeeds. Drill was a big guy, one of the enforcers. He's now out of the life, married a nice lady. I asked him, back then, to secretly help me persuade our father to walk away from you and Momma."

"You—you—" She gave her head a shake. "When was this?"

"Not long after I saw you at the Piggly Wiggly with Cletus Winston and he almost broke my nose." Crossing to the rail where she'd been earlier, I sat and looked out over the cold field behind the Winston homestead.

I had no regrets, but I didn't want to tell Jennifer how I'd cornered our father after he stepped out of his mistress's house, how I'd let my anger and resentment get the better of me. How I'd been the bully that time and he'd been the one who was accident-prone, accidentally stepped in front of a moving car, accidentally walked into my fist, and accidentally got hit with a baseball bat. I didn't regret it, but I wasn't proud of it. The memory still tasted sour.

"What happened?" she prompted at my prolonged silence.

Noting that little green remained in the wildflower field, probably due to the early frost, I looked at my sister. "Let's just say, we made a deal. He promised to divorce Momma and get off your back, stop controlling every part of your life."

My father had already been thrown out by my mother, his cheating exposed just the day prior to my visit, incidentally. But, knowing him, he had no plans to let my mother or her money go. Or my sister, since Jennifer had become the face of the bakery. During my visit to my father with Drill, he'd agreed to move out peacefully, leave Jennifer alone, and divorce my mother. For my part of the deal, I promised not to break his legs.

"I see." Close now, she met my gaze and openly studied me. "Then did you ever tell Momma the truth? Before she went on the run with that man, did she know about how Daddy left you in Nashville with nothing? Did she know it wasn't your fault?"

I shook my head slowly. "No."

"Why not? Why let her believe you were the one who abandoned us?"

"It's fine if she thinks that about me."

"Isaac! That broke her heart."

"No, Jennifer. Listen. You know how she is, how she was before she left. She felt guilty for staying with him for so long. Do you think her knowing would've done any good? She would've blamed herself for what happened, more guilt. That woman thinks she's strong, but she's wrong. She's not just soft, she's fragile. She *allowed* him to talk to us that way, do those things to us, and told us we were called to be obedient, to honor him as the head of the household."

"She was doing the best she could," Jennifer said weakly, her words lacking conviction.

I smiled, sad for my sister if she'd ever considered our mother reliable or capable. "Exactly. She couldn't even protect herself, didn't understand she needed to. How could she protect us? She drank the Kool-Aid for over twenty years, subscribed to the newsletter, bought the merch and wore the T-shirt until he *let* her leave him. And make no mistake, he let her. He never would've allowed it if I hadn't stepped in with Drill and made him do it."

Folks around town had gossiped about our parents' divorce, even on the fringes of society it was impossible to escape the rumors. They'd said it was nasty and contentious. I didn't think so. Our father put up a fuss about money, about bank accounts, and that's it. When I thought about what he might've done instead, it sent a shiver down my spine.

I truly believed Kip Sylvester would never have agreed to the divorce at all if Drill and I hadn't threatened him, using the promise of the Iron Wraiths' retaliation as a weapon. He would've held on to her and Jenn until the end.

It had been a bluff, of course. I couldn't use the resources of the Wraiths without claiming my sister and my mother as family. Drill, not a bad guy in the grand scheme of things, had kept our little adventure to himself, kept my secret safe from the brotherhood.

Staring at the floor of the porch, Jennifer wrapped her arms around her middle, her shoulders curling forward. I wanted to reach out and hug her. She was only two feet away. But she hadn't accepted my apology yet.

I shifted closer. "I know . . . I know I could've done things differently. I could've—I could've told you about my plans. But—"

"But you didn't trust me."

I breathed through another tight ache. "I did trust you."

"No. I was still influenced by wanting to honor my mother and father, wanting to be a good, obedient daughter." She lifted her sad eyes to mine. "It's taken me a long time to shred that skin, to ignore those impulses. Or rather, to reinterpret and change how I approach those ideas."

My instinct at this moment was to tell her how proud of her I was, but I didn't have the right.

Jennifer pressed her lips together, then sniffled. "I have one more question."

"Yes?"

"When Daddy was killed, did you think I had something to do with it?"

That had not been the question I'd been expecting. Even so, I answered honestly, "I didn't know."

"You thought I killed him?"

"I wouldn't have blamed you if you had."

She lifted her chin. "Because of the will reading? You thought I killed him for money?"

"No. But I was surprised you didn't appear to realize he'd named you as his sole heir. I thought, I hoped, you were still being decent toward him because of the money."

"You wanted me to be greedy? I had no idea about the will!"

"I know that now. And yes, I'd rather you be greedy than the alternative."

"What's the alternative, Isaac? That I'm not a terrible person?" she scoffed.

"The alternative is that you were being decent because you were still holding out hope that he'd change, Jennifer," I spelled it out, but quietly, gently.

She blinked and two tears trailed down her cheeks.

My eyes stung in response. I ignored it. "You didn't shut that door fully and cut him out of your life, despite everything he did to you and Momma and me, because you hoped he'd repent one day and see the light, that he'd be better for us. Right? You still hoped."

She didn't say anything, just looked at me with glassy eyes and a wobbly chin.

My chest ached all over again. "Jennifer. He was beyond saving. Some folks don't deserve your hopes, or your prayers."

"Funny." She sniffled. "That's what folks say about you, too."

Her verbal arrow found its mark and I grimaced. The sad part was, I'd be lying if I said I disagreed with those folks.

I should've found a better way; one that allowed us to know each other, see each other; one that didn't hurt her so badly and for such a long time. I had no defense to offer other than I'd been desperate and shortsighted when I first arrived in town. When I left, after the assignment ended, I didn't think I deserved a place in her life. I still didn't believe I deserved a place.

But none of that mattered now. The die had been cast, the future decided by the choices I'd made. I only had a few months left as Isaac Sylvester. She seemed happy here with the Winstons. Embraced, valued, protected but not coddled. Beau, Jethro, Billy, Roscoe—they were her big brothers, not me. They were her family now. If this family made her happy, what more could I ask for?

I wanted this short visit of ours to bring her a measure of peace, but not give her hope that I would be moving back to Green Valley.

Sucking in a deep breath, I pulled courage into my lungs. "On that note." I waited until she met my gaze before continuing. "My current assignment is my last as an undercover agent."

Jennifer stared at me, her mind plainly working.

Before she could make assumptions of what this might mean, I added, "When it's over, I plan to stay in town for a while, a few weeks or months. If you want to see me, please know I want to see you. Anytime. But then I'll be leaving for good and adopting a new identity."

"What does that mean? A new identity?"

"It means Isaac will be, for all intents and purposes, dead."

She reared back, blinking furiously.

I wasn't finished. "On the record, I will not be able to contact anyone who knew me under the name of Isaac Sylvester, not for a very long time, in order to keep my new identity secure and safe. And for their safety as well."

Betrayal stared back at me from her eyes. Betrayal and so much hurt. I held her gaze, forcing myself to look so I could remember this moment. It would be my punishment for not being smarter and stronger, for being too slow and thoughtless, for acting on my own, without her, for letting fear dictate my decisions. I would carry it with me and I would never forget.

"I don't understand—" she started, tore her eyes from mine and ground her jaw. "You can come back and live here. You just don't wish to."

"Jenn—"

"Listen, if this is about money, you don't need to work. When Daddy died, I took half that money and put it in an account for you. Cletus has been investing it. It's a lot. It's so much, you're set of life. Just quit your job and move back here."

Wincing at her dismissive tone, I stood from the railing. "Jenn, I can't just walk away—"

"Yes. You can. You walked away from me, why can't you walk away from a job? You could've reached out after your first assignment here was over, but you didn't."

I had no defense against this accusation. "You're right. I could've reached out after that assignment was over. We could've met in secret. I could've explained everything, asked for your forgiveness. But I didn't believe I had the right, nor did I believe—at the time—knowing me would make your life better."

"Then why can't you accept the money if it means you can stay?" she asked, her eyes flashing and pleading. "Cletus can save you from the remaining Iron Wraiths still in this area. We'll protect you. You want to work? Fine. Work at the lodge. Do whatever. Be the manager in charge of never returning my calls. Just . . . let me rescue you. Please."

I didn't know how to explain. What I did might've been just a job to her, but it wasn't just a job to me. My life, as it was now, wasn't something I wanted to be rescued from. As much as I wanted us to have a relationship, I'd saved myself without anyone's help and I was proud of the good, the difference I'd made in the world.

Maybe it wasn't her intention—I wanted to believe it wasn't her intention—but telling me to quit a job that brought me fulfillment and just accept our father's money or work a cushy job at the lodge belittled all I'd accomplished, every hour and minute of struggle I'd overcome. Did she think I had no pride? Or did she think so little of what I'd achieved?

I didn't know what to say.

In the face of my continued silence, my sister didn't cry. She didn't ask me to reconsider. She didn't rail against me or tell me to find another way. Her features grew hard and she walked away, her footsteps loud on the wooden porch. I heard her open the screen door, the back door, and then both shut in tandem, one right after the other.

Chapter Twenty-Two

HANNAH

"Seeds sown in dread never bloom because fear makes for shallow soil."

—Jeffrey James, *Totally Folked* by Penny Reid

"Are you okay?" Isaac glanced at me, speaking for the first time since we'd left the Winstons' house, shortly after talking to his sister. The whole day thus far had been very strange and now we were in his car going . . . somewhere. I hadn't asked and he hadn't volunteered.

"I'm fine." I took a moment to study him and noticed his hands were tight on the steering wheel. "Are you okay?"

He kept quiet for a beat, then said gruffly, "Not really."

My heart constricted, driving me to act without thought. In retrospect, I blamed the raw quality of his voice and the flash of vulnerability in his eyes for me instinctively reaching over and tugging his wrist, removing his hand from the wheel and threading our fingers together. It wasn't until we were holding hands that I realized how intimate the gesture now felt. Which, yes, odd, given the fact that I'd had my hand down his boxers two days ago. How backward was my life that holding his hand felt more intimate than giving him a hand job?

But it was too late to second-guess. I couldn't put his hand back on the wheel. *Just go with it!*

"Do you want to talk about it?" I dipped my head to the side, trying to see more of his face.

Again, Isaac seemed to think the question over before responding. "I think we have to."

My fingers tightened around his. "Okay. I've been told I'm a good listener. Go for it."

Isaac struggled around a swallow. "I'm afraid you'll need to participate in this conversation, and I shouldn't be driving for it."

Hmm. That sounded ominous. "Okay . . ."

"It'll take a bit to get where we're going." Isaac checked his rearview mirror for maybe the tenth time in ten minutes. "Will you tell me what happened this morning?"

"Sure." I turned in my seat to face him, bringing our joined hands to my lap. I told him about how strange the day had been, from Jenn Winston unexpectedly waking me up with the morning muffin and coffee I'd expected from Isaac, to her trying to sweet-talk me into attending a brunch at Jethro Winston's house by dangling the promise of meeting movie stars Sienna Diaz and Raquel Ezra there, and then producing a beautiful dress for the occasion, like she'd pulled a rabbit out of a hat.

I didn't have a lot of interest in meeting Ms. Diaz or Ms. Ezra—not because there's anything wrong with being a movie star, but what would be the point? Over the years, I'd spotted them both from afar around town, Sienna with her husband Jethro Winston and their kids; more recently, Raquel with Jackson James. Apparently they were dating. The ladies seemed nice, friendly enough, but I doubted we'd have anything in common.

Isaac nodded absentmindedly while I spoke. When I finished, he asked, "Why'd you agree to go with my sister to the Winstons'?"

"Well, for three reasons. First, she said she wanted to speak with you. She, uh, knew you'd been making frequent visits to the bakery without seeing or contacting her. This made her wonder if you wanted to meet, but she said doing so in normal situations, public or private, might prove troublesome for one or both of you due to your history with the Iron Wraiths. She thought no one would notice your arrival today among so many cars and visitors. She said she felt certain you would come if I was there. And, I guess, I wanted to help make that happen for y'all."

Isaac flipped on his blinker. "Thank you. I appreciate it. What were the other two reasons?"

"She said Simone Payton and Roscoe Winston would be there. We all went to high school together. It was nice to catch up. And the third reason was entirely selfish."

His eyes flickered to me then back to the road. "What's that?"

"I wanted to pick your sister's brain about social media strategies for small businesses and building a global brand."

Isaac's mouth curved up on the side I could see, his hand relaxing in mine. "I see."

"She's turned that bakery into something really special."

"Did she help you?"

"She did! She gave me some good ideas." Jennifer had been really, really nice this morning and afternoon, much kinder than I'd anticipated.

I'd been dismissive of Jennifer, growing up with her momma putting her in beauty pageants and such, and then when she'd donned the persona of the Banana Cake Queen, thinking of her like the town's self-appointed perfect princess. But I knew now a lot of that had been jealousy on my part.

Jennifer Winston had grown up in what appeared to be the perfect family, never needing to struggle to put food on the table or pay a mortgage or take care of an ailing parent. She seemed to get anything she wanted. Her momma took care of her, doted on her, bought her a flashy BMW to drive around town. She was famous and pretty and wholesome and sweet and so very, very sheltered. Basically, she had the life I wanted.

So, yeah, jealousy.

But then her parents had divorced, her family exploded, and the truth about the Sylvesters—about the daddy's cheating and stealing and horrible behavior toward his daughter and ex-wife—had spread through the gossip mill faster than wildfire.

It had taught me to never assume I knew what privileges or troubles a person faced without wearing their apron and baking their banana cakes.

"Good." Isaac pulled us onto the gravel road surrounding Bandit Lake. "I'm glad you two . . . got along."

"We did," I said, mostly to myself. Everyone had been perfectly nice to me at the Winstons' brunch. For a few moments there, I'd even forgotten that they were all respectable folks and a social divide existed between us.

But then at other times, like when Ashley—the only Winston sister—had kindly asked after my mother, it all came back.

Hank Weller had also been there with his fiancée, Charlotte Mitchell, and her four kids. He'd been playing the part of loving stepfather and caring partner. But the more I watched him, the more I realized it wasn't a part. He'd slipped into the role effortlessly. Hank had become a loving stepfather and caring partner. He'd become respectable.

Furthermore, I realized he would probably get away with it. Folks in town would let him move on from the Pony even though he was still dancing at the hen nights until we could find a permanent replacement for him. He wouldn't be forever branded by it because he was a businessman, independently wealthy, and now he was getting married, settling down with an instant family.

I was happy for my friend and mentor, but seeing him integrated into polite society, so quickly and so well, left me with that same sense of discomfort I felt whenever I spoke to my mother on the phone.

And so I'd spent a lot of the afternoon before Isaac arrived wondering what I was doing, all dressed up in gifted clothes, pretending I fit in.

Isaac finally pulled up to a two-story cabin surrounded by thick woods. The area wasn't well known to anyone but locals, difficult to navigate to and find, but I knew he didn't own this place. It must've either belonged to the government, or Isaac was borrowing it from a friend. None of the property around Bandit Lake could be sold to anyone but the federal government. The only other way to own a house here was to inherit it.

"Do you want something to drink? Eat? Tea?" Isaac asked as soon as we walked through the front door.

"Tea sounds good." I noticed he didn't remove his shoes. Following his lead, I trailed after him into building's efficiency kitchen while still wearing the white heels gifted to me by his sister.

He set to boiling water, pulling down cups, and setting a selection of teas in front of me. "Chamomile, peppermint, or Earl Grey?"

"I like my tea like I like my men," I said with a little smile, selecting the Earl Grey and pulling out a bag.

His expression had been cloudy since leaving the Winstons', but at my joke he seemed to perk up. "How's that?"

"Noble but gray." I winked at him.

His small smile was immediate, but it fell away almost as fast as it had appeared. "Here, let's sit while we wait for the water."

Isaac pulled out a chair at the small circular Formica table set in a space far too big for it and gestured for me to sit. Taking my mug and tea bag, I did. He claimed the chair across from me, not precisely wearing a frown. I got the sense he was working through something big and needed a few minutes to gather his thoughts.

Glancing around the room, I decided this place must've been government owned. No pictures hung on the wall and all the furniture—metal and particleboard instead of wood—felt sterile, with a public school or DMV sorta quality. No couch sat in the living room, no stools were at the breakfast bar. It felt bare and empty, soulless.

"Hannah."

Returning my attention to Isaac, I couldn't help but think he looked apologetic.

My stomach dropped but I hid it. "Yes?"

"There's an issue with the investigation you need to know about, a new development as of last night. I'd planned to tell you this morning, as soon as you woke up and I knew for certain why Levit came to the Pony two nights in a row."

I breathed out, feeling my body relax and realizing I'd tensed up because I worried Isaac was going to call off our courtship. And didn't that make me silly? *Priorities, Hannah.*

"Go on," I said, giving him an encouraging—and genuine—smile.

"Long story short, it seems Levit has an informant planted in our regional office. It can't be someone high up because you haven't been identified as our confidential informant, and Levit has no idea you're helping us or how we knew about the plans he discussed on Saturday. But we know he's aware we have someone helping us. He probably thinks it's someone inside his organization."

"Okay. So . . . are you saying he might find out it's me?"

"I don't know. He may never figure out you're our contact or that we've tapped your phone to gather intel. In which case you're not in danger. But if he does figure it out, you will be in a great deal of danger."

My good sense finally caught up with the topic of conversation and my brain immediately went into problem-solving mode. I had some contacts in Vegas, ladies who used to work at the Pony but had moved on to bigger venues. I could go out there and dance for a few months. It wasn't like there was anything or anyone keeping me—

"Isaac," I said and thought and brought him back into focus all in the same second. My stomach threatened to drop again because he was still watching me with a bracing expression. I spoke haltingly around a suddenly dry mouth. "Do I need to leave town? And, if so, what does that mean for us?"

"To address your first question, you don't need to leave town right now. If he knew your phone was the source of the leak in his organization, then you would need to leave town. He might find out in the future, which is why I need to ask if you're still comfortable helping with the investigation."

"I am." I nodded firmly at my own statement. "You said he is very dangerous, he hurts a lot of people. And as long as you're with me at the club, I want to help put him behind bars."

"Hannah . . ." Isaac seemed to be holding his breath, but then he breathed out, two wrinkles appearing between his eyebrows, his gaze open and searching mine. "To address your second question, nothing has changed for me. I still want to court you. I don't want to pressure you, but the logistics might've changed."

Studying him, I pondered over the word *logistics*. "Meaning?"

"I'd planned to talk to you about my future plans—as they are—during our first date tomorrow, give you some privacy after to decide whether or not you want a second one."

"You think I'll run off after one date? What do you have planned? Teaching me how to do and fold laundry?" He was certainly cute, that was for damn sure.

A bit of his hesitancy waned and he leaned back in his chair, like he was finally settling in for a longer conversation. "No. Like I said, a hike and dinner, my treat."

"Where are you taking me for dinner?"

"On a picnic," he said, crossing his arms, eyes bright and trained on me.

"A picnic?" Oh! I liked that. "Not a restaurant?"

"You don't seem to prefer public spaces, being around people who aren't *your* people, so I figured a picnic would suit us better."

How did he know that about me? Any danger that my stomach might drop with disappointment seemed impossible now, just as impossible as hiding my smile.

"I see you like the idea." Isaac's attention dropped to my mouth, his eyes seemed to warm, and I realized we needed to get this conversation back on track. Isaac was in very great danger of making eyes at me like he'd done on Sunday. And if he made eyes at me, we'd likely end up sleeping together, in this odd government-owned building, before our first date.

Clearing my throat in an attempt to clear my smile, I refocused on the issues at hand. "Back to you—uh—your plans for the future? What were you planning to tell me?"

The heat behind his gaze didn't lessen, but it did appear to be tempered by an abrupt sadness. "I'm retiring from undercover work after this assignment."

"Okay." This didn't sound like bad news, but the way he'd said it made it sound like bad news.

"After this investigation wraps up, and assuming it ends with you safe, your identity and contribution hidden, I'll be in Green Valley for a few more weeks, or a few months at the most, to tie up loose ends. But then I'll be moving to—uh—elsewhere."

"Where?"

"I can't tell you."

"You can't tell me?"

"Unless you decide you want to come with me."

"Go with—"

"But if you do, we should probably get married—"

"Pardon me?"

"—because I'll be adopting a new identity. And if you come with me, you'll need a new identity, too."

"Are you joking?"

"I'm not. Which is why I'm telling you now. This is—I know this is a lot to ask, and we haven't even gone on a date yet. But, Hannah, I like you a lot and I know I'm repeating myself. I've never—" He snapped his mouth shut, gave his head a quick shake. "Like I said, I can stay in Green Valley as Isaac Sylvester for a while. We can give things a try, see if it works out. I don't want you to feel rushed or pressured."

I wasn't really listening to him, my mind was all over the place. He was leaving. He'd known yesterday when he asked to court me that he was leaving.

"And when your time off runs out, I have to decide whether to leave with you, get married, and change my identity, or stay here and never see you again?" I tried to keep the bitterness out of my voice and mostly succeeded.

What a joke. Like he would marry me in three months. Did he think I was born yesterday?

"That's the gist of it." He sounded so grim.

"What does that mean, changing identity? Would you be able to—"

"No. We would have to leave Green Valley and everyone we know here behind. That includes your family and friends. Theoretically, you'd never be able to speak to them again. But, over time, it might be possible to meet in a third location—like a busy resort, a vacation spot where a lot of people fly in and out—and spend some time together. However, in general, the contact would be minimal."

Minimal contact. Never speak to them again. My neck felt hot. No one would ever agree to this. This was an empty offer. He'd never planned to court me at all. Or maybe dating for three months then leaving was his idea of courtship.

Hank had been right. The only person I could trust was myself.

You trust Hank, dummy.

THAT'S NOT THE SAME THING!

"Hannah?"

"Is this what you told your sister today?" I forced a small smile. "Is that why she was so upset when she walked back in the house?"

He grimaced. "We talked about a lot of things that might've upset her. But, yes, this was the last thing we discussed."

I nodded, my gaze losing focus as I worked to keep my cool.

Just date him, Hannah. Just date him, have a good time. So what if he leaves?

Now that the wheel of doom in my brain had started to spin I couldn't stop it. What if Isaac and I dated and I fell completely in love with him? What if we got to that three-month mark—or even before it—and he simply disappeared? And then he would leave forever and I would be stuck heartbroken, never able to see him again.

"You don't have to decide now," his steady voice interrupted my thoughts. "Like I said, we can date for a while as Hannah and Isaac. I have over three months of leave saved. I can keep working at the Pink Pony. And even if you leave with me and we get married, we don't have to live together. We can keep dating for as long as you want."

He sounded so sincere, talking about marriage. We didn't even know each other. He'd either lost his marbles or was a liar or some combination of the two.

The fact of the matter was, nothing ever worked out for me. This little contentment I'd carved out for myself at the Pink Pony, this small community where I felt valued, this was my safe place. I never should've believed him. I deserved this abundance of disappointment.

Life had taught me over and over that the only two good things in abundance were caution and condoms.

Rubbing my forehead, I felt a headache coming on. "Do you mind if—can I take some time to think about it?"

"Absolutely." He nodded, his voice sounding strange, tight, and his eyes dropped from mine to the table. "Do you still want to go out tomorrow?"

"Uh . . ." I tucked my hair behind my ears, then scratched the back of my neck to do something with my hands.

I wanted to go home. I wanted to sleep in my little room, not in the luxurious bed at the Donner family cabin. I'd slept too well there, too soundly, like a dream. It was time to get back to reality. I needed the safety of those cinder block walls, the low ceilings, the dark, windowless rooms of the Pink Pony. I could count on those walls.

"We could—"

Pushing back from the table, I interrupted, "Let's postpone. I'm not—I think I'll pass on the tea. I'd like to go home now."

Isaac nodded, his gaze still affixed to the table. "No problem," he said, his tone gruff.

But I didn't try to read him or his mood. I was too busy trying not to cry.

Chapter Twenty-Three
HANNAH

"Don't set yourself on fire trying to keep others warm."

— Duane Winston, *Beard in Mind* by Penny Reid

Isaac dropped me off at the Pink Pony Monday evening and I decided to give myself the rest of the day off. I didn't clean, I didn't paint or fix anything, I didn't do inventory or review payroll or review plans for the Halloween festivities coming up this weekend. I made tea for myself, read a book, and stayed in bed.

I also cried. In fact, I cried so much, my eyes were puffy the next morning and there wasn't a darn thing I could do about it. When I finally pulled myself out of bed on Tuesday, I found a morning muffin and tepid coffee waiting for me in the breakroom. Isaac must've quietly dropped them off and left. The sight of the bakery bag and paper coffee cup made me burst into tears and I spent a bit of time crying on the floor of the breakroom while eating the muffin.

Crying while eating was a whole journey, an entire mood, a level of pathetic wallowing that felt almost artistic in nature. I'd never done it before but I decided, once Isaac disappeared forever, I would do it all the time. Maybe I'd sell tickets and call it performance art.

Self-talk, minimizing, focusing on reasons to be grateful—none of it worked and I didn't understand why. I wasn't in love with Isaac Sylvester . . . I didn't think.

No! You're not in love with him. You don't even know him.

Then why was I taking it so hard? Why was this funk so deep and wide and inescapable?

At a loss, I ended up calling my momma Tuesday afternoon. She hadn't reached out for a few weeks and I knew I needed to get better at being the one to initiate contact. I needed to get over the unidentified discomfort I felt whenever we spoke.

"Hello? Hannah?"

"Hi, Momma." I'd closed myself in my little room with no windows and currently sat on the sliver of floor space, since it was either that or lie in the bed, but I'd left on the sunlamp. It didn't precisely brighten up the room in the aesthetic sense, but it was better than sitting in the dark.

"Hey, baby. This is such a nice surprise! How are you?"

"I'm good, I'm good." As usual, I'd pasted on a smile so she would hear it in my voice, even if I didn't feel like smiling. "How are you? How are the horses?"

"Great!" My mother spent a bit of time telling me about how she and Jedd had been busy making updates to the stables and were thinking about adding a new barn.

As usual I listened, feeling good sometimes—since she sounded so happy—but then also feeling uncomfortable and oddly angry—since she sounded so happy—until I couldn't wait to get off the phone. I decided calling her had been a mistake.

I needed to get over this odd, involuntary bitterness I felt about her great, fulfilling life. It wasn't right and it made me feel like a bad person. I'd spent so many years in that house with a thoroughly depressed version of her, a shell of her former self. After my father left us, after that horrible accident where she'd lost mobility in her legs, I'd done everything possible to be the sunshine in her life, to take care of her, to ease her worries and struggles, but mostly to shake her out of her perpetual sadness.

Now she was happy. So, why did I feel mad about it?

"How about you, baby? What have you been doing? Anything fun?" Her tone adopted that careful, overly cheerful edge. She did this whenever the conversation ventured anywhere close to my job or where I worked.

Usually, I'd give a vague answer because I knew the subject bothered her. But for some reason, I didn't want to do that this time.

"I finished the mural of the Pegasus out front. It's getting lots of traction online. We're seeing good traffic and chatter on social media about it, people taking pictures. And the merch store is going live this weekend so we can make the Christmas season."

"What do you mean, merch? What is merch?"

"Merchandise. T-shirts, mugs, that kind of thing." I nibbled on my thumbnail, suddenly feeling nervous. This was the most she'd ever asked about my new position, the most interest she'd ever shown.

"Oh. Well, is this a side business you're doing? That's great!"

"No. It's Pink Pony merchandise. The T-shirts have a simplified illustration of the mural I painted."

My mother was quiet for a moment, then asked, sounding honestly curious, "You think folks want strip club T-shirts for Christmas? For the Lord's birthday?"

My neck grew hot but I kept my smile in place. "I think so, yes. They're . . . they're real good quality." I had to clear my throat of a lump in order to keep speaking. "Thick cotton. And people have told me the illustration is very, uh, pretty."

"That's nice," she said, the words sounding both polite and strained, like she didn't think it was nice but wanted to be supportive, so she lied.

Tears pricked at my eyes and I decided I'd had enough. One would think I'd be out of tears, but apparently not. Tangentially, I wondered what I could eat while I cried. Maybe a taco. *Tacos and Tears* would be the name of my performance art show. *Or maybe* Melancholy and Muffins . . .

"Well"—I cleared my throat again and forced my smile wider—"it was good catching up—"

"Oh! Wait. Before you go, I have to tell you something. We won't have Thanksgiving at the farm this year. Jedd and I will be going to a convention out of town. I wanted to tell you with plenty of time so you could make alternate plans for the holiday."

I flinched, her news feeling like a sudden slap, and could only echo her words, "Alternate plans for the holiday . . ."

"That's right. I can't wait. We're going to meet some friends of his there and—"

I hung up. I hung up on my mother. I hung up and I threw the phone across the room. Don't worry, the phone didn't break because it didn't have far to go. My eyes darted around the small changing room, taking in the harsh sunlamp, the loft bed, the small dresser, and the narrow slice of floor.

Suddenly, this space didn't feel safe. It felt like a prison cell.

My heart was racing, as was my mind. Too many thoughts, most of them hateful and resentful, swelled in my brain, completely taking over. *I'm trapped here forever. I'm trapped here because of her choices and she's out there living her best life.*

Maybe the thoughts weren't fair, maybe they weren't rational. After all, she'd paid me back most of the money I'd spent on the farm. She didn't want me working at the Pony, especially now that her financial situation was better. She'd been pushing me to quit for a long time. She and Jedd had even offered me a job working for his business as an errand runner and laborer in the stalls. I didn't want to do that. My interests had nothing to do with farming and horses, and the job had nothing to do with my degree.

Yes, I'd tried to get a job in my degree major for a few months after graduation, but I'd been the one to give up after that awful manager harassed me. Quitting and not sticking it out had been my decision. And working here, staying here, taking the easier road and settling, that had been my choice, too.

So, no. The thoughts weren't true.

But it didn't matter because they felt true. Much truer than all the self-talk, minimizing, and lists of reasons to be grateful I'd been drowning myself in for years.

Picking myself up off the floor, I wiped my eyes and decided I would go ahead, eat that taco and cry. If I was going to feel sorry for myself, I might as well do so artistically.

* * *

By Thursday morning I'd pulled myself back together. I hadn't figured out why my reaction to Isaac's bombshells Monday afternoon were so intense. I shouldn't have gotten my hopes up in the first place. Regardless, I decided to stop thinking about it. Furthermore, I decided to stop thinking about anything difficult or unpleasant.

Since my usual coping mechanisms had abandoned me in this critical time of need, I had no choice but to deploy the repression nuclear option and simply stop feeling and thinking. I'd deployed this strategy when I was eighteen and it had worked great.

I'd saved my momma's farm, I'd driven her to all those medical appointments on time and paid all the bills without incurring more debt, I'd put food on the table. I'd survived. And survival was the only thing truly necessary when you got right down to it. Surviving was the cake, everything else was frosting.

Moving on.

As it turned out, my timing couldn't have been better because, instead of quietly dropping off the muffin and coffee like he'd done Tuesday and Wednesday, Isaac showed up to my office Thursday morning.

He knocked on the doorframe, drawing my detached attention away from the costume I'd been mending. Standing in the doorway looking big and strong and sexy and uncertain, he held the bakery bag and the paper coffee cup like he didn't know whether he'd be welcome or not.

I smiled politely. "Good morning."

He stared at me, not smiling, but not making eyes at me either. "Good morning, Hannah," he said softly, quietly, and the words carried an undercurrent of emotion I refused to dissect.

At the sound of his voice, my body tried to send a shiver down my spine but I would have none of that nonsense.

"What brings you here so early?"

Isaac's attention shifted from my gaze to my desk. He set down the coffee and muffin with all outward appearance of great care.

"Is it okay to say that I missed you?" he asked, the words causing an absolute riot between my brain, heart, and stomach.

Breathing out through my nose, I returned my attention to the mending in my hands and shrugged. "Sure. Why not? Sounds pretty."

I sensed him linger in the doorway, shift on his feet, then suddenly walk fully into the office. He sat in the empty seat and out of the corner of my eye I watched him pick up a costume and search for the large safety pin we used to mark tears. Then he set to work without me asking him to help.

He'd already done this once before, coming in here and sewing costumes with me silently. I caught myself staring at him after a time, my brain loud with curiosity about where he'd learned to sew such tidy stitches.

Just ask. What's the harm in asking?

Sitting straighter, I decided there was no harm in asking. "Where'd you learn to sew?"

Not missing a stitch, he said, "In the army."

"Really? You did a lot of sewing in the army?"

"Not a lot, but we were responsible for the care of our own uniforms. I didn't have much money, didn't want to waste any of it, so I taught myself with online videos."

Stretching my neck, I peeked at the whip stitch he used to repair a hem. "You do good work."

"No point in spending time, energy, and resources on something—or someone—unless you're fully committed," he muttered, eyes still on the garment.

Leaning back in my seat, I tried not to repeat his statement over and over in my head, scrutinize it too closely from different angles.

Thank goodness, before I could make myself batty with overanalyzing the words, he asked, "Where'd you learn to sew?"

"Oh. Well." I smirked at the memory. "It's actually boring story."

"I'd like to hear it."

I peeked at him again. His attention didn't waiver from his work but he'd sounded sincere.

Again, I decided there was no harm. "So, after my momma's accident, she couldn't work at all. The only job I could get was at the Front Porch as a hostess, and that was only because I'd tutored the owner's granddaughter, so they knew me. Anyway, we weren't making enough money and it got around town that we might lose the farm, so—one day—my aunt, Scotia Simmons, you might know her—showed up with a bunch of clothes that needed mending, completely out of the blue. She taught me how to do all the stitches over a week, and I started taking in laundry and mending after that."

I sensed Isaac grow very still and his lack of movement drew my eyes to him. He was staring at the fabric in his hands but wasn't making stitches with his needle.

"Isn't Scotia Simmons—I mean, wasn't your aunt Scotia very wealthy?"

"Uh. Well. Yes."

"Why didn't she just give y'all money so you didn't lose the farm? Why didn't she help you?" His gaze lifted to mine, heat behind his words.

"She did help me. She taught me a skill so I could make money for myself and helped spread the word about my stitching and laundry business." I angled my chin up defiantly. "But to answer your first question, my momma wouldn't take money from anyone. Folks tried to give us money but she sent it back, even the money from her sisters. She didn't want charity."

Isaac's eyes seemed to narrow, the glint behind them striking me as frustrated, or angry, or something like it. "I see," was all he said. His jaw flexed as he shifted his stare to the costume in his hands and resumed work on the hem.

We sat in silence for a while. At first, I had to keep pulling out the thread, my hands were moving too fast and the stitches were too tight. After a time, I finally relaxed back into the rhythm of work and the silence went from deafening to comfortable.

It was Isaac who interrupted the meditative quiet with, "I get the sense you don't trust people easily."

My hands stalled and I answered before thinking better of it. "I guess I don't."

"I don't either."

"I can see that," I drawled. His was not a revolutionary statement.

Then he said, "But I trust you."

My hands stalled again, my eyes cutting to him.

He was watching me again, his features open and earnest. "Why don't you trust me, Hannah?"

I gathered a deep breath, the question surprising me with its directness. But if he wanted to know, I'd tell him. "I don't know you."

"You should rectify that."

I smirked. "Oh? And how should I go about rectifying that?"

"Ask me anything."

Sure. Okay. I guess we're doing this. "Fine. Why do you like me? You don't know me very well either." Maybe he thought I was stupid, acting like he was considering marriage to me last week when we'd talked at the building on Bandit Lake. We barely knew each other.

"I do know you." The side of his mouth curved ever so slightly. "Except, what's your favorite book?"

"David Sedaris's *Me Talk Pretty One Day*, because it makes me laugh out loud." Also, the way the author dealt with sad or tragic situations helped me process tragedy in my own life, my own disappointments and sorrows.

But I wasn't going to tell Isaac that. I didn't trust him.

"Hmm. That's a good one." He nodded, it looked thoughtful, and his smile spread to the other corner of his mouth. "It suits you. Makes sense."

That had me wrinkling my nose, the mending on my lap forgotten. "Wait. Are you saying that's the last piece of my puzzle? Now that you know my favorite book you know everything about me?"

His smile almost showed teeth and his eyes seemed to dance as they moved over me. "I know what I need to know."

"What does that mean?" I wrinkled my nose harder, trying not to smile. Trying and failing because Isaac Sylvester was showing me a new side of himself today. The charming side. I suspected it might be lethal.

Ignoring my question, he said, "Since you claim you hardly know me. Why don't you ask what my favorite book is?"

Feeling a bit flustered, I admitted, "I know yours."

"You do?"

"Yes. It's *The Picture of Dorian Gray* by that funny playwright."

"Oscar Wilde."

"That's him." I picked up my needle again, inspecting the work in my lap and trying to figure out where I'd left off.

"How do you know that?"

"You used to carry it around all the time during choir practice, read it over and over. I guess I just assumed it was your favorite. Is it?"

"It is definitely one of my favorites if not my favorite."

"Will you tell me why?" *Darn my curiosity!* I hadn't meant to ask him that but I gave myself a pass. In fact, I decided to use this as an opportunity to ask all my most pressing questions about Isaac Sylvester. When would I get another chance? He might disappear at any time.

"It was . . . transformative for me at the time." I sensed him shift in his seat. "It helped me see things more clearly and . . . set me on a—a good—a better path."

"Tell me something about it. Like, why was it transformative?"

"Have you read it?"

"Yes. Three times, actually." The first time I'd read it was when we'd been teenagers and I'd spotted him carrying it around, but that was another truth I wasn't ready to admit to him. That first time, I'd been too young to understand the book. I'd read it again after Isaac showed up back in town, hanging out with Tina at the Pony. His reappearance reminded me of the book and how I'd liked it but couldn't quite pinpoint why. The third time I read it was just after Isaac had disappeared from town a few years ago. "I was in college the third time I read it and I think I finally understood it by then."

"What did you understand about it?" He shifted in his seat again, rolling it a little closer to me.

"I read a few essays other folks wrote about it, going over themes like individualism, morality of beauty and youth, appearance versus reality, Faustian bargains and the like." I hadn't discussed a good book with another person in a long time. It was fun and I almost forgot who I was talking to, that I needed to be on my guard. "Reading their interpretations helped, but for me, the thing that really stood out and something I didn't see discussed was that if you treat everything like it doesn't matter—like Lord Henry did, like he persuaded Dorian to do—then nothing matters and life becomes meaningless."

It was why I always balanced the minimizing of my feelings with gratitude. Gratitude made good things matter, while minimizing negative emotions made those feelings matter less.

At my answer, Isaac made a short noise, it sounded surprised, and he rolled even closer. "Yes. Exactly. People who play devil's advocate but don't have any beliefs other than in themselves, only play devil's advocate in order to invalidate the beliefs of others, those people are the most evil and should be cut from your life. They're destructive, deadweight. But it was also the theme of appearance versus reality that made an impact on me, the lies people tell, both to others and themselves, and how changing one detail in your description or representation of a thing can actually completely change another person's perception of that thing."

I'd never heard Isaac speak so much all at once, and he was speaking so fast, it was like he couldn't get the words out fast enough. It was enough to bring my eyes back to his.

"Do you remember the opening of the book?" he asked, looking more animated than I'd ever seen him. He was so cute, I could only nod. I didn't want to interrupt. I simply wanted to watch him. "When Wilde describes the flowering thorn bush? Obviously, he's talking about a rose bush. But he calls it a flowering thorn bush. He's fundamentally changed our perception of that plant by making it all about thorns and minimizing the role of the flower, of the rose, even though the rose is beautiful and the thorn is hurtful. I thought that was so brilliant at the time, and it made me realize and notice how people —manipulative people—used language. What they decide to focus on, what they describe and what they leave out of their description. They use language to change the perspectives and beliefs of those around them."

"It sounds like you're thinking about or talking about someone in particular."

Isaac blinked and—that quick—the light faded from his eyes. He sighed and rolled his chair back, staring at the unfinished mending in his hands. "My father," he said monotonically.

He sat very still for a moment, and then rubbed his forehead. "If you don't mind, I don't wish to discuss him."

"Fair enough. No pressure." I kept my tone gentle, his obvious agitation about the man wasn't something I had a right to ask about in any case. "We don't have to talk at all if you don't wish to."

"No. I want to talk. You said you didn't know me and I want you to know me." His hand dropped. "Ask me something, please."

Well, okay then. "Why'd you join the army?"

He huffed a laugh. "For a lot of reasons. But the only answer that's both true and not tragic is because I wanted to read."

Both true and not tragic . . . That sounded ominous.

"What do you mean?"

"I know I said I wouldn't talk about him, but my father didn't like me reading books that weren't the textbooks he approved. He said he didn't want me reading wrong things or bad history. But reading was what I loved to do. I would think about it all the time when I wasn't doing it, and I would find ways to sneak books into my room. You know Bethany Winston? She was one of the librarians when we were growing up."

"I remember. Roscoe Winston's momma. She died a few years ago."

"She used to read books out loud to me whenever my momma would take me to the library for one of her business meetings. Somehow, my father found out and almost got her fired for it. Said she was putting Satan in my mind." He huffed another laugh, his eyes fuzzy, then gave his head a quick shake as though to dispel a memory.

"Geez." This was a new point of view on my old high school principal but not a surprising one. I'd always thought Kip Sylvester was a real shithead. He had no sense of humor. Folks with no sense of humor were either wet blankets or psychopaths.

"I stopped going to the library after that. I didn't want to get her in trouble."

"Bethany Winston was a sweet lady." Finally finished repairing the tear in this tutu, I reached for the scissors.

"She was." His voice sounded far away, lost in another memory.

"So, what does reading books have to do with joining the army?"

"It's how I gained my freedom. Did you know I left town before I graduated from high school?"

"I knew you were homeschooled, but I thought you graduated." Swiveling in my chair, I picked another black costume from the pile so I wouldn't have to switch the color of the thread on my needle.

"No. I got my GED and then all I did was read. Or rather, yes. I had basic training and after that, deployment, but I could read at night, in the morning, during lunch, or whenever we had downtime. Most of my unit would go into town during leave and have their version of a good time. I'd go to the local library and read."

"You didn't surf the internet?" I snuck a quick look at him.

He shook his head slowly, his eyes still unfocused. "No. I didn't know much about the internet. I wasn't allowed to have access. My father called the internet the 'Devil's Wide Web.' I think my sister was allowed to have a laptop after I left home, but he did frequent and random checks on the device and had software installed to control what she viewed."

"How do you know about that? Don't you and your sister have a strained relationship?"

"When I returned to town for my first undercover assignment, the information man with the Iron Wraiths—a guy called Burro—helped me find out about my sister and my mother, how my father was treating them. He didn't prepare reports or dossiers or anything official. He verbally relayed all the details while making me sit and buy him drinks. The drunker he got, the more information he shared."

"Huh." My hands paused their search for the safety pin marking the tear. "Was your father a religious fanatic? I never knew."

"No. He wasn't."

"He wasn't?" Now I was confused.

"No. He only used religion as a weapon when it served his purpose. At home, when it was just the two of us, he often made fun of organized religion, called my mother a sheep for going to church. He said he didn't need religion or a pastor to understand God's word, but I think that was an excuse. I think he just didn't believe in any of it. He liked that she went to church every Sunday and took us kids. I'm pretty sure everyone knows by now, he cheated on my momma for years before they divorced."

"I did hear that he cheated on your momma." I swallowed around a small lump of uneasiness. This was a lot of sharing Isaac was doing and his expression still looked fuzzy, like he was speaking without thinking.

Should I stop him? Make a joke? These stories, these truths he revealed about his past, felt too personal.

Before I could figure out what to say, how to divert the conversation, he went on, "He used to say, used to tell me, that he was a high-value man and high-value men shouldn't be expected to have just one woman. He said he knew how to handle my mother when she acted out, and told my momma and sister that the number one quality in a good woman was obedience."

Finally, his gaze sharpened, focused on me. I held still under the intensity of his stare.

"I would never treat you that way, Hannah," he said, his voice low and gravelly. "Obedience isn't something I value, or want. It makes people small, it narrows their world. Obedience is for God, not for a partner."

Mesmerized by his expression and words, my question slipped out before I could stop it. "Then what do you want, Isaac?"

"You," he said, and the single word sounded both joyful and melancholy, like an invitation and a confession.

My heart warmed. I gave him a small smile that wasn't forced. He returned it. Then we resumed our work and silently finished the whole pile, my feet barely touching the ground, my head in the clouds.

It wasn't until hours later that I woke up from the spell he'd cast. He was so good at his sincerity act, I'd almost believed him.

I made it through the busy weekend with no additional prolonged conversations between me and Isaac, despite him making eyes at me all the damn time. Our interactions during his shifts had been nothing at all like the long discussion over mending we'd had Thursday morning before work. He'd reverted to his previous modus operandi: showing up out of nowhere and helping me silently. He didn't push. He didn't ask me what I'd decided about us.

I didn't know how to feel about all this quiet space and respect he gave me while we unloaded boxes, stocked shelves, cleaned bathrooms, and unloaded food crates.

Tavvy hadn't shown his face either—not on Saturday and not on Sunday—and I didn't know if that was a good or bad thing. I didn't ask Isaac about the investigation. Talking to him confused me.

Actually, it wasn't just the talking. Isaac was confusing in general. He seemed so sincere and earnest all the time, had shared so much of himself on Thursday while we repaired costumes, had me laughing and forgetting his plan to—with my permission—use me for a good time over the next few months, and then disappear.

The worst part was, even knowing he would leave me behind and all that talk of marriage must've been BS, I was still tempted to take him up on the time he offered.

Monday became Tuesday and he left the bakery bag and paper cup full of coffee in the breakroom both days. I couldn't bring myself to eat the muffin or drink the coffee, not because I'd grown tired of the taste, but because I'd grown to anticipate them.

Life hack: You can't miss something if you have no expectation of it in the first place.

Admittedly, I felt guilty when I threw away his offerings without touching them, but I told myself it was for the best. But then, out of nowhere, he appeared at my door Wednesday morning and—you guessed it—brought with him the morning muffin and coffee.

Leaning back in my chair, I mentally papier-mâchéd a mask of friendliness over my features and asked, "What brings you to my office on your day off?"

A small, plainly confused frown wrinkled his forehead. "It's not my day off. I'm here for the bachelorette party."

Well, shit.

A flare of something hot and miserable tried to break free from my state-of-emergency emotional lockdown and I yanked it back, suffocating the involuntary flash of feeling. I'd forgotten about his offer to step in over a week ago, which meant I'd forgotten to talk him out of it.

"It's today, right? Or did I get the day wrong?" He walked into my office, placing the coffee cup and muffin on my desk, and took a seat in the remaining chair. *Déjà vu.*

I slowly swiveled to face him while he picked up a costume, found the marker for the tear, and set about stitching it. Studying him, but not too closely, I decided a few things were true at the same time, and I debated how to proceed.

First, hen parties could get extremely rowdy. Women, just like men, felt emboldened when gathering in a group, engaged in behaviors they wouldn't otherwise. But it was often worse with women. Their minimal exposure to strip clubs, to the culture and the rules, and to sexuality in general meant they often took things too far. For most women, this would be their only time going to a strip club, and some saw it as their only chance to truly let loose.

Every member of the male dance team already possessed necessary, critical experience and knew how to diffuse a gaggle of horny, unrestrained, tipsy bridesmaids, out on the town and free in a way they'd never experienced before. Isaac, however, hadn't even witnessed one of these parties. At least Dave had watched a few before filling in as a backup. Putting Isaac in this position without any experience might spell disaster, especially considering his reaction to the lap dance I'd tried to give him all those weeks ago. If he thought what I'd done was shocking, he would be in for a big surprise today.

Second, we didn't one-hundred-percent *need* the empty spot filled, but it certainly would make things significantly easier from a customer service perspective. The time to alert the bride and her maid of honor—that there would be seven dancers today instead of the promised eight—had passed days ago. If they showed up today and we were down one dancer, experience told me they'd be really upset.

A bride's bachelorette party happened—ideally—once in a person's lifetime. Women rarely went to strip clubs otherwise. At worst, they'd throw a big fuss and leave negative reviews for the club everywhere, tanking our good ratings on every website. At best, they'd be upset and disappointed. Both were bad outcomes.

And third, but not really relevant anymore, I hated the idea of Isaac being part of the male dance team. I HATED it. I didn't want other women looking at him, touching him, and I certainly didn't want him touching other women—even if it was just removing their hands from his body—and making eyes at them the way he made eyes at me.

Yes, I was a hypocrite. Most folks are. Whatever. *Eat a dick, Wendy, and let me be a hypocrite.*

"Hannah?" Isaac had already finished mending the first costume and was in the process of cutting the thread.

"Are you—is everything okay?" he asked, glancing between me and the scissors.

I told myself to keep my mouth shut. I told myself Isaac was smart, was an officer of the law and likely knew how to handle a rowdy room without allowing things to spiral out of control. I told myself Hank would give him tips and pointers, keep an eye on him, keep him safe.

But when faced with my irrelevant jealousy, none of that seemed to matter and I blurted, "You don't have to do this."

Isaac lifted an eyebrow at my outburst but otherwise appeared unruffled. Eyes on me, he set aside the first costume and picked up another. "Do what?"

"Fill in for the missing dancer." I resisted the urge to scoot closer or touch him. "Our contract says eight, but we can easily call the maid of honor this morning and let her know. We'll just say someone is sick, offer a prorated amount on the event."

Isaac picked through the thread, presumably hunting for just the right shade of turquoise to match Piper's mermaid costume, and said calmly, "No. I said I'd help. I'll do it."

My fingers twisted in the fabric on my lap. "Are you sure?"

"Yes." His attention seemed to be focused fully on the needle he was trying to thread and I realized he hadn't looked at me much since walking in the room. My restrained emotions attempted to make a stir, mixing sadness together with disappointment, but I wouldn't let them. I still kept my thoughts and emotions under strict lock and key. The only feeling that successfully slipped past my internal feelings-security-system was jealousy.

If he didn't want to look at me, fine. I refused to be sad about it. But I took the opportunity of his absorption with the needle to stare at him, wondering how I could get him to change his mind. My stomach rolled, my lungs tight.

I wasn't surprised jealousy had been the emotion capable of breaking through all the boundaries. Jealousy was an old friend of mine, some form of it had kept me company most of my adult life.

I guess I'm just an awful, resentful person. That's who I am. OH WELL.

Tearing my gaze from his beautiful face, I said, "Okay then. As long as you're sure." Meanwhile my chest turned into a fireball of envy. I would do my best to remain professional when I greeted the bridal party, but I would not stay for the show. Just the thought of watching—

"I am sure," he said, cutting into my internal tirade. "But what do I need to do?"

Releasing a silent breath, I forced calm into my voice, responding, "Since you're filling in just the one time, you'll take one of the two pillar positions. You'll stand still and stare forward for most of it."

"That's it?"

"You'll be, uh, eventually wearing very little. But you and Dave will basically stand on either side of the stage, staring forward—which is why we call y'all the pillars—and hit your cues. You'll remove the parts of your costume when the lead dancers remove theirs." I set aside the costume I'd been mending, having no patience for the detailed stitches, and tucked my hair behind my ears.

"I'll be undressing in front of an audience?"

"It's ripping off Velcro clothes, not regular undressing, not like a striptease. Then you hold a pose on the stage for a bit. Eventually, you'll—uh—well, all the dancers go down to the floor, collect their tips, treat the ladies nice, and so forth. After a while, it's over and that's that. You should ask Hank for more details, he'll fill you in." I knew I was rushing and oversimplifying things, but I didn't want to think about it, let alone talk about it.

"You're saying I mostly stand on the stage while wearing nothing?"

"You'll have on something to cover your middle, depending on what the theme is, but your legs and chest will be, um, bare. Yes." I reached for the water bottle on my desk and gulped down most of its contents.

"I see . . ." He nodded, his expression thoughtful, his mending stitches impeccable.

"Are you sure you're okay doing this?" Like before, the words burst out of me. "I can offer a prorated rate to the maid of honor."

Isaac gave his head a little shake, lifting the costume and tilting it as though to see his stitches better, still not looking at me. "It should be fine. Like you said, I'll get Mr. Weller to explain the details."

"Okay. But if you want to change your mind, it's fine. Don't feel pressured just because we're dating—uh, I mean, we're—" *Shoot!* What was I saying?

We weren't dating! I'd postponed our date indefinitely and had been purposefully keeping my distance. We weren't dating at all. He was leaving and—

"Because we're dating."

I looked at him and found his eyes on me, wider than usual and tinted with something that looked like hope.

He lowered the costume to his lap and shifted in his seat. "Because we're dating, right?"

My feelings tried to break free but I shoved them down, down, down. Uncertain how to proceed with this hot potato of a question. Or statement. Or whatever it was. Unfortunately, he didn't give me even a full minute to reply.

Quite suddenly, Isaac was making eyes at me.

Chapter Twenty-Four
HANNAH

"If you can be replaced so easily in a person's life, then you probably don't need to be a part of that person's life."

—Dave, *Totally Folked* by Penny Reid

My heart ticked up then took off, staging a jailbreak and releasing all those uncomfortable *feelings*. I knew I was now breathing heavier than I should've been given the fact that I'd been sitting in this chair since he'd walked in, but I couldn't seem to slow my respiration as—despite the chaos in my mind and heart—a single question resounded between my ears.

Why not?

Why not date Isaac?

Why not date him until the investigation ended? And then date him while he was in Green Valley during his leave? And if he wanted to leave me behind, fine. I'd survive. I knew how to survive.

Isaac set aside the costume he'd been stitching, stood, walked to my door, shut it, and locked it. Being alone with him in my office again behind a closed and locked door had a similar effect as suppressing my feelings. Only, instead of feeling nothing, it was all too much. Overwhelming. No single thought or idea dominated.

Standing in front of me, he took my hand, tugging gently until I stood. "Hannah."

I closed my eyes, still breathing too hard. "Yes?" More than a shiver raced down my spine but I felt powerless to stop it. I was wound so tight, flashes of the last two times we'd been alone together in here with the door shut and locked played like a sexy slideshow against my closed eyelids.

Isaac bent to my ear and whispered, "I want to do something." He sucked the tip of my ear into his mouth, making me shiver again. "To you."

My hand came to his chest, my fingers curling into his shirt. "What—what do you want to do?"

He'd started backing me up toward the empty desk against the far wall, the desk where I'd been sitting when I'd reached inside his boxers over a week ago and made him come.

"I want . . ." Isaac's mouth lowered to my neck in tandem with his hand sliding under my skirt to cup me between my legs, his fingers pressing firmly, then caressing me slowly over my underwear.

A breath whooshed out of my lungs, my hands spasming and shifting to his shoulders. I needed to hold on for balance. And he was so strong and sturdy.

"Are you wet?" he asked, his voice a rasp. "Can I check?"

My head jerked with a nod. He'd done almost nothing but I was beyond speaking.

My backside connected with the desk and I sat obediently. Lifting his hand, he slid his fingers into the front of my underwear and nudged my knees apart, opening my legs wider. My breath hitched as his middle finger slid over my clit and straight into my opening, pushing deeply inside and making me gasp.

I sensed him lean back. In the next second he'd grabbed my jaw and lifted my chin.

"Open your eyes," he demanded.

I did, finding his staring intently at my face, like he didn't want to miss a single second of my reaction, like he was fascinated by it.

Pulling his finger out slowly, he seemed to catalog every change in my expression as he returned his fingers to my clit and stroked me, slow and soft. Over and over. Too soft. I whimpered, my eyes drifting shut.

"Open," he said, using the same stern tone as before. "I want to see your eyes."

Swallowing another whimper, I complied, but I felt so needy, especially as our eyes locked. For a man who didn't like to be teased, he sure did excel at it.

"Do you like it?" he asked, sounding sincerely curious, leaning forward to give my lips a biting kiss, his hand still holding my jaw. "Or do you want it harder?"

"Harder," I said without thinking.

This seemed to please him and he complied immediately, giving the very center of me a firm press and rub. I flinched, because it hurt, but it also felt amazing, especially after the barely there, whisper touches he'd been using. I knew my nails were digging into his shoulders over his shirt, but I didn't care. I needed—

He pushed two fingers inside and my whole body shook, my legs wanting to close instinctively at the roughness of the invasion even as the warmth low in my belly coiled tighter, loving his touch, how raw it was, how I felt completely at his mercy.

Holding my eyes, Isaac pumped his long fingers into me slowly, languid strokes with a controlled tempo, the pad of his thumb giving me those teasing, whispering touches at my center, making my toes curl. His hand released my jaw and caressed a wandering path down the front of my body, lifting my shirt up and off, pulling the strap of my bra down, reaching inside the cup, and palming my breast.

We stared at each other. I felt transfixed. A sound reverberated out of him, like a hum, and I felt his hips move restlessly between my thighs.

Isaac licked his lips, his eyes now hazy. "Can I put my tongue inside you, Hannah?"

I moaned, my breath hitching, because I was so close. And his dirty talk pushed me closer to the edge.

He must've seen how it affected me because he stepped forward, crowding me, rubbing the center of my breast roughly and pinching it with calloused fingers, his eyes moving between mine, dazed and ravenous.

"After you come like this, can I taste you here?" He removed his fingers at the center of my body and slid them up to my clit, using both to circle it, sending hot shivers down my legs. My body clenched, clamping down on nothing. The absence of his fingers was painful. I felt so empty.

"Please, please . . ." One of my hands moved to his neck and the other slid down his arm, holding the wrist between my legs, trying to force him to give me back his fingers. "I need . . ."

"What do you need?" he asked, his voice dark and sinful as he bent, moving the hand at my breast to my back between my shoulder blades and forcing me to arch upward so he could tongue my nipple, suck it, bite it.

"Isaac!"

"Tell me what you need. I want to give it to you, whatever you want."

He angled his hips to one side and I felt the length of him press against the interior of my thigh. He'd felt so perfect in my hands when I'd touched him on Saturday, so hard and smooth, hot and just the right size.

"If you don't tell me, I'll do what I want." The words sounded like a warning.

I couldn't think. What I really wanted was his fingers and his tongue and his cock. I wanted every inch of everything he had to offer all at the same time. I felt so out of my mind in the moment, I almost asked him to take me like this, right now, with no protection, my bra half on, my skirt shoved up. He could push my underwear to one side and slide right in, and wouldn't that ease every ache and hurt and desire? Then I wouldn't feel so empty.

In the moment, my silly body suspected that maybe his dick would solve all my problems, taking him inside me would be the answer to all my woes.

But before I could make this ridiculous request, Isaac said, "Fine. Then I'll do what I want," and slid down my body. He knelt in front of me. His fingers tugged roughly at the waistband of my underwear and shoved them off.

Grabbing my ankles, he pushed upward until my heels were perched on the edge of the desk, my legs spread wide. He bent forward and licked my slit with the flat of his tongue, humming again, deeper and longer, as though he loved the taste of me.

The sensation was too much, overwhelming, and once more, my knees instinctively wanted to press together. I felt overheated, dancing on the edge of something too big to process.

At my movements, his eyes cut to mine, a petulant-looking frown between them, a command. *Take it, Hannah. Let me. I want this so much. You want this. Take it.*

As though to punctuate this point, or maybe as a concession, he slid those two fingers inside and licked me again, humming again, pumping me again, and the wet, inelegant sounds of his touch and tongue made me wild. The look in his eyes, the slick friction of his tongue paired with the feeling of being suddenly filled sent me over the cliff.

My head whipped back. I'm sure I screamed or moaned or both, and loudly. Isaac paused only a second, maybe at the feel of my body clenching and releasing around him. I didn't know why he momentarily stopped. I couldn't think.

Abruptly, he increased his earlier tempo, stroking me fast and hard, licking me long and slow, like he didn't want to leave an inch untasted. Wave after wave crashed over me. Just when I thought it was over, a new brilliant burst of pleasure made me tense, made everything constrict and tighten so much I thought I might break. Then, I felt myself fall. Weak and replete. Boneless.

I couldn't catch my breath. My heart raced. And when he decided he'd tasted me enough, he stood and bent over where I lay on the desk, his fingers still inside, petting me slowly, like he would a cat.

"Open your eyes, Hannah." This time, the words sounded softer, a request and not a command.

Blinking my eyes open, I found Isaac above, his mouth wet. He waited a moment, simply staring, then licked his lips.

It was so, so fucking sexy. I shuddered, angling my chin, wanting that wet mouth on mine.

"I think I need you, Hannah," he said, just above a whisper.

This man was simply too good at appearing sincere, I almost believed he meant the words. I knew better than to take pillow talk seriously, though. Even so, tears pricked at my eyes.

"I like this part of your body. A lot." His voice deepened, another secret between us. He slid his fingers out and stroked them upward, teasing my clit softly. "I think I'll have a difficult time concentrating unless you let me touch it and kiss it every day."

Despite the sting in my eyes and my exhaustion, a sudden laugh burst out and I covered my face to hide it. He'd sounded so serious, so earnest. It made me self-conscious.

Isaac's mouth now on my breast, kissing and nuzzling, made me hot again. "If you like me, you should let me," he said, as though presenting evidence in front of a judge.

"I do like you," I choked out, but reminded myself that revealing this truth didn't mean anything. It wasn't a promise. My like of him was obvious given the multiple orgasms I'd just had. So what? Liking a person wasn't a contract. I didn't owe him. He didn't owe me.

He probably "dates" someone during each undercover assignment, seduces a woman to keep his bed warm. This is probably an old habit at this point.

Too many emotions and thoughts made forming sentences difficult. Thus, when he handed me the wet wipes and turned his back to give me privacy, I cleaned myself up wordlessly. And when he pushed my underwear back up my legs, righted my bra and skirt, and dressed me in my shirt, I let him. And when he sat in his seat and pulled me to his lap, stroking my back, encouraging me to lay my head on his shoulder, and giving me cuddles, I let him do that, too.

I hadn't asked for any of this sweetness. He offered it freely.

I wouldn't hope, I wouldn't trust, and I wouldn't make or ask for any promises. If he wanted to come in here and give me orgasms or let me love on his beautiful body, so be it.

When he left, I'd survive.

Chapter Twenty-Five
ISAAC

"No one expects an eighty-five-year-old Navy SEAL stripper. No one. And that was the beauty of George."

— Cletus Winston, *Beard Science* by Penny Reid

Hank Weller's knock on the door interrupted us. We hadn't been in the middle of anything except me quietly holding Hannah on my lap, her body soft and pliant and warm, while I rubbed her back. Amidst the peaceful moment, his voice sounded like nails on a chalkboard. Or a Chihuahua.

"Are you in there?" Hank's voice called out. "The fellas will be arriving soon. Where's this new replacement Tina promised?"

She heaved a sigh, then a chuckle, then stood and walked to the door. "I'm in here."

"Good. Where's this—" His eyes landed on me as soon as the door opened and it was as though the sun passed behind stormy clouds, the change in his expression was that quick. "Hello, Isaac." Hank Weller's voice oozed scorn.

I stood and gave him a short nod. "Mr. Weller."

Cutting his eyes to Hannah, he gave her a once-over. "Is he it?"

She nodded, saying nothing, but I could tell she found him amusing.

"Fine. Come with me," he grumbled, and then disappeared from the doorway.

I paused in front of Hannah on my way out, reaching for her hand and inspecting her eyes. She looked back at me, not smiling, but not frowning either.

Something wasn't right. I'd sensed it last Thursday when I'd arrived with her coffee and muffin. She didn't thank me. It was the first time she hadn't thanked me. The way she'd looked at me then and now, like I was an acquaintance, no one important, sent my stomach to my feet.

Last Thursday, I'd spent my time mending the costumes, frantically searching for what to say that might put things back on track. I'd told her I missed her. I'd told her I trusted her and asked what I needed to do for her to trust me. I'd shared more from my past than I ever had with anyone but my sister. I thought maybe, after I told her details about my father, we'd reached a breakthrough. But then at the end of the workday, Hannah went right back to being distant and polite.

I'd decided privacy was what she needed, so I didn't push. I waited. I wanted her to choose me without harassing her into it. I wanted her willing, just as I was willing, to give this a real shot.

Today, when I arrived once more with her muffin and coffee, I couldn't bring myself to look at her even though the urge to share her space, hear her voice, felt like a compulsion.

I'd never been one for fantasizing, or for physical urges and sexual gratification. I'd considered celibacy easy. Until Hannah. Now I was having wet dreams, waking up in the middle of the night in torment, thinking about her while I stroked myself during every shower, sometimes twice. Actually, most of the time it was twice. Rarely, it was three times. Not that it mattered.

And it wasn't just fantasies about us touching each other. About half of the time it was daydreams about us simply being together, sharing the same space, watching her laugh, maybe one day taking her to a movie or out to dinner, or on that hike and picnic I'd planned.

And then, just when I was about to leave the room earlier and end my pathetic pursuit for the day, she'd said the word *dating* in reference to us. Even though she'd cut herself off after the word, she'd said it and it had given me hope.

In hopeful desperation, I'd deployed Tina's advice from years ago: *If you really like a woman, offer to go down on her early and often. It's how she'll know you're boyfriend material and it might convince her to give you a real chance if she's on the fence. But don't cuddle after sex with someone you don't see yourself with long-term. It'll confuse her, make her think you like her a lot, and that's mean.*

I'd thoroughly enjoyed myself. Touching and tasting her, watching her come, had been a fulfillment of my fantasies and probably fuel for new ones, but I couldn't tell if it had worked. Hannah had seemed to enjoy herself. She'd cuddled with me, let me touch her, hold her. According to Tina, that meant she liked me. Hannah wasn't mean, so the cuddling meant she saw me as someone long term.

. . . Right?

"Have fun." She lifted to her tiptoes and pressed a quick kiss to my cheek. "And don't let him sass you. He's grumpy but he's not a bad guy."

Nodding, I allowed myself to study her for another moment, hoping the light behind her eyes would return and she'd look at me like she had before I spilled my guts at the safe house, as though I mattered to her.

"Let's go, loverboy!" Hank's taunt sounded from down the hall.

Hannah pulled her hand from mine and stepped back, crossing her arms over her middle and smiling softly.

With a cold lump in my stomach, I left. And when I was halfway to Hank, I heard her office door click shut. My chest spasmed at the sound and I wanted to rush back, ask her again what I could do to earn her trust.

I didn't. The possibility existed that I was overreacting, overthinking. I'd never been in a relationship before. Since falling for Hannah, I hated second-guessing everything about her, wondering if I was reading her right.

"You and Hannah are together now?" He tossed the question over his shoulder.

I didn't answer. It was none of his business and I didn't know, like, or respect him.

"Well, that's just fucking great," he said, which made me think perhaps our feelings about each other were mutual.

Turning, he stepped in my path and shoved a finger at my chest. "Now you listen, *Twilight*," he spat, using my old nickname from when I'd been undercover with the Iron Wraiths MC. "Hannah isn't meant to stay here in Green Valley, at this rinky-dink strip club. She's meant for bigger and better. Don't be the reason she stays. She's worth more than a hundred of you."

Those were not the words I'd expected him to say and I caught myself before I laughed or made any other outward sign of surprise. Masking the direction of my thoughts behind a cold stare, I set my hands on my hips and lifted my chin.

"You think she's too good for this industry?"

"No, turkey brains. It's not the industry, it's the size."

I didn't know what to pay attention to first: that he'd used the very same insult Cletus Winston and Tina Patterson had used on me weeks ago, or what he'd implied about Hannah and the industry versus size. "Pardon?"

Hank rolled his eyes and turned, waving me forward as he ranted. "She wants to keep working for clubs? Fine. Then it should be a nationwide chain. She should have a hundred direct reports, manage thousands of people. I always knew she was smart, but I had no idea what she was capable of until she took this place over. She could do it, she could do whatever she wanted. I don't care what industry she works in, that business degree makes her qualified to go anywhere, do anything. But the Pony, this city, it's too small for her. It's like putting a shark in a pond. What a waste."

I was still processing his words when Hank turned and shoved his finger at me again. "If you're going to be with her, *be* with her. And convince her to leave. Be supportive, and not a leech."

"Why don't you say this to her? Why don't you tell her to leave?"

"Because I know Hannah better than you ever will. If it comes from me, she'll believe I think she's doing a bad job. She'll think I want her to quit so I can replace her. That's how her brain works. She never believes good things are in her future. I mean, given what she's had to deal with, I don't blame her."

To stop him from turning again, I gripped his shoulder. "Then why the fuck did you hire her at eighteen? Why not turn her away?"

He brushed my hand from his shoulder, his eyes narrowing into aggressive slits. "Listen here, asshole. My parents were worthless, but at least I had a roof and food on the table. Hannah could never count on even that much. She was the sole provider starting at seventeen, working as a hostess at the Front Porch and running a laundry business out of her house. And by the time she turned eighteen, she and her mother were in massive debt, almost lost their house. She needed a job that paid more than just the bills."

"So you exploited—"

He lifted his voice over mine. "So, I taught her a trade and gave her a safe environment to apply it. I taught her how to do this job without letting anyone take advantage or gain an upper hand. She holds all the power when she steps on that floor, and I taught her how to do that. Don't give me whatever self-righteous bullshit speech about exploitation blah blah blah. Fuck off."

Gritting my teeth, I huffed a laugh. This guy was a real piece of work.

He wasn't finished. "Hannah made a shit ton of money here. She paid off that stupid farm. She paid all her momma's medical bills, saved a bunch, put herself through college, never once accepting a single cent of charity—not from me, not from anyone. I taught her independence, how to build a stable financial future, how to never be on the losing end of a deal, how to protect herself from scammers and good-for-nothing dipshits like you. What did you teach her? And while we're at it, tell me this: What other job exists that pays this much for a high school graduate in a desperate situation, living in nowhere Appalachia? Take a guess. I'll give you all day to think about it."

I stared at him, knowing there was no answer. No other *legal* job existed, especially not for a woman, and especially not in this part of the world.

Seemingly satisfied with my silence, he went on, "But now it's time for her to walk away. From her needy momma—bless that woman's heart—from that piece of shit farm, from this place, and probably from your trashy ass. Hannah should live her damn life away from here, away from small folks with small ideas, gossips and hypocrites, who care more about reputation than quality. She's earned it."

Giving me one last look of disgust, Hank Weller turned and marched to the main floor, not waiting for me to follow. I did follow, eventually. But first I took several moments to digest everything he'd revealed about Hannah. I knew some of this information already, but a few details were new. This trove of knowledge didn't make me feel sorry for Hannah. It reinforced how much I admired, respected, and liked her.

Tina had been right all those weeks ago. The urge to rescue Hannah and forcibly carry her out of this place, what Tina had called *white knight instincts*, nearly drove all the oxygen from my lungs. But Tina had also been right about Hannah not needing or wanting a rescue.

Swooping in and "saving her" wouldn't be saving her at all. It would be belittling her years of hard work and treating the life she'd built with scorn, exactly what I'd felt when my sister tried to give me money last week, telling me I should quit my job.

My choices hadn't been perfect, but I'd done my best. Hannah's choices hadn't been perfect, but she'd done her best. Neither of us needed or wanted a white knight to save us from any battles. What we needed was a partner in the fight.

I hoped she'd let me be hers.

* * *

"Okay, time for the body check," Hank said as soon as I walked out of the hallway.

I stopped in my tracks and glanced around the room at the guys assembled. I recognized Hank Weller, Dave, Louis, and Beau Winston. The rest of the fellas were strangers to me and seemed to return my stare with mild curiosity.

"Come on." Hank waved me over. "Stand here where the light is good and take off everything but your underwear, shoes, and socks."

My heart beat erratically. I ignored it. As I walked to where Hank indicated, I reminded myself I'd been in shoot-outs, I'd taken a bullet, I'd shot people in self-defense, I'd taken a beating I knew was coming, I'd worked undercover for years, hiding any trace of fear behind an impenetrable mask of indifference.

I could take my clothes off in front of strangers, no problem.

Once I reached the spot, I glared at nothing, undid my fly, shoved down my pants, then pulled off my shirt.

The men around me stepped closer, their eyes moving over my chest, torso, stomach, and legs. A few nodded then looked away, continuing their conversations my arrival must've interrupted.

Hank, who'd decided to circle me for a closer inspection, said, "You got a lot of stretch marks, huh?"

"Yes, sir."

He made a short, impatient sound as he came around to stand in front of me. "Don't call me sir."

"Fine. Yes, Mr. Weller."

"Don't—just—damnit. Call me Hank."

"Fine. Hank," I grit out.

"Was that so difficult, *Isaac*?"

"I got stretch marks too." This came from Beau Winston as he moseyed up, undid his fly, and shoved his pants down like someone asked him to.

I stared at the redhead, nonplussed. And were those Spiderman underwear he had on? How old was he, nine?

Lifting a leg out of his jeans, he pointed to his upper thigh. "I grew two inches in one summer. It hurt so bad, my momma gave me ice packs every night."

Dave and Louis bent over Beau's leg to inspect the marks. When they'd looked to their hearts' content, Dave nodded thoughtfully while Louis pulled off his shirt, showing off his torso. "I have stretch marks here and . . . here." On his sides and under his arms were the faint white lines and he walked around the room pointing them out to everyone. Even me, despite my complete lack of interest.

Pretty soon everyone but Hank wore nothing but their drawers, swapping stories of growth spurts, stretch marks, involuntary hard-ons, wet dreams, voice changes, and new body hair. The painful awkwardness of adolescence shared with nostalgic laughter, I felt the tension in me ease a bit. It reminded me of being back in basic training, or back in our unit during deployment. Those guys I'd served with had been just as goofy and immodest as these weirdos.

"How about you, Hank? Show us your stretch marks," Louis, who'd started making drinks but hadn't yet put his clothes back on, called from behind the bar.

"He has none." Beau, currently lounging in a chair with his sock-covered feet up on a table, still wearing nothing but his Spiderman underwear, folded his hands behind his head and grinned at Hank. "His parents were doctors. He has no visible flaws, just lots of invisible ones."

"No. I got both visible and invisible ones. But, it's true, I have no stretch marks, nor did I have growing pains either. I never shot up in height over a few months, I grew slow and steady and finally stopped at nineteen." He shoved his hands in his pockets and glanced around the room, his eyes settling on me. "What about you, Isaac? When'd you stop growing? I remember you were a lot smaller before leaving town."

Seeing no reason to withhold the information, I said, "I stopped around twenty-one."

"How much did you grow? You left at eighteen and you were short then. Shorter than your daddy, if I recall," Hank pushed.

I scratched the back of my neck, wondering if I could put my pants and shirt back on. "I grew, uh, four or five inches after I left." Was the body check over? Or what?

"Well, no wonder you have stretch marks." Hank crossed his arms. "Your growth spurt came late, your skin was less elastic."

"What are you talking about, Hank? 'His skin was less elastic.'" Beau snorted a laugh. "Where are you reading this shit?"

"'Cause he was *older*." Hank said the word *older* loudly, like maybe we were all older and hard of hearing. "Our skin gets less elastic as we age, Beau. Obviously."

"Ignore him, Isaac." Beau rolled his eyes, still perfectly content to lounge in his undies. "He's got strange ideas."

"All right, all right, it's time to get serious. Beau, Dave, and Isaac are filling in tonight. Charlotte and Kilby will be here later to help with crowd control and serve food. We got Joshua and Louis at the front of the house. But Joshua is going to make himself scarce, watching everything on the video monitors, unless needed." Sending me one last irritated, distrustful glance, Hank hopped up on the stage and walked to a big box. "These are our costumes for the night. Let's get started training the newb."

I couldn't help but wonder, if Louis wasn't dancing, then why had he been present for the body check? Why had he taken off his shirt and showed off his stretch marks? Perhaps the little dude liked the camaraderie? I didn't know much about him. Perhaps he was lonely . . .

Hank barked out directions and orders. All the guys I didn't know took a moment to introduce themselves to me. Soon we were on the stage in our positions. Hank and the rest of the professional dancers went through the routine once. Beau joined the second time and I got the sense he'd filled in a few times. After the sixth run-through, I sent a silent thanks to Tina for teaching me some dancing basics.

Hannah's descriptions earlier about what to expect were mostly spot-on. Dave and I stood on the edges and acted as pillars of a sort. Our job was to put props where the professionals could reach them for use during the show, and then clear the items away when they were done. Beyond that, we had a few steps to master and I learned how to pull off the tearaway clothes in sync with the other dancers.

Apparently satisfied once we finished the ninth run-through of the group numbers, Hank announced, "Okay, everyone but Isaac go take a break. You"—he pointed at me—"come over here."

Wearing the tearaway pants, my boxers, socks, and boots, I walked over to Hank and accepted the bottle of water he held out.

Just as I lifted it to my lips to take a drink, he said, "Hannah's your stand-in, right?"

It was a sheer miracle I didn't spew the water all over him, but I did choke.

He frowned at me. "Don't tell me, you do know what a stand-in is, right?"

"Yes," I rasped out. "I know what a stand-in is."

"Good. You need to start picturing Hannah as soon as you get on that stage. Every woman is her. You can't be up here sending these God-fearing bridesmaids your murder eyes. You'll scare them and they won't tip."

Swallowing a gulp of water, I nodded.

"Seriously." Hank took a step forward. "You're actually not as bad at this as I thought you'd be. But you have to look like you want to be here. No one is going to have a good time if you don't. They pay for the fantasy, and it's our job to give it to them. Don't force a smile—no one would believe it—but, come on. Give me something."

Continuing to nod, I drank the water and wiped my mouth.

He examined me for a long moment, his expression turning thoughtful. "After the choreographed part, are you planning to come down for tips?"

"Uh . . . I hadn't—"

Hank turned toward the bar. "Charlotte! Honey, please come here for a sec."

Frowning, I followed Hank's line of sight and spotted Charlotte Mitchell walking toward where we stood on stage. I knew Charlotte—or rather, remembered Charlotte—from the few years I'd attended a traditional school. She was younger than me but threw some punches when several bullies had ganged up on me during recess. Maybe I'd been in third or fourth grade, but she'd been in kindergarten and half their size. She'd also been one of the women who'd sent me stink eyes last week when I stepped on the back porch of the Winston house, just before I'd spoken with my sister.

Looking at her now, a wave of prickling heat slithered up my chest and burned my ears. I ground my jaw. When had other folks arrived? Who else had been watching us?

Hank hopped down from the stage and gestured for me to do the same. I complied, reluctantly. He wore nothing but the black boxer briefs that were part of the costume, socks, and boots.

Pulling an upside-down chair off one of the tabletops, he set it upright on the floor and smiled at Charlotte. "Hey, gorgeous. Sit here, will you?"

"Sure thing, but what's happening?" She grinned at Hank, then at me, then at Hank again.

"I'm going to teach Isaac some moves, how to give a lap dance, to see if he'll come down to the floor with the rest of us. He might try them on you, is that okay?"

She shrugged like it was no big deal, sat down, and I gaped at the couple, unable to comprehend what was happening.

He wants me to . . . with his . . . in front of him?!

"Make sure they're far enough from the table so you can straddle them, like this." Hank bent his knees and climbed on top of Charlotte. He didn't sit on her legs, but rather hovered over them, his crotch in her face. "It's up to you if you're okay with touching. But, just to warn you, with your abs, they're going to want to give them a poke."

I snapped my mouth shut, realizing it had been hanging open.

He didn't seem to notice. Placing his hands on the back of the chair, he lowered himself, but still didn't sit on her lap. "You have to tell them when you approach them where they can touch. If they deviate outside of your boundaries, walk away. And, no matter the circumstances, they may never touch you where your boxers cover. That's illegal. But more importantly, it changes the dynamic of power. Don't let them get the upper hand, ever. Stay in control. And if you feel like they're pushing you, if nothing about the interaction is fun, move on to someone else, someone more respectful, or go back to the stage."

I'd been about to opt out of the lesson and beg off, I had no plans to come down to the floor, but as Hank spoke, I couldn't help but listen, transfixed. This kind of instruction must've been what he meant earlier when he'd said, *I taught her how to do this job without letting anyone take advantage or gain an upper hand. She holds all the power when she steps on that floor, and I taught her how to do that.*

"You okay, gorgeous?" he muttered to Charlotte, giving her a small smile.

She smiled back. "I'm good. You good?"

His eyelids drooped. "I'm always good when I'm with you."

Charlotte laughed, her eyes twinkling even in the dim club.

"All right!" Hank glanced at me. "Hold on to the back of the chair, don't touch them if you can help it—ever. Again, that's a transfer of power. Never, never touch them with your hands unless you're removing or re-directing their hands. This is a big rule. Also, don't shove your crotch in their face. I don't know if a circumstance exists where a woman ever wants a crotch shoved in their face. Do you, Charlotte?"

"No." She shook her head, her tone serious. "Not unless she asks. And even then, don't shove it."

"Right. Bend your knees." He demonstrated by bending his knees. "And if you told her your safe zones, encourage her to touch you now. You can say something like, 'Come on, don't be shy.' They love that shit. Or, 'Aren't you curious what I feel like?' That one is another winner. If you were stripping for men, the whole dynamic would be different. Men don't like coy questions, they want to be told what to do."

My eyes widened at his last two statements but I caught myself before I gaped again. As before, he didn't seem to notice.

"Charlotte, pretend I told you my safe zones are my thighs, chest, stomach, and arms, but not my back or neck. You got it?"

Charlotte nodded and lifted her hands to Hank's body, sliding her fingers from his chest to his lower stomach, but not touching the fabric of the boxers.

"This position can feel awkward and you might be wondering how to move, 'cause you can't just squat over her lap without it being weird. Don't make it weird. What you gotta do is roll your hips, like this." Using his hand braced on the back of the chair, presumably for balance, Hank did exactly what he said he'd do. He *rolled* his hips. There was no other word for it and it reminded me of the body roll dance move Tina had made me practice over and over when she gave me dance and kissing lessons. "Imagine your stand-in, right? Then imagine you got her bent over, skirt flipped up, underwear off, and you're just getting started. Got that image?"

My mouth went suddenly dry, everything in me seemed to tense, and I stared at him stoically, neither confirming nor denying his question. But, for the record, yes. I definitely *had* that image now.

My lack of response didn't faze him. "That's what the movement is like. It's the beginning part of making love, when you're careful and slow, when you're making sure you're hitting all her right spots. It feels good for you no matter what you do. But for her, this is what's going to get the job done. Don't do the end part." Hank's hips changed tempo and his movements lost their gracefulness, becoming jerky and fast.

Charlotte, meanwhile, laughed again, clapping a hand over her mouth, her eyes shining up at Hank. He turned another grin on her and wagged his eyebrows, which only made her laugh harder.

And then there was me, still transfixed, feeling like a pervert even as my brain took notes.

Resuming his slow, languid rolling, his hips at the level of her chest, he pointed to his abdominal muscles. "See what happens here? They flex the whole time. Ladies love that. This move will get you lots of tips." Hank lifted his chin toward me. "You got the perfect body for up close dancing."

Self-consciously, my hand covered my stomach.

"When they're done, they'll stop touching you. That's when you get off their lap. I'll show you how in a minute. But if you're done, you can just remove their hands by gently grabbing a single finger. If more force is needed, grab their wrists." Hank, again, demonstrated. He lifted one of Charlotte's hands away by a single finger, and the other by gripping her wrist.

I nodded, absorbing this information, but then stopped myself because I still had no plans to go out on the floor later. All this careful instruction was pointless.

Well . . . not entirely pointless.

"There's a few ways to retreat from this position, I'll show them now." Hank demonstrated two or three different movements while I pretended to pay attention. But I wasn't paying attention. My mind was . . . elsewhere.

When he finally finished, he extended his hand to Charlotte and she took it. "Thank you, gorgeous," he said, giving her cheek a kiss.

"Any time," she said, leaning into the kiss and reaching around to give his backside a smack.

Watching them, I wanted to ask so many questions, many of which I knew would be more than strange coming from a grown man. In the end, I asked nothing. That felt safer.

"Got it? Any questions?"

I shook my head and realized I still held the water bottle from earlier. I lifted it and found only a sip remained.

Hank's inspection of me turned thoughtful, like it had earlier on the stage. He took another step forward and lowered his voice. "No need to come down from the stage if you don't want tips, but if you need a codpiece, no problem. You're more than good now, but if it deflates under pressure, we got you covered. Most guys stuff with black socks because they look surprisingly natural. Don't go full Buck Adams or anything. But you need to appear semi-erect for the whole show, especially on the floor."

Standing still as a statue, I stared at Hank Weller, thankful he'd waited for me to finish swallowing my water this time before speaking. I didn't know who Buck Adams was, but in context I caught his drift.

Was he teasing me? . . . *Is he fucking with me right now?*

The man gave me a small, tight smile—like, *good talk*—turned, and walked over to where the other guys were taking their break. Pointing at one of them, he shouted, "No Viagra, Ian! I told you to quit that shit. We have codpieces. Just say nope to dope, my friend."

Chapter Twenty-Six
HANNAH

"Folks who color outside the lines make the biggest difference."

— Charlotte Mitchell, *Folk Around and Find Out* by Penny Reid

I waited a few minutes after Isaac and Hank left, then took a ridiculously long shower, ignoring the cup of coffee and bakery bag on my desk, telling myself I'd throw it away later.

Although part of me felt morosely curious, most of me simply felt nauseous about Isaac filling in today. I decided I wouldn't stay for the show. I'd greet the customers, the bride and maid of honor, and ensure they felt pampered. Then I'd leave them with Kilby and Charlotte and go inventory the storage room. If anyone needed me, if there were any customer issues, I could be reached on my phone. I had no reason to be there and watch those women touch Isaac—

Squeezing my eyes shut, I rubbed the soap roughly over my face, then lifted my head up to the spray, letting the water wash away the suds. *Don't think about it. Don't think about any of it.*

Was he mine? No. Was I his? No. As of this morning, we were apparently dating until he left town. He'd said so, or asked, or a combination of the two, and I hadn't contradicted him. But after he left, we would be nothing. End of story.

Dressing in my party clothes—female customers seemed to like me dressed as though I was part of the bridal party, whereas male customers preferred business attire from their club managers—I applied minimal makeup, gave myself a big smile in the mirror and evaluated it for believability. When the smile looked 25 percent forced instead of 98 percent forced, I checked my watch. I still had some time. The bridal party wasn't set to arrive for half an hour.

Hank should be out on the floor right now finishing up the run-throughs of the main numbers. The male dancers would then head back to the dressing room and wait until the bridal party had a chance to order a few drinks, maybe some appetizers.

One of the reasons our bachelorette parties had been doing so well recently was because of our new novelty menus. Serafina and I had collaborated on the updates. The latest reviews online mentioned her penis-shaped shortbread cookies, which could be dipped in white frosting. They tasted as good as they looked, but mostly they were silly and helped get the party started, loosening people up.

Grabbing the tablet I used for inventory, I took it to the storage closet and set a timer on my phone. Time passed quickly. Too soon, I had to stop my counting of napkin packages and head to the club's entrance.

Going through the motions, I smiled my 25-percent-forced smile and showed the ladies around. The bride, a lovely woman by the name of Beth Diamond, seemed to be the least nervous of the bunch and the most ready to get down to business.

"Meghan said she paid for eight, but we have thirteen people here total. Is that okay?" Beth, who wore a little white veil, seemed very concerned that each of her bridesmaids be given equal time with a dancer. "I don't want anyone to be left out."

"No one will be left out." The maid of honor, a woman by the name of Meghan Long, reassured Beth before I got a chance to respond. "And eight was the maximum package available. I'm sure this place has dealt with large bridal parties before."

I was already nodding before Meghan finished her sentence. "Oh, yes. The dancers will approach every member of your party and give them a chance for some one-on-one time." I had an odd thought as the words left my mouth: *I sound like I'm talking about a petting zoo, not about a bunch of people.*

Vanishing the strange notion, I went on, "Sometimes the party includes more than just bridesmaids and the bride. We had one a few weeks ago where the mothers and grandmothers were also in attendance."

Beth's eyes grew impossibly wide and she shared a look with her maid of honor, both women laughing in a way that seemed anxious.

"I don't think my momma would approve. In fact, I think she'd have a heart attack if she knew where we were right now," Beth said.

"Well, don't give her a heart attack. Instead just enjoy yourselves. Louis is behind the bar and will take good care of you. We also have Kilby and Charlotte on staff, serving the tables tonight." I turned and indicated to the two women standing by the bar. Wearing full tuxedos, they both waved and smiled.

We never introduced the bouncers to the bridal parties as "bouncers." We always referred to them as servers or staff. They functioned as both waitresses and bouncers, a double purpose. The contract stated explicitly that at least two bouncers would be present to expel anyone from the premises who violated behavior policies, but Hank advised me to never point out who the bouncers were—or draw attention to their existence—during hen parties. According to him, it made women nervous, discouraged tipping, and dampened the mood.

So much of this job was psychology and encouraging people to let themselves have a good time.

"But if y'all have any questions, just have someone message me." I lifted my phone. "I'll be close by and will come right over."

"One more thing." Meghan pointed with her thumb toward one of their party. "Do y'all have a medical mask or something? One of our friends is just getting over the flu and the elastic band to her mask broke. She's probably not contagious but just to be on the safe side."

"We do." I lifted a hand toward Charlotte and waved her over. "We keep them behind the bar. Charlotte here will bring you a few."

"Thank you!" Meghan flashed me a big smile.

I placed a hand on Charlotte's arm and explained the situation, reminding her that the masks were behind the bar, and she promised to grab one for the bridesmaid.

Fears assuaged, the women rejoined their friends. It wasn't long before the entire room filled with sounds of merriment. Between pitching in with the initial food orders, taking photos for the bridal party, and serving drinks, I checked my watch to track the time, promising myself I'd leave two minutes prior to the show.

Before I was ready, the time had arrived and my phone beeped. I scanned the ladies once more, just to be sure all their requests had been addressed. Movement by the front entryway caught my attention.

"Tina? What are you doing here?" I faced her fully, surprised to see my friend on her day off.

"It hasn't started yet, right? I couldn't miss Isaac's debut. I thought about bringing a foam penis to wave around, but I didn't want to embarrass him." She glanced at me, her gaze moving down, then up, then she frowned. "What's wrong with you?"

"Nothing is wrong with me."

"You look constipated."

"I'm not—" I rolled my eyes. "Forget it. Have fun." I turned toward the back hall.

Tina grabbed my wrist, halting my departure. "Where are you going?"

"I have to do inventory. I'll be in the storage closet." I gave my arm a shake.

She didn't let go. "Are you kidding? They're just about to start. You're going to miss Isaac stripping."

"Oh well." I shrugged.

She blinked, like my reaction truly astonished her. "Hannah."

"What?"

Tina wrinkled her nose, pinched her lips, and widened her eyes, her signature *I'm irritated with you* expression. "Why are you being like this? Don't you think he'd appreciate your support?"

"Why would it matter to him if I'm here or not?"

"Because he's shy and modest." She tugged my arm. "He's actually a bit of a prude. And this is scary for him."

I wanted to roll my eyes again at her statement. This would be scary for him? For Isaac? The undercover agent?

Yeah, right.

Instead, I twisted out of her grip. "You're here."

"Yeah. But he's not in love with me."

"Tina. Come on." I glared at her. I also walked away. I wasn't entertaining her stupid teasing, not now. Probably not ever. There was no way Isaac was in love with me.

What a joke.

I'd made it just around the corner of the hallway when Tina grabbed me again. "Hannah. Stop walking away and stop being obtuse."

My expression flattened. "Where did you learn the word *obtuse*?"

Her gaze shifted to the left, then right. "Why? Did I use it wrong?"

"No. You used it right."

"Good. It was on my word-of-the day calendar this morning and stop changing the subject. If you leave him out there alone—"

"He won't be alone. There's thirteen women out there to keep him company." I lifted a hand toward the main area and the music kicked up, signaling the start of the show. My heart leapt to my throat as the bass beat reverberated in my chest. I'd planned to be safely in the storage room by now, where the sounds wouldn't reach me.

"—he'll be hurt," Tina spoke over me. "I told you your tires were safe from me because I assumed you'd be good to him. Don't turn me into a liar."

"Why are you making a big deal out of this? He's not going to care!" She was so weird sometimes and she was getting on my last nerve.

Tina huffed, visibly seething, and spat, "You're being a real bitch right now. What the fuck is wrong with you? Why are you acting like you don't know how he feels about you, what you mean to him?"

I flinched at the insult and fully embraced my rising temper, snapping back, "Sorry if you think I'm being a bitch, but you don't know what you're talking about. Isaac isn't 'in love' with me or whatever. We're casually dating—"

"No." She shook her head resolutely.

"Yes!"

"No, you twit!" Tina stepped forward and shoved her face in mine, punctuating her words by hammering her finger into my clavicle. "Isaac doesn't 'casually' do anything, and he definitely doesn't casually date. The man doesn't *date*, period. And he doesn't agree to fill in as a male stripper for just anyone, considering the fact that he's super private about his body, and he doesn't do bakery runs every morning for anyone else, and he doesn't go around inserting himself into conversations or other people's business, like he does with you and Louis whenever Louis flirts with you. Wake up. Smell the coffee he's been bringing you every damn morning!"

Finally, she leaned back, glaring at me as though to ensure all her points had landed.

"Well, I don't know him! How am I supposed to know what he does and doesn't do normally?" I threw my hands up, feeling defensive, because she made some good points about the muffins and such. Isaac did treat me differently from everyone else. And, according to her, he was helping today as a favor to me.

On the other hand, what was she talking about? Isaac wasn't private about his body.

"Ask him some questions, turkey brains. Get to know the guy so you'll know what he needs. And, in the meantime, trust his friends when they tell you what he needs. I'm telling you now—as his old friend—he needs you to be out there. He needs your support. Again, he's doing this favor for *you* and no one else. Stop being a selfish twat."

"Okay. Okay. Fine. I'll . . . go back out." I nodded and my chin wobbled for some reason. She was right, the least I could do was go out there and support him from the sidelines, even if the sight of it would make me feel wretched.

Tina huffed again, but this time it sounded sympathetic. "When you showed up and asked for a job here, I know Hank did what he thought was right for you at the time. And I think his influence and advice has saved you a lot of trouble. You were too soft, too sensitive, too trusting. But one thing he taught you—that he pushes on all of us, but you took it way too seriously—is to never let someone else have the upper hand. Never let yourself be vulnerable, not with anyone, and to always be hyperaware of power dynamics. Because if you are vulnerable, people will use you, hurt you, and rip your heart out."

Biting the inside of my lip, I swallowed convulsively to keep my tears at bay.

Tina lifted a hand and pointed in the direction of the thumping music. "Hannah, you need to trust me. That idiot loves you. Maybe he doesn't know it yet fully, maybe he's wrestling with it. But if Isaac wasn't in love with you, he would never touch you. And he certainly would never let you touch him."

"What are you talking about?" My question sounded like a squeak because my throat felt tight. "He used to get lap dances from you all the time, kiss you all the time. Was he in love with you? Are you saying he was in love with me when he showed up at my retirement party? I touched him then. He bought five lap dances—"

"Don't give me that shit. You know perfectly well that he thought I'd arranged the meeting in September. He never expected you to touch him then. Also, for the record, I never gave Isaac a lap dance, not once. And the kissing was for show, part of his cover. He never touched me when we were alone. And when we weren't alone, when he was forced to put on a show, he touched me only the barest amount necessary to make it seem real."

It seemed like she was trying to tell me something without having to say it outright. "So, you're saying he's a strict monogamist? That he only lets the woman he's interested in touch him?"

"No, Hannah, you obtuse obtusing obtuser! Listen to me! I'm saying, you're the first woman I've ever—and I mean *evvveeerr*—seen him with. You're the first person he's ever wanted to be with. That man is pure as new fallen snow. He's untouched. Except by you."

I snorted, wanting to laugh at the absurdity of this claim. "Right. Okay. Sure. If you say so."

"I know so."

"No, *I* know so. The stuff we've done so far—"

"He's only ever done with you, shortcake." She tapped my nose with the tip of her acrylic nail. "And the night you gave him the lap dance, that was the furthest he'd gone with a woman. And all this 'stuff' you've done together, it's been his first time, every time. Have you fucked yet?"

Stupefied by her words, struggling to make sense of them, I shook my head before my brain comprehended the sensitive and personal nature of the information I'd just revealed by the simple head shake. It wasn't any of Tina's business whether Isaac and I had slept together, and if I'd been in my right mind, I never would've told her.

"That's what I thought." She nodded once. "He's a virgin. But I bet, from the way he looks at you, he won't last another week if you're up for it."

My mouth opened and closed wordlessly for several seconds before I managed to wheeze out, "Are you—are you joking? Are you kidding with me? Is this—"

"No. Like I said, pure as new snow. Pure as, I don't know, really clean stuff. Pure as a—as a—whatever. You get the picture. And you get to plant that flag, the honor is all yours if you want it, because the boy is in love and is looking at you with heart eyes and a raging hard-on every time you—"

"That's enough." I shook my hands in front of my ears. "I can't—that's enough." Her statements were overwhelming.

"Think, Hannah." She tapped the side of my head. "I don't know what y'all talk about, what he's asked, what he's shared, but think back to all your conversations, and I guarantee you will see I'm telling the truth."

"But he's such a fantastic kisser!" I blurted, still trying to find evidence to contradict what I now knew was true. "Why is he such a good kisser if he's never dated anyone?"

"You can thank me for that." Tina glanced at her nails, sounding supremely satisfied with herself. "He used to be shit at it. And since we had to kiss anyway for his cover, like, all the time, I taught him how. I didn't want it to be —ugh, you know how it is with guys who don't know how? All slimy tongue and that weird stabbing thing they do, and no lips. Lips are great, why do they ignore lips? I hated it. So, I taught him. He's good, right?"

My mind on overdrive, our interactions rewound and played back in my memory on quadruple speed. How he'd reacted to our lap dance, how angry he'd been, how he'd treated me after. But then the sudden shift and apology when he realized I hadn't been lying to him, that I wasn't soliciting at the Pony. The way he looked at me since, quietly showing up and helping without asking for anything, his statement that he owed me, that he couldn't simply continue avoiding me, that he didn't want us avoiding each other.

Most damning, the memory of his confession at the Donner family cabin. He'd been so wholesome and sweet, uncertain and shy. I'd thought so at the time. A complete contrast to his typical confidence and stoicism.

What had he said? *I think I must be really bad at this. It's my first time.*

The man has no experience. You're his first everything. The realization stole my breath and it changed everything. The world tilted on its axis, the earth shifted, and the heavens parted.

Heck, even how he'd touched me earlier today in my office—either too soft or too rough—should've tipped me off to his lack of experience. I'd been so turned on, so lost to him and the moment, it had never occurred to me that a man with his life experience and of his age—

The sudden music change brought me back to the present and my heartbeat matched the frenzied tempo. Inventory forgotten, I jogged past Tina and into the main room, sending up a prayer of thanks that the stage would be lit but the room would be dark until they finished the first three choreographed numbers.

To hell with my hesitancy. To hell with my jealousy and envy. When the lights turned on, I wanted to be the first thing he saw. But mostly, I wanted to be worthy of being his first everything.

"Wait." Tina caught up with me, then grabbed my arm for a third time, bringing me to another stop.

"What? What is it?" I turned, impatient.

She'd scrunched her face, her gaze pleading. "Do me a favor and don't tell Isaac I told you he was a virgin."

"Pardon?"

She couldn't be serious.

"I don't want him thinking I spilled his secrets."

My mouth dropped open. "Tina. You *did* spill his secrets."

"I know!" She let me go and flapped her lashes at me, giving me a winning smile. "But there's no reason *he* has to know."

Chapter Twenty-Seven

HANNAH

"Think of how much better the world would be if people craved compliments about the beauty of their heart rather than the beauty of their face."

— Susie Moist, *Grin and Beard It* by Penny Reid

The main room had grown rowdy and the guys were still in the first half of the second dance number. Tina walked close behind me and I spotted Isaac at once. He stood on the far left end of the stage, his features clear of expression. He hit the cues impressively well considering this was his first time up there.

During our choir days, he had impeccable pitch and rhythm. I hadn't expected church choir to translate so well to . . . this. Just goes to show, no previous life experience is wasted if you're not picky about how and when to apply it.

I walked slowly to the bar, my heart climbing up my throat again. But not because Isaac was a virgin, or because of the other thing Tina had revealed: *That idiot loves you.*

My nerves were a direct result of my anxiety for him. If I'd known about his aversion to exposing his body, about his preference for modesty, I never would've agreed to his participation today. But he'd never seemed modest with me. He'd whipped his shirt off and kissed me. He'd let me reach inside his boxers like it was no big deal to him.

On pins and needles, I watched the show. They finished the second set and Tina shoved my shoulder, forcing me to look at her. Her grin was wide and she appeared proud.

"He's doing so great! My boy is all grown up." Wiping at fake tears, she sniffled. "And soon he won't be a virgin either. Make it good for him. Like, blow his fucking mind. He deserves it. And when y'all get married, you have to name your first child after me. No matter if it's a boy or girl."

A laugh left my lungs even though my stomach was in knots. "Okay, Tina. Sure thing," I muttered, returning my attention to the stage as the third number started.

Isaac didn't smile, not once, but that was okay. It sorta suited his persona on stage, gave him a sexy air of mystery and danger. Also, the man could dance. This third choreographed number was the most challenging, even for the pillars, but he only messed up once. I felt certain none of the women in the audience picked up on it. I only noticed because I'd watched the dance so many times.

The third number was also the longest and the one where they finally ripped off their Velcro pants. Getting those things off could be tricky because you had to grab them in just the right spot and tug in just the right way. His flew off with everyone else's and I clasped my hands beneath my chin, wanting to clap for him but knowing I shouldn't. Not yet.

But as soon as the dance ended, I was one of the loudest to cheer. And when the lights beyond the stage came on, I stepped slightly away from the bar and waved my hand in a small, mindless attempt to get his attention.

Isaac blinked, his eyes probably needing to adjust to the change in lighting, and then he scanned the room, swallowing. His hands were balled into fists and the slash of his mouth looked severe. Now that I knew he was modest, I could see he was unsettled by what he found, all the women staring at him and cheering.

But then his gaze found mine and his forehead cleared, the firm line of his mouth relaxing. I smiled widely, giving him two thumbs up, and I watched his chest rise and fall with a deep breath.

Oh my heart. He was something else. What had I done to deserve this man? I didn't know. A rush of tears stung my eyes, but this time they weren't the bad kind.

Hank said something over the microphone. The sound of his voice plus movement on stage had me tearing my eyes from Isaac's. I gripped the bar as all the professional dancers started making their way to the floor. Beau Winston, Dave, and Isaac were picking up props and costumes, tucking them away. Dave said something with a grin. Beau laughed and Isaac almost cracked a real smile. Then Dave gestured to the floor.

I watched, holding my breath as Beau glanced at Isaac, inspecting him while he held perfectly still, saying nothing, and time seemed to freeze, suspend itself. I'd almost forgotten that it was generally expected for everyone on stage to go down to the floor.

Screw that.

I prepared to step forward and intercede, stop Isaac from being pressured into it—because it was very clear to me now that he had no interest in walking among strangers and letting them touch his body—but before I could, Beau faced Dave and stepped in front of Isaac. He shook his head and waved the big man off with a smile. The redheaded Winston tossed a thumb over his shoulder and hit Isaac lightly in the chest.

In the next moment, Dave walked toward the stairs leading down to the floor while Beau and Isaac slipped through the back door off the stage, leaving the room completely. The relief I felt made my whole body sag.

Thank goodness for Beau Winston.

"I'll be back," Tina leaned close and whispered in my ear.

I nodded absentmindedly. Isaac had his own mind, but I didn't want him being pressured into dancing for tips. If Beau had joined the others, Isaac might've thought it was required, or that I would be put in a bad position if he declined. I never wanted him to do anything like this again, anything against his nature, outside of his comfort zone. He must be protected at all costs!

"Can I get you a drink?" Louis's voice asked.

I faced the bartender just as he set a glass down in front of me.

"Uh, no, thanks." I never drank during business hours. Hank used to. Not to excess, but one drink every so often. I didn't have a high tolerance so it was best to simply abstain.

"Then will you buy me a drink?"

My head tilted to the side and I frowned, not responding because this request struck me as strange. Louis never drank. At least, he never drank here. Not even during off-work hours.

"*Sooo* . . . you and mute-boy, huh?" Louis's lips twisted to the side wryly and I suddenly understood his request that I buy him a drink. As usual, I didn't need to guess the direction of his thoughts. The younger guy was too open with his feelings, and right now his gaze was laden with disappointment and wistfulness.

"If you mean, Isaac, then yes. Me and mute-boy," I said gently, hoping Louis wouldn't be too hurt about it. He was a good kid, but I'd been very clear from the beginning about my lack of interest. I'd built boundaries and he'd ignored them.

He nodded, pouring whiskey into the glass he'd set down. "Is it his 'murder eyes'? That's what Hank called them earlier."

A short laugh burst out of me and I shook my head at Hank's penchant for colorful descriptions. Hoping to keep the mood light between us, I joked, "Yes, Louis. It's his murder eyes. That's what won me over. A girl can't resist a guy with murder in his eyes."

Louis chuckled and downed the whiskey. When he recovered from the burn, he set his gaze on me again. "Thanks for being my first love, Hannah."

I reared back an inch, the words catching me off guard.

He wasn't finished. "I know I have no chance, and I'm not asking for one. But I do want to thank you. I'm proud you were my first love, even if it was unrequited. It made me realize I have great taste, and I don't need to worry about who I end up with. If they're half as smart and talented and funny and sweet as you, I'll be set."

My heart flip-flopped and I pressed a hand over the spot. He was a sweetheart. A frustrating, pushy sweetheart. "Louis—"

"No, no. It's too late now." He plucked the glass off the bar. "You had your chance. Go find your beloved, he's probably off scaring small children or something."

I laughed, but I also stepped back. I did need to find Isaac and talk to him. I needed to be vulnerable and honest about my fears. And I needed to keep an open mind and stop assuming life would give me the shit side of the stick.

This last one would take a while to unlearn, but I didn't want to miss out on the good in life because I always expected the worst.

* * *

I found Isaac hovering outside my office, wearing his own jeans and socks. No shoes were on his feet and no shirt covered his torso. My body seemed to really like this fact. Awareness blossomed in my lower stomach like a gentle wave moving through my body. Acute cognizance of his strength, size, and the intensity of his stare mingled with my wholesome intentions, making me feel a little dizzy and conflicted.

Get ahold of yourself, Hannah. Now is not the time to be turned on. He needs comfort, not your lusty admiration.

"Where's your shirt?" I asked, maintaining a safe distance. I reminded my overactive imagination that he shouldn't have to walk around here shirtless if he preferred modesty, no matter how gorgeous he was.

"I don't know. I can't find it," he said, looking only mildly frustrated by this fact.

"Do you want to come in?" I lifted a hand toward my office. As much as I wanted to soak up the vision of him in front of me, the beauty of his body on display, I also didn't want to make him uncomfortable.

"Can we talk somewhere else? We're always interrupted when we're in your office."

"Uh, yes." I debated where we could go, shoving my greedier impulses aside. I wasn't allowed in the dressing room today until the hen party ended since the male dancers—or their stuff—would be inside, which meant we couldn't access my small changing room. The only other truly private place in the club was the storage closet.

I grimaced at the thought. I'd spent so much time and energy keeping folks out of there for any reason other than to grab supplies or for inventory. I'd already taken Isaac in the closet once for a conversation, and my hypocrisy had bothered me since. Was I going to break my own rules again?

Glancing up at Isaac, at the force of his gaze paired with his state of undress, my mouth watered. I swallowed.

The devil on my shoulder told me, *It's not that big of a deal! You're the boss. Use the room. Y'all need to talk. It'll be fine.*

The angel on my other shoulder told me, *What the devil said.*

Ignoring the fact that both the angel and the devil sounded suspiciously like Tina Patterson, I grabbed his hand and pulled him after me.

"Okay, let's go," I said, leading the way.

Silently following, Isaac changed the hold of our hands, threading our fingers together instead of cupping our palms. Unlocking the closet, I searched our surroundings, craning my neck to ensure no one was nearby, then pulled him forward and into the compact space.

"Careful, don't let the door close," I whispered, releasing his hand and doing my best to face him without knocking something off a shelf.

Isaac propped the door open then turned to me. Wearing a small smile that looked a tad uncertain, he walked to me but left four feet between us.

I stepped forward and reduced the distance by two feet. "You did so great!"

"Thank you." He seemed to be inspecting me like he was searching for an answer to a question.

"Maybe you could give me some pointers," I teased, gently shoving his shoulder with my fingertips.

His ears tinted red but his smile widened. It still looked shy. *Oh my goodness. He is too cute.*

"If I'd known me filling in today would make you this happy, I would've volunteered to do it permanently," he said haltingly, his tone entirely earnest.

"No!" A spike of alarm had me lifting my hand. "No. Don't do that. I do appreciate you stepping in, but I don't want you to do it again, and it's not why I'm happy right now."

Still inspecting me, he asked, "It's not?"

Goodness, I didn't want him thinking he needed to do something that pained him in order for me to be happy. I didn't want that at all. I needed to clear the air and set him straight.

Shuffling my feet a step forward, I decided to spell it out. "I'm sorry. I've been distant and distracted. That's my fault. I—well, honestly, I doubted your sincerity and I'm sorry."

His hesitant smile disappeared. "And me helping out today proved to you that I'm sincere?"

"No. That's not it. Please don't think that. Actually, it was Tina who—" I cut myself off because Isaac's eyes widened and his normal façade of calm cracked.

If I read his expression correctly, a hint of panic sparked behind his gaze. Perhaps he was scared that Tina had told me about him never having a relationship. I didn't want to embarrass Isaac or make him feel self-conscious. If he wanted me to know about his past, he would've told me himself.

Also, Isaac being a virgin didn't matter to me. What mattered was everything else Tina had said, about all the evidence pointing to the depth of his feelings and how I never trusted people.

Wrapping my arms around his middle, I gentled my voice and began again. "It was Tina who pointed out my trust issues. She also spoke up for you, told me how great of a guy you are, told me you were—are—trustworthy. She called me some names, but she also called me out."

The panic receded from his gaze and his lips tugged downward. "She called you names?"

"No biggie. Being crass is her love language. But I am really sorry." My arms tightened, giving him a squeeze. "And I will do my best to talk to you about my doubts instead of packing them up and running away. That's my problem, and I'm sorry I made it yours."

Isaac opened his mouth but a sound I hadn't been expecting, like a door clicking shut, made us both blink and flinch. I leaned to the side and studied the angle of the door.

Oh cheesus. "The door closed!" I exhaled the words on a shocked breath.

Isaac turned his head just as Tina could be heard shouting from the other side of the door, "That's what you get! You said this room was only for inventory, not for conducting personal business."

"Tina!" I yelled. "Open that door right now!"

"No. Besides, I can't. I don't have a key."

"Dave has a key."

"Well, I'll go find him, but I'm going to take my time. You will stay in there until you learn your lesson. Or until you agree to change the lock back. I'll give you two hours."

"What are we supposed to do for two hours?" I hollered.

"Don't be so obtuse—and I know I used the word correctly that time. You got a half-naked man in there and at least four hundred condoms. Do with the time what you will, I'm sure y'all will find a way to make it pass pleasantly."

Chapter Twenty-Eight
ISAAC

"Put your best fuck forward."

—Cletus Winston, *Grin and Beard It* by Penny Reid

Hannah made a growling noise of pure frustration. "I am going to—she is—I swear to heaven—"

Chest tight, mind elsewhere, I struggled to keep my hands to myself. I wasn't upset about being locked in here together for two guaranteed hours. Alone. With no interruptions.

But it did set me on edge.

Hank had told me to imagine Hannah bent over in front of me, skirt flipped, underwear off. Ever since he'd spoken the words, they'd become a mantra, repeating over and over in my brain, conjuring the image on repeat.

Hannah bent over in front of me, skirt flipped, underwear off . . . bent over in front of me, skirt flipped, underwear off . . . bent over in front of me, skirt flipped, underwear off.

Currently, Hannah laughed lightly, giving her head a shake and taking a step back, her arms dropping from my torso. "Well. I guess we're stuck. Anything in particular you wish to discuss?"

I swallowed thickly and focused on regulating my breathing, intensely aware of the box of condoms behind me. I'd never worn one.

"Is it normal to be, uh, a little turned on after a show?" I asked, because I could. I trusted Hannah to answer my questions without making me feel stupid or callously teasing me.

Hannah peered up at me. "Um, sometimes. Depends on the show, I guess. Why?" She dipped her chin, looking at me like we were sharing a confidence. "Do you need me to distract you?"

"That might be a good idea." I backed up, bracing my hands on the shelves at either side.

"Okay." Hannah folded her fingers and leaned back against the paper towels behind her. "There are two things I want to talk to you about."

"Tell me." My brain informed me that she wore a skirt today. No stockings.

"First, I wanted to apologize again for what happened the night of my retirement party. I still feel *really* bad about it. I was thoughtless and greedy and, looking back, I fully understand why you were so upset. In this industry, clear, explicit consent is so important and I never should've assumed anything. I'm so, so sorry."

"I wish you would stop apologizing about it. I—I'm not upset." If anything, thinking about that night now was torture for a very different reason.

"Okay, okay. I'll stop." She peered up at me with remorse in her eyes and I think I fell a little in love with her. Her sensitivity and thoughtfulness for others was the main reason I trusted her so much.

Wanting to change the subject, I asked, "What's the second thing you wanted to talk about?"

"Oh. Yes. When we were at that place on Bandit Lake, you said you wanted us to date, even after the investigation is over." Her tone had turned businesslike, all the earlier remorse fading. "You said you could stay in town for a few weeks or months, but that you'd have to eventually leave."

"That's right."

"And when you left, you were leaving for good."

"Yes."

Her head tilted to the side an inch as she considered me. "But that I could go with you? If I did go with you, we'd have to get married and I'd also have to change my identity, leave my past behind."

"Correct, but I'm not trying to rush you."

"I know." She gave me a sweet smile that did nothing to help the situation I was presently struggling with. She was so fucking gorgeous when she smiled. And when she didn't smile. "Is that all true? You want us to start dating with marriage in mind? You want to take me with you? What about your job?"

"It's all true. I'm studying right now to take the trainers' exam so I can become a trainer for the agency. Some agents love the undercover work and never leave unless they're carried out in a pine box. But I'm tired of it."

"So, you were already planning to leave undercover work before coming here for your latest assignment?"

I paused, having to repeat her question in my head a few times before my mind could make sense of it because I was distracted by her button-down shirt. Finally, I nodded and said, "Yes."

"I see."

"Did that answer all your questions?" I wasn't wearing a shirt, but I was hot. So hot.

"It did."

"Does it—" I had to stop to breathe through another something tight in my chest. "Now that you're no longer—as you put it—doubting my sincerity, what do you think?"

"Part of me likes the idea a lot. But part of me doesn't know what to think." Her gaze moved beyond me.

Mine dropped to the front of her shirt, to the buttons. Since I thought I should probably say something in response, I said, "I see."

"It's complicated. I am so grateful to Hank for the opportunity he's given me here and I don't want to let him down."

"What if you weren't letting him down?" My voice sounded strained. I cleared my throat. "What if he gave you his blessing?" I wanted to adjust myself in my pants, I was so hard it was painful, but I didn't know how to do that without drawing attention to my, uh, big problem.

I wished she'd touch me. I wished she'd give me some sign she was as impacted by me as I was her. She had so many reasonable things to discuss while all I wanted to do was bend her over, flip her skirt, and—

"That would make a difference." She nodded, still not looking at me, her mind on other things. "But then there's also my momma. Until recently, we only had each other. She's been relying on me for a long time."

"Does she rely on you still? Do you think she'd be okay if you left?" I didn't want to come between her and her mother. If Hannah did leave with me, we'd have to work together to figure out how to ensure her mother continued to be safe and well.

What if Hannah can't leave her momma behind? What if—

I couldn't finish the thought. It made me feel desperate. And she had no idea. She had no idea I was standing here undressing her in my mind.

"I think she would, actually."

Fuck. What were we even talking about?

"I think my momma would be fine if I left." Her thoughtful gaze returned to mine and I dropped my eyes, not wanting her to see my struggle.

"Would you be okay if you left? If you could only have contact with your mom rarely? If you never saw the farm again?"

"I'd be perfectly fine if I never laid eyes on the farm ever again. And I'd miss my momma, but . . ."

I tried to distract myself by cataloging all the different kinds of paper goods that were stored in this tiny fucking closet. "But what?"

"But I think it's too late for us."

This statement from her cut through the haze of my yearning, sharpened my attention on her words. "For you and your mom? What do you mean?" I didn't want Hannah to be distraught, but the way she'd said *too late for us* had been stained with melancholy.

"She was someone else when I was little versus the rest of my childhood. Vivacious and sweet. She's that person again, finally. Or at least she's getting there. But all those years in between, she was so sad. Depressed. Angry at the world or checked out from it. I waited for so long, for her to become herself again. And now that she is, I'm too different. I'm the one who isn't the same. I can't . . . just enjoy her company. You know?" She gave me a half smile but her eyes were unhappy.

"I do know." I had similar thoughts about my own mother.

She wanted me to be someone I wasn't. She kept expecting me to turn back into the little boy she loved. I liked who I was now, but I was not the person she wanted me to be. Nor could I spend time in her company without feeling resentful.

She'd stayed with my father and bought into his BS, enabled him. She hadn't protected me and Jennifer. I resented that I had to be the parent and she'd been the child. I resented that I had to be strong because she couldn't.

Sniffing suddenly, Hannah shook her head as though to clear it and straightened her spine. "Since your offers were serious, then I will take them seriously, and I think your overall plan is a good one. We'll date each other, keep getting to know each other. But, just so you know, other than Hank, the Pony and its staff, and my momma, there's honestly nothing keeping me here."

These words were a huge relief, especially since I could tell she truly meant them. "Is it bad for me to say I'm happy that's the case?"

Her smile returned. "Because you want me to go with you?"

I nodded instead of saying, *Because I want to marry you. Because I want to build a life with you. Because I want to be a reason for you to smile. Because I want to be your partner in the fight, but also in times of peace.*

Books told me that falling in love with a person can happen instantaneously. Or overnight. Or over a few days or weeks. I'd thought, on the off chance it ever happened to me, it would take me years. I'd been so cautious, not allowing myself to look at another person with anything but platonic or professional interest, women especially. People were people; equal; genderless. To me, they were defined by their relevance to my investigation rather than a reflection of their hopes and dreams.

Yet, whenever I spent time in the same room as Hannah, her relevance to my investigation seemed incredibly irrelevant. I couldn't think straight. And I couldn't help but wonder about her hopes and dreams, notice all the things that made Hannah herself. Not just that, I also couldn't help but notice everything that made Hannah a woman.

I licked my bottom lip, pulling it into my mouth and biting it. My traitorous eyes lowered to the front of her shirt again. *Only seven buttons.*

"Isaac?"

"Hannah. I think I need you." As though pushed, I stumbled forward. My lungs were on fire. "Since we have a couple hours, maybe we could . . ."

I stopped myself. She had nowhere to go. She was already pressed against the paper towels. I didn't want to crowd or pressure her.

Hannah didn't respond right away, but her breathing quickened. At the signal of this change in her, I lifted my gaze from her shirt. She looked conflicted.

"We shouldn't . . . ?" Her tone made the words both an uncertain statement and a hopeful question. I doubted even she believed them.

"Hannah."

She lifted a hand. "Don't say my name like that."

I took a step forward, pushing my chest against her palm. "Why not?"

Her eyes focused on my body for a second, then she closed them. "Because it's really hard to be responsible when you—when you do . . . that."

Licking my lips again, I braced my hands on either side of her. Our history told me that if I touched her where and how I wanted, it would be over before she could fully think through the matter. I wanted her. But, more so, I wanted her mindful and making an active choice.

Bending, I whispered in her ear, "I think you'll like it." I would make sure she did.

She shivered. "I don't want your—I mean, *our* first time together to be in this storage closet, do you?"

"I don't care where it is." I was so beyond caring. I wanted inside her, didn't matter where we were.

"You can't mean that."

"I do." I bent my head lower and kissed her neck, licking the spot and whispering against her skin, "I just want you."

"You're letting lust dictate your choices."

"I don't think so. This isn't a sudden thing for me." Restless, I allowed one hand to release the shelf and lower to her shirt, unbuttoning the first of her buttons.

She let me, her breaths hot against my bare skin. "Just because it isn't sudden doesn't mean you—we—should settle for wherever."

"I don't feel like I'm settling. I suspect this will be memorable. Do you feel like you're settling?" I nuzzled her ear, softly biting the lobe and licking the tip.

I felt a shiver race through her. "No. No. This would not be settling for me at all. But I want you—a per—a couple's first time should be—it should be—"

"Hot."

"Yes. Hot. I mean, no!"

"It shouldn't be hot?"

She exhaled both a pant and a laugh. "You're being very bad."

"I'm okay with that."

"Isaac," she said, and it sounded like a plea.

I got the sense she was concerned about me, not herself. Abandoning her buttons, I slid my hand down the curves of her body, lifting her skirt and slipping my hand into the front of her underwear. I pushed a finger inside her. She was so wet. Knowing it was for me made me feel crazed.

I wanted to be buried in this tight heat. I couldn't stop thinking about it. Thoughts of us together had completely taken over, even more so since Hank's demonstration.

Hannah bent over in front of me, skirt flipped, underwear off . . . bent over in front of me, skirt flipped, underwear off . . . bent over in front of me, skirt flipped, underwear off.

I'd never been celibate because of an obsession with self-restraint, control, or because I had a masochistic desire to deny myself. It had always been about being smart, being cautious, being wary.

I didn't need to be cautious with Hannah. I trusted her completely, and I wanted her completely.

"Please . . ." She grabbed my wrist but didn't pull it away. Her chest rose and fell faster and faster as I stroked her. Finally, her head angled back and she glared at me. "Yes. Yes, please. As long as you don't care where it happens, I don't care either. I really, really don't."

Immediately, I withdrew my hand and made quick work of unzipping my fly. Her frantic fingers moved to help me, but then she hooked her thumbs in her underwear and yanked them down.

"Keep the skirt on," I said, shoving down my pants and boxers and hissing when my cock sprang free.

Her eyes dropped, widened; her movements stilled; she stared at me. "You're—you're already ready?"

Was she kidding?

Grabbing her hand, I placed her palm on my cock and wrapped her fingers around it. "Hannah. Love. I've been fantasizing about you for a long while," I said, wanting her to know.

An unintelligible noise slipped past her lips, her hand spasming around me. "What have you been fantasizing about?"

I marveled in the feel of her hand on my body. She simply held me, not moving, but her touch there felt essential. It felt like acceptance. Not a simple acceptance of this moment, but of me, of my desires, of who I was and how much I wanted to be a constant in her life.

Lowering to her ear again, I made quick work of her remaining six buttons. "You, bent over, skirt flipped up, underwear off."

"Is that how you want me?" The question was an airy whisper.

I hesitated, then asked, "Is that okay?"

Her hand gave me a stroke before letting me go so she could hurriedly shrug out of her shirt. "Honey, that is more than okay."

I reached behind me, grabbed a condom from the box, and lifted it up. "Will you help me put this on?"

Her attention flickered to the condom and her eyebrows pulled together, like my request confused her, and I immediately regretted it. It was probably strange for a grown man to ask for help like this.

But then she snatched the condom out of my hand and said, "Back up. You grabbed the wrong size."

Before I knew it, she'd ripped open a new wrapper with her teeth, extracted the condom, and put it in place. I watched her skillful fingers as she rolled it down. The action was so damn sexy and I was thankful for her experience.

In the next moment, she'd pushed me away, unfastened her bra and tossed it somewhere. Then she turned, leaned forward, and braced her hands on the shelf, her back arching.

All the air in my lungs fled and I'm sure part of my soul left my body.

There she was, bent over, skirt flipped, underwear off, her ass and pussy on display, her legs braced apart to accommodate me.

I didn't know where to look first, where to touch. I wanted to make this good for her, so fucking good. I wanted her to beg me to take her like this again.

Stepping forward, my cock jumped, sliding between her spread thighs and curving up. Palming her ass, I slid my hands down, loving the feel of her smooth skin. My hands caressed upward and to the interior of her legs. I used my middle finger to find her entrance, loving her little sounds of anticipation.

Bending over her slightly, I gripped her hips and rolled mine, causing my cock rub her clit and gritting my teeth at the overwhelming imagery and sensations. I wasn't going to last long. I wanted her too badly. Aligning myself, I pressed forward an inch and I thought maybe I should say something, something to make her hot. But words failed me and my hips jutted forward of their own volition, my cock invading her, filling her. My eyes rolled back in my head.

I cursed, needing a moment. Maybe needing forever.

"Isaac," she panted, her voice pitched high. She sounded desperate. Reaching behind her back, she grabbed one of my hands and pulled it around to her front. "Touch me. Touch me."

At first she brought my hand to her breast, then she slid our combined fingers between her legs and pressed them there, slowly rubbing her clit.

I nodded even though she couldn't see me and shook off her hand, telling my hips to move. Hank had said to go slow, to make sure I touched all the right spots. As best I could, I mimicked my memory of his movements, rolling my hips, making sure each slide was deep.

Another unintelligible noise escaped from her and she cursed. I watched her fingers dig into the paper towel rolls.

"Is there"—she paused and panted audibly—"anything you're not good at?"

My body picked up the pace without me telling it to, that hot spark gathering at the base of my spine urging me on. "You feel so good," I said, the words slipping out thoughtlessly.

"*You* feel so good," she groaned, her legs shifting restlessly. "Isaac. Isaac. I think I'm going to—oh!" Her muscles flexed and her bottom pushed back against my hips. "Faster! Harder!" The words lashed out, sharp demands, and so damn sexy.

Immediately, I complied, but I ended up shoving her more forcefully than I'd intended.

I was just about to apologize when she gasped, "Yes! Just like that. Just like that."

Surprised but more than willing, I removed my hand from her clit so I could hold her hips firmly. I pistoned into her body hard and fast, much harder than I ever would've thought she'd enjoy. She grew quiet except for little whines and hitches of breath, just like she had earlier today in her office when her body spasmed around my fingers, when my mouth had been on her, my tongue between her legs.

She was coming. I couldn't believe she was coming so soon. And the realization shoved my body toward the finish line. I lost control of my hips' movements, and I pumped into her without thought of anything but gratification. I would've felt a measure of guilt, for taking so much from her, for using her beautiful body this way, except she obviously liked it too.

Abruptly exhausted and gasping for air, I leaned further over her, my shoulders sagging, wrapping my arms around Hannah and bringing her back flush with my chest. Her heart pounded against my crossed forearms and she covered them, her hands finding mine to weave our fingers together.

"God. Isaac. Holy—wow."

I straightened us to stand, slipping out of her, and the crown of Hannah's head fell back on my chest like it was too heavy for her neck. She was still breathing hard and so was I, which made no sense. This had taken less than three minutes, tops.

I'd run sprints that were longer and hadn't been as out of breath afterward.

Thoughtlessly, I asked, "Is it always so short?"

She shook her head. "Not for women, no. I've never come so fast with anyone else." She opened her eyes and looked up at me, her eyebrows pulling together. "Although, I've never been with someone who's as good at foreplay as you."

"You think I'm good at foreplay?" I liked the sound of that and it made me want to research ways to improve my foreplay game.

"Yes. But it's not normal foreplay, or what most people think of when they use the word." She lifted a hand, cradling my jaw like I was precious to her. "It's how you're always looking at me like you're thinking about me. How you talk to me with so much respect and care. How you pitch in without me asking for help."

I stood straighter and my lips curved in an automatic response to her strange answer. I didn't understand her. How could all that be considered foreplay? "I'm not doing anything special, Hannah. I'm doing what I want to do."

"Exactly." She exhaled a laugh, grinning. "You're seducing me twenty-four hours every day by just being you. So, by the time we finally do touch each other, I'm ready to explode from wanting *you* so much."

Chapter Twenty-Nine
ISAAC

> "Freedom at the direct expense of another person's well-being was the worst kind of evil. It was selfishness masquerading as liberty, hypocrisy wearing the clothes of perseverance and grit. I wanted none of it."
>
> — Jason Doe, *Beard in Hiding* by Penny Reid

True to her word—*this time*—Tina opened the storage closet door two hours after she'd locked us in.

As we walked past my friend, she smirked at us in turn, a single eyebrow raised. "Did you have fun?"

Hannah said nothing, but she did turn her head toward Tina and glare at her.

I slowed my steps, waited until Hannah was a little distance in front of me, then lifted a fist without breaking my stride. Tina gave it a bump.

We hadn't conspired, I'd known nothing of her plans, but I believed her heart had been in the right place. *This time.*

"Your shirt is in Hannah's office," Tina whispered.

I nodded, then quickened my steps to catch up with Hannah, not surprised Tina had been the one to hide my clothes.

We left work together shortly after. Everyone else had already gone home except Tina and Dave. Hannah let me drive her to the Donner family cabin and we made plans for the night. She'd always wanted to try the lodge's farm-to-table restaurant, so I placed a take-out order and we had a carpet picnic in the living room.

She drank a glass of wine and so did I. She laughed a lot, like everything I said was funny or it made her happy, and I added making her laugh to my list of things I wanted to do every day.

Wracking my brain for more jokes as we finished dinner, I ended up resorting to cheesy ones just to keep her laughing. "What's a spy's favorite kind of shoe?"

"What?" she asked, looking up at me, already smiling. We were on the floor, the couch behind us, and she sat curled against my side, my arm around her shoulders, her hand on my leg.

"Sneakers."

She laughed. "That was so bad."

"I know, but I've run out of spy jokes."

She squeezed my leg, her temple resting against my chest. "Let me tell you some stripper jokes, then."

"Sounds good." I'd never done anything like this before, sit with someone and swap jokes back and forth. The members of my unit in the army used to do this and crack themselves up. Usually, I'd been reading a book and wasn't even half listening.

"What's an exotic dancer's favorite food?"

I gave it some thought but couldn't think of a punchline. "I don't know, what?"

"Chicken strips."

A surprised laugh barked out of me and suddenly I was laughing entirely too hard.

Hannah leaned forward and turned, watching me with a smile on her face. "That joke wasn't that funny, Isaac. Is this a pity laugh?"

I shook my head, wiping my eyes, not understanding it either. "I don't know. Right joke, right person, right time."

"Timing matters a lot, I guess." She leaned forward and placed her wine on the coffee table. She then lifted to her knees, faced me again, and held out her hand. "Come on, let's go."

I didn't ask where we were going. I could tell by the look in her eyes what she wanted.

Ignoring her hand, I stood, bent, and picked her up bridal style. A little squeal popped out of her, but she wrapped her arms around my neck and let me carry her to the bedroom. I placed her in the middle of the bed, bracing my hands on either side of her, and she gripped my shirt as though to stop me from leaving.

Tugging me forward, she lifted her chin and kissed me softly, but kept her eyes half open and on mine. "Isaac," she whispered. "Take off your clothes."

She let me go as I nodded, straightening, keeping my eyes on hers except when made impossible by removing my shirt.

She also took off her own skirt, shirt, and underwear, and the moment felt heavy with significance. The darkness partially veiled her from my view, her body either bathed in grayish light or completely in shadow. I assumed my body was similarly veiled. Only her eyes seemed to shine brightly.

This was the first time she'd initiated things between us if I didn't count the lap dance she'd given me on the night of her retirement party—which I didn't. We weren't together then, nor did we know each other. But she knew me now.

Watching what I could discern of her movements, I noted she took off her clothes slowly, with no artfulness, no seduction. Nor did she remove them with frenzied impatience. I could see from her gaze that thoughts of me clearly filled her mind and her hands were simply doing what needed to be done so that we could be together.

A lump formed in my throat.

Her body had always wanted my body, I'd never been in any doubt of that. But this felt like Hannah wanting Isaac.

Once we were both naked, she lifted to her knees and offered her hand again. I accepted it. She guided me to the bed, whispering, "Lie back," so I did.

The side of her leg brushed against mine and it felt warm and smooth. I wanted to touch her, very badly, but—in this instance, caught in the trance of her—I wanted Hannah to be the one who dictated how and when I put my hands on her.

Holding my eyes, she said, "I'm on birth control and I have no STDs. Do you still want to use a condom? It's fine if you do."

I shook my head. "Doesn't matter to me. Whatever you want to do."

We stared at each other. Eventually, she reached for the nightstand and opened the drawer. Pulling out a condom she must've placed there earlier, she ripped it open, and then proceeded to roll it on me with expert fingers. Her touch felt good, and watching her move, prepare to take me inside her also felt good.

In a fluid movement, she straddled my lap, her eyes back on mine. Looking at her naked body in this position—or what I could see of it—made me feel the best kind of restless.

Hannah lifted up, grabbing and positioning my wrapped cock between her legs, then lowered herself to take me inside.

I pressed the back of my head against the mattress, my hands fisting in the comforter, and I watched her. My mouth watered as my eyes devoured the expanse of smooth bare skin, the dark contrast of her nipples against the lighter skin of her breasts and how they tilted up slightly, how her body swayed and bounced.

Fuck. She was so hot. And watching my cock disappear inside her, even in shadow, even though she moved slowly, made me feel crazed but also so damn good.

I liked this slow pace she set. I liked how, when I lifted my eyes to hers again, she was looking right at me. I liked how this position felt entirely different, more intimate than what we'd done in the closet. My chest warmed at her expression and a surge of protectiveness made my lungs swell.

Taking her from behind had been like a fantasy. But this was a dream. It made my heart ache with how much I cared about her. It made my chest hurt as hopes and wishes completely unrelated to what we were doing swirled in my brain.

She was so beautiful to me. I wanted to give her everything. Not only all of myself, but the entire world. This kind of lovemaking was some kind of magic. I would've called it a spell, but it didn't feel temporary.

When her breath quickened, when she reached for my hands and *finally* put them on her body, when I filled my hands with her curves and bare skin, it felt like I was taking her inside myself, inside my heart, holding her there where I would keep her safe. Our eyes on each other, I got the sense she was doing the same.

And this time when we splintered apart, I had the odd notion that I didn't know where she started and I stopped because this time we were coming back together as one.

***

I drifted off to sleep after 2:00 AM, but then awoke with a start just before 6:00 AM. Discovering I was in bed with a fully naked Hannah and remembering all we'd done to each other last night, sleep became impossible. I was too . . . something. All of it good.

I both wanted and didn't want to wake her up, wondering how upset she'd be if I went down on her while she slept. Would she like to be woken up that way? I'd have to find out. But not right now.

Deciding she needed at least another three hours of shut-eye before I answered the question, I slipped out of bed and visited the facilities. I took a shower and resisted the urge to sing.

Wait a minute. I'd never sung in the shower before, but now it was an urge I had to resist? I hadn't thought having sex would change me.

It's not the sex. It's Hannah and it's happiness. This theory seemed valid. Bad sex doesn't make a person want to sing, but I suspected fantastic love-making would.

I brushed my teeth but I didn't shave, pulling on my clothes quietly and opting to go for a walk in order to release some of this pent-up energy. The sky was still mostly dark, but yellow had begun to leach into it, driving away the gray. When I cleared the forest path, I stopped and titled my head back, searching above me for any remaining stars.

"Isaac?"

At the sound of my name, I twisted at the waist, searching for the source, and finding my sister on the sidewalk some distance away. She looked at me with confusion, which was quickly giving way to wariness. My heart gave a sharp ache and, not thinking too much about it, I jogged forward.

Life with my father had been a chess game. My careful approach to every situation had made me an exceptional undercover agent and was likely thanks to him. His abusive treatment had taught me from a very young age to be cautious, to think and rethink before taking a single step.

But I didn't want to play games with Hannah or with Jennifer. Acting first and thinking later in the face of imminent physical danger was one thing, but not taking chances with the people I loved was quite another.

My time with Hannah had taught me to seize the moment, stop overthinking, stop being so damn careful all the time. With Hannah, taking chances had felt compulsory—touching her, asking for what I wanted, putting my pride on the line—my body and heart had conspired, leaving no room for my brain to intercede and ruin things with caution.

Jennifer stood in front of me now. This was my chance, maybe the only one I'd ever have. It was time to seize this moment.

As I approached, she surprised me by reaching out and grabbing my arms. "Isaac, I am so sorry. I am so sorry I was so horrible to you when we talked. It was years of built-up hurt, but that's—"

"Jennifer, I miss you."

She flinched slightly and blinked at my sudden confession. Maybe she had things to say, but I needed to speak before caution silenced me. I needed her to listen.

Sliding my arms out of her grip, I grabbed both of her hands. "I love you and I miss you. But I need us to figure this out together. We're both going to have to make compromises. I'll bend the rules. Hell, I'll break some. But I cannot stay in Green Valley more than a few months. That is not possible."

She seemed to have caught up in the conversation because her surprise gave way to faint grumpiness. "You say it's not possible, but if you left your—"

"I'm not quitting law enforcement. I believe in what I do. I'm retiring from this part of it, but I'm not quitting. Asking me to quit, telling me you'll save me, that belittles all the struggles I've been through, the life I've built from nothing."

She flinched a second time, her eyes round, like my words shocked her.

"Let's not try to rescue each other anymore, Jenn. Let's be a team and figure out how to see each other, talk to each other, after I go."

Jennifer stared up at me, her eyes growing glassy. Pulling both hands from my grasp, she punched me—hard—in the shoulder. "You are a real jerk, telling me this now. Why didn't you say this before? You said you were leaving for good and you broke my heart. Don't you know, I don't need you to stay in Green Valley, you don't have to live here. I just want us to talk, to see each other. I want you to stop trying to protect me while hurting me instead. That's all I want."

My mouth smiled and I didn't fight the gathering tears in my eyes, letting them come as I watched hers fall.

"I love you too, Isaac." She punched me again, but much softer this time. "And I missed you so, so much. All I wanted, all I want, is to know you." Her voice cracked and she took a few deep breaths before continuing. "But you've been making all these decisions on your own, cutting me out for years. What was I supposed to do? What was I supposed to think? So, yeah, I wanted to swoop in and solve all issues that were forcing you to leave because you didn't seem to want to stay."

"I don't want to stay here. This place, other than you and Hannah, and maybe Tina Patterson on one of her better days, holds nothing for me but bad memories. First at home, then with the Wraiths. This town is the last place I'll ever want to be. But I want to figure out a way to visit if you are here." My voice cracked this time and I cleared my throat so I could finish my thought. "I will come back for you, always."

My sister reached up and cupped my face, using her thumbs to wipe away my tears. "There you are." She smiled at me fondly. "There's my sweet brother. I'd wondered where you'd gone."

Her chest rose and fell with a deep, shuddering breath. "But you're still a jerk. I can't believe we just fixed years of frustration and hurt with a single conversation."

I laughed lightly and covered her hands with mine.

"Actually, I can," she amended. "I wish you'd come to me earlier, told me the truth."

"I know. I'm sorry. I didn't think I deserved a place in your life. I didn't want to burden you."

"Well, now you know that's not a possibility. You'll never be a burden."

"Same goes for you."

"Okay then." Her palms slipped from my cheeks and she turned her hands so that our fingers entwined. "Let's figure this out."

I nodded. "Okay."

"No going back on this." Her gaze narrowed, making the words she'd just spoken a threat.

"Okay."

"And you'll likely have to bend some pretty big rules."

"Okay."

Her eyes narrowed further. "We'll have to involve Cletus."

I was about to say okay but stopped myself just in time.

"Isaac!" She pulled her hands away and poked at me. "He's not that bad."

I frowned.

She laughed. "I remember this expression on your face. This is your real frown, not that scary one you throw around at people you don't know. But, I'm telling you, Cletus has friends in high places, he'll be able to arrange things so we can see each other. Secure video chats and phone calls not even the government can track. Private islands where we can meet without anyone knowing. You said you'd bend rules for me."

"I said I'd bend rules for *you*. Not for that guy."

"Compromise."

I hissed out a beleaguered breath, glancing above her head at the sun beginning to rise over the barren tree tops. "Fine. Fine, you can involve Cletus."

She hopped once, clapping her hands a single time, then placed her fingers on my shoulders. Lifting to her tiptoes, she pressed a kiss on my cheek. "I'm so happy, I could cry."

"You already did." I tried to flatten my features but my mouth wouldn't cooperate.

"So did you." She poked me.

I shrugged, swallowing, not trusting my voice. I didn't want her to cry again, and she would if I did.

"Then we're agreed?" She stuck out a hand for me to shake, her voice rough with emotion. "We'll work together."

Accepting her deal gladly, I fit our hands together, but I didn't let her go. I yanked Jennifer forward and pulled her into a long-overdue hug. Embracing me, she cried again. So did I. As the sun rose, we watched it through our tears, holding on to each other, and certain in the knowledge that neither of us would ever let go again.

Chapter Thirty
ISAAC

"Why can't a woman's words count for more than a man's violence?"

― Diane Donner, *Beard in Hiding* by Penny Reid

"Dave." I tapped the big guy on the shoulder.

"Isaac." He lifted his chin in greeting.

"I need to make a phone call real fast. Can I borrow the keys to the storage closet?"

"Sure thing." Dave reached in his pocket and passed me the keys. "We're closing in twenty. Place is still hopping, especially for a Thursday night. I'll get started and tell everyone it's last call, but I'll need your help in a bit to wrap things up."

I nodded, checking the time on my watch, already on the move toward the storage room. My call to Danforth tonight would be early. I wanted to leave with Hannah as soon as the club was locked up tight, take her back to the cabin, and have a repeat of last night. I didn't want to stay longer just to leave my *hey, nothing to report* voicemail for Danforth.

I couldn't remember ever being in a better mood.

This morning, I'd followed Jennifer to the bakery where we talked for hours in the office at the back of the kitchen before I realized how much time had passed. I didn't want to take a chance on someone seeing us meeting like this, so—after a renewal of promises to build our plan for continued contact collaboratively—I snuck out the back, circled around the building, stood in line for the bakery, and bought every single morning muffin they had in stock.

I also bought two coffees. One for Hannah and one for me.

When I returned to the cabin, Hannah was just getting up and she laughed when she saw all the muffins, but pushed them to the side in favor of snuggling with me in bed. I didn't get to go down on her like I'd wanted, but that didn't bother me much. We had plenty of time.

Eventually, we had to leave for work, and she brought the morning muffins in for everyone to share. The only person who didn't appreciate the gesture had been Serafina, who'd turned her nose up at the baked goods and said to me, "A cake is one thing, but you don't see my brother dropping off the Pink Pony's shortbread dick cookies at your sister's bakery, do you?"

Presently, I unlocked the storage room, flipped on the light, and was careful to keep the door propped open as I placed the evening call. Going through my spiel, I glanced around the small space, smiling when I spotted the box of condoms. I almost laughed, remembering how bitterly I'd regarded the box before.

When I finished making my report, I walked over and grabbed a handful in my size. Hannah showing me how to put one on yesterday had been fun. Maybe she could show me a few times tonight too.

I left the closet and glanced at my phone screen. We had another ten minutes until closing. It was time to flip on the lights and start pushing folks toward the door. Hannah kept strict hours, not wanting to overwork the dancers or stay open longer just because folks weren't ready to leave. I pulled the keys from my pocket as I approached Dave, holding them out to him.

"Thanks. All done."

He nodded, accepting the key ring absentmindedly, his eyes pointed elsewhere.

I followed his line of sight. Joshua stood by the champagne room doors, his arms crossed, trading a frowning stare with Dave.

"What's up? What's going on?" I scanned the room and spotted Louis at the bar also frowning in the direction of the room where the dancers gave their private shows.

"It's—uh." Dave sighed loudly. So loudly, it could be heard over the music. "Tavvy showed up. You know, that dipshit who makes Hannah wear those outfits?"

I reached out and placed a hand on Dave's shoulder, suddenly needing to hold on to something for balance. "What did you say?"

"So, he shows up, right? Asks for Goldie. But he's acting weird and, get this, he's got five guys with him this time instead of the usual two."

The rush of blood between my ears was almost deafening and I had to blink in order to see straight. "Where's Hannah?"

"She's in there already, said it was fine. Said he used to bring five guys when he came initially. And also, he didn't bring a costume today. Said whatever she wore was fine. Strange, right?"

"She's in there already . . ." I repeated, my stomach falling off a cliff as the room tilted in my vision. Ice entered my veins, cold fear.

I took a step toward the champagne room but then remembered where I was, who I was, and what I might encounter if I barged in there thoughtlessly. On the off chance nothing was wrong, it would look suspicious, but I didn't care about that anymore. I'd risk it because Levit had a mole at the regional office. He was probably already suspicious if he was here with five guys on a Thursday.

In the more likely scenario that something was wrong, they might be expecting someone to bust in to rescue her. Me barging in there would get everyone in the club killed, including Hannah.

"Dave," I turned to him, a plan forming in my mind. "Go to the security room and turn on the monitors. Right now. Text me what you see. And call the police on your way. 911. Tell them there's a federal agent who needs assistance. If they give you shit, give them this code." I was already typing out the code on my phone, sending it in a text message to Dave. It was used between agencies to signal an emergency.

"Wait, what? What federal agent? What—"

"Do it now."

Code sent to his phone, I marched over to the bar, reached behind it, and extracted the wicker basket the front house staff used to store our jackets, hats, gloves, and scarves. I already wore my jacket, but I wanted to cover my hair. I pulled on a black knit hat that seemed to live in the basket. I didn't know who it originally belonged to, but it was mine now.

I also grabbed a black medical mask from the dispenser box and shoved it in my jacket pocket.

I then crossed to where Joshua stood, his features uneasy. When I reached Joshua, I leaned close to his ear so we wouldn't be overheard, even if someone stood on the other side of the door, trying to listen for sounds of approach or conversation.

"Go tell Louis that you and he need to get everyone out, right now. Do it as quietly as possible and keep them calm. Don't turn off the music. Don't worry about closing out tabs. This includes the dancers. Tell them to leave, no time to change clothes. I want all the cars gone in less than five minutes. Say there's a slow gas leak, whatever. Do it now."

Frowning at me as he leaned away, he only searched my features for a moment before he nodded once and immediately jumped into action, crossing to Louis and giving him directions. I watched the two men move around the floor, quietly giving people the news that their tabs were paid and escorting them out. Joshua split off and whispered something to Kilby. Her eyes locked with mine for several seconds. Then she herded the rest of the dancers out of the room with startling efficiency.

I watched all this occur while splitting my attention with my phone's screen, waiting for Dave's text. I needed to know what was happening in that room and I was just about to run back to the office with the security monitors when three dots appeared next to Dave's name in my messages.

Dave: Police are on their way

I started typing out a message, asking what the status was in the room, when another message popped up.

Dave: GET IN THERE NOW

Dave: SHE'S GAGGED AND TIED UP

My heart jumped to my throat. I fought the rage clouding my vision and the almost irresistible urge to rush in. Caution interceded. I texted back rapidly.

Isaac: Send me a photo of the screen so I know their formation

Dave sent through the photo and I memorized their positions, forcing myself not to think about how they'd tied Hannah's wrists in front of her and were holding her up by her arms, a gag in her mouth.

Levit's mole had either discovered Hannah's identity through the regional system's case files or obtained a copy of the transcript from the monitoring department. If the latter was the case, I didn't understand how it was possible. Danforth had told me all the transcripts were replaced with summaries to mask Hannah's involvement. Regardless, the transcript would've pointed to Hannah's phone as the only possible source of the leak in Levit's organization and therefore would've revealed her part in the investigation.

I'd covered my hair earlier with the hat and I covered my face now with the black medical mask, not only to protect my identity and keep these guys from hunting me down, but also to protect my sister.

Then, I withdrew the gun I kept hidden in the back of my pants, I kicked open the door, and I immediately ducked, easily evading the man by the entrance since I knew he would be there waiting. I shot him in the knee. He fell to the floor, screaming in agony.

I announced my presence, my federal agency, told them not to move, told them they were under arrest, and told them they were surrounded. I hoped that by announcing which agency I belonged to, they would freeze in confusion. They didn't. Which meant I didn't hesitate to shoot the two perps who also drew their weapons.

My brain told me this would all be caught on camera. I couldn't shoot anyone who didn't try to attack me, draw their weapon first, or make a vocal threat on my or Hannah's life. What a shame.

Levit didn't draw a weapon but he did make a dive for cover. Since Dave had sent me the photo of the room first, I knew where Levit was and kneed him in the chest before he could make it across the room. He collapsed on the floor, wheezing, and I couldn't help but wish he'd drawn a gun. I then spun a kick and dropped the two men next to Hannah who'd been holding her in place but made no move to reach for their weapons. She immediately sunk to the floor and I realized they'd not only bound her wrists, they'd tied her ankles, too.

She'd also been hit in the face at least once, a trail of blood at the corner of her mouth.

In my peripheral vision, I saw another of the perps lift a weapon and in my cold rage and haste, I didn't shoot him in the leg or stomach like my training dictated. He wouldn't be getting up again and I wouldn't think about that now.

I bent and lifted Hannah over my shoulder, kicked Levit in the face with my steel-toed boot since he was on my path to the door, and then I ran. I ran for my car, unfolding her from my shoulder and placing her as gently as time would allow in the passenger seat, noting that all the dancers' and staff's cars were gone. Once I was inside the car, I started the engine, ignoring the seat belt chime and peeling out of the gated lot, out of the customer parking lot, and on to the road.

I checked the rearview mirror every three seconds and I didn't put on my headlights, thankful I'd spent so much time memorizing these winding mountain roads when I'd been undercover with the Wraiths. We'd taken them at fifty or sixty miles an hour with no lights. This was a piece of cake.

I heard the wail of a siren almost a half minute before the police cars sped past, obviously not seeing my black Ford Charger in time to stop. The sound of tires screeching on the road behind us made my foot press firmer on the gas.

I glanced at Hannah as I took another bend in the road. The movement shoved her against the door and I winced.

"Hannah. Hannah. Can you hear me?" I reached over and removed the gag, cursing myself for not doing so earlier.

Her head nodded and I realized she was quietly crying.

The sound made me want to die. But first, I wanted to kill every man in that room who'd touched her, who'd scared her. Slowly. With something dull and rusty.

"Hannah, honey. Can you put on your seat belt? It's going to be bumpy and I don't want you hitting the door again."

I watched her shaking hands, still bound, fumble for the seat belt and I bit back a curse, checking the rearview mirror. No one seemed to be behind us. I took a right at the next fork, which led to a straighter road down the mountain.

Do I want to go down the mountain?

I needed to get to the safe house—there were items there that could identify me, fingerprints—but not with Hannah.

It was doubtful my cover had been blown or that the safe house's location had been compromised. Evidence and case files—like the transcripts—were kept separate from operational resource details—like the location of safe houses. Similarly, regional offices didn't have any specs on undercover agents. Not gender, not skin color or eye color, not age. Just code names. I didn't care. If there existed even the smallest chance that the safe house had been compromised, I wasn't bringing her anywhere near it. Likewise, I wasn't bringing her near anything associated with Isaac Sylvester.

Until I spoke with Danforth, I wasn't taking chances, no matter how minute the risk. Hannah had already been through enough.

I could try driving out of town but immediately dismissed the idea. Hannah was in no shape for a long car ride and neither was I. My body was full of adrenaline now but I would have an adrenaline crash eventually. Three hours, four tops. It wasn't safe for me to be behind the wheel of a car when it happened.

The lodge was absolutely out of the question. I would keep my promise to Jenn, to find a way for us to talk and meet, but I wasn't going there and pulling her into this mess. It was bad enough that Hannah was involved.

Where do I go?

I couldn't go to my mom's empty place. It was locked up tight, and if Levit knew my identity, it wouldn't take him long to find out about my family's home. Iron Wraiths' safe houses weren't an option, even the two only Burro, Repo, and I—

Wait. Wait a fucking minute.

I checked my rearview mirror again and veered left at the next fork, heading back up the mountain.

Before my mother left Green Valley with the Iron Wraiths' former money man, before she'd been running from the law, she and Repo—the aforementioned former money man—had met at a hideaway off the map and off the Iron Wraiths' books, a place only he'd known about until he brought my mother there.

I knew about its existence because I'd helped her escape before the police could officially charge and arrest her with my father's murder. I drove there now, my lights still off, checking my rearview mirror every three seconds, but slowing down so Hannah wouldn't be continually bumped and bruised by the time we arrived since she didn't have her seat belt on.

"I'm taking you someplace safe," I whispered to hide the strain in my voice, also wanting to murder the person responsible for chimes in cars when seat belts weren't fastened.

Time passed in fits and starts. My hands started to subtly shake as we pulled on to the road for the hideaway, and I tightened them on the wheel. I flipped on my lights because finding the turnoff and driveway would be impossible without them.

Whispering a *thank God* under my breath when I found the driveway, I shut off the lights again, cut the engine, shifted the car into neutral, and rolled into the circular drive, studying the structure and searching for any sign of new ownership or anyone inside.

I doubted Repo would sell this place, but I needed to be sure. I couldn't have an angry homeowner coming out here and threatening to call the police. When the car came to a stop, I released the wheel, turned toward Hannah, and reached for her hands.

"Hannah. Are you okay? Let me cut this rope."

Her crying was still muffled and she nodded. "They scared me, but they didn't—they only hit me the one time."

They only hit me the one time . . . Rusty and dull. That's what I'd use.

She let me take her wrists and place them on my lap. I pulled a knife from my leg holster and gently sawed through the rope, careful not to cut her in the process. Task accomplished, I encouraged her to lean forward and put on my jacket and hat. She was in work clothes with no coat. She had to be freezing. I then lifted her legs, cut that rope, noted that she had no shoes, and slid my knife back in place.

"Can you stay here for a minute?" I whispered. "I need to make sure this place is empty before we go inside."

"Where are we?" She wiped at her tears, sniffling.

"Should be a safe place." I pulled out my phone and handed it to her. "If I'm not back in five minutes, take my phone, the car, and go. Go to Cletus Winston."

"No." She shook her head, pushing the phone away. "I'm not leaving you."

Sighing my frustration, I placed the phone in the cup holder and reached for her hands again. "Hannah, please. Please listen to me—"

My phone buzzed with a call, the sound like a gunshot in the dark against the soundtrack of our whispers.

I lifted it, stared at the screen, and read the caller ID several times as fear turned my veins to ice once more. Lifting the cell to my ear, I said, "Cletus? Is Jennifer okay? Did anyone—"

"Isaac. Jenn is fine. She's safe. She's doing science experiments in the kitchen and doesn't know what happened tonight yet because I just found out. You're at Repo's old safe house, am I right? I heard what happened at the Pony. Do you want some help?"

Startled, but grateful Jennifer was safe, I faced forward in the car, my mind spinning. "How did you know where—"

"Do you want help, yes or no?"

Gritting my teeth, I exhaled a hissing breath. "Yes. I want help."

"It'll cost you."

"Fuck off." I shifted the phone to end the call.

"Wait! Wait. It's not a big cost, and it's likely something you want anyway." His voice grew louder and his words had me bringing the cell back to my ear. "All I want is a favor."

"What's the favor?" I ground out. What a sneaky shithead, using this situation to his own benefit. Fucking vigilante asshole.

"As a show of goodwill, I'll tell you that the house you're parked in front of is vacant, but Jenn and I keep it tidy just in case your momma comes back and needs a hideout. You can find the key under the thornbush on the back porch."

"What's the favor?" I repeated.

"To be named later. And I'll fill Jenn in on the way. We'll leave soon. I'll take your grateful silence as agreement and see y'all in a bit."

Before I could say anything, Cletus ended the call.

I glared at the house. Did I go inside? If I did, I knew he'd make me pay for it later with whatever this favor might be.

Hannah's shaky inhale brought me back to the present. She was crying again and I saw a bruise starting to form on her jaw. *That settles it.*

I'd do whatever Cletus wanted later if it helped Hannah now.

Facing her again, I gently reached for and held her hands. "This house is safe. We're going inside. You can rest and clean up. No one is going to hurt you again, okay? And—and my sister is on her way. She'll be here soon."

Hannah nodded, her shoulders sagging with what looked like relief even as her crying became loud instead of muffled, making me suspect she'd been doing her best to hold it in, to be brave.

But now that she knew she was safe, she was letting it all out.

Chapter Thirty-One
HANNAH

"Why are you so anxious to build yourself a ceiling? Why don't you build a rocket instead?"

— Daisy Payton, *Dr. Strange Beard* by Penny Reid

Isaac carried me into the house, flipping on all the lights as we went, as though a bright room would drive away this nightmare. I wasn't afraid of the dark and I wasn't crying because I was afraid. I was crying because I could. Because it was over and we were together and he said we were safe.

He set me on a couch and placed a blanket on me, pushing my hair out of my face and staring into my eyes. "I'm not leaving. I'm just getting you tissues and ice. Okay?"

I nodded, unable to speak.

It had been scary. For a moment I thought I might die in that room. My life flashed before my eyes and it had been depressing as hell. Yes, there had been good things, good times, but in that moment I promised myself—if I made it out alive—I was going to quit my job and leave Green Valley.

I valued Hank and the Pink Pony and all my co-workers and friends. But I was going to quit and move away from here as soon as possible. I didn't want to live in this town anymore where I felt trapped, where I preferred cinder block walls and windowless rooms to going out in public. That wasn't living.

Maybe if I was a stronger person, if I enjoyed fighting with folks and raising their hackles, like Hank and Tina did, then I'd be able to stay and tough it out.

But I didn't want to be tough. I wanted to be soft.

Isaac returned, placed a warm, wet towel at the corner of my mouth, and gently wiped at my skin. When he discarded it on the table I saw it was stained with my blood. I didn't know how long I'd been sitting on the couch before he'd come back, the passage of time didn't register. He set a tissue box into my hands and held a cold pack to my face where he'd cleaned the skin.

I didn't wince at the feel of the cold pack, though the pressure did hurt. My mind was still swept up in determination. Like surrendering to the current on a river, I'd surrendered to my determination.

"Isaac."

"Are you hurt anywhere else? How are your wrists?" Holding the pack to my face, he lowered his gaze to my wrists and tugged on my fingers.

"Isaac." I shook off his searching hand and grabbed the front of his shirt, waiting until he met my eyes. "Let's leave. Let's leave Green Valley and never come back. Tonight."

His forehead wrinkled, his expression full of concern. "You're safe now—"

"I know. But I don't want to be here anymore. I love my momma, but I can't keep living my life for her—because of or in spite of whatever emergency she has. She's fine. She doesn't need me. And even if she did, I'm not her parent. I'm the child. She needs to stand on her own and I need to walk away and find my place in the world. And as much as I love Hank, as much as I'll forever feel grateful for him and the Pink Pony, my place in the world is not there. I'll miss my dancers and Dave, Joshua and Serafina. But I need to go. I need—"

The sound of the front door opening had Isaac dropping the cold pack to my lap, standing, and pulling out his weapon. He left the safety on.

"Isaac? Hannah?" Jennifer Winston's voice came from the entryway.

Isaac's shoulders slumped and he pushed the gun into the back of his pants. "We're in here," he called, lowering in front of me again and cupping my face. Hurriedly, he whispered, "You are safe, that's Jennifer."

"I know I'm safe now. I know—"

He spoke over me. "I don't know what the situation is with Levit. I left a message for my handler before he arrived at the Pony earlier tonight, and now I need to check in, do damage control."

"Wait." I covered his hand on my cheek, curled my fingers around his to keep him in place. "You're leaving?"

"I have to. But I'll be back. We'll talk when I get back."

"Isaac." I knew I sounded frantic, but I didn't want him to go. "Why? Why do you have to go?"

"I have to clear out the safe house." Isaac glanced to the side.

His sister and her husband had just walked in, but I wasn't ready for their interruption. "Could they be waiting for you there? Do they know who you are? Don't leave."

"I don't think they know my identity. I went in that room to get you wearing a mask, and I've been careful to keep out of sight the few times Levit came in with his crew to the Pony. But, Hannah, I have to go now." I got the sense he wasn't just talking to me, but also to Jennifer and Cletus, filling them in. "There are items at the safe house that will identify me. It's safer for me, and everyone I know, if I go now."

"But—"

Cletus interrupted. "He'll be fine. He's a professional."

Isaac's sister rushed over and tugged my hand. "Hannah, honey. Cletus and I will stay with you."

Isaac stood and I couldn't look away from his face. Fear told me this was the last time I'd ever see him and my heart felt like it was splintering.

Holding my gaze for only a second longer, Isaac ran past Cletus without saying a word and I heard the door shut behind him. Wracked with new tears, I tried to curl in on myself, but Isaac's sister wouldn't let me. She pulled me forward into her arms and held me tight.

"I know, I know. It's scary as hell," she said. Jennifer might've been talking to me, or she might've been talking to herself. Regardless, her lack of sugarcoating the situation made me feel better.

Probably because it reminded me of Isaac.

*** * ***

Once more, time didn't register. I cried until there were no more tears left and ended up zoning out while Jennifer Winston held me tightly, my uninjured cheek resting on her shoulder.

Eventually, she gently pushed me away and made me take a pill.

"It's just an anti-inflammatory," she said, dropping it into my palm. "You're going to get a headache if you don't have one already. The corner of your mouth is swollen. It'll help."

"I made some tea." Cletus set a mug down on the coffee table in front of me and took a seat in the armchair close to where Jenn and I sat on the sofa. "It's safe."

I frowned at him. "Safe?"

"That means it'll taste good." Jennifer picked it up and placed it in my hands. "Drink some. It'll help."

I nodded numbly and took a sip. She was right. It tasted good. Like honey and lemon and chamomile.

"Good?" Jennifer asked, her pretty eyes warm and compassionate.

"Yes. Thank you." My voice sounded nasally. I had a headache from crying. My lip throbbed. And when Isaac returned, I was going to really let him have it.

Who am I kidding? I was going to throw myself in his arms and never let him go.

Jennifer picked up the cold pack Isaac had brought over earlier and squished it between her fingers. "This isn't cold anymore. I'll go get a bag of ice and a towel instead. Cletus, keep her company." She stood and bustled out, leaving me alone with her husband.

"What happened?" Cletus asked after I took another sip of the tea, the heat feeling good on my scratchy throat. "It might help to talk about it. With someone. Like me. Since I'm here."

I stared at the auto mechanic, at his bushy beard and longish hair and open, interested expression. He'd always seemed so sweet and harmless. And odd.

Cletus once fixed my old truck for free but lied to me about it. I'd dropped it off on a Friday, and when I returned to pick it up a week later, he told me there was no charge, saying my truck was in perfect condition and he couldn't find anything wrong with it. He'd argued with me for close to fifteen minutes, telling me to take it to another mechanic shop, one where they would agree to fix *imaginary car problems.*

I'd been close to tears when I marched across the parking lot and yanked open the door. I sat inside my truck and prayed the engine would turn over in one breath while cursing Cletus Winston in the next.

But then, the engine turned over with no problem. And not only that, the noise it had been making was gone, and the gas pedal worked without having to pump it, and the brakes didn't screech, and I could use the radio and the wipers and the blinker all at the same time without the car simply shutting off, and the AC blew cold air.

There had been a ton wrong with my truck, obviously. And he'd lied to me, pretending the car had fixed itself, and refusing payment.

I'd always liked him after that, but I'd been surprised at first when Jennifer and he had ended up together. However, upon further contemplation, it made sense. Most everyone in town thought of Jennifer as simple, just like they thought of Cletus as simple. Simple and sweet.

"Since you're here, I might as well tell you," I agreed, forgetting my injury for a moment. My mouth smiled and I immediately winced at the sharp pain.

"I hope the other guy looks worse," he said, his eyes on my jaw and lips, and I'd never heard his voice sound so . . . menacing.

A flash of memory from when Isaac had busted into the room, the quick and lethal actions he'd taken, played in my mind, and I nodded, saying dully, "I think Isaac might've killed him."

Cletus nodded, not looking at all horrified or surprised, but he said, "Let's not talk about that. Maybe save that story for therapy and the trauma counseling in your future. Why don't you tell me what happened with you and Isaac. How'd you two end up together?"

"I'd like to know this story too, if you don't mind telling it." Jennifer returned with the bag of ice and a plate of shortbread thumbprint cookies, dollops of what looked like raspberry jam in their centers. Where she'd found the cookies—or how she'd conjured them—I had no idea.

"Uh, well." Now my memory rewound to the night of my retirement party. My lips wanted to smile, but I stemmed the instinct. "Y'all seem to know that Isaac is working undercover."

Jennifer nodded, handing me the bag of ice. "We've known for a while, yes."

"Well, he . . . he asked for my help with his latest investigation. Actually, he didn't ask." I chuckled without smiling, bringing the ice bag to my jaw.

"He didn't ask? Then, why did you help him? How'd that happen?" Jennifer nibbled on a cookie.

I shrugged, too tired and overwrought to be anything but honest. "I guess he sorta blackmailed me."

Jennifer gasped, a hand flying to her chest. "I can't believe he blackmailed you! That's terrible." She looked truly appalled. So upset, she put the cookie back on the plate.

"Yeah. Terrible," came Cletus Winston's dry agreement, his eyes sliding to his wife. "Who would ever do such a thing?"

Now her gaze sliced to his. "Cletus Byron Winston." His name sounded like a warning.

"A true miscreant of a human. Unconscionable." He made the reprimands sound like compliments, as though he admired Isaac for blackmailing me.

I was left speechless but also entertained. There was a story here between them, I was certain of it.

Jenn didn't appear speechless or entertained. She lifted a finger and wagged it at him. "This is not the same. You can't compare yourself to Hannah."

Cletus cleared his throat but made no attempt to wipe the small smile from his features. "Right, right. Not the same at all as when you blackmailed me into 'helping you.'" He put these last two words in air quotes. "And your dear, formerly estranged brother was blackmailing Hannah for the sake of catching bad guys. What were you blackmailing me to help with again? I've forgotten."

Jenn huffed while scowling at her husband.

"Alls I'm saying is, it must run in the family." He looked smug.

She scowled harder.

Cletus leaned forward, plucked her hand out of the air between them, and brought the back of it to his lips for a gentle kiss, his eyes bright as they moved over his wife. "You know I'm not opposed to blackmail, dearest. Not at all. I'm just pointing out that any future progeny will inherit it from both sides of our family trees. Two dominant extortion genes. I couldn't be happier."

* * *

Jennifer tried to get me to lie down and sleep, but I couldn't. Worry had me on a spin cycle. We ended up playing cards. After a while, I got the sense they were both letting me win, mostly because Jennifer lauded me with praise at the end of each hand like I was a child.

"Oh! Great job. You are so good at this game." Jennifer's genuinely cheerful exclamations were especially cute, like she'd taken it upon herself to be my personal cheerleader.

Whereas Cletus pretended to be upset every time he lost. "I'm not playing with Hannah. She cheats."

Jennifer would then smack his arm lightly and scold him for saying such things. He'd glare at me but the effect was ruined by the warm twinkle in his eye.

These two were adorable. Wholesome and in love in a way that reminded me of my grandparents.

My grandparents had died within hours of each other. My grandmother passed in her sleep, and my grandfather died later that afternoon while sitting in his rocker after her body had been taken away. My momma had always talked about their marriage like it was a fairy tale. I remembered them fondly, but I'd stopped believing in fairy tales a long time ago, deciding my memory of my grandparents—and my momma's memory—had been skewed and warped by time, fashioned by nostalgia, and our own wishes for a better life.

Looking at Cletus and Jenn, how they flirted and bantered, the light touches and long looks where they spoke with their eyes, I thought maybe such things as happily-ever-afters and true love existed.

Jennifer had just dealt a new hand when Cletus's cell buzzed on the table. He picked it up without checking the screen, saying, "Hello?"

I leaned forward, hoping it might be Isaac and further hoping I'd be able to hear his voice. Cletus didn't say anything for a while, just listened, and I couldn't tell if the person on the other side was Isaac or not. On the precipice of asking Cletus, I snapped my mouth shut as his eyes moved to mine and held.

"She's fine," he said. "Jenn made cookies, but I didn't save you any. We're playing cards. I'll let her know her momma is safe and is being protected by the sheriff's office, that your target is still at-large, that you're safe, finished at the safe house, and that you're on your way back. Furthermore, I won't tell her about you two needing to gett married ASAP."

"Cletus!" Isaac's shout was audible through the phone.

Jennifer's wide eyes cut to mine and we shared a startled stare. She rolled her lips between her teeth, giving no more of her thoughts away. Meanwhile, I didn't know what to feel first: relief about Isaac's safety, gratitude that he'd checked on my momma and took measures to keep her safe, worried about Tavvy still running around, or surprised about my impending marriage.

He's safe. That's all that matters. He's okay and he's coming back here.

And I wasn't really surprised about us needing to get married so quickly if I took a moment and thought the situation over. We were leaving together. I'd have to marry him eventually when we left. Now or later, didn't matter to me.

As Cletus hung up the phone, I had to fight a sudden yawn so as not to aggravate my mouth. My bones felt so tired, and my eyelids drooped. I leaned my elbows on the table and gripped my forehead.

"Are you okay, honey?" Jennifer placed a gentle hand on my bicep. "I'm here for whatever you need."

My mind was free of thought. Blank. My muscles felt rubbery and useless. And with every blink, I had more and more trouble keeping my eyes open. "I think I need to lie down."

Was that my voice? My words sounded slurred.

"Cletus." Jenn said his name like it was both a request and a command.

The next thing I knew, Cletus Winston had lifted me from the chair and was carrying me in his arms like I was a child. He walked me into a dark room, waited for Jennifer to pull back the bed's covers, then placed me in the middle of the mattress.

She arranged the comforter over me and the familiar smell of lye soap, sandalwood, and sweetness filled my nose. The same smell as the sheets in the Donner family cabin.

Tucking me in, Jennifer said, "Don't you worry about a thing. I'll take care of it all. Just sleep. We'll put some water by the bed if you get thirsty. Rest, sweet Hannah."

I nodded, my eyes closed, and I didn't hear her leave because I was already asleep.

Chapter Thirty-Two

ISAAC

"Everything always feels impossible, until it's inevitable."

— Cletus Winston, *Totally Folked* by Penny Reid

"He's gone underground." Danforth sounded like I felt. Extremely pissed off would be an understatement.

This was our second call of the night. I'd reached her through the emergency number and filled her in on the events of the evening while I drove to the safe house, answering her questions with facts, succinct and to the point. When you're in law enforcement, you learn the difference between "succinct" and "to the point." One has to do with the length of your answer, the other has to do with relevancy.

I hung up before we'd finished our conversation but after she'd confirmed for me that the safe house hadn't been breached. I'd reached the Bandit Lake turnoff. Clearing out anything that could identify me was a priority. It wouldn't do Jennifer any good if Isaac Sylvester disappeared but the fact that he was a federal agent was revealed. She'd be walking around this town with a target on her back. Retribution follows you everywhere in this line of work, even after death.

Driving the wrong way on the one-way loop, I'd parked the car about a half mile from the safe house, pulling it into the weedy driveway of a neglected and abandoned cabin. Then I pulled out my phone and checked the security video for myself, scrolling through the last twelve hours of our footage as well as the GPS infrared data and the neighbor's video footage by tapping into their system's app. I trusted the GPS infrared data the most.

I'd made it in and out with no problem, not pausing to destroy anything, but rather wiping down all surfaces myself and carrying my sparse belongings out the door with me. Instead of taking the black Ford Charger, I switched cars to one I'd stashed in the neighborhood just in case something like this happened, a car the regional office knew nothing about.

They wouldn't be able to track me unless I wanted them to. Right now, I didn't want.

This life was a chess game and it was time to get at least three moves ahead. It's not that I didn't trust Danforth. I didn't trust anyone. Not when the regional office had a mole who'd blown a giant hole in my investigation and almost got Hannah killed.

So when she asked on my drive back to Repo's hideaway, "Are you still near the safe house? Why can't I see your location? Where did you take the contact?"

I said, "This will be the last time we talk. Do you have any other questions for me related to tonight's events?"

Her sigh was loud in my ear. "I only ask because I have an update for you. The contact is now eligible for witness protection, if they want it. I rushed this through. You're welcome. We will find Epstein eventually, and the evidence from the club is enough to charge him and deny bail, especially if the contact testifies. This plus the recordings we got from their phone will keep Epstein behind bars."

"Once you catch him," I pointed out, careful to keep the anger out of my voice.

Now they wanted Hannah as a witness? *Now?* Maybe it was the adrenaline still coursing through my bloodstream, but I wanted to tell Danforth to fuck right off with the offer of witness protection, even though I knew she was trying to help.

I'd already started making arrangements for us to leave tonight. I'd arranged for one of the local sheriff deputies to contact Hannah's momma and ensure the woman was safe. They'd parked a surveillance car outside the farmhouse just in case Levit or one of his men showed up.

Then I'd called Cletus and gave him an update. He'd been a real dick about it, but what was done was done. Getting the marriage certificate would be no big deal, but I needed someone to marry us and I needed witnesses who were trustworthy. Assuming Hannah agreed.

Yet, whether Hannah married me or whether she went into witness protection wasn't my decision. It was hers. I'd tell her about the offer from Danforth, but I wasn't worried she would accept it. *She'll marry me.*

"Right. Well. This is it," Danforth said, sounding tired. "Thanks for your service, soldier. Good luck in the future and I hope we never speak again."

Despite the situation, that pulled a smile out of me. "Me too. Have a nice life. And take care of yourself."

"You too, McFly. You too." With that, she hung up.

* * *

Pulling into the circular driveway, I didn't bother to keep my approach silent. Caution and standard procedure dictated that I should have, just in case Levit had discovered Hannah's hiding place. But I didn't have the energy and it would delay seeing Hannah.

As much as I didn't like Cletus Winston, I did trust him to keep Jennifer and Hannah safe. Undoubtedly, he was a sneaky shithead. And just as undoubtedly, he loved my sister.

But I did text Cletus when I put the car in park.

Isaac: I'm back. Don't shoot me when I walk inside.

I didn't need him thinking I was a perp and knocking me out with a goofy gadget as I entered the house. I suspected, if there existed a person in world who would deploy booby traps and goofy gadgets, it was Cletus Winston.

Gingerly opening the door, I was a little surprised Cletus didn't have a bucket of hot tar fall on my head. But when Jennifer was the first person to greet me, I presumed he'd had plans which she thwarted.

"Everything okay?" My sister pulled me into a big hug. "You didn't encounter any trouble?"

I shook my head. "Thank you for staying with Hannah. How is she?"

"She's asleep. As soon as she heard you were safe, she passed right out." Jennifer proceeded to lead me into the kitchen and fill me in on what happened after I'd left. She also placed a plate of cookies in front of me, which I ate, taking satisfaction from the fact that she'd probably hidden them from Cletus.

My sister loved me and there wasn't a damn thing he could do about it.

"About the wedding . . ." Jennifer stood on the other side of the kitchen island, facing me where I sat on a stool and devoured the cookies.

"What about the wedding?" I asked around a bite.

"Cletus can marry you, but we'll need witnesses."

I lifted an eyebrow. "Cletus can marry us?"

"That's right." The man in question strolled into the kitchen. "It's one of the seven licenses I have."

"What are the others?" The question slipped out before I could stop it.

"That's need-to-know information," he said, coming to stand next to Jenn and draping an arm around her middle. "Who should be the witnesses? I assume you already have the marriage paperwork taken care of?"

I nodded, too tired to parse through his questions for landmines. I didn't have the paperwork yet, but I would soon. The adrenaline was finally starting to recede. Experience told me it would take a while and I'd get the shakes.

"Can we talk about this in the morning?" I asked, polishing off the last cookie. "I assume y'all will be sleeping here too? Or are you leaving tonight?"

"We'll sleep here," Jenn said before Cletus could speak. "There's two bedrooms. Hannah's in the main. But we'll head out early to prepare for the ceremony. Do you think I'd be overstepping if I brought her a dress?"

I shrugged tiredly. "I don't know. Ask her. But, Jenn, I appreciate the kindness and the gesture."

"She's going to be my sister-in-law. It's the least I can do."

Jennifer and I stared at each other, trading smiles as well as thoughts with our eyes.

Jennifer: I love you.

Isaac: I love you, too.

Jennifer: I'm so thankful we're back in each other's lives.

Isaac: You have no idea. I—

"All right! All right! Quit it." Cletus waved a hand between us within our line of vision. "Use words. I'm standing right here."

"Anyway." Jennifer turned in Cletus's arms and placed a kiss on his cheek. "We're going to bed now."

"That's more like it," he said, grabbing her hand and pulling her out of the kitchen.

I didn't watch them go. I walked to the sink and pulled my toothbrush out of the bag I'd taken from the safe house. After brushing my teeth and washing my face, I changed into new clothes, deciding the ones I'd been wearing needed to be burned.

Then I walked into the room where Hannah slept, crossed to an upholstered armchair, leaned back, and closed my eyes, waiting for the crash. I didn't want to get in bed with her, not until my body accepted it was over, not until I'd accepted we were safe.

* * *

"Isaac?"

At the sound of Hannah's voice I opened my eyes, blinking around the dark room. My shakes had subsided and I'd almost fallen asleep in the chair without meaning to.

"I'm here," I stood, my legs sore, and lay next to her on the bed but over the covers.

She scootched back and I curved my body around hers. "Are you okay?" she whispered. "No problems?"

"None at all," I said, inhaling deeply, pulling the scent of her into my lungs.

We were both quiet for several seconds. Or maybe several minutes.

I'd just drifted off when Hannah said, "I think I'm a little in love with your sister."

I snorted. "Join the club."

"And Cletus is so sweet!"

I'd been in the process of sleepily scratching my neck as she made this claim, and I froze. "Cletus is sweet?" My eyes opened.

"Yes. Of course. And they're sweet together."

Dropping my arm over her middle, I lifted an eyebrow. "Uh. If you say so."

"I do. He's helped me in the past."

"He has?" This was news to me, and I wondered what his help would cost us in the future. Cletus never did anything for anyone unless he got something in return. "What did he do to help you?"

Hannah told me a story about him fixing her truck, lying about it, and not charging her any money. At first bewildered, I listened. But then as she neared the end, I sighed an incredulous laugh. I thought back to the story Hannah had told me when we were mending the costumes in her office, about her aunt Scotia Simmons bringing over clothes to mend and launder, about how Hannah's mother was too proud to accept charity.

"You know why he did that, right?" I grumbled.

"Why'd he do it? To be nice?"

"I don't know about his motivations for fixing your car and not charging you, but I can tell you why he lied about it." I had to assume he'd make her pay for it eventually.

"Why do you think he lied about it?"

"Because your momma wouldn't accept charity. He wanted to fix your car for free—for reasons unknown—and so he made it happen in a way that wouldn't force you to turn him down."

She held still for a moment, then said, "Oh. Geez. He's so—"

"Sneaky."

She laughed lightly, then winced.

"Is your mouth okay?" I rolled her to her back and carefully placed my thumb under her chin to tilt her face so I could see the bruise.

"It's okay as long as I don't smile." She patted my upper arm as though to soothe me, then rolled back on her side. "Come on, lie back down and snuggle me."

Complying, I held her tighter, hating that she was in pain. *I almost lost her.*

I couldn't think about that. If I thought about it, this damn adrenaline would never leave my system and I'd be hyped up for the rest of the night. I wanted to relax with her. The fight was over. It was time to enjoy the hard-won peace.

"Hannah, I have something to tell you."

"Is it about us getting married?"

I hesitated, then said, "It's related. You have a new option. I've been informed that you now qualify for witness protection. Staying in Green Valley will be dangerous and difficult. Likewise, leaving on your own will be dangerous. I don't recommend either of those, but you could do it if you wanted. Or you could go into the program. Or you could marry me. Those are the options."

"Hmm . . . tough decision. Can I think about it?"

I grunted, only slightly irritated by her teasing, and teased her back, "No. Decide now."

"Fine. I guess I'll marry you." She said this like it was a chore.

I smiled against her neck and tightened my arms around her. "Good decision."

"Isaac," she whispered. "How did we get here?"

My heart gave a pinch. "I'm sorry if I messed up your life."

I felt her head shake. "No. I don't know why, maybe I'm still in shock, or maybe I need professional help, but I'm actually really good."

"Really? You're good?" I didn't believe that. She'd just gone through a traumatic ordeal. No matter where we ended up, she needed to see someone, talk about it, work through it.

I would, too, but mine would be mandated. And I'd save all my conflicted feelings and thoughts on the last twelve hours for my sessions. Undercover agents are required to undergo therapy after every assignment. Most law enforcement officers are required to undergo treatment if they discharge their weapon into another human. I'd gone to mandated therapy three times. It was a good policy.

"Yeah. It's like, you entered my life and it's been a whirlwind ever since." Hannah wiggled and I let her go. She turned in the bed and faced me, tucking her hands under her chin as we stared at each other in the dark. "You've disrupted everything, all my plans and assumptions. I feel like you were sent to me, a present to shake things up and force me to live my life. I'm so grateful for you."

"You think of me like a present?" I asked. *Oh. The irony.*

"Yes." She nodded. "Is that bad?"

"No. Not as long as you understand, I'm the one giving myself to you." I pulled a hand from beneath her chin and placed it on the bed between us, covering her fingers with mine.

"Good. 'Cause I'm the one giving myself to you, too." Her lips didn't smile but her eyes did.

"Good." I liked the sound of that. "You know, I used to dislike the idea of people being presents, but I'm not sure I do anymore. In the right context, I think it's okay."

"How so?" Hannah's voice was soft and quiet, and the sound of it in this dark room with just the two of us made me realize being with her was like being by myself. Obviously better. But I was just as comfortable with her as I was on my own. I also felt settled. Secure. She made me feel safe, like I didn't have to play chess with her because there were no wrong moves, no losing, only winning.

Also, I hadn't realized how lonely I'd been before Hannah, not until right that moment.

Jennifer and I used to whisper to each other in the dark. After our father went to bed, she'd sneak in my room and we'd whisper about hopes and dreams, but never talk about our hurts and woes. It had been a sacred time.

Now I had Hannah, and Hannah had me. And this also felt sacred.

"Isaac?"

Hannah's voice woke me to the present and I inhaled deeply, trying to figure out where we'd been in the conversation. *Ah, yes. Presents.*

"I like you thinking of me as a present," I reiterated. "But, like I said, only if I'm the one giving myself to you, freely and without reservation." I tightened my fingers on hers. "I don't expect anything in return except respect and kindness."

"Well, expect it. And more. I can't wait to know you better."

Scootching forward, I opened my arms and encouraged her to lie against my chest. She snuggled close as I said, "I can't wait for you to know me better, Hannah. And I only hope, as you keep unwrapping me, you'll like all that's revealed."

Hannah lifted her chin and kissed the underside of mine, just a gentle brush of lips, and said, "I'm pretty sure I'll love it."

Epilogue
HANNAH

"Stay away from the normals."

— Ashley Winston, *Beard Science* by Penny Reid

1 year (or so) later
Thanksgiving Day

"Oh, good Lord." This statement came from Jessica Winston. She held her son on her hip. According to Jessica, the toddler was usually a daddy's boy but Duane wasn't currently on the premises. "What is your momma carrying, Isaac?"

Standing at my other side on the balcony while the four of us looked down on the path leading to the beach house, Isaac sighed. "I think it's one of those big food gift baskets, with the crackers and cheese."

"It's huge. The Trojan horse wasn't that big. She should've placed it on wheels instead of making Jason carry it," Jessica said, her tone wryly amused. "Your momma is hilarious."

This would be my first time meeting Isaac's mother officially. Cletus had arranged for Diane Donner, Jason Doe—aka Repo, the Iron Wraiths' former money man—Jessica Winston, Duane Winston, their son Liam, Cletus, Jenn, Isaac, and me to meet on a remote Greek island for Thanksgiving.

Early on, Isaac had filled me in on the status of the investigation into Tavvy, specifically where the investigative team thought he might be hiding. After a while, I'd asked Isaac to stop telling me. I wanted to live my life and focus on my future. If they caught him, I wanted to know, but I didn't want unhelpful status updates that weren't really updates at all. They did end up catching the spy at the regional office, and that had felt like a win.

Luckily, Isaac had been able to get the time off from his new job as a trainer for the DEA training center so we could fly out here to Greece. He'd passed his exam with flying colors and had settled into the new job like a fish taking to water. I was so proud of him and I got the sense he liked the new challenge and rigor just as much as he liked the regular work hours.

Jessica, Duane, and Liam were world travelers, never staying put in one spot for any length of time, so I supposed it made sense for the family of three to meet Cletus and Jenn wherever they traveled. Their presence also gave Cletus and Jenn a reason to fly overseas, a cover story that didn't include meeting with Isaac and me—two people who no longer existed—or Diane and Jason—two people running from the law.

Isaac was now Zack and I was Anna, names close enough in sound to our own that none of our neighbors or co-workers in Las Vegas ever noticed when we made a mistake. Both Isaac and I had dyed our hair dark brown and started wearing glasses. The minor disguises helped me relax about having our photos taken during social or work events. We'd be calling each other Isaac and Hannah for this week, however. No reason not to with family.

"Hey, y'all!" Diane Donner hollered up at us, waving her hand like there was a chance we wouldn't see her next to the giant basket shaped like a turkey.

"Trojan turkey," Jessica muttered, chuckling to herself. "And how did she get it to the island? That's what I want to know."

"She has her ways . . ." Isaac waved at his mom but his movements weren't anywhere as exaggerated as hers.

I also waved, feeling shy. Some of my nerves dispelled when Ms. Donner waved back. Maybe Isaac sensed my flutter of anxiety because he placed an arm around my waist and tugged me close to his side.

We'd married the morning after Tavvy had tied me up. Jennifer and Cletus had slept at the house in the guest room but then left early the next morning, returning with a blindfolded Hank Weller in tow. It was too rushed to tell or invite my mother. Jennifer and Hank had been our witnesses, Cletus had married us, and it had been a simple ceremony. Before Isaac and I departed, Hank had surprised me with a hug.

I'd almost choked up, touched by the gesture, until he whispered in my ear, "Make him sign a post-nup. I'll have Cletus pass along a good template. Don't let him get your money." As he leaned away, Hank smiled at me fondly and said, "And remember to invest in real estate."

Settling in Vegas hadn't been a hassle at all. My new identity was very similar to my real one in terms of college degree, but instead of my work experience involving strip clubs, my alter ego had managed pole fitness studios. I'd considered working for one of the fitness studios in the city but eventually decided to open my own place. Also, I bought the commercial property where it was located, becoming both a business owner and a landlord in one fell swoop.

I loved it. I loved how busy I was with work and I loved seeing women—regular women—poke their heads in my studio, their eyes full of curiosity but not judgment. I loved watching them blossom, gain strength and confidence from learning how to work a pole. But most of all, I loved building *my* business, watching its social media presence gain momentum, seeing my income double then triple then quadruple due to my hard work and know-how.

And, who knows? Maybe one day my studio would become a national chain. For the first time in my whole life, it felt like anything was possible.

"I guess one of us should go help Jason," Jessica said on a sigh. "But I'm kinda enjoying watching him struggle under the weight of the basket."

"Me too." Isaac shared a glance with Jessica. She smirked. So did he.

We'd arrived only two days ago, but Isaac and Jessica had hit it off immediately. I'd caught him hiding smiles at her antics, sarcastic remarks, and especially how she sassed the Winston brothers like it was her full-time job.

Duane didn't say much. In that way, he reminded me of Isaac, and the two men got along just fine as far as I could tell. But their conversation thus far had been limited to sports, cars, and who was the more superior nineteenth-century French writer, Alexandre Dumas or Victor Hugo. The discussion hadn't grown heated even though they disagreed.

"He'll be fine." Jessica turned from the balcony and walked back into the white stone beach house. "If he didn't want to carry a giant turkey basket, he should've told her so when she bought it."

I felt Isaac's chest shake against my side and I peered up at him. He glanced down at me wearing a smile. He smiled a lot more these days, so much so, I'd almost grown used to seeing them on his handsome features.

"Should I go down and help?" I asked, feeling anxious about not helping.

He shook his head. "No. They're adults." Lowering his mouth to mine for a quick kiss, he turned us both from the balcony and used his arm around my waist to push me through the living room. "It's not our job to rescue them from their bad decisions."

* * *

"I have something to tell you."

"Oh?" I looked up from the pajamas I'd been pulling out of my suitcase. Dinner was over. I was more than full—both my heart and my stomach—and I couldn't wait to snuggle with Isaac in bed. Or do other things with Isaac in bed. I'd already called my momma and wished her a happy Thanksgiving via the secure line Cletus Winston had set up for us.

We didn't talk often, but our conversations had been better than they were before I left town. I think it helped that she wasn't allowed to know where I lived or what I did to earn money. She knew I was married, but not that I'd married Isaac. She knew I had to leave town for my own safety, but none of the particulars. We mostly spoke about her and the farm, books and movies, or current events. Sometimes I wished things could be different, but most of the time I was too busy being happy in my new life to fret over my momma or our past.

Over dinner, Diane had sent her giant grin to those gathered around the table, starting with her daughter, then her son, then me, then Jason, then everyone but Cletus. Cletus didn't seem to mind being left out.

Isaac had been right, the giant turkey had been filled with gift-basket items. Little packets of crackers, tiny jars of single-serving jams, cheese that didn't expire, remarkably long sticks of beef jerky that Liam and Duane used to play swords.

I'd been nervous about meeting his momma for nothing. Diane had fawned all over me the moment she and Jason finally made it inside the door. In the end, Isaac had helped bring in the giant turkey basket, earning him a thankful look from Jason and effusive praise from his mother. One thing was for certain, Diane Donner never did anything by halves. Whether it was giving Cletus the cold shoulder or welcoming me into her family, the woman was committed 110 percent.

Isaac scratched the back of his neck and leaned his hip against the dresser in our room like he needed it for support. "I don't know why I didn't tell you before now. I think, at first, I didn't want it to matter so I didn't say anything. But in retrospect, and after talking things over with my sister, I think I should tell you."

I stiffened, not wanting to be worried but old habits die hard. "What is it?"

"The thing is . . ." he started haltingly, his eyes communicating his fear even as the rest of his features seemed calm. "When we first got together, I'd never been in a relationship before. I'd never slept with anyone. You were my first—well, everything."

Breathing out my relief, I also breathed a laugh. "Oh! Oh thank goodness. The way you were talking, I was worried you were about to tell me you were still doing undercover work or something like that."

He seemed to stand straighter. "Why do you not seem surprised?"

"Tina told me."

"She what?" His voice dropped an octave with the question, the two words sharp and heavy with outrage. "She told you I was a virgin?"

I nodded. "She did."

"That—" He gritted his teeth and set his hands on his hips, giving his head a quick shake as he looked sightlessly around the room. Or maybe he was searching for Tina, like he might find her hiding in a corner so he could punish her. "I can't believe her."

Trying to subdue my smile at his cute reaction, I walked to him and slid my arms around his torso, leaning my head way back so I could see his gorgeous eyes. I loved his eyes. He still made eyes at me all the time and I hoped he'd never stop. "Don't worry about it. It's in the past."

He glared down at me. "Oh yeah?"

"Yeah."

"Well, how would you feel if I said Tina was the person who told me about your crush? That you'd been using me as a stand-in for a decade."

Flinching, I withdrew my arms and stepped back, my eyes growing wider with each passing second as past puzzle pieces clicked together. Anger set up a campfire in my chest. Soon, I'd set my hands on my hips too, searching the corners for Tina Patterson.

"That—" I cut myself off from the profanity, but I was mad. I was *so* mad. She couldn't be trusted, end of story.

Isaac's chuckle had me looking at him and I could see his anger had deflated mostly, leaving behind wry amusement. "You know, we should thank her."

"I'm not thanking her. *You* thank her." She'd betrayed my trust. She spilled my secrets. She—

"She's probably a big reason we're together," he said, plucking my hands from my hips and placing them around his neck. Stepping closer, he put his hands on my body, sliding them from the center of my back down to my bottom. All at once, Isaac was making eyes at me. "We're secretive people, Hannah. We guard ourselves closely. If she hadn't been so reckless with our secrets, it would've taken us years to tell each other the truth."

I opened my mouth to argue and he kissed me, saying, "Case in point, I'm just telling you now about my lack of experience. It's been over a year."

I heaved a sigh. He had a point.

"Well, I might be thankful, but I'm not thanking her. Since it's Thanksgiving, I'll thank you instead," I said, knowing I sounded grumpy.

Isaac lowered his lips to mine, kissed me once, then spoke against my mouth, "What will you thank me for?" His hands were moving very freely now, all over, and it felt like the best kind of massage.

"I am thankful to you for telling me the truth."

"Even though you already knew."

"Yes. Doesn't matter, you told me. And, let's see, I am thankful for our life together."

He stole another kiss and started backing me up toward the bed. "Go on."

"I am thankful for your lips and hands and—"

"My tongue?"

I shivered as the back of my knees connected with the mattress. "Of course. And . . ." I slid a hand down to the front of his pants and found him hard. Giving him a stroke, I nudged his nose with mine. "I'm also thankful that you love me. That I'm your first everything."

"My first and only everything," he said, lifting my skirt, his thumbs hooking into my underwear.

"That's right," I whispered. "And most of all, you should know, to me, you're the only one that has ever mattered."

This moment, our life, these words were a secret just for us, and I would never get tired of sharing secrets with Isaac.

Scan me to receive new book updates and news from Penny!

Scan me if you'd like a signed copy of this or any Penny Reid book!

About the Author

Penny Reid is the *New York Times*, *Wall Street Journal*, and *USA Today* bestselling author of the Winston Brothers and Knitting in the City series. She used to spend her days writing federal grant proposals as a biomedical researcher, but now she writes kissing books. Penny is an obsessive knitter and manages the #OwnVoices-focused mentorship incubator / publishing imprint, Smartypants Romance. She lives in Seattle Washington with her husband, three kids, and dog named Hazel.

Come find me -
Mailing List: http://pennyreid.ninja/newsletter/
Goodreads: http://www.goodreads.com/ReidRomance
Facebook: www.facebook.com/pennyreidwriter
Instagram: www.instagram.com/reidromance
Twitter: www.twitter.com/reidromance
TikTok: https://www.tiktok.com/@authorpennyreid
Patreon: https://www.patreon.com/smartypantsromance
Email: pennreid@gmail.com …hey, you! Email me ;-)

Other books by Penny Reid

Knitting in the City Series

(Interconnected Standalones, Adult Contemporary Romantic Comedy)

Neanderthal Seeks Human: A Smart Romance (#1)

Neanderthal Marries Human: A Smarter Romance (#1.5)

Friends without Benefits: An Unrequited Romance (#2)

Love Hacked: A Reluctant Romance (#3)

Beauty and the Mustache: A Philosophical Romance (#4)

Ninja at First Sight (#4.75)

Happily Ever Ninja: A Married Romance (#5)

Dating-ish: A Humanoid Romance (#6)

Marriage of Inconvenience: (#7)

Neanderthal Seeks Extra Yarns (#8)

Knitting in the City Coloring Book (#9)

Winston Brothers Series

(Interconnected Standalones, Adult Contemporary Romantic Comedy, spinoff of Beauty and the Mustache)

Beauty and the Mustache (#0.5)

Truth or Beard (#1)

Grin and Beard It (#2)

Beard Science (#3)

Beard in Mind (#4)

Beard In Hiding (#4.5)

Dr. Strange Beard (#5)

Beard with Me (#6)

Beard Necessities (#7)

Winston Brothers Paper Doll Book (#8)

Hypothesis Series

(New Adult Romantic Comedy Trilogies)

Elements of Chemistry (#1)

Laws of Physics (#2)

Irish Players (Rugby) Series – by L.H. Cosway and Penny Reid

(Interconnected Standalones, Adult Contemporary Sports Romance)

The Hooker and the Hermit (#1)

The Pixie and the Player (#2)

The Cad and the Co-ed (#3)

The Varlet and the Voyeur (#4)

Dear Professor Series

(New Adult Romantic Comedy)

Kissing Tolstoy (#1)

Kissing Galileo (#2)

Ideal Man Series

(Interconnected Standalones, Adult Contemporary Romance Series of Jane Austen Reimaginings)

Pride and Dad Jokes (#1, TBD)

Man Buns and Sensibility (#2, TBD)

Sense and Manscaping (#3, TBD)

Persuasion and Man Hands (#4, TBD)

Mantuary Abbey (#5, TBD)

Mancave Park (#6, TBD)

Emmanuel (#7, TBD)

Handcrafted Mysteries Series

(A Romantic Cozy Mystery Series, spinoff of *The Winston Brothers Series*)

Engagement and Espionage (#1)

Marriage and Murder (#2)

Home and Heist (#3, coming 2025)

Baby and Ballistics (TBD)

Pie Crimes and Misdemeanors (TBD)

Good Folks Series

(Interconnected Standalones, Adult Contemporary Romantic Comedy, spinoff of *The Winston Brothers Series*)

Totally Folked (#1)

Folk Around and Find Out (#2)

All Folked Up (#3)

Three Kings Series

(Interconnected Standalones, Holiday-themed Adult Contemporary Romantic Comedies)

Homecoming King (#1)

Drama King (#2)

Prom King (#3, coming July 2025)

Standalones

Ten Trends to Seduce Your Best Friend

Bananapants

Made in United States
North Haven, CT
30 January 2025